William Douglass

A summary, historical and political

Of the first planting, progressive improvements, and present state of the British

settlements in North-America

William Douglass

A summary, historical and political
Of the first planting, progressive improvements, and present state of the British settlements in North-America

ISBN/EAN: 9783742839329

Manufactured in Europe, USA, Canada, Australia, Japa

Cover: Foto ©Andreas Hilbeck / pixelio.de

Manufactured and distributed by brebook publishing software
(www.brebook.com)

William Douglass

A summary, historical and political

A

SUMMARY,

Hiſtorical and Political,

OF THE

Firſt Planting, Progreſſive Improvements, and Preſent State of the BRITISH Settlements in NORTH-AMERICA.

CONTAINING

I. The Hiſtory of the Provinces and Colonies of New-Hampſhire, Rhode-Iſland, Connecticut, New-York, New-Jerſeys, Penſylvania, Maryland, and Virginia; their ſeveral original Settlements and gradual Improvements; their Boundaries, Produce and Manufactures, Trade and Navigation, Laws and Government.

II. Their Natural Hiſtory, Religious Sectaries, Paper Currencies, and other Miſcellanies.

III. Several Medical Digreſſions, with a curious Diſſertation on the Treatment of the Small-Pox, and Inoculation.

By WILLIAM DOUGLASS, M.D.

VOL. II.

HISTORIANS, like ſworn Evidences in Courts of Law, ought to declare the WHOLE TRUTH (ſo far as comes to their Knowledge) and nothing but the TRUTH.

LONDON,

Printed for R. and J. DODSLEY, in *Pall-mall.*

MDCCLX,

Thomas . Miller Esq.

THE

CONTENTS

Of Vol. II. Part II.

CONTENTS.

Province

CONTENTS.

A
S U M M A R Y,
HISTORICAL and POLITICAL,
O F

The firſt planting, progreſſive improvements, and preſent ſtate of the *Britiſh* ſettlements in NORTH-AMERICA.

VOLUME the SECOND.

A Supplement to the firſt Volume;

And Introduction to the ſecond Volume.

THE writer of this hiſtorical ſummary, does not affect a ſtudied elegancy. This is a plain narrative of inconteſtable facts delivered with freedom, a collection or common-place of many years obſervations, deſigned at firſt only for the writer's private amuſement or remembrancer; but at the deſire of ſome friends it is publiſhed for the benefit of the public, and for the uſe of future hiſtorians: Deus nobis hæc otia fecit. As the writer is independent, being in no public office, no ringleader of any party, or faction; what he writes may be deemed impartial: If facts related in truth offend any governor, commodore, or other great officer, he will not renounce impartiality and become sycophant.

As this summary has been discontinued many months from an [a] incident which may in course be mentioned by way of a digressional amusement; I find myself inclined to continue the history of sundry affairs down to this time, April 1750.

I. The naval affairs upon the continent coast of British North-America. Here [b] ends (a peace being concluded at Aix la Chapelle) our naval war with France and Spain upon the coast of North-America; the peace of Aix la Chapelle was signed October 7th, 1748, and proclaimed in Boston, May 10, 1749.

In autumn 1747, Commodore Kn——les arrived in the harbour of Boston with a squadron of men of war from Louisbourg of Cape-Breton, ordered all our [c] men of war, stationed for the protection of the North-American trade, to join him at Boston, to prosecute some secret expedition against the French and Spaniards in the gulph of Mexico; the reduction of St. Jago de Cuba was the principal design, and was not effectuated; but, en passant, he happened to surprize the French fort of Port Louis of the island of Hispaniola, and had the better in a sea engagement with a Spanish squadron off the Havannah of the island of Cuba; these occurrences are not within the limits of our history, which is confined to the British continent settlements in North-America; and the admiral Kn——'s conduct in these expeditions, as it is said, is now upon the carpet at home. Our coast being

[a] The great man of the province for the time being, finding that the writer, though of his personal acquaintance, was not a sycophant, but wrote transactions with a true and impartial freedom, endeavoured that his own management might remain obscure, and not stare himself and the publick in the face; this he attempted in many forms, in diverting, impeding, or rather defeating this publick-spirited laborious undertaking.

[b] The sea bickerings of Georgia and St. Augustine are left to the section of Georgia.

[c] They were only frigates, not fit for line of battle, or for battering of land forts.

thus

thus left naked, in May 1748 about fourteen French and Spanish privateers were roving from South-Carolina to New-York: They sailed up Delaware bay and river so high as New-Castle, and with their armed boats to within five miles of Philadelphia: Philadelphia newspapers say, " foreign trade is now at a stand, and the " port as much shut up as if the river was frozen." In Chesaepeak bay of Virginia, they went so high as Repahanock river and carried off several ships. In September 1748, two Spanish privateers sailed up Cape-Fear river of North-Carolina, landed Men, plundered Brunswick, took possession of six vessels, but from some casual disasters, they soon returned down the river. Here was a fine opportunity given to the French and Spaniards to plunder our continent ports, or put them to high contributions; but the French and Spanish pusillanimity favoured us.

II. A treaty of peace with the [d] Abnaquie or eastern Indians, or, rather the formal submission of these Indians by their delegates to the government of New-England, Vol. I. p. 564, ended our account of the late French and Indian incursions in New-England; since that account, there have been only some small damages done by a few scattered Indian banditti.

As this Indian treaty or submission to King GEORGE II, is very plain, easy, and voided of some antiquated wild fooleries which usually accompany such affairs, we

[d] The St. John's Indians of Nova-Scotia, are of the Abnaquie nation, but were not in the congress, because lately they seem chiefly to associate with the Mikmak Indians of Nova Scotia.—The Pigwaket tribe of Abnaquie are almost extinct, they did not engage in this war, but retired and lived amongst the English, during the war, in the county of Plymouth; fourteen of them, men, women and children, were present at this congress— The Masisassuck Indians on the east side or Dutch side of Lake Champlain or Corlaer, are in the Abnaquie division, but never do associate with the Abnaquies. The small tribe of Scatacooks, on Houssuck river, east side of Hudson's great river, and the scattered Mohegins on Hudson's river, though Abnaquies, are under the protection of the Mohawks or Iroquies, great nations.

shall

shall insert it here by way of a specimen of Indian treaties.

There was first a previous general meeting of the Indian delegates from all the tribes in a general council, to pray the government of New-England for a treaty of peace.

Some time in June 1749, nine delegates from the several tribes of Indians came to Boston, to make proposals for a peace; they proposed the sage governor Dummer's treaty to act upon, and that the congress should be at Falmouth in Casco-Bay, about 100 miles eastward from Boston.

The congress began at Falmouth, September 27, 1749, between the commissioners of Massachusetts-Bay, viz.

Thomas Hutchinson,   Israel Williams,
John Choate,   John Otis, Esqrs.

And of New-Hampshire, Theodore Atkinson, John Downing, Esqrs. on the one part; and the delegates of the eastern Indians on the other part, viz.

Eight from the tribe of Norridgowocks;

Toxus,	Soosephnia,
Eneas,	Naktoonos,
Magawombee,	Nesaqumbuit,
Harrey,	Pereez.

Five from the tribe of [e] Penobscot;

Eger Emmet,	Esparagoosaret,
Maganumba,	Neemoon.
Nictumbouit,	

Six from the tribes of [f] Arresuguntoocooks, and Weweenocks;

Sawwaramet,	Sauquish,
Aussaado,	Wareedeon,
Waanunga,	Wawawnunka.

[e] The Penobscots jocosely said, that they could answer for their young men if they were not drunk.

[f] These by the French, are called the mission of St. François and of Besancourt; both lie upon the south side of St. Laurence, or Canada river,

All

All the Indian delegates were not arrived until October 15. The New-Hampſhire commiſſioners returned home before the treaty was finiſhed, and left a power with Roland Cotton, Eſq. to ſign in their name. — The colony of Connecticut, though deſired by the government of Maſſachuſetts-Bay, did not ſend any commiſſioners; perhaps they reckoned themſelves out of the queſtion, being covered by the whole breadth of the province of Maſſachuſetts-Bay; Nova-Scotia was alſo invited.

Roland Cotton, Eſq. was clerk.

Capt. Joſeph Bean was interpreter; both under oath.

Toxus of Norridgowocks was reckoned the chief of theſe Indian tribes, and their ſpeaker; he ſaid, " Ever ſince governor Dummer [g] treated with us, all the Indians liked it well, and have reckoned it well ever ſince." Mr. Hutchinſon, chairman of the commiſſioners from Maſſachuſetts-Bay, in his ſpeech to the Indians, " You have always ſpoke well of governor Dummer's treaty, and the Engliſh have liked it well, and it laſted long; this we propoſe to be a plan for a treaty.

The Treaty is as follows,

" We the Indians inhabiting within his Majeſty's territories of New-England, make ſubmiſſion to King GEORGE II, in as full and ample a manner as any of our predeceſſors have heretofore done.

1. We Indians in all times coming will maintain a firm and conſtant amity with all the [b] Engliſh, and will never confederate to combine with any other nation to their prejudice.

one forty the other thirty leagues above Quebec; their joining with the other tribes of the New-England Indians in this ſubmiſſion to King GEORGE II, of Great-Britain, may well be uſed as an argument for New-England's reaching naturally and in the opinion of theſe Indians, to the ſouth ſide of Canada river.

[g] That treaty was anno 1725.
[b] The deſignation Engliſh is uſed, as more familiar to the Indians than that of Britiſh.

2. The

2. That the Englifh fubjects may peaceably and quietly enjoy their rights and fettlements; referving to the
Indians all lands not formerly conveyed to the Englifh, as
alfo the privilege of fifhing, hunting, and fowling, as
formerly.

3. The trade to be under the direction of the Maffachufetts government.

4. All controverfies fhall be iffued in the due courfe
of juftice of Maffachufetts government courts.

5. If any of our Indians commit hoftilities againft the
Englifh, we fhall join the Englifh to bring them to
reafon.

6. If any tribe of Indians make war upon any of the
now contracting tribes, the Englifh fhall affift and bring
them to reafon.

Moreover, it is agreed that there fhall be truck-houfes
at George's and at Richmond. The Indians defire a
truck-houfe alfo at Saco river.

III. A fhort and general continuation of the [i] Nova
Scotia affairs, particularly as to the Chebucta fettlement.

[i] See p. 305, 317, 566, vol. I. There was a government fcheme
of this nature fet on foot 1732; it was too much Utopian, and therefore
impracticable: I mean the fettlement of the province of Georgia in the
fouthern parts of South-Carolina, a frontier againft the Spaniards of Florida,
in a dry, fandy, parched foil: the fcheme was pompous, viz. to raife great
quantities of rice, wine, cotton-wool, indigo, cochineal, filk, hemp, flax.
Hitherto they have done nothing, though a great charge to the crown, in
civil and military eftablifhment; from 1733 (1733, the parliament granted
10,000 l. fterl. 1735, 26,000 l. fterl. &c.) to 1743 inclufive, the parliament grants for the civil eftablifhment amounted to 120,000 l. fterl. from
1743, to 1749, their civil and military grants were blended together;
1749, the parliament granted for their civil eftablifhment, 5,304 l. fterl.
their military eftablifhment has been very chargeable, the pay and victualling of one regiment and feveral independent companies of regular troops,
armed fchooners and rangers.

The patent for erecting Georgia into a province or corporation, paffed
the feals 1732. In Feb. 1733-4, the whole number of perfons that had
been fhipped to Georgia were 320 men, 113 women, 102 boys, 83 girls,
in all 618 perfons, whereof one quarter were foreigners; fince that time
many people have been imported, but not long fince in that province were
to be found only 602 perfons. July 1748, in Mr. Whitefield's Bethefda,

The

The general of Canada fince the conclufion of the late peace, by letters to the prefident of Nova Scotia, and to the governor of New-England, claims the greateft part of Nova Scotia or L'Accadie : the French Coureurs des Bois and their Indians, 1749, have made fome fmall appearances to intimidate our new fettlers. 1. A number of French and Indians came before our block-houfe at Minas without effect; they furprize and carry off about eighteen ftragglers as captives. 2. In September, eight Indians as traders came aboard Donnel a trading floop in Chicanecto bay, by furprize with their long knives they kill three of his men, while feveral Indians on fhore waited the event; in this fcuffle, the Indians loft feven of their men. 3. Beginning of October, a company of about forty Indians, as was fuppofed, furprized eight of Gilman's timber-men near the faw-mills, eaft fide of Chebucta bay; they killed four of Gilman's men, three efcaped to the flanker of the block-houfe, one man is miffing, fuppofed to be captivated to make difcoveries ; the Indians did not attempt the block-houfe :—Afterwards there was a more general rendezvous of Indians, but having no profpect of any advantage, and the St. John's Indians differing with the Mikmaks, they broke up and went home.

The chief fettlement will be the town of [k] Halifax or Chebucta, laid out and fettled in a few months; [l] for defence round it at proper diftances are five picquetted block-houfes containing barracks for Warburton's regiment.

(12 miles from Savannah) were only one mafter, two women, four menfervants labourers, and eighteen children, whereof two paid for their board ; in his vagrancies this was his great cant fund to beg money and other effects from weak chriftians. Here I inadvertently anticipate what properly belongs to the fection of Georgia.

[k] So called from the earl of Halifax, the principal encourager of this fettlement.

[l] Idlenefs and intemperance, the bane of all our plantations, efpecially confidering the nature of the firft fettlers of this place, are more dangerous than any parcels of defpicable ftraggling Indians.

In

In our firſt vol. p. 566, we juſt entered upon the late
projected, but now vigorouſly proſecuted [m], re-ſettle-
ment of Nova Scotia, by the indefatigable governor
Cornwallis: the firſt parliamentary allowance or encouragement was 40,000 *l.* ſterl. towards tranſporting to
Nova Scotia, and maintaining there, for a certain time
after their arrival, ſuch reduced officers and private men,
lately diſmiſſed from his majeſty's land and ſea-ſervice,
and [n] others as ſhall be willing to ſettle the ſaid colony.
Col. Cornwallis with his fleet of one frigate of twenty
guns, one man of war ſloop—tranſports—with ſettlers,
proviſions and ſtores, arrived in Chebucta bay, end of
June; ſoon after arrived the French tranſports (who had
brought from France the troops that took poſſeſſion of
Louiſbourg) from Louiſbourg with the Britiſh troops
who had evacuated Louiſbourg, conſiſting of the two
regiments of Fuller and Warburton, and a detachment
of the train; the regiment of late Fuller's, to recruit
Warburton's, and to leave ſome ſettlers, was reduced to
thirty-five private men per company, half their former
complement, and ſent home.

In this bay of Chebucta, is built a uniform elegant
town, called Hallifax, after the earl of Hallifax, a great
promoter of this ſettlement. This harbour of Chebucta is
a moſt convenient place of arms for our American men of
war, and a certain check upon the French of Louiſ-

[m] I am ſorry to write, that from 1710, to 1749, being near the ſpace
of forty years, the French have been ſilently allowed to keep poſſeſſion in
all reſpects of the province of Nova Scotia, the fort of Annapolis and its
banliew excepted.

[n] A riff-raff of diſmiſſed ſoldiers and ſailors habituated to idleneſs and
vice, by their labour can never ſettle a new colony; but two or three
young vigorous regiments (ſuch as Warburton's) cantoned all over the
country, paid and victualled from home for two or three years, (from New-
England we can ſupply them with wives, good breeders) and when thus
habituated to the country, and to huſbandry, with proper encouragement
of land, they may be diſmiſſed from their military ſervice; and make laſting good ſettlements —No old men paſt their labour, no women but ſuch
as are of the ages of breeders, that is, none exceeding 35 æt. be admitted,
excepting parents of numerous children, to ſerve as their guardians.

bourg:

bourg: it is well situated for making dry cod-fish, being about the middle of a long range of Cape-Sable coast fishing banks, and may prove the best cod-fishery hitherto known. I heartily wish success to the settlement, but we cannot expect that it should answer so well for husbandry, that is, for tillage and pasture, as our colonies farther south. I conclude with the words of Bacon lord Verulam, "Settling plantations is like planting "of timber, we must wait patiently some years, before "we reap any benefit [o]."

IV. A short recapitulation and conclusion of the Louisbourg affair; the Cape-Breton islands, for reasons of state, are now restored to the French dominions; and after some political remarks, we shall take our final leave of them. See vol. I. p. 335, &c. and p. 347, &c. The French of Canada and Cape-Breton had more early intelligence of the French war than we of New-England; it was proclaimed in Boston June 2, 1744. Louisbourg of Cape-Breton surrendered to us, June 17, 1745. Autumn following to garrison Louisbourg, were shipped off from Gibraltar, Fuller's and Warburton's regiments of foot, and three companies of Frampton's regiment, with a large

[o] In the late treaty of Aix la Chapelle, October 7, 1748, there were many things in relation to trade, and to the claims and boundaries in the respective plantations to be settled with France and Spain, which required a considerable time to be adjusted, and therefore could not be inserted in the body of the treaty, but referred to a convention of commissioners: as the French court in their various negotiations are noted for appointing men of merit and real knowledge in the various affairs with which they are intrusted, doubtless our ministry will use gentlemen of practical knowledge in trade, and habituated to plantation affairs; men of a quick clear thought, and of a distinct clear elocution.

In the present state of things, the well-being of the European mother-countries depends much upon their plantations; plantations make a country rich; Holland is rich, not from its produce or manufactures, but from its East and West-India plantations, its trade and navigation. France never flourished so much as in the administration of cardinal Fleury; his principal attention was to their plantations and trade; the empire of Germany, Sweden, &c. though they abound in labouring men, for want of plantations and trade, are very poor.

detach-

detachment from the train; it was too late in the year before they arrived upon our winter coaft, and were obliged to winter in Virginia; a few of them put into New-York; they arrived at Louifbourg May 24, 1746, and relieved the New-England militia confifting of about 1500 men, who had kept garrifon from the furrender of the place; commodore Warren was at that time governor; after him commodore Knowles was pro-tempore governor; admiral Townfhend from the Weft-India iflands with a fmall fquadron is ordered for the protection of Louifbourg, and fails for England in November 1746. Mr. Knowles in his time, at a very great charge, repaired the town and fort, as if they were to remain to Great-Britain for ever. Commodore Knowles in the autumn 1747, with a fmall fquadron came to Bofton, and proceeded upon a fecret expedition to the Sugar iflands, and Mr. Hobfon lieut. col. of Fuller's regiment is appointed governor of Louifbourg. Peace drawing near, Shirley's and Pepperell's regiments, from a complement of 100 private men per company, were reduced to feventy men; the private men of the three companies of Frampton's regiment, were incorporated by way of recruits with Fuller's and Warburton's regiments, and their commiffion officers, ferjeants, corporals, and drums fent home; Pepperell's and Shirley's regiments in Louifbourg were entirely [p] difmiffed June 24, 1749; their arms and other accoutrements were detained by the government. The Britifh troops evacuated Louifbourg, July 12, 1749, and were carried by the French tranfports to Chebucta, and the French troops being about 600 men took poffeffion of the place.

It is a fpreading pufillanimous opinion amongft the lefs thinking people, that the great advantage of Louifbourg's falling into our hands was its ferving as a propitiatory free offering to France, and without reftoring it we fhould have had no peace: but we ought to obferve 1. That both parties in the war were low in cafh and cre-

[p] They were put in pay, Sept. 1, 1745.

dit.

dit. 2. The French navy, trade, and navigation, were
ſo reduced, that they could not avoid deſiring a peace;
we had taken as many of their men of war as might have
been ſufficient to reduce the remainder; we had taken
great numbers of their South-Sea, Eaſt and Weſt-India,
Turkey, and other Ships, and what remained were obliged
to continue in port, (in fear of our numerous privateers)
having no convoys or men of war to protect them.
3. The corruption which prevailed in Holland was like
to be extirpated, and the Dutch became active. 4. The
army of our auxiliary Ruſſians were upon their march to
join us; for ſome reaſons of ſtate they ſeem to have been
retarded in their march. If Louiſbourg had not fallen
into our hands, the reduced towns and forts in Flan-
ders muſt have been returned, that is, evacuated; it
ſeems that in all modern negotiations for a peace the ba-
ſis is reſtitution of all land conqueſts on both ſides, excepting where equivalents or antiquated claims fall in
the way.

The court of Great-Britain cannot cordially approve
of this infinitely raſh New-England corporation adventure, though beyond all military or human probability
ſuccefsful; it involved the nation, already deeply in debt,
in an additional ſum of about 800,000 *l.* ſterl. in the
ſeveral articles of reimburſement-money, extraordinary
ſuperfluous repairs, tranſport ſervice, ſtores, garriſon
officers, a large detachment from the train, and a numerous garriſon of regular troops: this place was una-
voidably to be evacuated and reſtored to the French upon
a peace, and, as it happened, in a better condition, and
without any reimburſement or equivalent; cui bono! I
cannot perceive any real advantage acquired by the reduction of Louiſbourg. The ſmall Britiſh ſquadron ſta-
tioned at Boſton, without any additional national charge,
would have been an effectual check upon the Louiſbourg
privateers; commodore Warren from the Weſt-India
iſlands was ſent for the protection of the coaſt of New-
England

England and Nova Scotia in the spring 1745, and our trade in the northern parts of America could not have suffered above two or three per cent difference of insurance, which is as nothing compared with the great charge of 800,000 *l.* sterl. before the charge was fully known, I estimated it at 500,000 *l.* sterl. or less [*q*].

I sum up the Louisbourg affair. 1. It was infinitely rash, a private corporation adventure, without any orders or assured assistance of men of war from home; thirty-six hundred raw militia (some without proper arms) without any discipline, but at random, as if in a frolick, met together; no provision of cloathing or ships: by this and small care of the sick, and want of discipline, we lost about one half of our men by scurvys and putrid slow fevers; in a military way we lost only about sixty men killed and drowned, and about 116 prisoners to the French,

[*q*] If the Canada expedition which was recommended home by governor ——had proceeded and succeeded, after another great addition to the national debt; for reasons of state, without any equivalent or reimbursement, it must have been evacuated and restored to the French; New-England was at considerable charge towards this intended expedition in levy-money, victualling, transport service, bedding, &c. for want of proper application, Massachusetts have received no reimbursement of this: Rhode-Island, by application have received their reimbursement.

Another extra-provincial perquisite expedition was the sending off 1500 men towards the reduction of Crown-Point, a French fort, near Lake Champlain in the province of New-York; this involved our province in some charge (never to be recovered) by sending provisions, ammunition and other stores by water to Albany; an epidemical distemper in the county of Albany luckily prevented us; if it had been reduced, it must either have been kept by us at a very great charge equal to the opposition of all the force of Canada; or we must have demolished it, to be re-built by the French at one tenth of our charge in reducing of it.

Another project towards ruining our province was the charge of building a fort at the Carrying-place in the government of New-York, between the falls of Hudson's river and Wood-Creek: this was attended with the same inconveniencies as the former.

Sending off troops to assist the six Indian nations of New-York—All these idle proposals, were not resented by the government of New-York, as, if that rich government had been incapable or neglectful of self-protection, but silently admitted of Sh—— Quixotisms; our house of representatives in their journal say, the people of New-York were much abler to protect themselves.

in

in the rafh foolifh attempt upon the ifland-battery : during the fiege, by good fortune, we had conftant dry favourable weather : but June 18, next day after we had poffeffion of the town, the rains fet in, which certainly from our men being ill cloathed and ill lodged, muft infallibly have broken up the fiege. We had a wretched train of artillery, or rather no artillery (they were voted by the affembly not worth the charge of bringing back to Bofton) in a Quixote manner to demolifh a French American Dunkirk, in which were 1900 armed men, whereof 600 were regular troops, 125 good large cannon, nineteen mortars, with ftores and provifions fufficient for fix months. 2. The military fuccefs was miraculous, but the cunning part of the project was natural, and could not mifs of fuccefs. 1. A neceffary enormous multiplied emiffion of a depreciating paper currency, enabled the fraudulent debtors to pay their debts at about ten fhillings in the pound difcount. 2. Vaft perquifites to the manager [r].

CURRENCIES. [s] The parliament of Great-Britain, before the commencement of the late French war, had

[r] As writers and preachers forbear publifhing ****** which are fingular, rare or new, left they fhould prove of bad example, I fhall only fum up thefe perquifites in this manner: In the fpace of four years, viz. 1741, the introductory gratuities from the province, and from ***** of many thoufands of pounds, and the unprecedented perquifites in the three expedition years of 1745, 1746, and 1747, from a negative fortune, was amaffed a large pofitive eftate, and the loofe corns built a country-houfe at the charge of about fix thoufand pound fterling. The predeceffor, an honeft gentleman of a good paternal eftate, after eleven years adminiftration, in a meffage to the general affembly, July 21, 1741, reprefents, that he had been obliged to break in upon his own eftate fome thoufands of pounds, to fupport the character of a king's governor; in faithfulnefs to his truft he refufed a certain retaining fee.

[s] This accurfed affair of plantation paper-currencies, when in courfe it falls in my way, it proves a ftumbling-block, and occafions a fort of deviation. In the appendix, I fhall give a fhort hiftory of all the plantation paper-currencies; it may be a piece of curiofity for times to come. Maffachufetts-Bay was the leader, and exceeded all the colonies in this fraud; from their firft emiffion 1702 (I take no notice of Sir William Phipps's Canada bills, they were foon out of the queftion) to 1749, the laft year of Mr. Sh—— adminiftration, our bills of publick credit or ftate-notes
under

under their confideration fome regulations concerning the plantation currencies; and now that war being ended, this third feffion of the tenth parliament of Great Britain hath refumed the confideration thereof.

fuffered a difcount of eighty-eight per cent; in France, in the worft of times, when Mr. Law had the direction of the finances, the difcount upon their ftate-notes was only fixty-five per cent: Maffachufetts publick bills of credit 1749, were pejorated to eleven for one fterling.

In the few years of Mr. Sh—— adminiftration, this fraudulent currency from 127,000l. old tenor, was multiplied to about two and a half millions, and by this depreciating contrivance the fraudulent debtors paid only ten fhillings in the pound, and every honeft man not in debt loft about one half of his perfonal eftate. The money-making affemblies could not keep pace with him in his paper emiffions; 1747, the governor infifting upon further emiffions, the affembly reprefents, " If we emit more bills, we " apprehend it muft be followed by a great impair, if not utter lofs of the " publick credit, which has already been greatly wounded;" and in their journal 1746, p. 240, " We have been the means of actually bringing " diftrefs, if not utter ruin upon ourfelves—When any complaints were " offered to the affembly concerning depreciation, by—contrivance, they " were referred to committees, confifting of the moft notorious deprecia- " tors." See Journal, Auguft 17, 1744.

By way of amufement. I fhall produce fome different managements of adminiftrations with refpect to a fraudulent paper medium—1703 by contrivance of Mr. W—— from New-England, Barbadoes emitted 80,000l. at four per cent (common intereft was ten per cent) upon land fecurity, payable after fome years; thofe land-bank-bills immediately fell forty per cent. below filver; upon complaint home the court of England fent an inftruction to governor Crow, to remove from the council and all places of truft, any who had been concerned in the late paper credit; thus currency was fuppreffed, and their currency became and continues filver as before.—Governor Belcher of New-England, 1741, from integrity and faithfulnefs to the publick, when a wicked combination called LAND-BANK, became head ftrong; he refufed their bribe or retaining fee, negatived their fpeaker and thirteen of their counfellors, and fuperfeded many of their officers, civil and military.—Soon after this fcheme was damned by act of parliament, governor Sh—— I fhall not fay in contempt, but perhaps in neglect of this act, promoted their directors and other chief managers to the higheft offices, of counfellors, provincial agents, judges, juftices, fheriffs, and militia officers preferrable to others.

When there was an immediate publick emergency for raifing money, the borrowing of publick bills, already emitted, from the poffeffors, would not have increafed a paper currency, but prevented depreciations; fome merchants and others offered to lend thefe bills at a fmall intereft; fome gentlemen faid, that they had better let them without intereft than that their perfonal eftates from multiplied emiffions, fhould depreciate at a

Maffa-

Maffachufetts-Bay, as they have at prefent no province bills out upon loan for terms of years, have previoufly fettled their currency by act of affembly, approved of by the KING in council; it is intituled, An act *for drawing in the bills of credit of the feveral denominations, which have at any time been iffued by this government, aud are ftill out-ftanding; and for afcertaining the rate of coined filver in this province for the future.* By this act it is provided that the treafurer fhall be impowered to receive the [t] reimburfe-ment money to be exchanged after the 31ft of March 1750, at the rate of forty-five fhillings, old tenor, for a piece of eight; and one year more is allowed for exchang-ing the faid bills—After 31ft of March 1750, all debts and contracts fhall be payable in coined filver only, a piece of eight at fix fhillings, one ounce of filver at fix fhillings and eight-pence [u], as alfo all executions with fuch ad-dition according to the time of contracting, as the laws of the province do or fhall require; the feveral acts of affembly, whereby fome fund of taxes, for cancelling province bills of credit, have been poftponed gra-dually, to 1760 are repealed, and the tax of 1749, to-wards cancelling thefe bills, fhall be three hundred thou-fand pound old tenor. Penalty to thofe who receive

much greater rate than after the value of an accruing intereft: but this would have effectually defeated the fcheme of the depreciators, the frau-dulent debtors, therefore the propofal or expedient was rejected by the advice of———

For paper currencies, fee vol I. p 310, 314, 308, 493.

[t] This reimburfement money arrived at Bofton, Sept. 18, 1749, in a man of war frigate, confifting of 215 chefts, (3000 pieces of eight at a medium per cheft) of milled pieces of eight, and 100 cafks of coined copper. Connecticut, a government of fagacious hufbandmen, feems to have acted more prudently than Maffachufetts-Bay; by their affembly act, Oct. 1749, they allow three years (to prevent a fudden confufion) to can-cel their bills gradually; and in their reimburfement money to fave the charges of commiffions, freight, infurance, and other petty charges, they are to draw upon their receiving agent, and thefe bills will readily purchafe filver for a currency.

[u] This is not in proportion, a milled piece of eight is feven eightfis of an ounce, and at fix fhillings per piece is fix fhillings and ten pence, one third of a penny better per ounce.

or

or pay filver at any higher rate, fifty pound for every offence; and after 31ft of March 1750, the penalty for paffing any bills of Connecticut, New-Hampfhire, or Rhode-Ifland, fhall be fifty pound for every offence; and from thence to March 31ft 1754, all perfons entering into any town affairs, conftables, reprefentatives, counfellors, all officers civil and military, [x] plaintiffs in recovering of executions, tavern-keepers, and retailers of ftrong drink, fhall make oath that they have not been concerned in receiving or paying away any fuch bills.

As the exportation of fterling coin from Great-Britain is prohibited by act of parliament, Spanifh pieces of eight are reckoned the plantation currency, and are efteemed as fuch in the proclamation act fo called, for plantation currencies; but although the Britifh or fterling fpecies could not be a plantation currency, the Spanifh coin might have been reduced to their denominations at 4 s. 6 fterl. per piece of eight, and all the colonies reduced to the fame fterling denominations of Great-Britain, which would much facilitate the trade and bufinefs of the plantations amongft themfelves, and with their mother-country: thus we fee in Portugal a millrée, though no fpecie or coin, but only a denomination, is the bafis of their currencies; and in the fame manner with the plantations, a pound or crown fterling, although no fpecie or coin in the colonies, might have been the general bafis of our denomination or currencies.

I may be allowed to drop a tear, I mean fome expreffion of grief, over the languifhing ftate of my altera patria, the province of Maffachufetts-Bay, formerly the glory of our plantations; but now reduced to extreme mifery and diftrefs, precipitately brought upon us by the adminiftration of **** and a party of fraudulent debtors. At his acceffion he was lucky to find a ftanding irrefiftible party formed to his mind, and not empty-

[x] That is, all delinquents are out-lawed; a very fevere penalty: this may introduce a habit of forfwearing or perjury.

handed;

handed; they effectually depopulated the province by the lofs of many of our moft vigorous labouring young men, the only dependance or life of a young plantation; they peculated the country by ruinous unneceffary expence of money—Our prefent commander in chief in his firft fpeech to the affembly, Nov. 23, 1749, modeftly expreffes the late peculation and depopulation of the province; " deliver this province from the evils and " mifchiefs (particularly the injuftice and oppreffions) " arifing from the uncertain and finking value of the " paper-medium—the cultivation of our lands and ma-" nufactures are greatly impeded by the fcarcity of " labourers." Mr. Sh——'s own affemblies fometimes complain. June 3, 1748, the council and reprefenta-tives, in a joint meffage to the governor, enumerate the " great lofs of inhabitants for hufbandry and other la-" bour, and for the defence of our inland frontiers; " the vaft load of debt already contracted, and the un-" paralleled growing charges, infupportable difficul-" ties!" The houfe of reprefentatives upon a certain occafion, complain, " with publick taxes we are bur-" thened, almoft to ruin;" in their journals 1747. " Should the whole fum expended in the late expedi-" tion be reimburft us, we have ftill a greater debt re-" maining, than ever lay upon any of his majefty's " governments in the plantations." Mr.—— had no fympathy with the fuffering province, becaufe [y] de-preciations of currency, and our unfufferable taxes did not affect him.

[y] Depreciations, by his fucceffive affemblies were made more than good in advancing his allowances and other perquifites: he is ex-empted from taxes by act of affembly. Whereas all perfons of the pro-vince not in debt, have loft about one half of their perfonal eftates, by depreciations in this fhort adminiftration; and the provincial poll tax of two fhillings and three-pence, O. T; this tax is equal to rich and poor, and befides poll tax, there are provincial rates upon eftates and faculties, excife, impoft, tonnage; and befides provincial taxes, there are country and town poll rates, &c. Mr. Belcher, by his wife and honeft manage-ment, had brought all our publick debts or paper credit and currency, to be cancelled in one year 1741, being 127,000 l. O. T. but

By the province being depopulated, labour is dear, and all countries can afford to underfell us in produce and manufactures; in confequence our trade is loft: I fhall adduce a few inftances: 1. When Mr. Belcher was fuperfeded 1741, in Bofton at one and the fame time were upon the ftocks forty top-fail veffels of about 7,000 ton, all upon contract: at Mr. Sh —— going home 1749, only about 2,000 ton on the ftocks, whereof only four or five fhips upon contract, the others upon the builders account to wait for a market, and to keep their apprentices to work, and to work up their old ftores of timber. 2. 1741, in Marble-head, our chief fifhing town, were about 160 fifhing fchooners of circiter fifty ton each: 1749, there were only about fixty fifhing fchooners. 3. For many months lately there were not to be found in Bofton goods (nay not the coarfeft. of goods, pitch, tar, and turpentine) fufficient to load a middling fhip to Great-Britain; but under the prefent adminiftration and ma-nagement of affairs our trade and navigation feem to revive.

In the feveral SECTIONS or HISTORIES of the feveral colonies, may generally be found, but not in the fame ftrict order, the following particulars.

1. When the colony was firft difcovered and traded to by any European nation; when firft colonized by the

---

Mr. —— and his party being afraid of lofing hold of this accurfed fraudulent currency, they refolved (the province was at that time in its greateft profperity) that 127,000 *l.* O. T. was an inconvenient fum to be cancelled in one year, and therefore divided it among three fubfe-quent years; by this neft egg in a few years they increafed the brood to two and a half millions; and the g—— upon his call home 1749, for certain reafons which may be mentioned, (by the advice of his trufty friends) contrived two years exceffive taxes of 360,000 and 300,000 O. T. to be collected in not much exceeding one year, when the country wa, depopulated, peculated, and much reduced in trade and bufinefs: this fudden and quiet reverfe change of fentiment in this party is unac-countable; but quicquid id eft timeo, perhaps they expect confufion; they have practifed fifhing in troubled water.

Englifh:

Englifh : and what revolutions have happened there from time to time, in property and jurifdiction.

2. Its boundaries, if well afcertained, or if controverted in property or jurifdicton.

3. Wars with the French, Spaniards and Indians.

4. The numbers of whites, or freemen, and flaves.

5. The laft valuation, that is, the number of polls and value of eftates, taken to adjuft the quotas of taxes for the feveral counties, diftricts, towns, and parifhes.

6. The militia upon the alarum-lift, and how incorporated or regulated.

7. Houfe of reprefentatives, their nature and number : the qualifications of the electors, and of the elected.

8. Courts of judicature.

1. The nature of their juries, and how returned.

2. The jurifdiction of a juftice, and of a bench of juftices, and of their general quarter feffions.

3. Inferior or county courts of common pleas.

4. Superior, fupreme, or provincial courts for appeals.

5. Chancery, or courts of equity, if in ufe.

6. Jufticiary courts of oyer and terminer.

7. Ordinary for probate of wills and granting adminiftration.

8. Courts of vice-admiralty.

9. Jufticiary court of admiralty for crimes committed at fea.

10. The prefent taxes, viz. polls, rates, impoft, and excife.

11. Produce, manufactures, trade, and navigation.

12. The number of entries and clearances of extra-provincial veffels, diftinguifhed into fhips, fnows, brigantines, floops, and fchooners.

13. The various fectaries in religious worfhip.

In moft of the fections there is a digreffional article, to prevent repetitions, concerning fome things which are in common to feveral colonies, but inferted in that fection or colony the moft noted for thofe things; thus 1. in the fection for Maffachufetts fhould have been in-

ferted

ferted the affair of paper currencies, as they did originate
and were carried to the greateſt diſcount or fraud there:
but as by a late act of aſſembly confirmed by the king in
council, paper currencies are terminated in that province, we drop it. 2. As Piſcataqua, alias New-Hampſhire, has, for many years, been noted for royal maſting
contracts, we choſe to inſert in that SECTION, ſome things
concerning maſting, lumber, and other timber for conſtruction or building ; for joiners and for turners work:
and if that article does not ſwell too much, we may inſert ſome other foreſt trees and flowering ſhrubs fit for
boccages, parks, and gardens. 3. As Rhode-Iſland
has been noted for ſectaries, from no religion to the
moſt enthuſiaſtick, there is deſigned ſome account of
our plantations or colony ſectaries ; though at preſent
Penſylvania exceed them in that reſpect, where beſides
the Rhode-Iſland ſectaries, are to be found a ſect of free-
thinkers who attend no publick worſhip, and are called
keep-at-home proteſtants ; publick popiſh maſs-houſes ;
and ſome ſectaries imported lately from Germany, ſuch
as Moravians called unitas fratrum or united brethren,
who have had ſome indulgencies by act of parliament
1749.   4. Connecticut, a colony of ſagacious laborious
huſbandmen, firſt in courſe naturally claims the digreſſion concerning grain and grazing ; it is true New-
York, Jerſies, and Penſylvania at preſent much exceed
them in grain and manufacturing their wheat into flour.
5. Maryland and Virginia for tobacco, and maſt for
raiſing ſwine or pork.   6. The Carolinas for rice, ſkins,
and hides.   7. Georgia as an inſtance of an Utopian unprofitable colony.

To render this hiſtory as compleat as may at preſent be
expected, I have annexed ſome maps of the ſeveral colonies, not borrowed from borrowing erroneous hackney
map publiſhers, but originals compoſed and lately printed
in the ſeveral countries : For inſtance, with the ſection
of the colony of Connecticut, the laſt of the four New-
England

England colonies, I annex a [z] correct map of the dominions of New-England, extended from 40 d. 30 m. to 44 d. 30 m. N. Lat. and from 68 d. 50 m. to 74 d. 50 m. W. Longitude from London. To the colony of Penfylvania is annexed a [a] map of New-York, the Jerfies and Penfylvania, publifhed 1749, by Mr. Evans in Penfylvania, much more accurate than any hitherto publifhed. To the colony of North-Carolina is annexed a map of North-Carolina, [b] and fome parts of South-Carolina, principally with regard to the fea-coaft and lands adjoining; this large inland country is wafte or vacant, and confequently delineated at random by col. Edward Mofely of North-Carolina.

[z] This map is founded upon a chorographical plan, compofed from actual furveys of the lines or boundaries with the neighbouring colonies, and from the plans of the feveral townfhips and diftricts copied from the records lodged in the fecretaries office and townfhips records, with the writer's perambulations: when this plan is printed, the author, as a benefaction, gives gratis, to every townfhip and diftrict, a copper plate copy; as the writer of the fummary had impartially narrated the management of a late g———— which could not bear the light; to check the credit of the author, the g———— endeavoured (as fhall be accounted for) to divert, impede, or defeat this publick generous-fpirited amufement, but in vain. The writer in his journeys upon account of his chorography and other occafions (formerly ufed to fuch amufements in the gardens of Paris and Leyden) has en paffant, but with fome fatigue, made a collection of above eleven hundred indigenous plants, claffically defcribed and referred to icons in Botanick writers which have the neareft femblance, as the fpecifick icons could not conveniently be cut here; this is an amufement proper for gentlemen of eftates and leifure; it is not quite fo ridiculous as our modern virtuofo amufements of fhells, butterflies, &c. The medical or medicinal part of botany is fmall, and foon becomes familiar to people of the profeffion; the fame may be faid of the other branches of the materia medica from animals, minerals, and chemical preparations of thofe; but to proceed further as a naturalift, is only proper for gentlemen of fortune, leifure, and leifibabbers as the Dutch exprefs it; or otioforum hominum negotia.

[a] From 43 d. 30 m. to 38 d. 30 m. N. Lat. and from 73 d. 30 m. to 78 d. Weft Long. from London.

[b] From 33 d. to 36 d. 30 m. N. Lat.

S E C T.   IX.

Concerning the province of New-Hampſhire.

AS the four colonies of New-England were originally ſettled by the ſame ſort of people called [c]
Puritans; their municipal laws, cuſtoms, and œconomy are nearly the ſame, but more eſpecially in New-
Hampſhire, which was under the aſſumed juriſdiction
of Maſſachuſetts-Bay for many years; therefore to ſave
repetitions, we refer ſeveral things to the ſection of
Maſſachuſetts-Bay.

The preſent poſſeſſors have no other claim to their
lands but poſſeſſion and ſome uncertain Indian deeds.
Upon Mr. Allen's petition to queen Anne, deſiring to be
put in poſſeſſion of the waſte lands, the aſſembly of
New-Hampſhire paſſed acts for confirmation of their
townſhip grants and of their boundaries, without any
ſaving of the right of the general proprietor; upon Mr.
Allen the proprietor's application, the queen in council
diſallowed and repealed thoſe acts.

The crown aſſuming the vacant lands, until the proprietors claiming in right of Mr. Maſon ſhall make formal proof, that Mr. Maſon ever was in poſſeſſion of
theſe lands; this appears by an action of ejectment
brought by the claiming proprietor Mr. Allen againſt
Waldron and Vaughan; Allen, being caſt in coſts, appealed home, but his appeal was diſmiſſed becauſe he
he had not brought over proof of Mr. Maſon's having
ever been in poſſeſſion, and was ordered to begin de
novo. The collective body of the people by their repreſentatives in aſſembly, have no [d] pretenſion to the
vacant or waſte lands, and therefore have no concern in

[c] See vol. I. p. 367.
[d] The other three colonies of the dominions of New England, by
their reſpective royal charters, have the property or diſpoſal of their
vacant lands lodged in the repreſentatives of the collective body of the
people.

granting

granting of unoccupied lands; all grants or charters of thefe lands, according to the governor's commiffion and inftructions, are vefted in the governor and council, with this claufe or referve, fo far as in us lies;— this refervation feems to favour the claims under Mr. Mafon; as is alfo a claufe in the royal new charter of Maffachufetts-Bay 1691, " Nothing therein contained " fhall prejudice any right of Samuel Allen, Efq. " claiming under John Mafon, Efq. deceafed, of any " part of the premifes."

The jurifdiction of this province is indifputably in the crown. In property there are many and various claimers, [*e*] 1. As it is faid that Mr. Mafon and his heirs and their affigns never complied with the conditions of the grant, in confequence it reverts to the crown; and che crown at prefent is in poffeffion not only of the jurifdiction but property of lands hitherto not granted. 2. Capt. John Tufton Mafon, heir in fucceffion, as he fays, to the original grantee capt. John Mafon, lately made a conveyance of his right for a fmall confideration to fourteen or fifteen perfons of New-Hampfhire; by their advertifements in the Bofton news-papers, they feem to make a bubble of it. Bofton poft-boy, Nov. 9, 1749. " The prefent " claimers under the late Samuel Allen of London, " will find upon trial, they have no right to any of " thefe lands; that the faid claimers under John Tufton " Mafon, will be able to make out the right to be in " them, and are willing to difpute the point in law, as " foon as any perfon will give them opportunity."

John Hobby, grandfon and heir of Sir Charles Hobby, fays, that Thomas Allen, heir to col. Allen, by deed of fale, Auguft 28, 1706, conveyed one half of thefe lands to Sir Charles Hobby of New-England, Knight, See vol. I, p. 505.

[*e*] Upon any judgment in the provincial courts of New-Hampfhire, by an appeal home, all thefe claims may be finally fettled by the king in council, and prevent all bubblings of property in New-Hampfhire.

3. Hobby and Adams claiming under Mr. Allen by their bubbling advertiſements, Nov. 9, 1749, publiſhed in the Boſton poſt-boy, November 20, 1749, in theſe words, " Whereas ſundry gentlemen in the province
" of New-Hampſhire, claim a right to all thoſe lands
" in the ſaid province and elſewhere which were granted
" to capt. John Maſon of London, by letters patent
" from the council eſtabliſhed at Plymouth, dated
" March 9, 1621, and confirmed to him by charter
" from king Charles the firſt, dated Auguſt 19, 1635;
" which lands the ſaid gentlemen claim under capt.
" John Tufton Maſon, the now pretended heir to the
" ſaid original patentee : This is therefore to inform
" whom it may concern, that although it ſhould ap-
" pear, that the ſaid Tufton Maſon is the lawful heir
" to the ſaid original patentee, (which is yet to be
" doubted) it evidently appears that John and Robert
" Tufton Maſon, undoubted heirs to the ſaid original
" patentee, did, by an abſolute deed of ſale, dated April
" 27, 1691, in conſideration of the ſum of 2750 *l.*
" ſterling, convey all their right and title to the ſaid
" lands to Samuel Allen of London, afterwards go-
" vernor of New-Hampſhire aforeſaid, which con-
" veyance we doubt not will be . . .' to appear legal
" and valid, the ſaid Samuel Allen'ſ claim having been
" allowed and confirmed by king William and queen
" Mary, as appears by their charter to the government
" of the province of the Maſſachuſetts-Bay ; and that
" Thomas Allen, only ſon and heir to the ſaid Samuel
" Allen, did, by deed of ſale, dated Auguſt 28, 1706,
" convey one half of the ſaid lands to Sir Charles Hobby
" of Boſton, New-England, Knight, under whom
" John Hobby late of Barbadoes, but now reſiding at
" Boſton, grandſon and heir at law to the ſaid Sir
" Charles Hobby, together with John Adams, of
" Boſton, have a lawful claim to the ſaid half of the
" ſaid lands ; and the heirs of the ſaid Thomas Allen
" or their aſſigns, have a right to the other half; all
" which

" which will foon be made to appear: And whereas
" the firft-mentioned claimers are granting fundry tracts
" of lands to people who apprehend their title to be
" good, it is thought proper to advife fuch perfons to
" be cautious in fettling the faid lands, till it appears
" whofe the property is, which may probably be very
" fpeedily, when the wafte lands may be granted; and
" alfo thofe perfons already poffeffed of lands may be con-
" firmed in their poffeffions on eafy terms."

4. The claim of Mr. Allen's heirs, if Mr. Mafon's
heirs fulfilled the conditions of the grant, feems to be
the beft. It is true, the Mafons and affignees in favour
of their claim, fay, that thefe lands were entailed, and
therefore could not legally be conveyed to Mr. Allen;
but Mr. Allen's heirs fay, that upon Mr. Allen's pur-
chafing of Mr. Mafon's grant, he obtained a feigned or
common conveyance of thefe lands; the effect of this fort
of recovery is to difcontinue and deftroy eftates tail, remainders and reverfions, and to bar and cut off the en-
tails of them.

5. Wheelright and affociates claim to lands in New-
Hampfhire, by Indian deeds; this was revived by Mr.
Cook and others, about thirty years fince, but without
effect. See vol. I. p. 410.

6. Million purchafe, fo called. See vol. I. p. 419.
This interferes with the late conveyance of the prefent
Mr. Mafon to fome New-Hampfhire gentlemen; as
thefe claims will never be of any confequence, it is
not worth while to difintangle them. This million purchafe claim was revived about twenty-eight years fince,
and lately by an advertifement in the Bofton gazette,
June 21, 1748.

7. Not many years fince, when the affair of the property of their lands was to be referred to the king in
council; the governor and council, fo far as in them
lay, granted to themfelves and friends, (in all about
fixty perfons of New-Hampfhire,) a tract of land called
Kingfwood, laying upon and near Winepefiakee lake

or

or pond, containing almoft the whole of the wafte lands in Mr. Mafon's grant, and perhaps farther than Mr. Mafon's grant extended.

In the reign of Charles II. the king in council at fundry times appointed trials of the claims of the colony of Maffachufetts-Bay, and of Mafon's heirs concerning the difputed lands between Neumkeag and Merimack rivers, but without refult or iffue; at length by charter of William and Mary, October 7, 1691, conform to the old charter of 1629, that tract of land was confirmed to the province of Maffachufetts-Bay abfolutely as to jurifdiction, but with a referve of col. Allen's claim under Mr. Mafon as to property.

The corporation, or company called the council of Plymouth or council of New-England (fee vol. I. p. 366, 386.) made many grants of property, but could not delegate jurifdiction; therefore to fupply this defect, fome of thefe grantees obtained additional royal charters with power of jurifdiction; Mr. Mafon 1635, Sir Ferdinando Gorge 1639, obtained royal patents; here we may obferve, that although the jurifdiction of the lands from Neumkeag to Merimack river are included in Mr. Mafon's patent, this patent was pofterior to the Maffachufetts old royal charter, which included that jurifdiction.

Originally the extent of this province from three miles north of Merimack river to Pifcataqua river, was twenty miles fea line, and fixty miles inland; by the determination of the king in council 1739, the fea line continues the fame, and weftward heading the province of Maffachufetts-Bay, it extends from Newichawanack river about 115 miles to New-York bounds; northward towards Canada it is indefinite, or rather not determined.

The fucceffive changes in property and jurifdiction, are as follows. Mafon's firft grant, fee vol. I. p. 418.

Towards

Towards the end of 1635 dies capt. Mason, and by will leaves New-Hampshire to John Tufton (to be called Mason) and his heirs: John dying before he was of age, it came to his brother Robert Tufton Mason an infant, who was not of age till 1650: during his minority the servants in New-Hampshire embezzle every thing, and the civil wars preventing any legal relief, the Massachusetts people, at the desire of the inhabitants of New-Hampshire, took all those lands into their own disposal and jurisdiction.

1661, Robert Tufton Mason petitioned king Charles II. to be relieved as to his property of these lands; Sir Geofry Palmer, attorney general, made report, that these lands were the undoubted right of the said Robert Mason, grandson and heir of the said John Mason. The inhabitants of New-Hampshire, and province of Main, incapable of protecting themselves against the incursions of the Canada French and their Indians, desired the protection of the colony of Massachusetts-Bay; the assembly of Massachusetts assumed the property of the vacant lands and jurisdiction of that country. The colony of Massachusetts-Bay by their agent, that is attorney at home, purchased the property of the province of Main, July 20, 1677, from the heirs or assigns of Gorge; the property and jurisdiction was confirmed to the province of Massachusetts-Bay by their new charter.

1675, Mr. Mason still continuing his petition, the king refers them to the attorney and solicitor general; they report his title good, and the king sends a mandatory letter [*f*] dated March 10, 1675-6, to the Massachusetts-Bay colony: William Stoughton and Peter Bulkley are sent over agents to answer Mason's complaints; they

---

[*f*] This letter is directed: To our trusty and well beloved the governor and magistrates of our town of Boston in New-England. N.B. in those times the colony of Massachusetts-Bay (a hard word) was called the Boston colony.

as attornies legally conſtituted in the name of Maſſachuſetts colony diſclaim thoſe lands before the court of
King's-Bench.

1679, the proprietors and inhabitants of New-Hampſhire not capable of protecting themſelves againſt the
Canada French and their Indians, deſired of the crown
to take them under their immediate protection ; accordingly the king commiſſioned [g] a preſident with
ten counſellors for the government thereof, Sept. 18,
1679, and the lands granted there by the Maſſachuſetts colony, were directed to pay Mr. Maſon's heirs
ſix-pence in the pound quit-rent, as incomes at that
time were valued by way of compoſition ; at the ſame
time a court of record is conſtituted, to try and determine all cauſes, reſerving an appeal home when the
value is fifty pound ſterling and upwards ; Robert
Maſon may make out titles to the preſent poſſeſſors
at ſix-pence in the pound value of all rents of real
eſtates, as quit-rents ; the unoccupied lands to remain
to the ſaid Maſon.

1682, May 9, King Charles II. appoints Edward
Cranfield, Eſq. lieutenant governor. When the crown
was endeavouring to re-aſſume all charters and patents,
the patentees made another formal ſurrender of juriſdiction to the crown ; and Cranfield 1684 was
commiſſioned governor, but ſoon went to Barbadoes,
and lieutenant-governor Uſher had the adminiſtration.

Robert Maſon the patentee's caſe was recommended
by the crown ; he came over to New-Hampſhire ; ſome
few of the poſſeſſors took leaſes, but they generally re-

[g] For the honour of thoſe families, who in theſe times were reckoned
principal original ſettlers, we ſhall tranſmit them by name, viz. John
Cuts, preſident ; the ten counſellors were Richard Martyn, William
Vaughan, and Thomas Daniel of Portſmouth ; John Gilman of Exeter ;
Chriſtopher Huſſy of Hampton, and Richard Waldron of Dover, with
power to chuſe three others to conſtitute the firſt council ; the preſident
and five other counſellors to be a board.

fuſed

fufed this propofal.   Mr. Mafon brought writs of ejeᴄtment againft Mr. Waldron, and about thirty others ;
he recovered judgment, but was oppofed in the execution, and his life threatened.   1684, Mr. Mafon
brought a writ of ejeᴄtment againft William Vaughan,
Efq. and recovered judgment ; Mr. Vaughan appealed to his majefty in council ; this appeal was difmiffed and the former judgment confirmed, and cofts
given againft the appellant.   Mr. Mafon defpairing of
any accommodation with the people, and his ,life
threatened, returned to England, and foon after died,
leaving two fons John and Robert Tufton Mafon.

1691, April 27, John and Robert Tufton Mafon by
their deed lawfully executed for the confideration of
2750*l.* fterl. did grant to Samuel Allen of London, Efq.
all their [*b*] right to lands in New-England.

[*b*] An abftraᴄt of Mafon's deed to Allen. 1691, April 27, John
Tufton Mafon and Robert Tufton Mafon, fons of Robert Tufton Mafon, fome time of the parifh of St. Martin's in the fields, in the county
of Middlefex, Efq. deceafed, did fell to Samuel Allen of London, Merchant, in confideration of 2750*l.* fterl. a portion of main land in
New-England, from the middle of Merimack river to proceed eaftward
along the fea-coaft to Cape-Anne and round about the fame to Pifcataqua harbour, and fo forwards up within the river of Newichawanock, and to the fartheft head of the faid river, and from thence north-
weftward till fixty miles be finifhed from the firft entrance of Pifcataqua
harbour; and alfo from Néumkeag through the river thereof up into
the land weft fixty miles; from which period to crofs over land to the
fixty miles end accounted from Pifcataqua through the Newichawanock river to the land north weftward; and alfo all the fcuth half of
the ifles of Shoals, together with all other iflands and ifelets as well
imbayed as adjoining, laying, abutting upon or near the premifes
within five leagues diftance, not otherways granted by fpecial name to
any at any time before April 18, 1635, called by the name of New-
Hampfhire. Alfo ten thoufand acres at the S. E. part of the entrance of Sagadahock, called by the name of Masonia. Alfo a portion of land in the province of Main, beginning at the entrance of
Newichawanock river and fo upwards along the faid river, and to
the fartheft head thereof, and to contain in breadth through all .the
length aforefaid three miles within the land from every part of the faid
river, and half way over the faid river. Alfo that part of the fea-coaft
of New-England, on a great head land or cape north eaftward

1692, March 1, Col. Samuel Allen was commissioned governor of New-Hampshire, and his commission was from three miles north of Merimack river to Piscataqua river, &c.

1700, Col. Allen came over to New-Hampshire to prosecute his claim, and found there were twenty-four

of a great river of the Massachusetts, stretching into the sea eastwards five leagues or thereabouts, in the lat. between 42 d. and 43 d. known by the name of Tabigranda or Cape-Anne, with the north, south and east shores thereof; the back bounds towards the main land beginning at the head of the next great river to the southward of the said cape, and running into the main land westward, and up a river supposed to be called Merimack, north westward of the said cape to the fartheft head of the said river; from which period to cross over land to the other great river, which lies southward of the aforesaid cape, and half way over, that is to say, to the middle of the said two rivers within the great island called Isle Mason, laying near or before the bay, harbour or river of Agawam, with all islands laying within three miles of the said sea-coaft, known by the name of Mariana. Also all those lands and countries bordering on the rivers and lakes of the Iroquois or nations of Indians inhabiting up into the landward, between the lines of the west and north weft, conceived to pass or lead upwards from the rivers of Sagadahock and Merimack, together with the lakes and rivers of the Iroquois, and other nations adjoining, the middle part of which lake lies near about 44 d. or 45 d. as also all lands within ten miles of any parts of the said lakes and rivers on the south east part thereof, and from the weft end or sides of the said lakes and rivers, so far forth to the weft, as shall extend half way into the next great lake to the westward, and from thence northward into the north side of the main river, which runneth from the great and vaft western lakes, and falleth into the river of Canada, including all within the said perambulation, which portions of lands, rivers, and lakes, are commonly called the province of Laconia. As also the towns and ports of Portsmouth, Hampton, Dover, Exeter, Little Harbour, Greenland, Salisbury, old Salisbury, Concord, Sudbury, Reading, Belerica, Gloucefter, Cape Anne town, Ipswich, Wenham, Newbury, Haverhill, Andover, Rowley, Bafstown, Woburn, and all other villages, towns, ports and harbours in the aforesaid tracts of land called Masonia, Mariana, Isle Mason, and province of Laconia, with all mines, minerals, &c. and all royal letters or patents, deeds, writings, rentals, accounts, papers, and evidences of land whatsoever relating to the same.

It is said that Mr. Mason (called treasurer and pay-mafter of the army,) 1634, sent over about seventy servants with stores and provisions to carry on the settlement of New-Hampshire; and Mr. Mason dying towards the end of 1635, that his eftate in New Hampshire inventered, amounted to about twenty thousand pounds fterl.

or

or twenty-five leaves torn out of the records; thefe
leaves contained the records of former judgments of
ejectment obtained by Mafon.   He enters new writs of
ejectment againft Waldron, Vaughan, &c. the juries
brought in for the defendants cofts; the king in council
difmiffed his appeal without cofts, becaufe he had not
brought proof of Mr. Mafon's poffeffion, and was allowed to begin de novo. Col. Allen petitioned Q. Anne
in council to be put in poffeffion of the wafte lands, &c.
the petition was referred to the board of trade and plantations; they advifed with Sir Edward Northey, attorney general, who reported that her majefty might fafely
put him in poffeffion of the unimproved land, but where
the inhabitants had poffeffion he might bring his writs
of ejectment: an order was fent to governor Dudley (at
this time Dudley was governor of the province of Maffachufetts-Bay, and of the province of New-Hampfhire,
by two diftinct commiffions) to put col. Allen in poffeffion of the wafte lands, but for land improved he was
to bring writs of ejectment, and when the trials came
on governor Dudley was directed to go into court and
demand a fpecial verdict; accordingly upon a trial of
ejectment againft Waldron, governor Dudley was notified to attend, but for certain reafons at that time beft
known to himfelf, and a great indifpofition of body (as
he faid) he proceeded no further than Newbury; the
defendants obtained cofts of fuit: Col. Allen appeals
to the crown, but dies before the appeal was profecuted, leaving one fon and four daughters. His fon
Thomas fucceeds him in thefe claims, and was caft in
his writs of ejectment with cofts, a fpecial verdict
being refufed; he appealed, and died before it could
be heard, leaving two fons and one daughter infants.
To cut off the claim of Mr. Allen's heirs to wafte
lands, fo far as in them lies, lately this government
have made a grant of the wafte lands by the name of
Kingfwood, to about fixty of their principal inhabitants

tants poſſeſſors, that there might remain no waſte lands
in Mr. Maſon's grant.

The lands lately adjudged by the king in council, not
to belong to the Maſſachuſetts Bay grant, are now crown
lands, but at preſent under the juriſdiction of the province of New Hampſhire; they lay north of Maſſachuſetts, and when the boundaries with Canada are ſettled may
prove a good diſtinct inland province for produce.   By
an order of the king in council 1744, it is directed, that
if the government of New-Hampſhire do not provide for
fort Dummer, there will be a neceſſity for returning that
fort with a proper contiguous diſtrict to the province of
Maſſachuſetts Bay : but ſo it happened, that during the
late French war, the province of Maſſachuſetts-Bay by
the contrivance of—for ſake of perquiſites maintained
that fort and many block houſes within the diſtrict of
New-Hampſhire, without any conſideration or allowance
for want of proper application at home.

As Mr. Maſon's grant lies indented in the province of
Maſſachuſetts Bay, (the old colony of Maſſachuſetts-Bay
is weſtward, and the province of Main by the new
charter annexed to Maſſachuſetts-Bay is eaſtward) perhaps it would be for the intereſt of Great-Britain and for
the good of the inhabitants, to annex this ſmall country
to the neighbouring government by an additional charter.   The property of the vacant lands of Maſſachuſetts-
Bay being in the repreſentatives of the collective body
of the people, and the property of the vacant lands in
New-Hampſhire being in the crown, is no obſtacle, ſee-
ing the vacant lands in Sagadahock or duke of York's
former property, though annexed by charter to Maſſachuſetts, continue the property of the crown, that is, not
to be aſſigned by the government of Maſſachuſetts-Bay,
without conſent of the crown.   New-Hampſhire is too
diminutive for a ſeparate government or province; the
numbers of their people and the value of their commerce
are inſignificant: in fact the governor of Maſſachuſetts-Bay for many years was alſo governor of New-
Hampſhire;

Hampshire with a distinct commission, but about ten years since the assembly of New-Hampshire enter a complaint to the king in council against the joint governor of that time, in relation to the case of settling the boundaries between the two provinces; that he was partial in favour of his more profitable government of Massachusetts-Bay, by adjourning and proroguing the assembly of New-Hampshire, when the case was in agitation; this complaint, by the king in council, was judged true and good, therefore a separate governor for New-Hampshire was commissioned anno 1740. In such diminutive governments, the governor may domineer and act in a more despotick manner, than his sovereign can possibly in Great-Britain; it is said that a governor and such of the council as he thinks proper to consult with, dispense with such provincial laws as are troublesome or stand in their way in procedures of their court of equity, so called.

Here is at present subsisting a dispute (interrupting all publick business) between the governor in council, and the house of representatives, concerning the governor's prerogative of negativing a speaker, and his qualifying so many towns and districts, as he shall think worthy to send representatives. And in this insignificant government, it may be called Lis de lana caprina, but in our considerable colonies it is an affair of great consequence, therefore I shall here insert a small digression concerning these prerogatives and privileges.

A Digression, concerning some disputed points relating to the legislatures of the several British colonies in America; particularly where the prerogatives of the crown governors seem to clash with the privileges of the representatives of the collective body of the people or settlers, in general court assembled.

Perhaps, in our colonies after a legislature is constituted by royal charters as in New-England, as by proprietary patents of government as in Penſylvania, Maryland, &c. or by royal commiſſion or inſtructions [*i*] to the firſt crown governor in the king's governments; further inſtructions from the court of Great-Britain, though obligatory upon the negatives of the country's repreſentatives, who naturally may be ſuppoſed, and doubtleſs were intended, as a check upon inſtructions from the boards at home not well verſed in plantation affairs.—On the other ſide, as to prerogative, the plantation acts ought to have a ſuſpending clauſe, that is, not to be obligatory (thus it is in Ireland, a Britiſh colony or acquiſition, an ancient precedent) unleſs confirmed by the Britiſh court.

Thus in general, there are two ſupreme negatives in the legiſlatures of our American colonies; the king in council, and the particular legiſlatures of the ſeveral colonies.

In a colony where there is a royally conſtituted legiſlature, perhaps their publick acts, after being approved of, or not diſapproved after a certain time (Maſſachuſetts-Bay charter expreſſes it after three years) cannot be diſannulled but by the legiſlature of Great-Britain called the parliament, who in all Britiſh caſes and over all perſons, according to the Britiſh conſtitution, are abſolutely ſupreme and the dernier reſort.

If any innovations were to be made by the adminiſtration at home upon the eſtabliſhed conſtitution of our colonies, they naturally will begin with ſome inſignificant colony, ſuch for inſtance is this of New-Hampſhire, where the people have no money nor intereſt lodged at home to maintain their privileges; and from precedents of ſuch impotent colonies, proceed to impoſe upon the more rich and valuable colonies. Thus it was in the latter end of the reign of Charles II. and in the ſhort abrupted reign of James II. when all corporation valuable privileges were deſigned to be abrogated;

[*i*] The inſtruction is, that after *** a limited time, they ſhall iſſue a ſummons for convening a general aſſembly.

they

they began with the infignificant impotent borough corporations.

A governor perhaps by foliciting at home and giving
adequate gratuities and fees to the proper leading clerks
of the feveral boards, may obtain additional inftructions
fuitable to his intereft or humour.   I do not maintain,
but only mention, that we feem to have a late inftance of
this in the province of New-Hampfhire. In 1744-5, there
was a difpute between the governor and houfe of reprefentatives concerning the houfe's not admitting of members from the governor's new conftituted townfhips and
diftricts, but not qualified by the houfe; the governor
by folicitations, &c. at home, obtained in the king's
abfence, from the lords juftices an additional inftruction,
as follows.

" By the LORDS JUSTICES.

Gower, P. S.	Additional inftruction to Benning Went-
Bedford,	worth, Efq. his majefty's governor and
Montagu,	commander in chief, in and over the
Pembroke.	province of New-Hampfhire, in New-
	England in America; or to the comman-
	der in chief of the faid province for the
	time being.
(Seal)	Given at Whitehall, the 30th day of
	June, 1748, in the 22d year of his ma-
	jefty's reign.

Whereas it hath been reprefented to his majefty, That
you having in his majefty's name, and by virtue of your
commiffion, iffued a writ to the fheriff of the province
under your government, commanding him to make out
precepts, directed to the felect men of certain towns,
parifhes, and diftricts, therein mentioned, for the election of fit perfons qualified in law to reprefent them in
the general affembly, appointed to be held at Portfmouth, within the faid province, on the 24th day of

January 1744-5; by which writ, the towns of South-Hampton and Cheſter, and the diſtricts of Haverhill, and of Methuen and Dracut, and the diſtrict of Rumford, were impowered to chooſe repreſentatives as aforeſaid; the ſaid general aſſembly did refuſe to admit the perſons duly elected to repreſent the ſaid towns and diſtricts to ſit and vote in the choice of a ſpeaker: And whereas the right of ſending repreſentatives to the ſaid aſſembly was founded originally on the commiſſions and inſtructions given by the crown to the reſpective governors of the province of New-Hampſhire, and his majeſty may therefore lawfully extend the privilege of ſending repreſentatives to ſuch new towns as his majeſty ſhall judge worthy thereof:

It is therefore his majeſty's will and pleaſure, and you are hereby directed and required to diſſolve the aſſembly of the province, under your government as ſoon as conveniently may be, and when another is called, to iſſue his majeſty's writ to the ſheriff of the ſaid province, commanding him to make out precepts, directed to the ſelect-men of the towns of South-Hampton and Cheſter, the diſtricts of Haverhill, and of Methuen and Dracut, and the diſtrict of Rumford, requiring them to cauſe the freeholders of the ſaid towns and diſtricts to aſſemble, to elect fit perſons to repreſent the ſaid towns and diſtricts in general aſſembly, in manner following, viz. One for the town of South-Hampton, one for the town of Cheſter, one for the diſtrict of Haverhill, one for the diſtrict of Methuen and Dracut, and one for the diſtrict of Rumford: AND it is his majeſty's further will and pleaſure, that you do ſupport the rights of ſuch repreſentatives, when choſe; and that you do likewiſe ſignify his majeſty's pleaſure herein to the members of the ſaid general aſſembly."——

This would be nearly the ſame, as if the patricii of Rome (in our colonies they are called governor and council) had aſſumed the prerogative of regulat-

ing

ing the [*k*] tribuni plebis, or reprefentatives of the people.

The writs or precepts for electing of reprefentatives for the feveral townfhips and diftricts returned into the fecretary's office, were produced in the houfe, Jan. 5. 1748-9, being the firft day of the fitting of a new affembly.   They confifted of

3	from Portfmouth.	1	from Newington.
3	Dover.	1	New-Market.
2	Hampton.	1	Stratham.
2	Exeter.	1	Greenland.
2	Newcaftle & Rye.	1	London-derry.
1	Kingfton.	1	Durham.
1	Hampton-Falls.	—	
		20	

There were fome other members returned by fome new towns, Chefter, South-Hampton, and three other diftricts, but not admitted to fit: Richard Waldron, Efq. a worthy man, chofen fpeaker by all the votes, excepting one, was negatived or difallowed by the governor, becaufe the reprefentatives from the new towns were not admitted to fit and vote in the choice. The houfe were ftrictly required by the governor to admit thefe new reprefentatives, the refufal of them being the higheft contempt of the king's authority, as he faid, and to proceed to a new choice of a fpeaker.   This was abfolutely refufed by the houfe; denying the governor's power of negativing a fpeaker, and of introducing [*l*]

[*k*] When the patricii or optimates came to lord it too much over the other people of Rome, thefe people infifted upon their having reprefentatives in the publick adminiftration, called tribuni plebis, to maintain the liberties and privileges of the commons, againft the power of the optimates; perhaps the houfe of commons in the Britifh legiflature had fome fuch original.

[*l*] If the king fends inftructions to his governors of colonies, concerning the negativing of fpeakers, and qualifying any new towns or diftricts that fhall be thought worthy to fend reprefentatives to their

members not warranted by law, uſage, cuſtom, or any other authority.

This houſe ſtill ſubſiſts (June 1750) by many prorogations and alternate meſſages, but have done no publick or ordinary provincial buſineſs ; whether the governor or houſe of repreſentatives are in fault I do not determine ; I only relate matters of fact, and refer it to proper judgment.

As to a governor in the Britiſh colones NEGATIVING A SPEAKER, it is ſaid to be a controverted point, therefore ſhall make a few remarks in relation to it.

1. As the king at home, and his governors in the plantations abroad, never pretended to negative the election of a member for a county, town, or diſtrict; it ſeems inconſiſtent that they ſhould claim a negative upon a ſpeaker, or chairman, or moderator, choſen amongſt themſelves.

2. In Great-Britain towards the end of the reign of Charles II. all charters and other privileges of the people were deſigned to be ſacrificed to the prerogative ; there was a diſpute between the prerogative and the privilege of the commons concerning the court's negativing of a ſpeaker ; but ever ſince, this controverſy lies dormant; it is a tender point, a noli me tangere ; and plantation governors, who endeavour to revive the like in their diſtricts, by ſlily procuring inſtructions from the court at home, in favour of ſuch a negative, are perhaps no true friends to their colony, nor to the Britiſh conſtitution in general.

3 Notwithſtanding that, in the new charter 1691 of the province of Maſſachuſetts-Bay, it is expreſly ſaid, that the governor ſhall have a negative in all elections and acts of government ; in their additional or expla-

general aſſemblies ; it ſeems an ancient eſtabliſhed cuſtom or practice, that is, privilege of the houſe to admit or refuſe novel practices, it being a notorious privilege in the Britiſh conſtitution for the repreſentatives of the people to regulate their own members.

natory

natory charter 12 Geo. I. in the king's abfence granted by the guardians or juftices of the kingdom, it is faid, that no provifion was made in the faid charter, of the king by his governor, approving or difapproving the election of a fpeaker of the houfe of reprefentatives. In confequence of this new charter, not by any abfolute royal command, but by the voluntary confent and act of the reprefentatives themfelves, the commander in chief is allowed to negative the fpeaker. Thus perhaps an act of the general affembly of New-Hampfhire or their tacit fubmiffion, might inveft their governor with the like power, but not to be affumed in any other manner.

4. The exclufive right of electing their own fpeaker is in the houfe of commons or reprefentatives; the confirmation by prefenting him to the king, or to his governors, is a mere form in courfe. Thus the lord mayor and fheriffs of London are prefented in the king's exchequer-court, but no negative pretended; and perhaps if the king in a progrefs fhould happen to be in any corporated city or town at the time of the election of, their mayor and fheriffs, in compliment and form they would be prefented to the king.

As to the governor's difpute with the houfe of reprefentatives, concerning his fummoning NEW MEMBERS FROM UNPRIVILEGED PLACES OR DISTRICTS, we make the following remarks.

1. The prefent governor of New-Hampfhire, without any prudential retinue or referve, impolitically expofing fuch an arbitrary proceeding, menaces them with ten more fuch reprefentatives; he means an indefinite arbitrary number in his meffage, Feb. 15, 1748-9.

2. For many fcores of years, which is generally conftrued a prefcription; there have been no royal addition of members of parliament; and at the union of the two kingdoms of Scotland and England, to prevent multi-

plying

plying of members, the ſmall royal corporated towns of Scotland were claſſed, that is, four or five of them jointly to ſend one member or repreſentative; therefore as the royal appointing of new repreſentatives in Great-Britain has been diſcontinued time out of mind, why ſhould the general conſtitution be infringed upon in our colonies, and from the caprice or private intereſt of a governor, the aſſembly members be [*m*] multiplied to an inconvenient and chargeable number? excepting where the cultivation of wilderneſs lands may require new townſhips or diſtricts, and, if inconveniently remote from a former ſhire or county town, they require a new ſeparate county or ſhire.

3. As an inſtance or precedent of a royal regulation in the colonies; in the charter of Maſſachuſetts-Bay it is expreſsly declared, " that the houſe of repreſentatives " with the other branches of the legiſlature, ſhould de- " termine what numbers ſhould be afterwards ſent to " repreſent the counties, towns, and places;" therefore the affair of repreſentation in the legiſlature is not abſolutely in the governor and his devotees of the council.

[*m*] In the province of Maſſachuſetts-Bay, from 1730 to 1741.(the reaſons or inducements of this procedure, I ſhall not account for) by erecting of new townſhips and ſplitting of old townſhips into many corporations, the members of the houſe of repreſentatives were likely to be increaſed to an impolitick number; therefore in the following adminiſtration, (ſee vol. I. p. 490.) the governor had an inſtruction, in granting new townſhips to exclude them from ſending repreſentatives. This ſeems inconſiſtent with the Britiſh conſtitution, whereby all freeholders of forty ſhillings per ann. income and upwards, are qualified to be repreſented in the legiſlature and taxation; in particular, freeholders are not to be taxed, but where their agent or repreſentative does or may appear.

A vote of the repreſentatives to regulate their own houſe, is not a general act of government.

Governors have a conſiderable advantage over their aſſemblies; when he ſends them any impoſing meſſage of importance, but not reaſonable, to prevent any repreſentation of its inconvenianency or illegality, he adjourns or prorogues them.

4. In

4. In the neighbouring province of Maſſachuſetts-Bay, by charter each townſhip was qualified (by, a late inſtruction, the newly granted townſhips are diſqualified) to ſend two repreſentatives, whereas they generally ſend one, and at times exclusively the houſe of repreſentatives excuſe ſome towns from ſending, and mulct other townſhips for not ſending.   In Great-Britain, there are many borough towns or corporations not privileged to ſend members or repreſentatives to parliament; but as there are county repreſentatives, as freeholders they are repreſented in their county ; whereas in New-England there being no county repreſentatives, theſe unprivileged diſtricts are not repreſented, which is an [n] infringement upon the Britiſh conſtitution.

5. All new townſhips and diſtricts, who by a governor's precept are required to ſend repreſentatives, their qualifications ought to be confirmed by an act of aſſembly, before they are allowed to ſit, otherwiſe the governor to ſerve a turn may multiply the houſe of repreſentatives to any inconvenient number and unneceſſary publick charge, where the repreſentatives are upon wages ; together with the general damage of calling off from labour and buſineſs, many perſons invincibly ignorant of publick affairs.

6. The laſt charter of the city of New-York, in the king's province of New-York, was confirmed by act of their provincial aſſembly, 1730; and by its laſt clauſe it is provided, that, " this preſent act ſhould be reputed,

[n] To obviate or rectify this, the counties by act of aſſembly may be allowed county repreſentatives, or the new townſhips and ſubdiviſions of old townſhips may be claſſed, and jointly ſend one or more repreſentatives.   As in the nature of things, nothing, no conſtitution is perfect ; where any inconveniency from time to time appears, it ought to be rectified.   This introducing of county repreſentatives, or of claſſical repreſentations of towns, is not conſiſtent with a late inſtruction from the court of Great-Britain, that in granting of new townſhips, a proviſion be made that the number of repreſentatives be not thereby increaſed, or with a ſuſpending clauſe, i. e. It ſhall not take place till confirmed from home.

"'as if it were a publick act of aſſembly relating to the " whole colony." This is an inſtance of corporations in the plantations, being confirmed by act of aſſembly.

I ſhall here inſert ſome obſervations concerning general aſſemblies or houſes of repreſentatives, which were omitted in the ſection of Maſſachuſetts-Bay.

1. Conſtituting townſhips with all corporation privileges, but expreſly excluding them from the privilege of ſending repreſentatives, ſeems ANTI-CONSTITUTIONAL; eſpecially conſidering, that there are no county repreſentations of freeholders in New-England. See vol. I. p. 459.

2. By act of the aſſembly of Maſſachuſetts-Bay forty members are required to make a QUORUM in the houſe of repreſentatives. As this is not by charter, it may be rectified by act of aſſembly. In the houſe of commons of Great-Britain conſiſting of 558 members or returns, forty make a quorum; why ſhould the houſe of repreſentatives of Maſſachuſetts-Bay, which this year 1750 conſiſts of only about ninety returns, have the ſame number forty for a quorum? As many towns are delinquent in ſending repreſentatives, and ſome members of the other towns negligent in their attendance, it may ſometimes be difficult to make a quorum of forty, and conſequently publick buſineſs impeded.

3. The old act, that a repreſentative muſt be a reſident in the townſhip for which he is elected, may be ſalutary for ſome time in a new country not much concerned in commerce and policy; but a trading politick country, ſuch as is Maſſachuſetts-Bay, for a country-man not uſed to trade or money, to preſcribe in ſuch affairs, is not natural. See vol. I. p, 506.

4. As in England, ſheriffs of counties are excluded from being members of the houſe of commons, ſo in the colonies the ſame regulation may take place, becauſe a ſheriff may be ſuppoſed to be under the influence

of

of the court or governor, his conftituents, and his perfonal prefence feems required in his bailywick.

5. That the counfellors and reprefentatives may ferve
their country gratis : thus we fhall have generous members, not hirelings eafily to be corrupted. This year
1750, the town of Bofton and fome country townfhips
by way of leading examples have made an introduction.
Anciently in the parliament of England, a knight- of
the fhire was allowed four fhillings, and a citizen or
burgefs two fhillings a day, by the refpective places for
which they were chofen ; at prefent they have no wages ;
the houfe of lords, the king's hereditary council or fecond branch in the legiflature, never had any pay. It
is full time that our colonies fhould conform to this
example ; feveral provinces have conformed, particularly in New-England our neighbouring colony of
Rhode-Ifland ever fince 1746. See vol. I. p. 507. This
will be a confiderable article of faving in the ordinary
charges of government.

A Digression, concerning the national claims of Great-
Britain and France relating to difputed countries on
the continent of North-America and fome of the
Caribbee Weft-India iflands.

The crown lands lately taken from the province of
Maffachufetts-Bay, and the lands north of Mafon's grant,
have lately pro tempore been annexed to the jurifdiction
of this fmall province of New-Hampfhire ; they extend
from weft to eaft from New-York eaft line (which is
twenty miles eaft of Hudfon's river) to the weft line of
the province of Main about 115 miles ; north they extend indefinitely to a line dividing the American Britifh
dominions from the dominions of France called New-
France or Canada ; this line is now upon the carpet in Paris, to be adjufted by Britifh and French commiffaries[o].

[o] This line does not immediately affect the province of Maffachufetts Bay ; it affects Nova-Scotia, Sagadahock, (the jurifdiction pro tem-
Mr.

Mr. Bollon, agent for Maſſachuſetts-Bay, has an [*p*] inſtruction from their aſſembly to repreſent the encroachment which the French are making upon our ſettlements in North-America.

The late exorbitant French claims of extending their boundaries in America, beyond all the limits which have hitherto been challenged or allowed, gave occaſion to the following paragraphs.

M. La Janqueriere governor general of Canada or New France, by his inſtructions from home, lately ſent

pore.but not the property of Sagadahock or duke of York's grant, is in the province of Maſſachuſetts-Bay, as was alſo Nova Scotia by the preſent charter) the late crown land of New-Hampſhire, New-York, &c.

[*p*.] That the curious may have ſome notion of our colonies agencies at the court of Great Britain, I ſhall here inſert, by way of inſtance, an abſtract of the laſt body of inſtructions to agent Bollon voted by the aſſembly, January 19. 1749-50.

1. To ſolicit the payment and reimburſement of the charges of the late intended expedition againſt Canada.

2. To ſolicit the payment for the provincial cloathing made uſe of by admiral Knowles for his majeſty's ſea and land forces at Louiſbourg

3. To ſolicit the charge of ſupporting fort Dummer, and defending the frontiers of New-Hampſhire.

4. To make application, that the governments of Connecticut, New-Hampſhire, and Rhode-Iſland, be obliged to a ſpeedy and equitable redemption of their bills of publick credit.

5. To repreſent the encroachments made and making by the French on his majeſty's territories in North-America.

6. To enquire into the ſtate of the line, between this province and the colony of Connecticut as formerly ſettled, in order to have it confirmed, if not already done.

7. To make application that ſeveral governments on this continent be obliged to bear a juſt proportion of men and money in caſe of another war.

8. To ſolicit the exemption of ſea-men and others in this government from impreſſes on board any of his majeſty's ſhips that may come into this province.

9. That he apply to the court of Great-Britain for pay for the ſnow Eagle and Dominique, taken from the captors at Louiſbourg, and employed in his majeſty's ſervice to carry home priſoners to France.

10. The agent being impowered to receive what money ſhall be obtained at Great-Britain for this government, he is to lodge the ſame at the bank of England for the further order of the general aſſembly.

letters

letters to the commandant of Nova Scotia and to the governor of Maffachufetts-Bay, claiming a great part of Nova Scotia, and from thence fo far as Quenebec river in New-England. At this writing M. La Corne, a French officer from Canada with a confiderable [*q*] force, lies cantoned on the north fide of Chicanicto bay and river, to prevent us from extending further north than the peninfula, fo called, and from building a fort upon the neck, where is the barcadier by the Bay Verte to Canada. Major Laurence of Warburton's regiment with about 450 men was fent to diflodge them, but finding the French too ftrong, and inftructed to repel force by force, as alfo the houfes burnt to prevent any lodgment there, he retired to Minas.

The French court has appointed as commiffaries the marquis de la Gliffoniere late commandant general of New-France, and M. La Houettes; with two commiffaries nominated by the court of Great-Britain, Mr. Shirley, late governor of Maffachufetts-Bay, and Mr. Mildmay; to regulate all the refpective pretenfions of the two nations in America, and the contefts ftill remaining on fome prizes made on both fides during the war. It is thought, that for fome time they may avoid coming to any determination, and perhaps inftead of a definitive may come to a provifional treaty of Uti, &c.

There was lately a difpute concerning the property and jurifdiction of the ifland of Tobago in the Weft-Indies, between the governor of Barbadoes and the general of Martinico; this difpute ended in a provifional treaty; this with fome other of the windward Caribbee iflands commonly went by the name of [*r*] Neutral Iflands.

[*q*] This force confifts of three companies of marines, about 400 Indians of Canada, St. John's, Cape Sable, and Penobfcot, fome Canada militia and Coureurs des Bois, and French neutrals, as they are called, of Nova Scotia.

[*r*] The imprudence of our commanders and other officers, in giving the denomination of neutrals to the French fettlers of Nova Scotia, per-

Soon after the peace of Aix la Chapelle, which was concluded October 7, 1748, the French began to ſettle (erect batteries) the neutral Caribbee iſlands of [ſ] Tobago, St. Vincent, St. Lucia, and St. Dominico. Theſe and ſome other Caribbee iſlands called Neutrals are expreſly mentioned to keep up the claim, in both [*t*]

haps gave occaſion to the preſent French claim of a great part of Nova Scotia, and of ſome part of New-England, ſo far as Quenebec river.

[ſ] Tobago was formerly the property of the dukes of Courland; they had a ſettlement on the coaſt of Guinea, called Fort St. Andrew, to ſupply it with negro ſlaves: in the beginning of the reign of king Charles II. they were diſpoſſeſſed by the Dutch; this occaſioned **James, duke of Courland** by treaty November 17, 1664, to make over to Charles II. the ſovereignty of the ſaid iſland and fort of St. Andrew's, reſerving liberty of trade to the Courlanders and Dantzickers. Upon this the Dutch ſeem to have quitted the iſland, and the Courlanders never repoſſeſſed it; thus it remains at leaſt a fief of the crown of Great-Britain.

It was firſt diſcovered by the Spaniards, and had its name from Indian tobacco ſmoakers. When the Engliſh firſt ſettled Barbadoes, there being no Spaniſh ſetlers in Tobago, the Engliſh from Barbadoes frequented it, and Charles I. made a grant of it to the earl of Pembroke; the ſubſequent civil wars prevented his ſettling of it. Soon after about 200 Dutch people ſettled there, but were expelled by the Spaniards and Caribbee Indians. Next James Kettler duke of Courland, god-ſon to James I. of England, made a ſettlement there; but was diſpoſſeſſed by the two Lampſons, Dutch merchants from France; they had the titles of counts and barons of Tobago; and from the Dutch Weſt-India company had a grant of the iſland, and with conſent of the States they ſent over M. Bavean governor. It was in diſpute between the Engliſh and Dutch in Charles II. Dutch War. The houſe of Kettler being extinct, it reverted to England.

[*t*] The preſent governor of Barbadoes, his commiſſion runs thus; Henry Grenville, Eſq. captain general and chief governor of the iſlands of Barbadoes, St. Lucia, St. Vincent, Dominico, and the reſt of his majeſty's iſland colonies and plantations in America; known by the name of the Caribbee Iſlands, lying and being to windward of Guardaloupe. The preſent governor of Martinico, his commiſſion runs thus; Marquis de Caylus, governor and lieutenant general of the iſlands of Martinico, Guardaloupe, Grande and Petite Terre, Deſiada, Marigallante, the Saints, Dominico, St. Lucia, St. Vincent, Bequia, Cannaovan, Caricacocoan, Grenada, and of all the iſlands and iſlets commonly called the Granadillos, Tobago, St. Bartholomew, St. Martin, Cayan, and the continent comprehended between the river of the Amazons and Oranoke.

com-

commiffions of the governor of Barbadoes, and the French general of Martinico. Beginning of December 1748, the French governor of Martinico iffued a proclamation, prohibiting the Englifh, Dutch or Danes, from trading there without licence from the general of Martinico, on pain of forfeiting veffel and cargo. Upon information of thefe proceedings the governor of Barbadoes fent capt. Tyrrel with fome frigates to Tobago. Capt. Tyrrel fent aboard the French commodore to enquire what bufinefs he had there; who roundly told him, he was come to fettle that ifland, and if obftructed therein, was to make the beft defence he could. Capt. Tyrrel returned to Barbadoes for further orders.

When complaint was made to the French court by the court of Great-Britain, concerning the French affuming the ifland of Tobago; the court of France by way of recrimination anfwered in April 1749, that the Englifh were the aggreffors, by prefuming laft November in a clandeftine manner to ftick up a proclamation in that ifland, commanding the French fubjects there to quit the place within the fpace of thirty days, upon pain of military execution: this (as they pretend) induced the general of Martinico, without previous orders from his court to prevent the fame, by fettling inhabitants and batteries there.

Martinico, November 27, 1749, a provifional (not definitive) treaty was figned between commodore Holbourn, authorized by governor Grenville of Barbadoes, and the marquis de Caylus governor of Martinico, for the reciprocal evacuation of the ifland of Tobago, as well as for the immediate demolition of all the works and fortreffes which the French have raifed on Rockley-Bay, or any other part of the faid ifland: that neither nation fhall make fettlements there, but may wood and water there, catch fifh, and build temporary huts to fcreen them from the weather during their fifhing and

4	wooding,

wooding, but ſhall not cut down any trees other than
for fire-wood, nor gather any ſimples or valuable plants.
Accordingly a Britiſh man of war ſloop from Barbadoes, and a brigantine from Martinico, ſailed to Tobago, having each of them an officer on board charged
to ſee that iſland evacuated by the ſubjects of both
crowns.

The wars of New-Hampſhire with the Canada French
and Indians their allies, is generally comprehended in
what is wrote in the ſection of Maſſachuſetts-Bay [*u*].
Moreover, 1. Towards reduction of Louiſbourg, on
Cape-Bretton iſland, they contributed a regiment of 350
men under col. More. 2. Towards the ſecond reinforcement of 1000 men ſent from New-England for
the protection of Nova Scotia, they contributed 200
men, whereof only forty that were ſent to Minas did
any duty, the reſt in ſome trifling diſguſt ſoon returned to Portſmouth in New-Hampſhire. 3. In the
late French and Indian wars, they were neither capable

[*u*] As we hinted in the firſt volume, during the late French and Indian war, at the requeſt of the preſident and council of Nova Scotia,
repreſenting the weak ſtate of Annapolis as to their garriſon, and the
ill condition of their fortifications ; there were three reinforcements of
men ſent from New-England to Nova Scotia. 1. From Maſſachuſetts-
Bay 200 men ; they were of good uſe in the beginning of the French
war in ſummer 1744 ; the other two reinforcements were of no uſe.
2. In the winter 1746-7, a reinforcement of 500 men of Maſſachuſetts-
Bay, 300 of Rhode-Iſland, and 200 of New-Hampſhire, in all 1000
men, to be cantoned amongſt the French at Minas to keep them in due
ſubjection, and at the ſame time to eat up their ſpare proviſion which
uſed to victual the French and Indian parties : from ill contrivance and
worſe management, being indiſcreetly cantoned, no ſnow ſhoes, and ill
provided with ammunition, they ſuffered a diſmal maſſacre by a French
and Indian party from Chicanicto ; our forces happened to be only 470
men, the 300 Rhode Iſland men never arrived, having ſuffered ſhip-
wreck ; of the 200 New-Hampſhire men, only forty marched to Minas,
the reſt ſoon returned home. 3. Was a reinforcement of 270 men
from Maſſachuſetts-Bay ſent in the winter 1747-8, when the peace with
France was as good as concluded.

nor

nor willing to protect their own Frontiers; the g——
of Maffachufetts-Bay gladly embraced this opportunity of further perquifites, and procured the affembly
to take them under protection at a confiderable provincial charge, but hitherto without any reimburfement.

This province makes only one county or fhire: anno
1742, it contained about 6000 rateable whites, and
about 500 negroes or flaves.

Their complement of counfellors is ten; when much
deficient, the governor may appoint pro tempore. The
new grants of lands or townfhips are not from the reprefentatives of the collective body of the people, but by
the governor and council conform to the governor's commiffion and inftruction, at a certain nominal quit-rent,
e. g. London-derry to pay yearly one bufhel of potatoes
when required. The conftitution of their houfe of reprefentatives, fee vol. II. p. 37.

The juries are returned by the fheriff.

Their courts of judicature, befides the jurifdiction of
a juftice of the peace, and of a bench of juftices, are

1. The general feffions of the peace held quarterly.

2. Inferior courts of common pleas held four times a
year, confift of four judges, whereof three make a
quorum.

3. A fuperior court of judicature or common pleas
held twice a year, confifts of a chief judge and three
other judges, whereof three make a quorum; from
thence are allowed appeals to the governor and council,
or to a court of appeals in cafes where the value in difpute exceeds 100 *l.* fterl. and to the king in council,
where the true value of the thing in difference exceeds
300 *l.* fterl.

4. Courts of oyer and terminer, affizes, or general
goal delivery, are fpecially appointed by the governor
and council.

5. At prefent the fame judge of vice-admiralty and other officers, ferve for Maffachufetts-Bay, Rhode-Ifland and New-Hampfhire.

6. The officers of the court of probates, are appointed by the governor and council, with appeal to the gover-hor and council.

7. Court of equity. The commander in chief with the council, fuftain by way of appeal from the court (having jurifdiction) next below; directly without any new procefs, is tried on the fame original writ or pro-cefs brought to the firft court, and comes in ftatu quo exactly, faving that either party may bring new evidence if they pleafe: after a hearing, perhaps fome weeks or months may elapfe before fentence is pronounced; and from thence appeal may lie to the king in council.

In this province there is only one collection or cuftom-houfe, kept at Portfmouth. By the quarterly accounts from December 25, 1747, to December 25, 1748, fo-reign voyages

Cleared out,		Entered in,	
Ships	13	Ships	11
Snows	3	Snows	1
Brigs	20	Brigs	7
Sloops	57	Sloops	35
Schooners	28	Schooners	19
	121		73

befides about 200 coafting floops and fchooners, which carry [x] lumber to Bofton, Salem, Rhode-Ifland, &c.

---

[x] By lumber is meant all forts of wooden traffick that is bulky and of fmall value. In North-America, ranging timber, fpars, oak and pine plank, oak and pine boards, ftaves, heading and hoops, clap-boards, fhingles and laths, are called lumber. In the act of parlia-ment 1722, giving further encouragement for the importation of naval ftores, lumber is fpecified, viz. deals of feveral forts, timber balks of feveral fizes, barrel-boards, clap-boards, pipe-boards, or pipe-holt, white boards for fhoemakers, boom and cant fpurs, bow-ftaves, capre-vans, clap-holt, ebony-wood, headings for pipes, hogfheads and barrels, hoops for coopers, oars, pipe and hogfhcad ftaves, barrel ftaves, firkin

‡   whereof

whereof about one half enter in with freight from these parts.

Their produce is provisions, but scarce sufficient for their own consumption; masts, timber, deal-boards, joists, staves, hoops, clap-boards, shingles, and some dry cod fish.

Their manufactures are ship-building; lately a good fifth rate man of war called the America was built there. Bar-iron; the noted iron-works on Lamper-eel river were only bloomeries of swamp or bog ore. These works were soon discontinued; they never made any considerable quantity of bar-iron, they wanted water in the drought of summer and in hard frosts of winter, and their ore became scarce.

Their excise upon strong liquors may amount to about 1000 *l.* O. T. per annum; this with 1000 *l.* O. T. from the interest of loan-money per annum is the present salary of their governor. In New-Hampshire as in Massachusetts-Bay, there are two sorts of licences for selling of strong drink. 1. A licence to keep an open tavern. 2. A licence to retail liquors out of doors only. This liberty or licence is first to be obtained of the select men of the township, afterwards to be confirmed by the justices of the county in their quarter sessions.

Mr. Brown, missionary at Portsmouth of New-Hampshire, anno 1741, writes to the society for the propagation of the gospel in foreign parts, that there were in New-Hampshire about fifty or sixty families of the church of England, the rest were Independents; that they had no quakers, baptists, separatists, heathens, or infidels, amongst them.

MISCELLANIES. About 1623, Mr. David Thompson attempted a settlement at Piscataqua now called New-Hampshire; it soon vanished, and the very memory of it, is lost.

staves, trunnels, speckled wood, sweet-wood, small spars, oak plank, and wainscot.

New-Hampfhire printed law-book begins July 8, 1696.

Ufher, Partridge, Vaughan, and John Wentworth, Efq. were fucceffively lieutenant governors; the fucceffive governors of Maffachufetts-Bay being governors in chief, until July 1741, when Bennin Wentworth, Efq. was appointed governor in chief of New-Hampfhire.

John Wentworth, Efq. was appointed lieutenant governor 1717; he died Dec. 12, 1730.

1731, in July, arrives col. Dunbar as lieut. governor; he was alfo furveyor general of the woods in North-America, with four deputy furveyors, principally to prevent wafte of the mafting trees. Anno 1743, he relinquifhed thofe pofts, and was by the directors of the Eaft-India company appointed governor of St. Helena; there has been no lieut. governor appointed fince, and governor Wentworth fucceeded him as furveyor of the woods.

A Digreffion, concerning Timber, Wood, Lumber, and Naval Stores; the growth and manufacture of North-America.

T HIS is a fubject fo copious as to require a peculiar volume, but the [y] character of Summary does not permit to expatiate upon this ufeful fubject.

The timber trees of North-America for [z] conftruc-

[y] For this reafon I feldom mention their quadrupeds commonly called beafts, their birds, their fifhes, their ferpentine kind, and their infects: I avoid the ufelefs virtuofo part of natural hiftory concerning figured ftones, curious marcafites, extraordinary petrefactions and cryftallizations, fhells of all forts, &c. Men of that fort of curiofity may confult peculiar authors, e. g. in botany, father Plumier a Minim of Marfeilles, in his four voyages to America difcovered 900 new plants, efpecially in the capillary tribe; in this tribe, North-America exceeds any country upon our earth or globe.

[z] New-England perhaps excels in good ax-men for felling of trees, and fquaring of timber.

tion of fhipping and framing of houfes, may be reduced to two general kinds, pine and oak.

The PINES may be fubdivided into the mafting, or white pine, the pitch pine or picea, and others of the pine kind ufed as lumber. I fhall not ufe any ftiff [a] fcholaftick enumerations, which can be of no common ufe, but fhall endeavour to exprefs myfelf in an intelligible manner.

The WHITE PINE or [b] MASTING PINE may be called pinus excelfa, cortice lævi, foliis quinis anguftis perpetuis ex eodem exortu, conis longioribus; Tournefort calls it, Larix Americana, foliis quinis ab eodem exortu. Plum. Some are of very large dimenfions. An. 1736, near Merimack river a little above Dunftable, was cut a white pine ftrait and found, feven feet eight inches diameter at the butt-end; the commiffioners of the navy feldom [c] contract for any exceeding thirty-fix inches

[a] P. Tournefort, M. D. for many years profeffor of the royal garden in Paris, (a defervedly celebrated antiquary and naturalift, as appears by his voyage au Levant, 4to, 2 vol. Paris 1717) in his Inftitutiones Rei Herbariæ, feems upon too frivolous differences, that is, from the number of leaves or needles from the fame theca or fheath, to tranfer the noted naval ftore pines, the white and pitch pine to the larix. Claffing of plants, efpecially trees by their general habit, feems to be more obvious or fcientifick, than the minute infpections of their flowers and feed. We find Tournefort himfelf, the prince of botanifts, recede from this rigour in claffing of his leguminous trees by differences in the leaf, viz: foliis fingularibus, foliis ternis, et foliis per conjugationes. When he comes to ufe this laft deviation with regard to the pine kind, inftead of the obvious habit, he feems not to diftinguifh well: his general diftribution of the pine tribe into coniferous and bacciferous is natural; but his fubdivifion of the coniferous into abietes or firs foliis fingularibus, pinus foliis binis, larices foliis (or needles) pluribus quam binis ex eadem · theca, or fheath, is not natural, becaufe the foliis pluribus quam binis in their external habit agree with the foliis binis, and ought to be called pines.

[b] In New-Hampfhire and the province of Main, is much good fhip timber and mafting trees: in the duke of York's grant, called Sagadahock, not much of either.

[c] Col. Partridge fome years fince had the mafting contract for ten years, no maft to exceed thirty-fix inches diameter at the butt-end, he fent home a few of thirty-eight inches and two of forty-two inches.

E 3　　　　　　　　diameter

diameter at the butt-end, and to be ſo many yards in length as they are inches in diameter at the butt-end.

From time to time the commiſſioners of the navy agree with contractors to furniſh certain numbers of ſpe-cified dimenſions of maſts, yards and bowſprits, with his majeſty's licence for [d] cutting ſuch trees : the late con-tracts have been from Piſcataqua harbour in New-Hamp-ſhire, and Caſco-bay in the province of Main. The maſt ſhips built peculiarly for that uſe, are generally about 400 ton, navigated with about twenty-five men, and carry from forty-five to fifty good maſts per voyage. By act of parliament there are [e] penalties for cutting of maſting trees without licence, cognizable by the court of vice-admiralty.

Col. William Dudley ſome years ſince, in his frequent ſurveys of new townſhips about fifty or ſixty miles in-land, obſerved white aſh trees, ſtrait and without branch-ings for about eighty feet, and about three feet dia-meter at the butt-end; it is as light and much tougher than white-pine. Would not thoſe make ſtronger maſts than white-pine, and in all reſpects better ? It is true, the land carriage for ſo great a diſtance is inconvenient— The black aſh has a ſmaller leaf than the white aſh.

White pine is much uſed in framing of houſes and in joiners work ; ſcarce any of it to be found ſouth of New-England. In joiners work, it is of a good grain, ſoft, and eaſily wrought ; but ſoon loſes its good complexion by mildewing; priming or painting may hide this in many caſes, but in ſome caſes it is not to be hid, e. g. in flooring ; the ſoftneſs of its texture ſubjects it to ſhrink and ſwell hygrometer like, and conſequently it never makes a good joint. The beſt white pine is from the up-land; thoſe from ſwamps or marſhy lands, are the moſt apt to mildew, make a bad joint, and ſhake or ſhiver upon

[d] Hard winters are good for the ſledging conveyance, but hard froſts render the edges of their falling axes inconveniently brittle.

[e] See vol. I. p. 379.

the

the leaft violence.   The apple pine is of the white pine kind, but more frowey [*f*].

New-England abounds in faw-mills of cheap and flight work, generally carrying only one faw.   One man and a boy attending of a mill may in twenty-four hours faw four thoufand feet of white-pine boards ; thefe boards are generally one inch thick, and of various lengths ; from fifteen to twenty-five feet; and of various widths; one foot to two feet at a medium ; it is reckoned that forty boards make 1000 feet.——Thefe mills moftly ftand upon fmall ftreams, becaufe cheap fitted, but with the following inconveniencies.   1. As the country is cleared of wood and brufh, fmall ftreams dry up.   2. In living fmall ftreams they do not afford water fufficient to drive the wheel in fummer.   3. In the winter they are frozen up.   The furveyors of the woods mark the mafting trees, and furvey the logs at the mills, for which they have fome perquifites from timber-men.   A timberman's eftate confifts in mills and oxen ; oxen are a more fteady draught than horfes ; in [*g*] logging the fnow muft not exceed two feet deep.

Spruce or true [*h*] fir grows ftrait and tapering, is very beautiful, is ufed as fpars, it is apt to caft or warp,

---

[*f*] Norway red deal boards anfwer for upper works of fhips, becaufe their fplinters are not fo dangerous as oak.   Norway white deal boards are from nine to ten feet long, and from one and a quarter to one and a half inch thick.

[*g*] Mifunderftandings with the Indians are a great hindrance in our timber and lumber trade; therefore the Indians ought to be awed by four or five forts at proper diftances upon our inland frontiers ; kept in a refpectful condition by the appearance of fome military force ; and enticed by proper affortments of goods to exchange, with their furrs, fkins, and feathers.

[*h*] The commonly called Scots fir, is properly pinus foliis binis ex eadem theca.

I fhall enumerate five abietes or firs of the growth of New-England; this volume fwells too much.   I can only mention them.

1. Abies pectinatis foliis Virginiana, conis parvis fubrotundis. Pluk. Hemlock.   It is cut into deal boards, but much inferior to the white pine.   Its bark is ufed by the tanners.

E 4   and

and being too flexile is not fit for maſts or yards of any
conſiderable largeneſs; its twigs with the leaves are
boiled with a beer or drink made with molaſſes, and is
eſteemed good in the ſcurvy and the like foulneſſes of

2. Abies tenuiore folio, fructu deorſum inflexo, minore, ligno exal·
bido. The white ſpruce fir of New-England. All the abietes, eſpe·
cially the ſpruce ſo called, grow in ſwamps or marſhes; the extremity
of a branch is well repreſented by T. I. R, H. fol. 354, and its cone
or fruit in fol. 353.

3. Dit. ligno rubente, red ſpruce.

4. Dit. ligno obſcuriore, black ſpruce.

5. Abies tenuioribus foliis abſque ordine diſpoſitis fructu deorſum
inflexo, balſamifera Accadienſis: The fir turpentine tree of Nova Scotia,
commonly called the balſam of Gilead tree of Nova Scotia. From
the tumors or bliſters in the bark, by inciſion is gathered a thin fragrant
fir turpentine, which from its citron-like fragrancy, ſuch as that of the
Levant balſam, has been called balſam of Gilead; it is very hot. Some
years ſince, when balſam capivi was wanting here, I uſed it in gonor-
rhœas; but it increaſed the ardor urinæ and ſome other ſymptoms to
ſuch a violent degree, I was obliged to drop it. The name of balſam of
Gilead gives a prejudice in its favour; but from its great heat and at-
traction in all recent wounds, bruiſes, and other ulcers, it induces violent pains, inflammations and fluxions upon the part.

It is a miſtaken notion of many people, that all our medicinal balſams
or liquid roſins are from various fir-trees; I ſhall here by way of amuſement rectify thoſe errors, by enumerating and deſcribing the medicinal
natural balſams.

1. Opobalſamum, balſamum verum, Gilead, Syriacum, Judaicum,
e Mecha; is a liquid roſin, fragrant as citron, of a ſyrupy conſiſtence,
from a ſmall tree or ſhrub with pinnated leaves ending in an impar;
on the top of the ſtalk are hexapetalous whitiſh flowers, ſucceeded by a
roundiſh rugged fruit; this fruit is called carpobalſamum, and the
wood is the xylobalſamum of the apothecary ſhops, but at preſent not
in practice.

2. The balſam of Gilead or fir turpentine of Nova Scotia, Newfoundland and Canada, is from the abies tenuiore folio, already deſcribed.

3. Terebinthina communis, one of the enumerated naval ſtores, is
from the pinus foliis ternis ex eadem theca; it is whitiſh, thick, and
opaque.

4. Straſburg turpentine, from the abies mas Theophraſti: Picea
major prima five abies rubra, C. B. P. Red fir. This turpentine is
clearer, paler, of a thinner conſiſtence than Venice turpentine, of a
pleaſant lemon-peel ſmell.

5. Venice turpentine is from the larix folio deciduo conifera, I. B.
The larch tree; this is browner and thicker than the Straſburg tur-

the

the blood and other juices; it is much drank in the northern parts of North-America, especially in Nova Scotia and Newfoundland.

What is further to be said of the pine kind, is referred to the paragraphs of lumber and naval-stores [*i*].

pentine. The cedrus Libani et Palestinæ præcelsa. Lob. belongs to the larices.

6. Chio, and Cyprus turpentine, is not from the pine kind, but from the terebinthus vulgaris, C. B. P. The turpentine tree. It is a tree shrub with pinnated leaves, ending in an impar; the fruit is a longish hard nut. This, though not of the pine kind, gives name to all the rosins of the pine kind. It is thicker and more tenacious than Venice turpentine, and of a pleasant smell; that from Chio is clear and almost transparent; that from Cyprus is full of dross and browner.

7. Balsam capivi. Balsamum Americanum. C. B. P. It comes to us from the Dutch plantations of Surinam. It is from a large tree with long rounding leaves; its fruit is in short pods. This balsam is of a bitter hot or rough taste; does not give that remarkable violet smell to the urine, that turpentine occasions. By experience I have found it the most effectual of all the natural balsams, in internal ulcerations, dysenteries, diseases of the lungs, kidneys and bladder; in the fluor albus and gonorrhœa: it inviscates the acrimony and prevents the colliquation of our juices.

8. Balsam of Peru from the Spanish West-Indies in earthen jars; it is of a reddish dark colour, about the consistence of a thick syrup, fragrant, warm, aromatick taste: from a middling tree with almond tree like leaves, and a fox-glove flower. This balsam is also a nervine medicine internally and externally used.

9. Balsam of Tolu, comes in small calabashes from Tolu in the Spanish West-Indies; is of a yellow brown colour friable by age, of a fragrant smell and aromatick taste: with this is made the syrupus balsamicus, used in the affections of the lungs. It is from the soliquæ arbor sive ceretia, I. B. with a pinnated leaf and soliquous fruit.

There are several other natural Balsams, but hitherto not introduced into the materia medica.

[*i*] Here, once for all, I shall insert some general annotations concerning vegetable produce.

There is such a lusus naturæ in the herbs, shrubs, and trees between the tropicks, or in hot countries, they are scarce to be reduced to tribes.

Most of the fine flowers in the gardens of Europe came from the Levant or Asia. The sultans and their mistresses or seraglio women take pleasure in fine flowers and delicious fruits; the bashaws and other governors of the several provinces supply them with the most gay, fragrant, and elegant; most of the orchard, especially the stone fruit, came from thence.

The

The White Oak or Oak for Construction of Shipping may be called Quercus ligno exalbido duriore

Syſtematick writers in any part of literature, are much inferior to thoſe who write only of ſuch things as were diſcovered or obſerved in their own time and place. I ſhall mention a few in the affair of plants. Cornuti Canadenſium plantarum hiſtoria, 4to Paris 1635; he was a ſmall-rate botaniſt. Hortus Malebaricus, containing elegant deſcriptions and icons of 475 Eaſt India plants, done by the direction and at the charge of Draakenſtin governor of the Dutch Eaſt-Indies, in folio, publiſhed in twelve parts from anno 1678, to 1693. Tournefort, Corollarium rei herbariæ, 4to Paris 1703, in 3 vol. containing 1356 new plants which he diſcovered in his voyage or travels to the Levant, that is, the iſlands of the Archipelago and the Leſſer Aſia, at the charge of the king of France; as a ſupplement to his Inſtitutiones rei herbariæ, 4to Paris 1700, in 3 vol. whereof two volumes are compoſed of elegant icons, the other volume contains a catalogue of 8846 plants. His Hiſtoire des plantes, qui naiſſent aux environs de Paris, avec leur uſage dans la medicine, is a finiſhed uſeful piece of 1037 plants, printed at Paris in octavo 1698.

As to the time and place in general with regard to our mother-country, anno 1696—laſt edition in 8vo, Mr. Ray a naturaliſt in his Synopſis methodica ſtirpium Britannicarum, has 1480 plants, whereof 113 are trees and ſhrubs. With regard to the country near Boſton in New-England, I arrived to the deſcriptions of about eleven hundred indigenous plants, but was interrupted by * * * * * * * * * * * * * *
* *

Plukenet in his Phytographia and Almageſtum botanicum publiſhed in folio, London 1691 to 1696; he mentions Beniſter's catalogue of Virginia plants not publiſhed at that time. Sir Hans Sloane a noted liefbebber or virtuoſo, his Catalogus plantarum inſulæ Jemaaca, &c. London 1696; there are no deſcriptions; the plants generally were not in his own knowledge, but an immethodical rapſody of ſynonima copied from ſundry writers concerning the Weſt-India ſettlements. There are enumerations of many American plants with elegant proper coloured icons in Cateſby's natural hiſtory of Carolina and the Bahama iſlands. See Phil. tranſact. vol. xxxvi. p. 425; vol. xxxvii. p. 174, 447; vol. xxxviii. p. 315; vol. xxxix. p. 112, 251; vol. xl. p. 343; vol. xliv. p. 435. Cateſby's eſſays are in eleven ſets.

Father Plumier in his deſcription of the American plants publiſhed at Paris near ſixty years ſince, gives an account of more Weſt-India or American plants than all the botaniſts of that age; he made four voyages to North-America, on purpoſe, and obſerves, that it remarkably abounds with capillary plants.

The two brothers Lignons in the French iſlands, and Saracen in Canada, in quality of royal botaniſts with ſalaries, have deſerved well. Dierville a French ſurgeon in Nova Scotia ſent ſome curious plants from

cortice

cortice cinereo leviter rimoſo.   We have [k] great variety of oaks, but this is the only oak required by contract with the ſhip-builders for conſtruction.   Black

Nova Scotia or L'Accadie to Tourneſort.   In New-England hitherto we have no botanick writer.

Frequently I find ſome difficulty to reſtrain myſelf againſt excurſions. I ſhall conclude this excurſion by obſerving that in the ſixteenth century, the moderns began to apply themſelves to the knowledge of plants in ſome method ; before that time, plants were ranged according to their general appearances, or virtues, and in a very looſe manner ; in that century many good botaniſts appeared ; Geſner the father of all natural hiſtory, born in Switzerland 1516, died of the plague 1565 ; his botanick writings were moſt of them loſt and never publiſhed ; Tournefort followed his method of claſſing the plants by their flower and ſeed.

[k] Theſe botanick excurſions muſt prove tedious to moſt readers ; I ſhall therefore ſlightly deſcribe only a few of the oaks that are moſt common in New-England, partly by their claſſical Latin names, and partly by their common Engliſh appellations.

1. The white oak of the ſhip builders, is a large tree, with aſh-coloured bark of ſmall and frequent crevices, the leaves reſemble thoſe of a dwarf oak, robur III. Cluſii, or rather like that of T. I, R. H. tab. 349. on inch pedicles, the acorns ſometimes, more than one from a common half inch pedicle from the ſinus of the leaves near the extremities of the ſurculi, paraboloid, exos, one inch, tranſverſe diameter three quarters of an inch, of a pleaſant taſte, the cupulæ are ſhallow and verrucoſe.

2. The red oak ; while young, all the bark is ſmooth like the beech tree ; when old, the bark of the lower part of the tree becomes rough ; it is a large ſpreading tree with a large ſhining leaf eſculi diviſura, that is, laciniated to ſharp points, a large acorn but no pleaſant taſte, generally the wood is of a reddiſh caſt and very porous ; this ſpecies is ſubdivided into many diſtinct ſorts, viz. red, grey, blue, yellow, &c.

This oak being very ſpungy is of ſhort duration in uſe, it rives eaſily into ſtaves for molaſſes, bread, and dry caſk.

N. B. Quercus parva ſive phagus Græcorum, et eſculus Plinii, C. B. P. or the eſculus of the ancients, is a ſhrub oak with a deeply laciniated leaf, its name is from the peculiar ſweetneſs of its acorn ; for this reaſon in Maryland, Virginia and Carolina, all acorns, beech nuts, walnuts, and other nuts of the foreſt are called maſt from maſticare, and when plenty, it is ſaid to be a good maſt year for feeding of ſwine or making pork.

3. Black oak, perhaps ſo called from its dark coloured bark, may be called quercus Americana magna, patula, cortice obſcuriore rimoſo, foliis majoribus eſculi diviſura ; may be uſed as plank in the under water parts of a ſhip ; it makes the beſt charcoal.

oak

oak for the bottom of veſſels always under water an-
ſwers well, and being very acid, as I am informed, is
not ſo ſubject to the eating or boring of the teredines or
worms of the hot countries ; ſome think that black oak
may be uſed as timber but not as plank. In Virginia and
the Carolinas there is an oak called live or ever green oak,
quercus latifolia perpetuo virens, caudice contorto et valde
ramoſo ; it is of a very hard, ſtubbed ſhrub trunk, but of a
groſs grain fit for compaſs timber, that is, for crooked
riſing timbers, ſtandards, and knees ; but not for plank.
Excepting this live oak, all oaks ſouth of New-England
are ſoft and ſpungy ; they rive well for ſtaves, but in ſhip-
building they ſoon rot. In Great-Britain and Ireland there
is no other diſtinction of oaks but upland and marſh oak;

4. Swamp oak is from ſtrong moiſt land, ſuch as white pine requires;
it is of a midd!ing ſize, its leaf like that of the ilex, (T. I. R. H. tab.
350.) but not ſo rigid and ſpinulous ; the acorns are oval, of a pleaſant taſte, in duſky ſcally cups.

5. Cheſtnut oak, ſo called from the inequalities or rimæ of its bark,
reſembling the bark of cheſtnut trees : it is of a fine grain, and by ſome
uſed in conſtruction.

6. Common black ſhrub oak, grows from five to ten feet high,
patulous, ſmooth bark, deeply ſinuated, ſomewhat rigid leaf, acorns
ſmall from the body of the trunk on ſhort pedicles, bitter taſte, and
ſcaly cup.

7. A leſſer black ſhrub oak reſembling the former, but of a diſtinct
ſort.

8. White ſhrub oak, three or four feet high, vimineous, leaf dented
like that of the ſwamp oak, acorns ſmall as a pea, ſeſſile in the ſinus of
the leaves, and ſcaly cup.

9. A leſſer white ſhrub oak, reſembling the former, but of a diſtinct
kind.

N. B. Such waſte barren lands as in Great Britain are called heaths,
in New-England are called ſhrub oak and huckleberry plains, from
theſe ſhrubs which are their only produce. In Great-Britain there are
ſeveral ſpecies of heaths, the moſt common is the erica vulgaris humilis
ſemper virens flore purpureo et albo. I. B. common heath; in New-
England are ſeveral ſpecies of ſhrub oak, the moſt common is the
large black ſhrub oak, and ſeveral ſorts of the vitis idæa, or huc-
kleberries; the moſt common may go by the name of vitis idæa communis foliis ſubrotundis non crenatis, fructu nigro minus ſucculento in
faſciculis.

4

their

their oak is quercus vulgaris brevioribus et longis pe-
diculis, I. B. 1. 70. The leaves refemble thofe of our
fhrub white oak, the leaf has a fhort or no pedicle, un-
equally laciniated or deeply dented with four or five
dentations each fide of the leaf; the acorn, fome have
fhorter fome longer pedicles. Great-Britain does not
afford oak fufficient for their own ufe, they import much
from the Baltick or eaft country. Pomerania fhips off
the beft oak timber and plank; Konigfberg in Ducal
Pruffia fhips off confiderably; the beft eaft country oak
timber and plank comes down the Oder to Stetin, and
down the Viftula or Wefer to Dantzick; this river of
Wefer is navigable a long way up into Germany and Po-
land, and is the chief mart in Europe for importing of
herrings and exporting of grain.

The next oak in goodnefs, if to be ufed in fhip-
building or conftruction, is fwamp oak fo called; fee the
annotations.

The black oak; fome find that it may do for timber;
not long fince a gentleman by way of experiment built
a fhip, timber and plank of black oak, called the Black
Oak Galley.

Live oak in the fouth parts of North-America is ufed
for conftruction; it is a fhort ftubbed tree, hard wood.

Mahogany wood of the Weft-Indies between the tropicks is ufed in fhip-building there; it is durable, and
in receiving fhot does not fplinter: for cabinet and
joiners work it is excellent, much furpaffing the red
cedar of Carolina and Bermudas, which has a difagree-
ble perfume.

Cedar of Bermudas, fee vol. I. p. 148. It is excellent
for floops, the worm does not feize it, it is light and of
quick growth, may be cut every twenty years, plank
thin and narrow; crooked timber, beams, and mafts,
are brought from the continent, for the floops.

In Newfoundland they build fifhing and coafting veffels of many forts of wood.

From

From the cupreſſus of Carolina they make canoes and periauges, that may carry fifty barrels ; it is of a good grain, but ſoft.   It is of the cedar or berry-bearing kind of pine, grows tall, affords good boards and ſhingles.

The AMERICAN PITCH PINE. This is the mother of the naval ſtores of turpentine, tar, pitch, roſin, and oil of turpentine, and may be expreſſed by a ſhort [*l*] deſcription. Pinus Americana communis, ſive picea, patula, cortice ſcabro rimoſo, foliis ternis ex eadem theca, conis mediocribus turbinatis duris quaſi ſeſſilibus vix deciduis.   It grows on a dry ſandy ſoil.   The leaves about three inches long, with a prominent longitudinal rib inſtead of a ſulcus ; T. I. R. H. tab. 355. fig. A. well repreſents its amentaceous flowers, and fig. G. repreſents its freſh cones.   In New-England there is another diſtinct pitch pine, called yellow-pine ; it is taller, bark not ſo rough and dark, wood with a yellow caſt and not ſo knotty, does not yield turpentine ſo plentifully. In the Carolinas, much pitch pine, harder than that of New-England, ſo as to ſink in water ; it is ſawed into boards for the Weſt-India iſlands ; it is uſed for maſting, being ſtraiter than that of New-England.

1. TURPENTINE of North-America is a liquid roſin, gathered by boxing the pitch pine trees in the lower part of their trunk. 2. White pine boxed affords a turpentine brighter than that of the pitch pine, but not in plenty, and therefore neglected or not followed.   3. The abies or ſpruce gives a very liquid turpentine by inciſion of bladders or tubercules in the bark ; it is not gathered in quantities, therefore of no general naval uſe. 4. From the white cedar is gathered from the bark in lumps or grains a ſolid dry roſin, being concreted exudations, and by ſome is called olibanum or frankincenſe. 5. Pitch pine knots boiled in water, gives a top by way of ſcum, a ſemiliquid roſin reſembling Burgundy pitch.

[*l*] The name of a plant expreſſing a ſhort deſcription thereof, is of great uſe in botany, being the moſt natural.

New-England turpentine is of a honey confiſtence, that of the Carolinas is leſs liquid, reſembling tallow or fluſh.   New-England turpentine yields about three gallons of oil per ct. wt. that of the Carolinas not exceeding two gallons.   Turpentine reſiduum in diſtillation is about 7 12ths, called roſin, the ſtill not exceeding one half full of turpentine, left it ſhould boil over. Our chemical and pharmacopœa writers ſeem not to be practical diſtillers ; Quincey, much conſulted by young practitioners, adviſes to add water to the turpentine, whereas the more phlegm in the turpentine, the more tedious and dangerous is the diſtillation.   In diſtilling, if the turpentine boils up, a ſprinkling of water makes it ſparkle and fly, but a large quantity of water ſoon quells it.—The ſtills in Boſton are ſmall ; three barrels of turpentine of 300 wt. each may be wrought off in three hours.   The principal care in diſtilling, is in the beginning, left the phlegm boiling over ſhould blow up the ſtill ; as the phlegm goes off the ſtill ſubſides, and the danger is over.   At firſt comes over more phlegm than oil ; the proportion of phlegm gradually diminiſhes to the ceaſing of the watery ebullition, and for a ſhort time oil only paſſes, and more abundantly, but ſoon comes turbid, and if the fire is not removed the reſiduum or roſin is ſpoilt ; after the oil is drawn off and the fire removed or extinguiſhed for an hour, the roſin is to run off from the ſtill.

Varniſh is from one half roſin and one half oil of turpentine boiled up together, and is ſold at the ſame price with oil of turpentine.

Tar is from light wood ſo called, the knots of fallen pitch pine ; every fourteen years they reckon that the pine lands afford a ſufficient crop for the tar kilns.   In the Carolinas the people are not ſo much indulged as formerly in gathering of touchwood at random in the proprietary lands, and the exports of tar and pitch from the Carolinas is not ſo much as formerly.   The largeſt kiln of tar in Carolina in my knowledge was of 960 barrels ;

rels; this is too great a risk, because in blowing up all is lost. Four hundred barrels is a good kiln, and the running of the first 100 barrels is not much inferior to that of Stockholm. Anno 1746, the difference in price between Swedes and American tar was twenty-one shillings Swedes, and sixteen shillings New-England per barrel; Swedes tar is cooler and better for cordage. By act of parliament only the first half of the running of a kiln is to be used as tar, the other half to be boiled into pitch; penalty forfeiture of the kilns; this act is not put in execution. Green tar which has an additional premium, is made from green pitch pine trees stript of the bark eight feet or thereabouts up from the root of each tree; a slip of the bark of about four inches in breadth, having been left on one side of each tree, and such trees shall stand one year at the least before cut down for making of tar. No certificate bill shall be made out by any officer of the customs for any tar, &c. imported from the plantations, nor any bill made out by the commissioners of the navy, to entitle the importer of tar to any premium; unless the certificate of the governor, lieutenant governor, collector of the customs, and naval officer, or any two of them, to express that it has appeared to them by the oath of the owner that such tar, &c. — Tar that leaves a yellowish stain is good; a black stain is of a bad burning quality.

Pitch is made by boiling three barrels of tar into two barrels: in South-Carolina this is done in coppers; in North Carolina it is done in clayed cisterns by setting fire to the tar. At present scarce any tar is made in New-England, and very little turpentine is gathered — A barrel of tar should gauge thirty-one and a half gallons, a barrel of pitch should be two and a half ct. wt. neat. Tar should be free from water and dross; pitch free from all dirt and dross; turpentine free from water and chips, and stones.

The

The horn-beam trees, or carpinus dod, and the but-ton-tree (fo called from its feeds growing In clufters re-fembling buttons,) or platanus occidentalis, becaufe of their crofs or confufed grain not liable to rive or fplit, are ufed for windlaces, blocks, and turners-work.

This fection fwells too much, I fhall refer lumber and other woods to the article of natural hiftory in the Appendix, and at prefent only mention the following obfervations.

Shingles are made by cutting, fplitting and fhaving of certain woods into the form of a flate or flat tile for covering the roofs of houfes ; in New-England they are made of white cedar, or cedrus excelfior ligno ex-albido non olente in udis proveniens. This wood is eafily fplit and managed, but may be furrowed by the rain, therefore fhingles from white pine are preferable ; thefe may continue good twenty or thirty years. In Carolina fhingles are made of pitch pines and cyprus. In Jamaica they ufe bullet wood, which may laft 100 years.

Clapboards for facing of houfes, and laths for plafter-ing, are made of the fame woods.

Red cedar, or cedrus folio cupreffi atro, medio lig-no rubro duro. This is of excellent ufe for pofts fixed in the earth, it will hold good for a century.

The common cheftnut of North-America, or caftanea ampliffimo folio, fructu moliter echinato T. I. R. H. The fruit is fmaller, and capfula not fo much echinated as in Europe. It rives well, and is moft durable in rails in fencing of lands.

In North-America are many [m] varieties of walnuts. The hunters of the woods fay that there are almoft as great a variety of walnuts as apples ; their general

[m] Hickery or white walnut. This is the moft common walnut of New-England, a middling tree, the central laminæ or annuli with age become dark like black walnut ; the nuts are fmall, oval and fmooth, too hard to be cracked by the teeth. This is our beft fire wood.

diftinction is into black and white, from the colour of the wood.

Vitis or grape vines in New-England, natives, are five or fix diftinct forts [*n*] that are in my knowledge.

Cerafus, or cherries, natives of New-England, in my knowledge are four or five diftinct [*o*] kinds.

2. Nux juglans virginiana nigra, H. L. B. Black walnut; the wood is of a dark brown, is much ufed in joiners and cabinet work.

3. Nux juglans fructu tenero, fragili putamine.' C. B. P. Shagbark of New-England. It is not fo common as the hickery, and of a fmaller habit, the bark exfoliates in coats (as the birch and button tree) the nut is eafily broke by the teeth.

4. Nux juglans porcorum, the pig nut, a middling fpreading tree, exfoliating bark; the putamen or fhell of the fruit is not fo brittle as the fhag-bark, nor fo hard as the hickery; the nucleus is confiderable and of a pleafant tafte.

[*n*] 1. Vitis Americana fylveftris, uvis nigris pruni fylveftris magnitudine foliis magnis, vulpina dicta Virginiana. Pluk. The fox grape or wild vine with black grapes. It is the moft common of all our grapes, grows generally near ponds, not exceeding four to feven in a racemus, ripen into grapes, not much fucculent, and of a difagreeable tobacco tafte.

2. Dit. Uvis albidis, vulpina Virginiana alba. Pluk. White fox grapes differ from the former only in colour, and lefs frequent.

3. Vitis quinquefolia Canadenfis fcandens, T. I. R. H. Five-leafed ivy of Virginia, or Virginia creeper. It creeps and climbs to a great extent, leaves of a bright green color, makes agreeable arbours, very plenty in the woods: the racemi or clufters are lax, the grape or fruit is in form and bignefs of the uvæ Corinthiacæ or currants ufed in puddings.

4. Vitis fylveftris Americana, platani folio, uva racemofa, acinis rotundis parvis acidulis nigro-cæruleis. The fmall American grape vine with large leaves and fmall black grapes, in lax clufters.

5. Vitis Americana fylveftris, platani folio, uva recemofa, acinis rotundis parvis rubris; differs from the former only in the deep red colour of its grape.

[*o*] 1. Cerafus fylveftris rubro fructu Americana. Common wild cherry. It is frequent in the woods, and flowers more early than the racemofæ; is an arborefcent frutex, in tafte flatter than the cerafa fativa, or common red cherry.

2. Cerafus fylveftris Americana racemofa præcocior fructu majori nigro. The greater wild clufter cherry or birds cherry. A middling tree, the racemus of the flowers and fruit is from the extremities of the branches, not from the finus of the leaves as the padus. I. B. The

Our

Our apple trees are all from Europe ; ten or twelve buſhels of apples are required to make one barrel of cyder, one barrel of cyder gives not exceeding four gallons of proof ſpirit : beginning of October is the height of cyder making.

Saſſaphras ex Florida, ficulneo folio. C. B. P. is plentiful in New-England, and not ſo ſtrong a perfume as farther ſouth : it is an ingredient in the decoction of the woods ſo called, and uſed in venereal and other pſorick diſorders.

I omitted in the proper place to inſert, that the right merchantable hoops are from the ſaplins of white oak and of hickery ; white oak is the beſt.   Staves for tight caſk are from the white oak ; red oak ſtaves are uſed for molaſſes and dry caſk.   One thouſand ſtaves make from thirty to thirty-five hogſheads of 100 gallons each.

cherry is larger than the following, black, ſucculent and ſweet ; its wood is uſed in joiners and cabinet work.

3. Ceraſus Americana ſylveſtris racemoſa, fructu minore nigro dulci. The common bird cherry of New-England, a middling tree, flowers and fruit in racemi, like the ribeſia, and ſomewhat larger ; in New-England it is uſed in place of the officinal or ceraſus ſylveſtris fructu nigro. I. B. the ſmall birds affect it much.

4. Ceraſus Americana ſylveſtris humilis fructu nigricante non eduli. The American dwarf crabbed birds cherry, does not exceed the height of ſeven or eight feet ; it is not a padus, becauſe the racemi are not from the ſinus of the leaves, but from the extremities of the branches or twigs ; this cherry is ſmaller than the former, of dark red, and an acerb choaky taſte.

I have not room to mention the great varieties of wild roſes, gooſe-berries, currants, brambles, raſp-berries, &c.

All the apple trees in New-England are exoticks ; as I formerly hinted.   La Hontan perhaps is miſtaken in ſaying, that he did ſee ſe-veral European fruit trees natives upon the river Illinois ; probably they are the relicks of a former Fr nch ſettlement there.

Thuya Theophraſti, C. B. P. Arbor vitæ. Cluſ. Tree of life of New-England, is by miſtake called ſavine. Sabina is not well deſcribed by botaniſts. Some with Boerhaave ſay, it is bacciferous, ſome with Ray call it conifer : the ambiguity may proceed from its bearing ſel-dom, and not till very old.

Some miscellany observations relating to this Digression.

In New-England ship-building, a vessel fitted to sea, two thirds of the cost is a profit to the country; the other third is iron, cordage, sail-cloth, and small stores from Great-Britain.

Timber, if of too old growth, is dotted; if too young, 'tis sappy; neither of them fit for construction.

There are several good acts of the British parliament, and of the legislatures of the several colonies, concerning the seasons and times of falling of timber; as also concerning the proper seasons of killing these beasts that afford fur, skins, and hides: but little attended to, and perhaps never put in execution.

Clearing a new country of wood, does not render the winters more moderate, but conduces to its being more healthful: the damp of wood-lands produces intermitting, pleuritick, peripneumonic, dysenterick, and putrid fevers.

Where trees and other growth are large, it is a sign of good land. Chestnut, walnut, and beech trees, are symptoms of good land. Alder is good meadow ground.

We have in the woods variety of beautiful flowering shrubs; but few of them flower in winter, the most valuable qualification for a flowering shrub.

For peculiar things of this kind, if we consult the most celebrated dictionaries we are led astray; for instance, Bailey describes tar, " A sort of gross fatty li-" quor issuing from the trunks of old pine trees."

In middling climates timber or wood is generally spungy or light by alternate relaxations and bracing from heats and colds, consequently of no good use or duration; thus it is from New-England to Carolina: farther north the timber is solid and heavy, fit for permanent construction, e. g. in New-England, Nova Scotia, and Canada; still farther north the timber is too

small,

fmall, fhrubby and gnarly; in the hot countries are many
fpecies of hard wood of flow growth, good for wainf-
cotting and other joiners work; this fummary does not
allow me to enumerate them.

Summer-built veffels are of better ufe than thofe of
any other feafon.

The fire wood near Bofton is much exhaufted; we
are under a neceffity of fetching it from the province of
Main, and territory of Sagadahock. A wood floop
with three hands makes about fifteen voyages per ann.
from the eaftward to Bofton, may carry about thirty
cord fire wood each voyage.—A cord of wood is eight
feet lengthwife, per four feet height, of four fticks or
logs. A kiln for charcoal or furnaces, bloomeries and
refiners of iron, is generally of twenty cord of wood, and
generally may yield ten cart load of charcoal at 100
bufhels per load.

At fmelting furnaces they obferve that young black
oak makes the beft coal. One acre of wood land at a
medium yields about forty cord wood; one cord of
wood yields forty to fifty bufhels of charcoal.

Our feafons are uncertain; in open winter the fap rifes
too foon, and a fubfequent hard froft makes the bark
fplit and peel off; thus at times our fruit trees particularly fuffer.

Timber under twelve inches is called ranging timber,
above twelve inches it is called tun timber; ftandards
and knees are called compafs timber; the compafs timber to the northward is beft.

Our trees, efpecially the oaks, while growing, are
much fubject to the [p] teredo or worm, therefore in all

[p] There are varieties of teredines or wood eating infects: I fhall
upon this occafion only mention two. 1. An afcarides or maggot-like the
teredo, which preys upon the wooden wharfs in Bofton and elfewhere.
2. The xylophagus marinus major navibus infeftus, it is pernicious to
fhips in hot countries, efpecially in their firft voyages; lately it did
damage in the harbour of Newport of the colony of Rhode-Ifland.
This is not the fame with the infect which makes the worm-holes in our

new-

new-built ſhips theſe worm-holes in the plank muſt be carefully ſpiked.

The ſhips built in Boſton exceed all of other building-yards, the many merchants and ſhip-maſters, good connoiſſeurs, tranſiently inſpect them, and every bad piece of timber or length of plank is cenſured. In Newbury where they are not much inſpected, the builders act at pleaſure, and as the contracts are generally to be paid in goods, they build accordingly; thus a noted builder T. W. jocoſely ſaid, that he had built for —————— a callico ſhip. The other country building places are ſtill worſe, particularly North River, where, inſtead of what is reckoned ſhip-timber, they uſed foreſt-wood of any ſort; theſe veſſels with repairs laſt only two or three voyages, and are deſigned as a bite upon ſhip buyers at home.

Timber uſed green, or with the ſap up, is like fœnum madide repoſitum, it ſoon tends to putrefaction : this ſap may be extracted by macerating or ſoaking in ſalt water. In ſhip-building, they ought to uſe only white oak for timber, plank, and trunnels; and theſe as much as may be without ſap, [q] rot, or worm-holes.

timber trees while growing : neither is it that which a few years ſince, 1730, and increaſed for eight or nine years, ſeized the piles or paalen of the dykes in Holland, threatening an inundation, but were deſtroyed by a hard froſty winter.

[q] The annuli or annuolex increments of trees begin from the center of their tranſverſe ſections or heart of the tree; and in the decline (trees like animals, for many years according to the nature and conſtruction of individuals of their ſeveral ſpecies increaſe, then for ſome years are at a ſtate or ſtand, and afterwards are upon the decline ; thus our firſt or ancient growth of timber is not good, our ſecond growth perhaps may equal that of Great-Britain) the dottedneſs, carioſity, or tabes begins naturally, progreſſive from the center ; this is moſt remarkable in the ſpungy timber of red oak. One may blow ſpittle through a ſtave of four feet long; its annuli, or circular laminæ, in the tranſverſe ſections are noted, and after ſurveying, if red oak, and ſome other trees, are uſed for monument trees, by the number of the ſurcreſcent laminæ we compute the number of years from the ſurvey ; therefore it is better to mark monument trees upon the bark, which does not alter, than upon the woody ſubſtance where the marks are yearly inveloped.

[r] Oak

[r] Oak if long ſeaſoned or dried, becomes vapid or dry-rotted, and does not laſt; we have lately had a notorious inſtance of this; cordfire wood to the N. E. of Boſton cut before our late war with the French and their Indians, during the war of a few years, could not be carried off; upon a peace it was ſhipped to Boſton, it burnt like ſtubble, of no duration, leaving no coal, and the aſhes not profitable to the ſoap-boiler.

[s] Oak timber from thick wood lands is not good.

Next to the ore, in all iron works, wood or charcoal is the moſt eſſential. Here we may obſerve, that iron works require only three men who may be called artificers, viz. a forgeman, a carpenter, and collier; the others are only common labourers.

When the ſun does not ſhine, les hommes des bois, ſwampeers or wilderneſs men, diſtinguiſh the courſes or corners of winds by, 1. Moſſes growing moſt plentifully on the north Side of old dotted trees. 2. Pines branching moſt ſouthward. 3. Trees reclining generally eaſtward, from the prevailing of the weſterly winds there; Sir John Narborough obſerved the ſame in South-America. This obſervation holds good all over America. 4. The rings in the tranſverſe ſection of trees, which are moſt compact northward.

[r] A wood fire is more pleaſant to the ſight and ſmell than that of pit coal, but its warming influence is not ſo diffuſive; it ſearches more, but is not ſo ſteady and laſting, its ſmoke and vapour is more offenſive to the eyes, it diſcolours and dry-rots paper prints more than pit coal. We have lately in Charles-town adjoining to Boſton made an eſſay for diſcovering of pit-coal; if it ſucceeds, by act of aſſembly wood ought to be prohibited for uſe in firing in and near Boſton; otherways than in charcoal for the uſe of furnaces of bloomeries and refineries.

[s] Oak timber called day oak, from places well cleared, is better than that from wood lands where there is not the benefit of the ſun and free air; or ſecond growth of timber or paſture oak is almoſt equal in quality to that of Great-Britain.

In all oak timber there is an acid juice which corrodes iron (therefore the French ſpiking does not anſwer ſo well as our trunneling of ſhip plank) and the timber itſelf; therefore it ought to be ſeaſoned either by drying, or by (this is better) ſoaking in ſalt-water to extract this corroſive acid.

There

There is no author who has wrote tolerably well concerning the natural hiftory of New-England [*t*].

When Sweden began to impofe upon Great-Britain
in the exportation of their naval ftores, an act of parliament was made allowing certain premiums upon the
importation of certain naval ftores from Englifh
America [*u*].

In rope-making, by the addition of tar the cordage
acquires one fifth more in weight, the rope-makers great
gains.—A rope-walk for merchants ufe need not exceed
200 fathom: becaufe 200 fathom yarn when twifted
makes 120 **fathom cable**.

In the mifcellany article of a fection, I fometimes infert things which fhould have been inferted in their proper places but were forgot.

Here fhould have been inferted fome fhort account
of Dr. Berkley's tar-water ufed as a medicine; but as
moft readers are not in the tafte of natural hiftory, I
have already exceeded too much in that refpect; and
here fhall only obferve, that his directions for making

[*t*] Joffelyn frequently quoted, arrived at Bofton 1663, and refided
in New-England many years; publifhed a fmall book called eight years
obfervations, printed in London 1672, as a natural hiftory of the
country; it abounds with grofs miftakes, v. g. " fome frogs when they
" fit upon their breech are a foot high, and fome as long as a child
" one year old. Barley frequently degenerates into oats." Here he
was impofed upon, by fome oat and barley feed intermixed as frequently happens: " In New-England, no woodcocks, no quails." N.B.
they are very plenty.

[*u*] The premiums at prefent are, for mafts, yards, and bow-fprits,
per ton of forty feet girt meafure, —— —— 1 *l*.

Merchantable tar	eight barrels	——	2	4
Green tar	——	ditto	——	4
Pitch	——	ditto	——	1
Turpentine	——	ditto	——	1 10

There muft be a plantation certificate that they are the growth or produce of our colonies: upon landing the pre-emption to be offered to the
commiffioners of the navy: if twenty days after landing the commiffioners do not contract for the fame, the owners may difpofe of them at
pleafure, and receive the premium.

of

of it are: A gallon of cold water to a quart of tar worked thoroughly together with a flat ftick for five or fix minutes, after three days the tar being thoroughly fubfided, decant the above, and bottle it for ufe; at a medium one pint drank per diem at intervals upon an empty ftomack: it may be made weaker by a lefs proportion of tar or lefs ftirring, according to the con-ftitution and ftomach of the patient.   As Dr. Berkley favoured Bofton with fome fermons agreeable to the people in New-England, his medicine ex verbo facer-dotis is much ufed there, and I have had the opportunity of obferving the effects thereof.   1. In ladies of a foft fine fair complexion, a long ufe of it gives their counte-nance a fallow, that is, a yellow greenifh caft.   2. As tar is a creature of the fire, and therefore cauftick, I ob-ferve, it has a bad effect in all hecticks and hæmorrhages, and inflammatory cafes.   3. In vapid diforders of the nervous fyftem it is of good ufe, if not ufed too long; if ufed too long, its effects are more violent and de-ftructive to the conftitution, than the habitual drinking of rum or brandy.   N. B. Of all thefe I can produce fpecial vouchers.

4. This is no quack medicine, becaufe it is no no-ftrum, and publifhed by a benevolent clergyman without any defign of lucrative profit; his friend in publifhing a confiderably large book of many hundreds of cafes ex-actly in the form and univerfality of quack recommen-dations, is a difparagement.

The prerogatives of provincial governors multiplying members or reprefentatives from new places to the gene-ral affembly ad libitum, is a matter of great confe-quence to our colonies: as this has been lately affumed in the fmall government of New-Hampfhire, I cannot clofe this fection, without taking fome further notice of the fame.

There is a law of this province called the triennial act, by which the qualifications of members, and of thofe thoſe who may elect them, is ſtated; the method of calling and governing the meetings of the electors is regulated, and the longeſt term an aſſembly may ſubſiſt limited.   June 4, 1648, the aſſembly became diſſolved in courſe by virtue of this law; from which time to the third of January following there was no aſſembly in being; in this interval the governor received the inſtruction, vol. II. p. 35. and beſides the places mentioned in the ſaid inſtruction, the freeholders of Pelham and Methuen are ordered to unite and chuſe one repreſentative for both places at a joint meeting held at Pelham. This was a novel thing, to aſſemble the electors of two or five towns in one body. In Scotland, where by the act of the union parliament (not by prerogative) four or five towns were claſſed to ſend one member or repreſentative, each town voted ſeparately for a repreſentative, and thoſe repreſentatives by vote ſent one of their own number as a member of parliament; but in a different manner the freeholders of the towns of Dunſtable, Merrimack, Holles, Monſon, and Nottingham-weſt, are ordered to unite in one meeting to be held at Dunſtable, and chuſe one member for the whole as a conſolidated body; this was done, but no return made, as I am informed.

After the late running of the line with Maſſachuſetts-Bay government, ſeveral parts of townſhips and other ſettlements formerly in Maſſachuſetts-Bay fell within this province; as the aſſembly were deſirous that the polls and eſtates of theſe annexations ſhould contribute to the charge of government, by a temporary act, they incorporated them by the name of Diſtricts, with the ſame appellations as before; and the fragments from the Maſſachuſetts townſhips, viz. of Almſbury and Saliſbury were made one diſtrict: from Methuen and Dracut one diſtrict; Haverhill one diſtrict, &c: this act was frequently renewed for ſhort periods, only that they might contribute towards the charge of government; but after repeated application of the inhabitants, they had the
privi-

privilege of townships added, but still temporary. Some of these districts were made townships by charter : thus Dracut was made a town by the name of Pelham. about seven months after calling the assembly the last district act expired; notwithstanding their legal exist-ence expiring, Methuen, e. g. had a representative in the assembly.

By the triennial act, the select-men of each place sending representatives, are to call the qualified voters within their precincts to meet and proceed to a choice; but there was no legal authority for the select-men of one town or district to call a joint meeting of the electors of two or five places, and therefore was in propriety a tumultuous assembly : thus were two of the excluded members chosen.

The governor was from home required to commu-nicate the lords justices additional instruction of June 30, 1748, to the members of the general assembly con-cerning this affair, which he never did in form; they only obtained a transcript of it by the courtesy of a private hand as a favour; and the governor's friends insisted that they should first admit these disputed mem-bers, and afterwards enter upon the merits of the case. I have no concern in the affair, and endeavour only im-partially to represent facts.

N. B. By the royal charter to the colony of Rhode-Island, their assembly is to determine what towns have power to send representatives to the assembly.

As this is a petty inconsiderable province or govern-ment, very irregular and factious in their œconomy, and affording no precedents that may be of exemplary use to the other colonies; I omit (to ease the Sum-mary) many articles which in the other colonies are de-duced at length, as of good use and information.

4   Perhaps

Perhaps if this government were annihilated, and annexed to the neighbouring province, it might be of benefit, for their protection in cafes of war with the neighbouring French and Indians, or infurrections, and for good order, and to eafe their charges of government.

S E C T.   X.

Concerning the colony of Rhode-Ifland.

I Shall not repeat what I have already mentioned in general, concerning the earlieft European difcoveries and fettlements in America [*x*].

This colony was not originally or immediately from England, it proceeded from the neighbouring colony of Maffachufetts-Bay; and was at firft made up of the emigrants and [*y*] banifhed from thence, becaufe of diffenting from their generally received way of religious worfhip; thefe emigrants were puritans of puritans, and by degrees refined fo much that all their religion was almoft vanifhed: afterwards it became a receptacle of any people without regard to religion or focial worfhip; and their modes of civil goverment were very variable and defective.

There were fome incidents, which favoured the firft Englifh fettlements. 1. A few years before the Englifh

[*x*] See vol. I. p. 63. &c, For the firft Britifh difcoveries and fettlements there, fee p. 109, &c. and p. 203, &c. the firft fettling of New-England, p. 364, &c.

[*y*] Thefe banifhments were under pretence of preferving the publick peace, and preventing of fectary infection; and as is natural to all zealots and bigots, they fell into the fame error of rigidity, which they complained of upon their emigration from the church of England. At a general fynod in Newtown near Bofton, which was called Auguft 30, 1637, eighty erroneous opinions were prefented, debated, and condemred; and by the general affembly or legiflature of the colony, October 2 following, fome perfons were banifhed.

came

came to New-Plymouth, there prevailed some malignant, contagious, very mortal diftempers amongft the Indians from Penobfcot to Narraganfet, which made room for a fafe fettlement. 2. Several of the neighbouring Indian nations were inftigated to deftroy one another: thus the Narraganfets affifted the Englifh to deftroy the Pequods 1637; Myantomy the great fachem of the Narraganfets was made prifoner by Uncas the fachem of the Mohegins, and was put to death 1643.

In the Britifh acts of parliament, this colony is named Rhode-Ifland, Providence Plantations, and the Narraganfet Country or King's Province: originally thefe were diftinct affociations or plantations, but fince have been united, and by charter incorporated into one colony or jurifdiction. I fhall briefly mention the origin of thefe feveral diftinct fettlements.

Mr. Roger Williams came over from England to Salem 1630; he fucceeded Mr. Shelton minifter of Salem 1634; and becaufe of his antinomian, familiftical, brownift, and other fanatical doctrines, though in other refpects a good man, 1635 he was excommunicated and banifhed from Maffachufetts colony by their affembly or legiflature as a difturber of the peace of the church and commonwealth, and removed to Seàconck, now called Rehoboth, and procured a grant of lands from Maffafoit fachem of the Pakanokat Indians; the magiftrates of the colony of Plymouth, Seaconck being within their jurifdiction, obliged him to remove; in the fpring following, with fome of his friends and adherents he fettled on the other fide of Patuket, the boundary river at Moofachick, by Mr. Williams called Providence, and the Narraganfet fachem made them feveral grants of lands; one of the grants is dated Nantiganfick the twenty-fourth of the firft month commonly called March, the fecond year of our plantation or planting at Moofachick or Providence; Mr. Williams lived in Providence forty years; 1640 the twenty-

ſeventh day of the fifth month about forty perſons [z]
voluntarily formed a ſort of civil government.   When
for the eaſe of the inhabitants, the colony, formerly all
in one county as is at preſent the ſmall province of New-
Hampſhire, was divided into three counties, the townſhip or plantation of Providence was divided into four
townſhips, Providence, Smithfield, Scituate, and Glo-
ceſter ; Providence ſends four repreſentatives to the general aſſembly, the other ſend two each.

Duke of Hamilton's grant from the council or company of Plymouth in April 1635, was from Providence
or Narraganſet-Bay eaſt, to Connecticut river weſt,
ſoutherly upon the ſea, and northerly up inland ſixty
miles, or ſo far north as to reach the Maſſachuſetts
ſouth line. This takes in all the colony of Rhode-Iſland,
and the eaſtern parts of the colony of Connecticut; the
duke of Hamilton had a further grant of 10,000 acres
eaſt of Sagadahock adjoining to lord Ware's grant; that
family have at ſundry times eſſayed to revive their
claim, but as they never fulfilled the conditions of the
grant or ſettling, they never proſecuted the affair to effect. There were ſeveral other vague grants, but as they
are now obſolete, and claims not like to be revived, we
ſhall not mention them.

In the year 1637, the ſynod at New-town in Maſſachuſetts-Bay having condemned the opinions of many
ſectaries, and by the ſubſequent general court or aſſembly perſons being ill uſed, theſe perſons with their

---

[z] To perpetuate the memory of the firſt conſiderable ſettlers and
of their families, I ſhall in the hiſtory of our ſeveral colonies mention
ſome names.   The firſt twelve perſons who with Mr. Williams were
concerned as proprietors of the Providence lands ; William Arnold,
John Greene, John Throgmorton, Thomas James, William Harris,
Thomas Olnay, Richard Waterman, Francis Weſton, Ezekiel Holli-
man, Robert Cole, Stukely Weſt-coat, and William Carpenter ; afterwards were aſſociated Chad. Browne, William Fairfield, J. Warner,
E. Angel, J. Windſor, R. Scot, Wm. Reinolds, Wm. Wickenden,
Gregory Dexter, &c. at length they amounted to the number of 100
proprietors of Providence, being the value of twenty miles ſquare.

friends

friends and adherents went to Aquatneck, now the ifland of Rhode-Ifland, and by deed, March 24, 1637-8, purchafed the ifland from the Indians; eighteen perfons [a] without a patent did voluntarily incorporate or affociate themfelves; the eafterly end of the ifland with Seaconet was called Pocaffet. This fettlement increafed faft, and was called Ifle of Rhodes or Rhode-Ifland; 1644 it was divided into two townfhips, Newport its eafterly part, and Portfmouth its wefterly part; lately Newport is fubdivided into Newport and Middletown. In the beginning, the œconomy or government was variable; 1640 they agreed that the government fhould be in a governor, deputy-governor and four affiftants; [b] they held their offices until the patent of incorporation.

1642-3, Jan. 12, Showamet was purchafed of the Indians by eleven affociates [c], and called Warwick in honour to the family of the earl of Warwick, who had a grant (but never profecuted) of a large tract of land in thefe parts; they were by directions from this minifter incorporated in the Province of Providence Planta-

[a] Thefe eighteen perfons were William Coddington, John Clark, William Hutchinfon, John Coggefhal, William Apinwal, Samuel Welborn, John Porter, John Seaford, Edward Hutchinfon, jun. Thomas Savage, William Dyree, William Freeborn, Philip Sherman, John Walker, Richard Corder, William Raulifton, Edward Hutchinfon, en. Henry Bull. *N. B.* Some Families returned to the Maffachufetts-Bay colony, the Hutchinfons, Dummers, Savages, &c.

[b] William Coddington, governor, W. Brenton, deputy governor, N. Eafton, J. Coggifhal, W. Hutchinfon, and S. Porter.

[c] Rendal Holden, John Wickes, Samuel Gorton, John Greene, Francis Wefton, Richard Waterman, John Warner, Richard Corder, Samfon Shelton, Robert Patten, and William Woodeal. *N. B.* Gorton was a preacher or exhorter, of many wild peculiar opinions in religion, different from thofe of the other New-England fectaries, and ufed a myfterious dialect; his followers were called Gortonians; he came to Rhode-Ifland 1638, was banifhed from thence 1640; he was of a good amily in England; he difowned the Puritans, and oppofed the Quakers; e fettled at Patuxet, and kept a peculiar religious fociety for upwards f fixty years, and lived to a great age; but as this fect is utterly extinct, we fhall not revive the memory of it in the digreffion concerning the Britifh plantation fectaries.

tions.

tions. About this time ſome people began a ſettlement
at Patuxet river [d], whereof at preſent part is in the
townſhip of Providence, and part in the townſhip of
Warwick. Warwick is lately ſubdivided into the townſhip of Warwick, four repreſentatives, and country two
repreſentatives.

1643. Mr. R. Williams went to England as agent,
and by the aſſiſtance of Sir Henry Vane, obtained from
the earl of Warwick, governor and admiral of all the
Engliſh plantations for the parliament, a ſort of charter
of incorporation of the ſeveral ſettlements by the name
of " the incorporation of the Province Plantations in
" the Narraganſet-Bay in New-England; may ſettle
" themſelves into any form of government the majo-
" rity of the freemen ſhould agree upon, ſuitable to
" their eſtate and condition, and make ſuitable laws,
" agreeable to the laws of England, ſo far as the nature
" and conſtitution of the place will admit, &c." dated
1643-4, March 17. Their firſt general aſſembly was
not called until May 19, 1647; this aſſembly eſtabliſhed
a body of very good and wholſome laws, and erected a
form of government for the adminiſtration of theſe laws,
and for making further laws that may be found requiſite.
Their legiſlature, called a court of commiſſioners, con-
ſiſted of ſix members from each of the four towns of
Providence, Newport, Portſmouth, and Warwick; but
the ſupreme power to be in a regular vote of all the [e]
freeholders of the colony or incorporation; the freemens
vote ſuperſeded or repealed the acts of the court of com-
miſſicners and made them void. —A preſident and four
aſſiſtants yearly choſen were judges of the court of
trials, aſſiſted by the two wardens or juſtices of the

[d] Meadows upon a river have, in our northern plantations, always
and every where been an inducement to begin a ſettlement; as being
immediately furniſhed with food for their cattle in winter.

[e] At preſent there remain in our plantations, only two populace or
popular colonies, where the ſupreme power or dernier reſort is lodged
in the community, viz. Connecticut and Rhode-Iſland.

particular town, in which this court fat from time to time. Every town chofe a council of fix perfons to manage the prudential town affairs, and had the trial of fmall cafes, with the wardens or juftices of the town, but with an appeal to the court of prefident and affociates. There was a fhort interruption of this form of government, October 2, 1652, by order of the council of ftate from England; but foon refumed, and continued until the prefent charter took place.

The prefent charter is dated July 8, 1662, 15 regn. Carol. II. in which it is enumerated, that they were people who left their fettlements in the other colonies, becaufe obliged thereto by their different fentiments in religion; and did by good providence tranfplant themfelves into the midft of Indian natives, and made land purchafes of thofe natives, fit for building of veffels, making of pipes ftaves and other lumber: that their defign was to live quietly with liberty of confcience together, and to convert the Indians. They are by charter made a body politick or corporate by the name of the governor and company of freemen of the Englifh colony of Rhode-Ifland and Providence Plantations in Narraganfet Bay in New-England.

Grants liberties of confcience in religion [*f*], a power to make a common feal, to call an affembly annually, firft Wednefday of May, and laft Wednefday of October, or oftener: compofed of the governor [*g*], deputy governor, ten affiftants; and reprefentatives of towns, whereof Newport not exceeding fix, Providence four, Portfmouth four, Warwick four, and two for each other place or town, to be elected by the majority of freemen in each town. The majority of the affembly, whereof the governor or deputy governor

[*f*] Without excepting Roman Catholicks or any others.
[*g*] In the charter, for the firft year, the king nominated Benedict Arnold, Efq. for governor, William Brenton deputy governor.

and fix of the affiftants at leaft to be feven; [b] to have power to appoint the time and place of their meetings, to make any man free of the company, to nominate proper officers, to make laws, &c. not repugnant to thofe of England, to appoint courts of judicature with their proper officers, to determine what towns have power to fend reprefentatives to the affembly, to pardon criminals, to make purchafes of the native Indians; when the affembly does not fit, the governor with the major part of the affiftants to have the direction of the militia. The governor, fix of the affiftants, and major, part of the reprefentatives of the freemen in affembly, have power of making war againft the Indians or any of the king's enemies, but not to invade the Indians of any neighbouring colony without the confent of the government of that colony: allowed the liberty of fifhing and of curing fifh on any of the coafts of New-England: perfons born there, to be denizens of England: all perfons and manner of goods may be tranfported thither from England: any difference arifing with the neighbouring colonies, to appeal to the king in council: to have a free trade with all the other Englifh colonies. The bounds of tne colony to be wefterly, the middle channel of the middle great ftream of Pokatuke, alias Narraganfet great river, fo far as it lies up the country, and thence by a line due north to the foutherly line of the Maffachufetts colony; northern bounds, the foutherly line of the Maffachufetts colony fo far eaft as three miles to the E. N. E. of the moft eaftern and northern parts of the Narraganfet-Bay; the eaftern bounds, as the bay lieth or extendeth itfelf from the ocean into the mouth of the river which runneth into Providence; and from thence higher along the eafterly

[b] As in the majority of voters there muft at leaft be the governor or deputy governor and fix of the affiftants, it was the fame cafe as if the governor and affiftants were a feparate board or houfe; therefore after fome years by act of affembly they were conftituted a feparate houfe, and the governor in cafe of an equivote in the board of affiftants, to have the cafting vote, but no negative.

bank

bank of the said river called Seaconck river, up to the falls called Patucket-falls, being the most westerly line of Plymouth colony; and from the said falls in a straight line due north, till it meets with the south line of Massachusetts: southern bounds, the ocean comprehending all the islands and banks in Narraganset-Bay, Fisher's Island excepted.   To hold of the king as the manor of East-Greenwich, in free and common soccage, paying the fifth of all gold and silver ore found there: Any clause in a late grant to the governor and company of Connecticut colony notwithstanding. Signed Howard.

Their first assembly met at Newport, March 1, 1663, and enacted, that on the first Wednesday of May annually by a majority of the votes of the freemen of the colony, shall be elected a recorder or secretary, a sheriff [*i*], an attorney general, and one treasurer general.—All purchases of the Indians without consent of the assembly, to be void, and the purchasers finable.   All inhabitants of competent estates christians (Roman Catholicks excepted) to be accounted freemen, and have power of choosing and of being chosen deputies and other officers.

This competency of estate has been varied from time to time; anno 1746, the assembly enacted, that the qualification for a freeman should be freeholds of 400 *l.* currency in value, or that shall rent for 20 *l.* per ann. or the eldest son of such a freeholder; and to be proposed to their respective town meetings three months at least before their admission. As briberies in the elections of assembly men and general officers were become frequent and notorious, by the same act no man is admitted to vote until he has taken oath or affirmation, that he will use his freedom for the good of the government without any other motive, and shall not receive nor expect any reward or promise of reward in elections. The same assembly enacted, that no assistant (member

[*i*] At present the sheriffs of the several counties are appointed by the general assembly.

of

of the council) or member of the house of representatives should be allowed any wages or pay for their service. Several other such wholsome and exemplary [k] laws have at times been enacted, when the government was in good hands.

.From time to time there were some English trading houses, with small purchases of lands from the Indians, in the Narraganset country. 1657, the island of Canonicut was purchased of the Indians, and 1678 incorporated by act of assembly, and named James-Town. Some gentlemen of Rhode-Island and other parts of New-England made a considerable purchase of Petaquamsecut (from the Indians) which with the adjacent lands were incorporated a township by the name of Kingston 1674: but since divided into three townships, South-Kingston, North-Kingston, and Exeter.

Misquamicut purchased of the Indians, 1665, was constituted a township 1669, by the name of Westerly; this is lately divided into three townships, Westerly, Charles-Town and Richmond; in Charles-Town is the Narraganset Indian reserve (Ninigret is sachem,) of two miles from E. to W. and of about six miles from north to south; which is generally farmed by the friends of the Indian guardians appointed by the assembly, upon long leases and small rents.

Manisses or Block Island, 1672, was constituted the township of New-Shoreham.

1677, the township of Greenwich, was incorporated, and lately divided into the two townships of Greenwich, and West Greenwich. By this time all the colony or general lands were reduced to private property; see a subsequent table, p. 89.

When the court of England, in a bad administration, were resolved to vacate charters of any nature, because restraints or obstacles to a despotick power; a writ of Quo Warranto was issued out against the colony Oct. 6,

---

[k] Exemplary to the other colonies.

1685.

1685, and delivered June 2, 1686, by Edward Randolph, Efq. The freemen of the colony by their ballots or written votes called proxies, by a majority gave in their opinion to the general affembly, in conformity to which, the general affembly, after the example of many corporations or charters in England, determined not to ftand fuit with his majefty, but by an humble addrefs to the king, pray for the continuance of their privileges and liberties according to charter : the king promifed them protection and favour; they were put under the government of prefident Dudley, who was foon fuperfeded by governor Andros. 1686-7, Jan. 12, Sir Edmond Andros's commiffion as governor of New-England, was publifhed in Rhode-Ifland, and all the colony formed into one county.

Upon the Orange revolution, by a general vote of the freemen in May 1689, it was concluded, that Sir Edmond Andros's authority, by his confinement in Bofton, was terminated or filenced, and therefore they re-affume their former government or charter; and as their charter never was vacated in a due courfe of law or judgment, the court of England allows them to continue in the poffeffion and ufe of it to this day.

Each townfhip is managed by a town council, confifting of the affiftants who refide in the town, the juftices of the town, and fix men freeholders chofen annually by the freemen of the town; the major part of them is a quorum, with full power to manage the affairs and intereft of the town to which they refpectively belong; to grant licences to publick houfes; and are a probate office for proving wills and granting anminiftration, with appeal to governor and council as fupreme ordinary.

On any urgent occafion the governor, or in his abfence, the deputy governor, may by warrant call a general affembly.—The direction of the militia is in the general affembly of the colony; but when the affembly does not fit, the governor and affiftants have the power of the militia.

At

· At the township meetings in March annually, the Freemen of the town bring in their written votes called proxies, for a governor, a deputy governor, ten affiſtants, recorder, treaſurer, and attorney general ; theſe votes are ſealed up and ſent to Newport for next May general election ; the governor has no negative in elections, has no negative in paſſing of bills or reſolves; only in the houſe or board of aſſiſtants in caſe of an equivote, he has the caſting vote. All other officers civil and military are appointed by a joint vote of the board of aſſiſtants and houſe of repreſentatives. The legiſlature of Rhode-Iſland colony ſtile themſelves, The governor and company of the Engliſh colony of Rhode-Iſland and Providence Plantations in New-England in America ; the enacting ſtile is, Be it enacted by the general aſſembly of this colony, and by the authority of the ſame it is enacted. The aſſembly adjourn themſelves for any time. The governor for the time being has the cuſtody of the colony's charter, ſeal &c. and appoints the naval officer; the governor's ſalary is 300 l. per ann. currency, and all his perquiſites do not exceed 1000l. [*l*] There are yearly two aſſemblies or elections of repreſentatives ; they ſit on the firſt Wedneſday in May at Newport; the ſecond aſſembly meets on the laſt Wedneſday of October at Providence and South-Kingſton alternately. In all grand committees, and elections of officers, the board of aſſiſtants and houſe of repreſentatives ſit and vote together.

In the laſt [*m*] election of general officers on the firſt

[*l*] At this writing 1750, the deputy governor has a ſalary of 300 l. currency or O. T. per ann. the treaſurer 200 l ; aſſiſtants and repreſentatives have no wages.

[*m*] Formerly the parties in elections and publick tranſactions were upon ſectary footings; but for ſome years paſt the oppoſite parties are, they who are againſt multiplying a fallacious fraudulent paper-currency, and they who encourage it for private iniquitous ends ; majority of the preſent houſe of repreſentatives are of the paper money ſide, notwithſtanding a growing depreciation : from April 1, 1750, to Sept. 1, 1750, their paper currency from par ſuffers a diſcount with the

Wedneſday

Wednesday of May 1750, were chosen William Greene governor, Robert Hazzard dep. governor; assistants, George Wanton, Jonathan Nichols, John Potter, John Bowen, Benjamin Tucker, Robert Lawton, James Arnold, William Richmond, Daniel Coggeshal, Jeffry Watson ; Thomas Ward secretary, Daniel Updike attorney general, and Thomas Richardson general treasurer. [*n*] When the charter first took place 1663, there were only 18 representatives, 6 from Newport, 4 from Providence, 4 from Portsmouth, and 4 from Warwick ; at present, 1750, besides these, there are 2 from each constituted township incorporated from that time, and at present are 58 members.

Massachusetts paper currency above 20 per cent, that is, a piece of 8 in Boston sells for 45s. O. T. in Rhode-Island it sells for 56s. O. T ; by selling, I mean, it is merchandize, and will continue such until the paper money is generally annihilated, or by its small quantity arrive at a just par with silver : I shall mention a palpable instance of the good effects of paper currency being gradually annihilated (if the transition is too sudden, it may occasion a stagnation of business, confusion and uproars, which ought carefully to be avoided, as tending to sedition) by sinking of our paper medium ; within these last six months (this is wrote September 1750) exchange with London is fallen from eleven and a half, for one sterling, to nine and a half, for one sterling good bills or well endorsed.

[*n*] The fallacious plantation paper money currencies are a most disagreeable topick, and fall too often in my way : here I cannot avoid observing, that the habitual practice of this paper money cheat, has had a bad influence not only upon profligate private persons, but upon the administration of some of our New-England governments : for instance, one of the legislature, a signer of the Rhode-Island colony bills, was not long since CONVICTED of signing counterfeit bills: Men are chosen into the legislature and executive parts of their government, not for their knowledge, honour, and honesty, but as sticklers for depreciating (for private ends) the currency, by multiplied emissions: this year, 1750, the parties amongst the electors of assembly men were distinguished by the names of paper money makers, and the contrary: the paper money makers have got a majority in the lower house, and propose a new emission of 200,000 l. O. T. ; it is probable the house or board of assistants will not concur ; it is not for want of paper currency ; at present they have more than ever ; Massachusetts-Bay, where the bulk of their bills were lodged, have sent them back accompanied with the bills of New-Hampshire ; their design is by quantity to depreciate the value of

A
s

As a table is the moſt conciſe and diſtinct form of repreſenting ſeveral numeral articles relating to a colony; I ſhall here repreſent each townſhip, their late numbers of proxies or freemen voters, their repreſentatives in general aſſembly, their juſtices, their companies of militia, perluſtration (1748) of whites, negroes, and Indians.

their bills; and lands mortgaged for publick bills will be redeemed in thoſe minorated bills, at a very inconſiderable real value. In the neigh-bouring province of Maſſachuſetts-Bay the principal directors and ſig-ners of bubbling or notorious cheat bills (in the act of parliament, 1741, it is termed a miſchievous undertaking and publick nuſance) were by votes concurred by gov. Sh——y, made councellors, ſigners of publick bills of credit, judges, juſtices, &c. This to an impartial reader muſt appear the greateſt diſregard of a miniſter (all governors are in a miniſterial capacity) to acts of parliament. To prevent this nuſance, in all acts of aſſemblies concerning paper money currencies, there may be a clauſe, that any perſon convicted of making, ſigning, or uttering any falſe, fraudulent, or counterfeit bills, be rendered inca-pable of any place of profit or truſt in the ſaid province or colony.

In Maſſachuſetts Bay province December 1748, the act for drawing in their bills of credit, expreſsly declares, " that the bills of the neigh-bouring provinces have paſſed promiſcuouſly with the bills of our pro-vince; and the inhabitants of Maſſachuſetts-Bay province will thereby be liable to greater evils than they have as yet ſuffered, if the bills of the neighbouring governments continue current within the province; therefore, &c." particularly every perſon ſo accounting (extra provincial bills reckoned up to a perſon or otherways evading in negociation) receiving, taking, or paying the ſame, ſhall forfeit the ſum of fifty pounds new tenor for every ſuch offence. There has lately hap-pened a publick controverſy in the Boſton weekly news papers for Sept. 1750, concerning the word accounting: this ought to be ex-plained by ſome ſubſequent act of aſſembly; as there is a diſcovery of a principal manager, negociating in Boſton (in a manner as he thought evadable in the law) ſome bills of New-Hampſhire: as he was a principal agent in reſtraining the currency of bills of the neigh-bouring provinces, if intereſt had not prevailed againſt common pru-dence, he would have evaded the negociating of theſe bills in any manner though evadable in law.

N. B. To annihilate plantation paper currencies in a general ſenſe, is very laudable; but to do it ſuddenly or in the ſpace of one year, when there is no other medium or currency, puts a ſtop to all trade and buſineſs; this obſtruction may divert our commerce into ſome other channel: we have a notable inſtance of this in the province of Maſſachuſetts-Bay, 1750.

Townſhips.

Townships.	1748. 1749. Proxies.	Repref.	Juftices.	Whites.	Negroes.	Indians.	Companies Militia.
Newport	96	6	9	5335	110	68	4
Providence	32	4	13	3177	225	50	5
Portfmouth	25	4	5	807	134	51	1
Warwick	21	4	8	1513	176	93	3
Wefterley	23	2	6	1701	59	49	4
*New Shoreham	23	2	0	260	20	20	1
North Kingfton	30	2	7	1665	184	86	3
South Kingfton	21	2	5	1405	380	193	3
Greenwich	17	2	6	956	61	27	2
James Town	4	2	0	284	110	26	1
*Smithfield	45	2	5	400	30	20	3
Scituate	58	2	4	1210	16	6	3
Gloucefter	11	2	4	1194	8		3
Charles-Town	9	2	3	641	58	303	1
Weft Greenwich	25	2	4	757	8	1	2
Coventry.	12	2	6	769	16	7	2
Exeter	24	2	4	1103	63	8	2
Middletown	20	2	4	586	76	18	1
Briftol	13	2	5	928	128	13	1
Tiverton	102	2	4	842	99	99	2
Little Compton	107	2	5	1004	62	86	1
* Warren	82	2	4	600	50	30	1
Cumberland	73	2	3	802	4		1
* Richmond	11	2	5	500	5	3	1
	888	58	119	28439	3077	1257	51

N. B. The numbers of whites, blacks, and Indians for the townfhips of New Shoreham or Block-Ifland, Smithfield, Warren, and Richmond, are only eftimates, and not an actual cenfus.

When the qualification of a freeman, as formerly, was low, the proxies or voters never exceeded 1300 : at prefent the qualification is better or higher, and anno 1749, the proxies were only 888.

The valuation or cenfus anno 1730, was whites 15,302, blacks 1648, Indians 985, in all 17,935 ; the valuation anno 1748, was whites 28,439 blacks 3077, Indians 1257, in all 32,773 ; from thefe deduct Briftol, Tiverton, Little Compton, Warren, and Cumberland, a
late

late addition taken from the juriſdiction of Maſſachuſett
Bay, and added to Rhode-Iſland colony, of 4196 white
343 blacks, and 228 Indians, remain 24,243 white
which is an increaſe of near 9,000 whites, upon 15,50
circiter, in 18 years; this is more than one third increaſ
ed in the ſpace of 18 years.   The cenſus of their black
and Indians perhaps is not exact ; that ſmall colony doe
not poſſeſs more negroes, than the much larger provinc
of Maſſachuſetts-Bay ; it is true, their late Guinea trad
exchanging of negroes for horſes, ſtock, and proviſion
ſhipt off for the Weſt-India iſlands, has added conſider
ably to the number of their negroes.   Here is an in.
creaſe of 44 Indians, whereas they are obſerved every
where to be upon the decreaſe from the intemperate uſe
of Britiſh ſpirit, and from their being ſent to ſea, and
upon expeditions.   The 51 militia foot companies are
formed into 4 regiments, being one regiment foot in
each of their four counties of Newport, Providence,
King's-county, and Briſtol ; there are alſo one troop of
horſe in the county of Newport, and a troop in the
county of Providence.

Concerning the boundaries of the colony of Rhode-Iſland.

KING Charles, anno 1630, made a grant to the earl
of Warwick from Narraganſet-Bay, weſtward along
ſhore 40 leagues, and in length from ſea to ſea: he
aſſigned this grant to William viſcount Say and Seal [o],
lord Brooks, lord Rich, and eight more aſſociates : the
conditions of the grant were never compiled with by
ſettling, &c. and the grant is become void.   A ſubſequent
grant to duke Hamilton, 1635, for the ſame reaſon is
null.

[o] Seabrook at the mouth of Connecticut river is ſo called from the
name of viſcount Say and lord Brook.   This humour of joint names
for townſhips is ſtill practiſed in the colony of Connecticut ; thus a
townſhip granted lately to Hartford and Windſor jointly, is called
Harwinton, from the initial ſyllables of theſe two townſhips.

In

In the beginning of our settlements, the country not being well investigated, sundry succeeding royal grants interfered with former grants [*p*]. King Charles II. having received complaints concerning the wrong description of places and grants, not to be determined at a distance, but by commissioners to be sent expressly upon the spot; accordingly 1664, four commissioners, col. Nichols (afterwards governor of New-York) Sir Robert Ker, &c. were sent over to settle all the controverted boundaries of the provinces, and to be determined by the concurrence of any three of these commissioners, or of two of them, whereof Nichols to be one. [*q*]   Three of those commissioners gave the Attleborough Gore to

[*p*] For instance, Plymouth old north line, from Conahasset due west to Patuket river, and Massachusetts south line, from 3 miles south of the southermost part or head of Charles river, extended E. and W. overlap one another several miles; Attleborough Gore is plainly included in Plymouth grant, and also in the grant to Rhode-Island. Some of the lands of Tiverton and Little Compton, seem to be in both these grants. In equity perhaps the prior grant should take place; but this was not observed in the late determination of Rhode-Island easterly bounds; the validity of the Plymouth grant as to jurisdiction being questioned. Rhode-Island colony pretended to the settlements of Tiverton, Little Compton, Dartmouth, Rochester, Sandwich, and Cape-Cod townships, because Plymouth grant is not said to be bounded upon the ocean: but as this claim was not brought before a late court of commissioners appointed by patent from Great-Britain to settle the eastern boundaries of Rhode-Island colony, it may be supposed drort and silenced. Lately in Rhode-Island, they have imagined a claim of jurisdiction further north than their present line; taking in part of Wrentham, Bellingham, Mendon, Uxbridge, and Douglass; they were encouraged to this by their late success in the eastern claim; but when they complained at home concerning the encroachments of Massachusetts-Bay, upon their eastern borders, they made no complaint of northern encroachments; which if any, might have been adjusted by the same commission without further charge; and when commissioners were appointed, December 18, 1749, by the general assembly of Massachusetts-Bay, to join with commissioners from the jurisdiction of Rhode-Island, to run and renew the line agreed on and settled by both governments, Jan. 19, 1710-11; the Rhode-Island commissioners did not appear.

[*q*] The Rhode-Islanders construed it that nothing could be concluded without the concurrence of Nichols; and because Nichols hap-

Plymouth

Plymouth colony, that is, Patucket alias Blackftone [r] river to be the dividing line between thefe two colonies; the king's pleafure concerning this determination was never fignified ; as it was not confirmed at home, it con-tinued many years in difpute, and at length, was deter-mined by commiffioners 1741, and confirmed by the king in council 1746, in favour of Rhode-Ifland ; it is now called Cumberland townfhip, in honour to his royal highnefs the duke of Cumberland, and is annexed to the county of Providence.

Rhode-Ifland eafterly line dividing it from the prefent province of Maffachufetts-Bay was fettled by commiffi-oners [s] 1741. Maffachufetts government appealed home againft every part of the judgment as grievous and injurious ; but the judgment in the whole was confirmed 1746, by the king in council. In autumn 1746, the go-vernment of Rhode-Ifland fent to the government of Maffachufetts-Bay, a copy of his majefty's order in coun-cil, affirming the judgment of the court of commiffion-ers, for fettling the boundary line between the two go-vernments, and by act of affembly appointed commiffion-ers to run (Dec. 2, 1746) this late adjudged line with commiffioners from Maffachufetts-Bay ; the affembly of Maffachufetts-Bay could not be informed of this ap-pointed time until their next fitting, December 24; thus Rhode-Ifland contrived to run this line *ex parte*. For a minute defcription of this line, fee vol. I. p. 399.

For Rhode-Ifland northerly line dividing this colony from the province of Maffachufetts-Bay, fee vol. I. p.415.

---

pened not to be one of the three that concurred in the determination of the Attleborough Gore, they alledged the determination was not perfect, whereas Nichols was plainly intended to have only a cafting vote when two are againft two.

[r] This river was fo called by the name of Mr. Blackftone, who removed from Maffachufetts-Bay and lived in this Gore, upon that river, many years.

[s] The fettling of this line coft each government about 4,000 l. O. T. The commiffioners had from each government 6s. fterl. per diem, with all charges in coming, at, and returning from the congrefs.

Southerly

Southerly the colony of Rhode-Island is bounded upon the sea or Atlantic ocean.

Its westerly line dividing it from the colony of Connecticut was settled by commissioners from both colonies September 27, 1728 ; was ascertained by a direct line extending west from the rock at the uttermost point of Warwick neck, 20 miles, to a considerable heap of stones in a cedar swamp, the S. W. corner of Warwick purchase. From this monument the line with Connecticut is determined by running first N. 7 d. E. by compass, 23 miles 10 rods to a large heap of stones in a valley being between two marked pine trees in the south line of the province of Massachusetts-Bay, and for the first 7 and a half miles were made monuments every half mile, and from thence northward to the Massachusetts south line, were made monuments at the end of each mile : from the said monument the S. W. corner of Warwick was made a southerly running of 15 miles and 9 rods S. 11 d. 20 m. W. to the mouth of Astrawage river where it falls into Pakatuke river; and from thence Pakatuke river is the boundary to the sea.

Signed	Roger Woolcot, James Wadsworth, Daniel Palmer.	} For Connecticut.
	William Wanton, Benjamin Ellery, William Jenkes.	} For Rhode-Island.

The colony of Rhode-Island have been very little concerned in the British North-America wars with the adjacent Indians, and their encouragers to rapine the French of Canada ; from the Quaker principles of many of the inhabitants, and as not being immediately exposed to the ravages of the French and their Indians. In the expedition against Port-Royal in Nova-Scotia, an. 1710, and in the abortive expedition against Canada, 1711,
they

they had some forces: towards the feint or intended
expedition against Canada, in the summer 1746, they
fitted out 300 land men with a warlike sloop of 100
seamen; they were ordered for Nova-Scotia, but in their
voyage suffered disasters, never proceeded, and after
some time this expedition was countermanded. They
have been noted for privateering against the French and
Spaniards in time of war. They have built a good fort
upon Goat-Island, an island in the harbour of Newport.

The numbers of their whites, slaves, and other lists,
may be seen in the foregoing table.

Concerning their courts of judicature.

FORMERLY the colony of Rhode-Island made only one
county: not long since it was divided into three counties,
Newport, Providence, and King's county; lately they
have constituted a fourth county called Bristol, comprehending the late addition from the province of Massachusetts; Cumberland is in the County of Providence.
Newport county contains Rhode-Island (the townships
of Newport, Portsmouth, and Middletown,) Block-Island
(the township of New-Shoreham) Canonicut-Island (the
township of James-Town) Prudence-Island, and Patience-
Island, with the lately adjudged parts of Tiverton and
Little-Compton. Providence county comprehends the
townships of Providence, Smithfield, Scituate, Gloces-
ter, Warwick, Coventry, Greenwich, West-Greenwich,
and Cumberland. King's county includes South-Kingston, North-Kingston, Exeter, Westerly, Charles Town,
and Richmond.

The legislature, called the general court or general
assembly, sits the first Wednesday in May annually at
Newport, and at Providence and South-Kingston alternately the last Wednesday of October.

The form of their judicial oath or affirmation does
not invoke the judgments of the omniscient God, who
                                                    sees

fees in fecret, but only upon the peril of the penalty of perjury [*t*].

Juries. The town council of each townfhip take a lift of all perfons liable by law, and whom they fhall judge able and well qualified to ferve in juries, and lay the fame before a town meeting called for that purpofe ; and the names of all fuch perfons written on feparate pieces of paper, fhall be put in a box to be delivered to the town clerk, to be by him kept under lock and key. When the precept or notification for returning of jurors is iffued, at a town meeting the box fhall be unlocked, and the town clerk fhall draw out fo many tickets, as there are jurors required, to be returned as jurors ; fuch as in the judgment of the town meeting are unable to ferve at that time, their names fhall be returned into the box and others drawn in their ftead ; the names of the perfons returned to ferve, fhall be put in another box from time to time, until all the tickets be drawn as aforefaid ; then they fhall be returned into the firft, to be drawn from time to time as aforefaid. The town council fhall once a year lay before a town meeting fuch other perfons as may from time to time become qualified, to be put in the box. If by reafon of challenge or otherways there are not a fufficient number of good and lawful men to make up the jury, the jury fhall be filled up by the fheriff or his deputy *de talibus circumftantibus.*

Justices of the peace. The general affembly in their May feffions, chufe for each town fo many juftices of the peace as they may find requifite, to be commiffioned by the governor of the colony under the feal of the colony ; their power extends all over the county. A juftice may join perfons in marriage, take the ac-

[*t*] This does not feem to be a facred or folemn oath, and may be illuftrated by the ftory of two profligate thieves ; one of them had ftolen fomething, and told his friend of it : well, fays his friend, but did any body fee you ? No : then fays his friend, it is yours as much as if you had bought it with your money.

knowledgment

knowledgment of a deed or other inſtrument ; take de
poſitions out of court, the adverſe party being notified
Two or more juſtices may hear, try, and adjudge al
manner of debts, trefpaſſes, and other actions, not ex
ceeding five pounds currency ; titles of lands are ex
cepted, and ſuch other actions as are excepted by any
particular law of the colony. Three or more juſtices
of the peace may try all perſons ſuſpected of thieving
to the value of ten pounds currency. Appeals in civil
caſes are allowed to the inferior court of common pleas,
and in criminal caſes to the court of the general ſeſſions
of the peace : the judgment of which court, on all appeals from the juſtices court, is final.

Sessions of the peace. In each county are held
twice a year, a court of general ſeſſions of the peace,
five juſtices of the county making a quorum, impowered
to hear and determine all manner of matters and things
relating to the conſervation of the peace, the puniſhment
of offenders ; and all pleas of the crown (capital crimes
excepted) are therein cognizable. Any perſon aggrieved
at the ſentence of this court, may appeal to the next
ſuperior court of judicature, court of aſſize and general
goal delivery.

Inferior courts of common pleas are held twice
a year in each county ; three juſtices of the ſaid court
are a quorum : they have cognizance of all civil actions
ariſing or happening within the county, and tryable at
common law, of what nature, kind, or quality ſoever :
but no action not exceeding five pounds currency, is
brought into any of theſe courts, unleſs where any man's
freehold is concerned, or by way of appeal from any
juſtices court. Liberty of appeal from theſe inferior
courts of common pleas, is allowed to the next ſuperior
court of judicature, &c.

Superior court of judicature, courts of aſſize
and general goal delivery, are holden twice a year in
each county ; three judges are a quorum : they have
cognizance of all pleas, real, perſonal, or mixt ; as alſo

pleas of the crown, and caufes criminal, and matters relating to the confervation of the peace, punifhment of offenders, and generally of all other matters, as fully and amply to all intents and purpofes whatfoever, as the court of common pleas, king's bench or exchequer in his majefty's kingdom of England have, or ought to have, and are impowered to give judgment therein, and to award execution thereon, and make fuch neceffary rules of practice, as the judges fhall from time to time fee needful; but no caufe, matter, or thing (writs of error, capital crimes, &c. excepted) are brought into this court by an original writ or procefs, but by appeals from the inferior courts of common pleas.

APPEALS TO HIS MAJESTY IN COUNCIL are allowed, where the matter or thing in controverfy is the value of three hundred pounds new tenor, unlefs from judgment obtained upon a bond, which has no other condition but for the payment of a fum or fums of money. They appeal to the king in council not only on perfonal, but alfo in real actions.

A COURT OF CHANCERY or delegates not long fince was erected; but on their iniquitous proceedings in difpenfing with all laws, no man's property was fafe; it was therefore difcontinued.

THE ORDINARY FOR PROBATE OF WILLS, and granting adminiftration, is in the refpective town councils, with appeals to the court of governor and affiftants.

THE COURT OF VICE-ADMIRALTY confifts of the fame individual officers or perfons that officiate in Maffachufetts-Bay, or by deputations from them.

THE JUSTICIARY COURT OF ADMIRALTY is much of the fame nature with that of Maffachufetts-Bay, with an addition of the governor and fome of the council of the neighbouring province of Maffachufetts-Bay.

Their prefent taxes of all kinds are very inconfiderable; the intereft of their publick loans generally defray all charges of government and other needfuls both of the colony and particular towns.

Navigation. Newport of Rhode-Iſland is their prin-cipal trading town at preſent; lies in 41 d. 35 m. N. lat. it is of eaſy and ſhort acceſs, being near the ocean, but for that reaſon not ſo well ſituated for home con-ſumption. Providence is about thirty miles farther up Narraganſet-bay inland, therefore in a few years it muſt be their principal place of trade. For the ſafety and conveniency of ſailing into the harbour of Newport, in ſummer 1749 was erected a light-houſe in Beaver-tail at a publick colony charge.

LIGHT-HOUSE.

The diameter at the baſe is twenty-four feet, and at the top thirteen feet. The height from the ground to the top of the cornice is fifty-eight feet, round which is a gallery, and within that ſtands the lanthorn, which is about eleven feet high, and eight feet diameter.

The ground the light houſe ſtands on is about twelve feet above the ſurface of the ſea at high water.

The following are the bearings (by the compaſs) of ſeveral remarkable places from the light houſe, viz.

Point Judith		S. W.	3	Deg. S.
Block-Iſland N. W. point		S. W.	8	S.
Ditto	S. E. point	S. W. b. S.	5	S.
Whale rock		W.	9	S.
Brenton's reef		E. S. E.	4	E.
Seal rock		E. S. E.	10	E.
S. point of Rhode-Iſland		E.	7	S.
Watch houſe on Caſtle-hill		E. N, E.	4	E.
Brenton's point		E. N. E.	4	N.
Fort on Goat-Iſland		E. N. E.	5	N.
S. eaſtermoſt of the Dumplins		N. E. b. E.		
Kettle bottom rock		N. E.	4	E.
Anchoring place between the town of Newport and Coaſter's harbour		N. E. b. E.		

N. B. There

N. B. There is a small sunken rock lies off due S. and at
the distance of about 200 yards from the light-house.

The entrances and clearances of vessels in the collection of Newport for the last year of the late French
and Spanish war ; and for the first year of the present
peace.

From 25 March 1747 to 25 March 1748.
Ships, Snows, Brigs, Sloops, Schooners.

Entered in 2	3	20	27	4	**Total 56**
Cleared out 4	5	33	71	5	118

From 25 March 1748, to 25 March 1749.

Entred in 2	2	30	37	4	Total 75
Cleared out 8	11	49	9	83	160

The vessels used here are generally brigantines and
sloops. Their trade in time of war consists much in
privateering ; this last war they had bad success ; not
much trade with Europe ; much used to smuggling of
contraband and uncustomed goods ; they export for the
West-India islands, horses, live stock of several kinds,
butter, cheese, lumber, and rum of their own distilling ;
their trade seems to be upon the decline ; they import
or rather carry to Boston, sugar, molasses, and other
West-India island produce, a few negroes from Guinea,
and logwood from the bay of Honduras.

Ever since 1710, their most beneficial business has been
banking or negociating a base fraudulent paper money
currency, which is so contrived, that amongst themselves
it comes out at about two and half per cent. per ann.
interest and lend it to the neighbouring colonies at 10 per
cent [*u*] a most barefaced cheat. Of the interest of these
publick iniquitous frauds, one quarter goes to the several
townships to defray their charges, the other three

[*u*] I shall only mention their emission 1744, of a publick paper
money credit of 160,000 *l.* O. T. upon pretext (as the preamble expresses it) of the present Spanish war, and of an impending French
war ; but was shared amongst themselves by way of loan at four per
ct. per ann. interest, for the first ten years, and after the expiration of
those ten years, the principal to be paid off gradually in ten years more
without any interest.

quar-

quarters arc lodged in the treaſury to defray the government charges of the colony.

PRODUCE. Rhode-Iſland colony in general is a country for paſture, not for grain ; by extending along the
ſhore of the ocean and a great bay, the air is ſoftened by
a ſea vapour which fertilizeth the ſoil ; their winters are
ſofter and ſhorter than up inland ; it is noted for dairies,
whence the beſt of cheeſe made in any part of New-
England, is called (abroad) Rhode-Iſland cheeſe.

Anno 1687, when by act of aſſembly taxes were receivable in produce of certain ſpecies, Indian corn was
valued at 18 *d,* per buſhel, butter 4 *d.* per pound, ſheeps
wool at 8 *d.* per pound; currency at that time, pieces
of eight at a denomination of 33 3 quarters worſe than
ſterling.

The moſt conſiderable farms are in the Narraganſet
country. Their higheſt dairy of one farm, communibus
annis, milks about 110 cows, cuts about 200 load of
hay, makes about 13,000 wt. of cheeſe, beſides butter;
and ſells off conſiderably in calves and fatted bullocks.
A farmer from ſeventy-three milch cows in five months
made about 10,000 wt. of cheeſe : beſides cheeſe in a
ſeaſon, one cow yields one firkin of butter, from ſeventy
to eighty wt. In good land they reckon after the rate of
two acres for a milch cow.

In this colony there is no college or ſchola illuſtris;
lately ſome gentlemen, lovers and encouragers of the liberal arts and ſciences, to promote literature in the colony, have in Newport, the metropolis of the colony of
Rhode-Iſland, lately founded a library. That this may
be of exemplary uſe to our other provinces and colonies,
I ſhall give ſome account of it. 1747, Abraham Redwood, Eſq. beſtowed 500 *l.* ſterl. in books, being
volumes, 206 folio's, 128 quarto's, 712 octavo's, and
251 duodecimo's ; ſeveral other perſons have beſtowed
ſome valuable books ; a gentleman of noted liberality
has promiſed an experimental philoſophy apparatus, and
to erect a ſpiral monument with an obſervatory. Some

4

gentlemen incorporated by an ample colony charter have contributed, and upon ground, given by Mr. Henry Collins, merchant, erected a regular building for a library, at the charge of about 8,000 *l.* currency O. T..

The building for the library confifts of one large room where the books are kept, thirty-fix feet long, twenty-fix feet broad, and nineteen feet high, with two fmall offices adjoining. The principal or weft front is a pediment and portico of four columns after the Dorick order; the whole entablature of which, runs quite round the building. The two offices are placed as wings, one on each fide the portico, and connected with the body of the building, fo as to form two half-pediments proceeding from the lower part of the entablature. Thefe two wings, befides the conveniencies they afford, have a very good effect in extending as well as adding variety to this front. The eaft front confifts of a plain Dorick pediment fupported by a ruftick arcade of three arches, in the recefles of which are placed three Venetian windows, after the Ionic order. The outfide of the whole building is of ruftick work, and ftands on a bafe about five feet high from the ground, and the entrance is by a flight of fteps the whole width of the portico. Their charter conftitutes them a body politick, by the name of the company of the Redwood library, with power to chufe annually eight directors, a treafurer, fecretary, and librarian; to admit new members, make laws, &c.

It is to be wifhed that a tafte for learning and books with the better fort of people may prevail in all our colonies. In Philadelphia, fome years fince, a company of gentlemen, well-wifhers to letters, have conftituted a confiderable library; of this we fhall give fome account in the fection of Penfylvania. In Charles-town of South-Carolina, is lately formed a library company; April 21, 1750, they confifted of 128 members; their firft general meeting was the fecond wednefday of July 1750; they are to have four general quarterly meetings yearly, whereof one is the general annual meeting for election

of

of officers, viz. preſident, vice-preſident, treaſurer, ſecretary, librarian, correſpondent and ſteward. The contribution of the members to be [*x*] five ſhillings currency per week: the books to be lent to any of the ſociety, giving a receipt for the ſame, to be returned within a limited time, a pamphlet in ——— days, an octavo or duodecimo in ——— weeks, a quarto in ——— weeks, a folio in ——— months; of this we ſhall give a further account in the ſection of South-Carolina.

Rhode-Iſland government [*y*] pretend to an extent of juriſdiction farther north than is at preſent ſettled, (this we hinted at p. 91. of vol. II.) and takes off from the juriſdiction of Maſſachuſetts-Bay, conſiderable parcels of the townſhips of Wrentham, Bellingham, Mendon, Uxbridge and Douglaſs. Commiſſioners were appointed by the general aſſemblies of the province and colony as is uſual, to run their diviſional line laſt autumn 1749 reſpectively; they did not meet, and the Rhode-Iſland commiſſioners run the line ex parte. Jonathan Randal,

[*x*] Eight pence ſterl. which is about thirty-four ſhillings ſterl. per annum.

[*y*] The provincial taxes and townſhip rates having lately in the province of Maſſachuſetts-Bay, from the wrongheaded management of ——— been ſo oppreſſively great, that, 1. Upon a diſpute between the province of Maſſachuſetts-Bay and colony of Connecticut, lately broached concerning ſome townſhips of the province indented with the colony; the Maſſachuſetts townſhips of Woodſtock, Somers, Enfield, and Suffield, did in a voluntary manner withdraw from the juriſdiction of Maſſachuſetts, and put themſelves under the juriſdiction of Connecticut; and by force or menace prevent the civil officers of Maſſachuſetts from exerciſing any authority and gathering of taxes. 2. The Maſſachuſetts townſhips adjoining to the northerly line of Rhode-Iſland colony, allowed the Rhode-Iſland men (in an actual treſpaſs) to run a line, without any oppoſition; chuſing rather to be under the juriſdiction of Rhode-Iſland, where the publick or colony taxes are very ſmall, and ſometimes nothing, and no pariſh or miniſterial rates, a very ſtunting or diſcouraging article in the poor new ſettlement: theſe diſputes cannot be compoſed, but by applying to the court of Great-Britain at a great charge. Here we may obſerve, that ill deviſed exorbitant taxes occaſion diſcontent amongſt the people, with a charge and confuſion to the governments.

Thomas

Thomas Lapham, and Richard Steern, Efq. [z] were appointed in Auguft 1749 commiffioners to run the line according to charter: the commiffioners with Henry Harris, Efq. furveyor, and two chairmen, by themfelves run a line to their own mind, and made report laft Tuefday of February 1749-50; that, 30th of October 1749, no commiffioners from Maffachufetts-Bay appearing, we proceeded: " We [a] could find no ftake or monument
" of Woodward and Safferey, but from the place de-
" fcribed in our commiffion, viz. we found a place
" where Charles river formed a large crefcent foutherly,
" which place is known by the name of Poppolatick
" pond, which we took to be the foutthermoft part of
" the faid river; from thence we meafured three miles
" on a plain in Wrentham, one quarter of a mile N.
" eafterly from the dwelling-houfe of Thomas Man,
" and about a quarter of a mile S. eafterly from the
" houfe of Robert Blake, where we marked a pine-tree
" and erected a monument of ftones, and found the fame
" to be in lat. 42 d. 8 m. north, which we deemed the
" N. E. bounds of the colony. From the faid pine-tree
" we proceeded to run the northern boundary line in a
" weft courfe of eight and half degree variation, and in
" this courfe marked many trees, the faid line paffing
" over the foutthermoft part of Manchoag pond [b], and
" terminated about thirty rods eaftward of a fmall
" pond called Graffy Pond at a black oak tree which we
" marked with a monument of ftones about it, as the
" north weftern bounds of the colony, being about

[z] In Rhode-Ifland government are fquires many, becaufe annually elective, and once a fquire always a fquire; not long fince, a facetious gentleman met upon the road a Rhode-Ifland juftice of his acquaintance, bare legs and feet, driving a team in very foul weather; he faluted him in this manner: Your fervant, fquire—I am furprized to fee a gentleman of your noted frugality, to wear his beft ftockings and fhoes in fuch dirty weather.

[a] Perhaps, according to inftructions they defignedly did not find this proper monument.

[b] In the northern parts of Douglafs.

" twenty-

" twenty-two miles from the aforeſaid pine-tree to the
 ſaid black oak."
.. Some time afterwards a new commiſſion was iſſued from
each of the governments to perambulate the northern boundary of Rhode-Iſland colony, by the ſtake ſet up by Natha-
niel Woodward and Solomon Safferey, purſuant to the a-
greement of the province and colony, Jan. 19, 1710-11.

There is a caſe concerning ſome MINISTERIAL LANDS
in this colony of conſiderable value, claimed by the
church of England, and by the preſbyterians or congregationaliſts. This caſe has been depending almoſt thirty
years in the colony courts of common law, called the
courts below, and before the king in council, and hitherto not iſſued : a particular account of the caſe may
be agreeable to the devotees of both ſides.
     Anno 1657, the chief ſachems of the Narraganſet
country ſold to John Parker, Samuel Wilbore, Thomas
Mumford, Samuel Wilſon of Rhode-Iſland, and John
Hull, goldſmith of Boſton, Petaquamſcut-Hill for ſixteen
pound ; next year the ſachem of Nienticut, ſold for fifteen pound ſome lands north of the ſaid purchaſe, to the
ſame purchaſers. The whole purchaſe was about fifteen
miles long, and ſix or ſeven miles wide ; afterwards they
aſſociated Brenton and Arnold, jointly they were called
the ſeven purchaſers. Another company, called Atherton's
company, 1659-60, purchaſed lands of the Indians north
of the ſaid Petaquamſcut perchaſe ; theſe two companies
had ſeveral controverſies concerning their boundaries;
anno 1679, they came to a final accommodation.
     Anno 1668, the Petaquamſcut purchaſers by deed gave
300 acres of their beſt land, for an orthodox parſon to
preach God's word to the inhabitants : from this proceeds the diſpute, who is the orthodox miniſter ? By the
Rhode-Iſland charter all profeſſions of chriſtians ſeem
to be deemed orthodox ; by one of the firſt acts of their
legiſlature, 1663, all men profeſſing chriſtianity, and of
competent eſtates, and of civil converſation, and obedi-
                                                    ent

ent to the civil magiftrate, though of different judgment in religious affairs, Roman catholicks only excepted, fhall be admitted freemen, and fhall have [c] liberty to chufe and be chofen officers in the colony, both civil and military.

The boundaries with the Atherton company being finally accommodated, the Petaquamfcut purchafers, 1693, made a final divifion amongft themfelves, and amongft other company grants (120 acres to a mill, &c.) confirmed the grant of 1679, of 300 acres to an orthodox miniftry, which were furveyed and lotted.

Thefe minifterial lands not being claimed by any orthodox minifter, anno 1702, Mr. Henry Gardiner enters upon twenty acres of it, and James Bundy upon the remaining 280 acres.

Moft of the grantees feem to have been of the church of England, but many of them fell off to an enthufiaftick fect in Warwick, called [d] Gortonians, now extinct; perhaps at that time there were no Prefbyterians or congregational people in Rhode-Ifland, and at this time it is faid there are in South-Kingfton more people of the church of England than of the prefbyterians and congregationalifts.

1702, Mr. Niles, not ordained in any manner, preached in the faid diftrict for fome time, but never had poffeffion from Bundy of the 280 acres; in 1710, he left Kingfton and fettled at Braintree of Maffachufetts-Bay.

1719, George Mumford bought of Bundy the poffeffion of the faid 280 acres.

[c] They were not originally of fo catholick and chriftian fpirit in Maffachufetts-Bay colony; the Maffachufetts firft fettlers left England, becaufe of an oppreffive teft act, notwithftanding (fuch is the nature of zealous, furious bigotry and ent ufiafm) upon their firft fettling, 1631, in Maffachufetts was made a teft act, that no perfon could be free of the colony, who was not in full communion with fome of their churches in the independent congregational model. Here we fee that priefts and bigots of all religions are naturally the fame ; the people of New-England are become good chriftian catholicks.

[d] From Mr. Gorton their leader, this fectary is now loft or extinct; it did not furvive Mr. Gorton, the father of the fect.

Several

Several inhabitants of the Narraganſet country havi
petitioned the biſhop of London, and the ſociety
propagating the goſpel in foreign parts, for a miſſiona
Mr. Mc. Sparren was appointed 1721, and Mr. Gardiᵤ
delivered his twenty acres which he had in poſſeſſion,
the church of England incumbent. Mr. Guy before M
Sparren's time had been appointed miſſionary, but ſo
left it ; Mr. Mc. Sparren upon a writ of ejeƈtment 17
againſt Mumford for the 280 acres, grounded upon t
confirmation 1679, and the laying out 1693, the o
ginal grant of 1668 being ſecreted, was caſt in two tria
he appealed to the king in council, but the ſcociety ſ
propagating the goſpel refuſing to meddle in the affa
the matter reſted, and Mumford kept poſſeſſion.

The preſbyterian incumbent miniſter, Mr Torrey, t
firſt incumbent of ordination, brought an aƈtion verſ
Gardiner for the twenty acres, but was caſt; and M
Mc. Sparren, the church of England incumbent, broug
and recovered ejeƈtment againſt Robert Hazard tena
to Mr. Torrey.

1732, Mr. Torrey brought an aƈtion of ejeƈtme
againſt Mumford; both inferior and ſuperior court ga
it for Mumford; but upon Torrey's appeal to the kiᵣ
in council, theſe verdiƈts were diſallowed, and poſſeſſi
ordered to the incumbent Mr. Torrey, 1734—Tl
members of St. Paul's church of England in Narraga
ſet, April 7, 1735, addreſſed the ſociety for propagatiᵣ
the goſpel, &c. for their aſſiſtance in advice and expenᵢ
but to no purpoſe.

1735, by advice from England, Mr. Torrey conveyᵉ
the ſaid 280 acres which he recovered of Mumford,
Peter Coggſhal and five others in fee in truſt for himſ₁
and his ſucceſſors in the preſbyterian miniſtry : the ſa
truſtees leaſed the ſame to Hazard for a few years.

1739, the original deed of the miniſterial land in P
taquamſcut purchaſe, which had been ſecreted, comin
to light, Dr. Mc. Sparren in behalf of himſelf and ſu
ceſſors in St. Paul's church of South-Kingſton, by t

advice of his lawyers, capt. Bull, col. Updike, and
judge Auchmuty, brings a new writ of ejectment againſt
Hazard, the occupant or tenant of the ſaid 280 acres,
was caſt in the courts of Rhode-Iſland, but allowed an
appeal to the king in council, which, for ſome reaſons
has not been entered, nor petitioned for a hearing.

For the information of the curious, of after-times, I
ſhall here inſert the VALUATION or quota of each town-
hip towards a publick colony rate of 5000*l.* new tenor,
Anno 1747.

	£.		£.
Newport	825	Glouceſter	118
Providence	550	Charles-town	75
Portſmouth	276	W. Greenwich	79
Warwick	239	Coventry	60
Weſterley	270	Exeter	125
N. Shoreham	83	Middletown	149
North Kingſton	325	Briſtol	175
South Kingſton	450	Tiverton	140
Eaſt Greenwich	125	Little Compton	167
James-town	100	Warren	115
Smithfield	274	Cumberland	84
Scituate	132	Richmond	64

The affair of currencies in general is left to the appendix ; at preſent we ſhall only hint, that in the colony of
Rhode-Iſland from the votes of their general aſſembly, it
appears, that in February 1749-50, their publick bills of
credit current were 525,335 *l.* O. T. (whereof upon funds
of taxes 135,335 *l.* the reſt upon loan not to be finiſhed
until 1764) which is ſufficient to carry on the trade and
buſineſs of the colony even at their preſent depreciated
value ; and the preſent deſign of emitting 200,000 *l.* O. T.
more upon loan, is not as a further medium of trade, but
a knaviſh device of fraudulent debtors of the loan money,
to pay off their loans at a very depreciated value ; the
threatnings of Connecticut government to prohibit the
currency

currency of Rhode-Ifland bills in cafe the Rhode-Iflan
ers emit more, will be an advantage to the fraud; b
caufe Rhode-Ifland will then have fuch a drug of the
own and New-Hampfhire bills as to render them of litt
or no value, confequently a real debt or mortgage ma
be difcharged by a little or no value.   ··· ·

In Attleborough Gore or Cumberland of this colon
are great variety of iron-rock ores, but unprofitable
here we fhall give a fhort account of the metallick ore
and minerals hitherto difcovered in New-England; fe
p. 540. vol. I.

Mr. Baden, an ingenious miner and effayer, not man
years fince, was fent over to New-England from Eng
land by a company of gentlemen in queft of metallic
ores and minerals; he found, 1. Iron ore, (both rocl
and fwamp or bog ore) in plenty but not profitable. 2
Lead ore near Merimack, and Souhegan rivers, but no
plenty, and fo intermixed with rock and fpar, that it i
not worth working. 3. Copper ore in Simfbury hills, i
the colony of Connecticut, near Connecticut river; thre
different companies (Belcher and Cafwel, Mr. Bowdoi
and company, Goff and company; this laft was a bubbl
of Shodes) have wrought thefe mines with a confiderabl
lofs, and for fome years have been neglected; Mr. Bel
cher erected a fmelting furnace in Bofton for his coppe
ore, but to no purpofe. 4. Silver ore in Dracut nea
Merimack river; a furnace was erected in Bofton fo
fmelting this ore, but the ore proved a cheat of co
- V—m's, and all mifcarried.

In Attleborough Gore fome copper ore was intermixe
with iron ore, which is a detriment to the iron ore, an
of no profit as to copper.

We have fome alum-flate or ftone, but no fa
fprings, no pyrites of vitriol ftone, fuch as is found c
both fides of the river Thames along the Kentifh ar
Effex fhores in England, no lapis calaminaris. W
have plenty of feveral forts of earths, called boles

okers, such as black lead in Brimfield of Massachusetts-Bay near Connecticut river, ruddle or red oker in many places, and some small quantities of yellow oker, which is the only valuable oker.

Our only metallick ore at present under the improvement is that of iron, and may be reduced under the folowing heads. 1. Furnaces for smelting of rock ore into pigs; in Attleborough, now Cumberland, annexed lately to the jurisdiction of Rhode-Island, were erected at a considerable charge three furnaces; the country was well wooded for coal, but the ore proved not good or profitable, and is neglected; they were of some small use in the late war in casting of small canon, bombs, and bullets. Here is a magnetick iron ore, which yields a red shot iron, not good. 2. Smaller furnaces for smelting of swamp or bog ore into hollow or cast ware, pots, kettles, &c. which we can afford cheaper than from England or Holland. 3. Bloomeries, which from bog or swamp ore without a furnace heat, only by a forge hearth, reduce it into a bloom or semiliquidated lump to be beat into bars; commonly three tons of this ore yield one ton of bar iron, much inferior to the bar manufactured by the refiners of pig iron imported from the New-York, Jersies, Pensylvania and Maryland furnaces.

Col. Dunbar, late surveyor general of the woods in America, anno 1731, reported to the board of trade and plantations, that in New-England were six furnaces, meaning hollow ware furnaces, and nineteen forges, meaning bloomeries, for at that time we had no pig furnaces, no pig refineries.

In New-England, we have two slitting mills for nail rods, one in Milton eight miles from Boston, and another in Middleborough about thirty miles from Boston, which are more than we have occasion for. Our nailers can afford spikes and large nails cheaper than from England, but small nails not so cheap.

Religion,

Religion, or rather the various religions in the colon of Rhode-Iſland. The Rev. Mr. Cotton Mather in folio hiſtory of New-England, which he calls Magnalia &c. writes, that anno 1695, (book VII. chap. 3. p. 20. " Rhode-Iſland colony is a colluvies of Antinomians " Familiſts, Anabaptiſts, Antiſabbaterians, Arminians " Socinians, Quakers, Ranters, and every thing but Ro " man catholicks, and true chriſtians ; bona terra, mal " gens," he ſhould have added ſome Browniſts, inde pendents, and congregationaliſts, but not formed into ſocieties or congregations.

In this colony are no townſhip or pariſh rates for the ſupport of eccleſiaſticks of any denomination ; only the church of England miſſionaries, miniſters, and ſchool maſters have ſalaries from England by the ſociety for propagating the goſpel in foreign parts ; and the congregationaliſt miniſter in Weſterly, as a miſſionary amongſt the Narraganſet Indians, has an exhibition from an incorporated ſociety in Scotland, called a ſociety for propagating chriſtian knowledge.

In the addreſs of the ſeveral plantations, ſince united by charter into one colony called Rhode-Iſland, to the ſupreme authority in England 1659, they call themſelves a poor colony, " an out-caſt people, formerly from our " mother nation in the biſhops days, and ſince from " the new Engliſh over zealous colonies."

The plantations of Rhode-Iſland were originally ſettled by people privately whimſical in affairs of religion, Antinomians, rigid Browniſts, &c. Their firſt embodied ſocieties of publick meeting were anabaptiſts (the true enthuſiaſts were only tranſients or vagrants) and to this day ſeem to have the majority in the colony.—In general they differ from the other two branches (preſbyterians and independents of the profeſſions in England tolerated by licence) ſolely in their admitting only of adults to baptiſm, and that not by ſprinkling, but dipping or immerſion ; private perſons among themſelves differ in particular tenets, ſuch as, it is unlawful to pray with

or

or for any practical unbelievers—That human learning
is no way necessary for a gospel-preacher—differences as
to grace and free-will, &c——

Some have no particular place of meeting or worship:
We shall give a more particular account of the sectaries
amongst the anabaptists in the digressional article of British plantation sectaries in religious worship.

The quakers, persecuted in Massachusetts-Bay, first
came to Rhode-Island 1656, and several of the most enthusiastick amongst the anabaptists joined with them;
the congregational way did not take place until 1698;
Mr. Honyman the first settled church of England missionary, fixed in Newport of Rhode-Island 1706; he
was the senior church of England missionary, and died
lately.

The baptists or anabaptists of Providence, 1654, divided into two sects concerning the essential necessity of
laying on of hands (ordination) as a qualification in a
person to administer baptism: the laying on of hands at
length generally obtained—There is a strict association
of the ordination baptists by itinerant yearly meetings
all over New-England once a year.—1665, a baptist
church or congregation was formed in the new plantation of Westerly, and generally embraced the seventh
day or saturday sabbath, and are at present a large society,
called sabbatarian baptists—1671, from the sabbatarian
baptist church of Newport some drew off, and formed a
first day sabbath church.

1720, in Newport was gathered a society in the congregational way; 1728, another church of congregationalists proceeded from them; their first considerable
appearance, but without any place of publick worship,
was 1698.—There is a congregational society in Providence, but do not thrive.—There is a congregational
meeting in South-Kingston, which we have mentioned
at length in the account of the ministerial lands of Peta-
quamscut.—There is a congregational church in Westerly, the minister has an annual exhibition from the Scots
society

ſociety for propagating of chriſtian knowledge amongſt the Narraganſet Indians as his province; the fund was partly the donation of the Rev. Dr. Williams of London. —There is a congregationaliſt ſociety in Shoreham called Block-Iſland.—And ſome in townſhips lately taken from the province of Maſſachuſetts-Bay, and annexed to the colony of Rhode-Iſland.

The church of England ſociety for propagating the goſpel in foreign parts, in this colony have four miſſionary miniſters at Newport, S. Kingſton, Providence, and Briſtol; and occaſional worſhip at Warwick and Weſterly; two ſchool-maſters with ſalaries; and lately in Newport a catechiſt or ſchool-maſter, a donation of their late collector of the cuſtoms, Mr. Keys.

Here is no preſbyterian congregation after the model of the church of Scotland, Holland, Geneva, and the French huguenots.

Many quaker meetings all over the colony.

Civil officers are choſen indifferently out of every religious ſociety; ſome years ſince Mr. Cranſton was continued governor many years as an impartial good man; he did not aſſociate with any ſect, and did not attend any publick meeting; as the charter grants an univerſal liberty of conſcience, he was a keep-at home proteſtant.

A ſmall congregation of Jews, who worſhip at a private houſe, where a clerk or ſubordinate teacher regularly officiated at all conſtituted times.

A Digreſſion concerning the various ſectaries in religion, in the Britiſh ſettlement of North America.

With regard to religion, mankind may be diſtinguiſhed into three general ſects, 1. infidels, 2. ſcepticks, 3. the religious, properly ſo called, conſiſting of many peculiar modes or ſchemes of practical devotion.

The religious are divided into chriſtians, &c. there we write concerning chriſtians only.

The

The sacred scriptures, called our Bible, is the magna charta of all christian societies ; this book or bible is a most valuable collection of moral precepts, sometimes delivered in plain literal sentences, but generally by way of mystery, fable, allegory, allusion, and the like, as was the manner of the eastern sages and writers of those times. I am a catholick christian, no libertine, no enthusiast, no bigot ; what I relate is purely historical ; bishop Tillotson writes, " the zealots of all parties have " got a scurvy trick of lying for the truth."

It is the general opinion of politicians, that a proper deference to a well regulated clergy is requisite in a commonwealth ; notwithstanding, and not inconsistent with his due deference, I may be allowed to make the folowing remarks concerning the conversions or propagaion of christian knowledge among our American Indians : I shall premise the observations of some good men who were knowing in this matter, before the missionary societies took place. [*e*]

Mr. Elliot minister of Roxbury near Boston, with much labour learnt the Natick dialect of the Indian languages. He published an Indian grammar, preached in

[*e*] At our first arrival among the American Indians, we found no laces and times of religious worship, only some priests called Powers, a kind of knavish cunning conjurers, like those in Lapland, who pretend to converse with familiar spirits.

After some years communication with the neighbouring Indians, these Indians of themselves established some good and natural regulaons ; such as—If any man be idle a week, or at most a fortnight, he shall pay five shillings.—If an unmarried man shall lie with a young woman unmarried, he shall pay twenty shillings.—Every young man, not a servant, shall be compelled to set up a wigwam (a house or hut) and plant for himself—If any woman shall not have her hair tied up, but hang loose, or be cut as men's hair, she shall pay five shillings.—Whoever shall commit fornication, if a man, shall pay 20 shillings ; and if a woman, 10 shillings.—None to beat their wives, penalty 20 shillings. The Powowers, are the Indian phycians as well as priests ; any persons inclinable to the christian rel* ion, when sick, and weak minded, are used as we christians of diferent sects of religion use one another, that is, damn them if they do ot assent to the faith of the priest.

Indian to ſeveral of their tribes, and tranſlated 1664 ou
bible and ſeveral books of devotion into the ſaid India
language ; he relates ſeveral pertinent natural queri⟨
of the Indians relating to our religion.   Whether Jeſu
Christ, the mediator or interpreter, could underſtan
prayers in the Indian language ? How man could be th
image of God, ſince images were forbidden in the ſe
cond commandment ? If the father be nought, and th
child good, why ſhould God in the ſecond command
ment be offended with the chiid ? with many other in
tricate queſtions concerning our accounts of the creatio⟨
and the flood, particularly, how the Engliſh came t⟨
differ ſo much from the Indians in their knowledge o
God and Jesus Christ, ſince they had all at firſt bu
one father ? Mr. Elliot was ſo much approved of, tha
in relation to the Indians, in the acts of the general aſ
ſembly, the acts run thus, " By the advice of the ſai⟨
" magiſtrates and of Mr. Elliot ;" Mr. Elliot travelle⟨
into all parts of the Maſſachuſetts and Plymouth colo
nies, even ſo far as Cape-Cod.

Mr. Mayhew, a noted Engliſh evangeliſt, [*f*] or itine
rant miſſionary among the Indians, more eſpecially wit⟨
the Indians of Martha's-Vineyard, Nantucket, and Eli⟨
zabeth iſlands ; he learnt the Indian language, that h⟨
might be in a capacity of inſtructing the natives in th⟨
chriſtian faith ; his father had a kind of patent fron
home, as proprietor and governor of theſe iſlands.

All our miſſionaries who have endeavoured the con
verſion of the Indians, have been guilty of a grand fun
damental miſtake, which if not amended, will for eve
render their real converſion impracticable. The clerg
miſſionaries began by inculcating the moſt [*g*] abſtruſ

[*f*] In his voyage to England 1657, the veſſel foundered at ſe⟨
and he was loſt.
[*g*] As it is generally agreed amongſt chriſtians, that revelation
and myſteries or miracles are ceaſed ; religion is become a rational a
fair, and ought to be taught in plain intelligible words. The ba⟨

and myſterious articles of the chriſtian religion. Mr. Mayhew in his journal, writes, " That the Indians declared

of all religions and myſteries, is, the belief of the exiſtence of a ſupreme incomprehenſible BEING, director of the univerſe; this we can
inveſtigate no other ways but by reaſon : the TRINITY ought to be
introduced by ſome rational obvious analogies, ſuch as : We offer our
praiſes and prayers to the ſupreme being, called GOD THE FATHER ;
invited and encouraged thereto, from the conſideration of the divine
clemency and benevolence, that is, by the mediation of GOD THE
SON ; with the aſſiſtance of the DIVINE SPIRIT, GOD THE HOLY
GHOST ; all three being the attributes of, or perſonated by one and
the ſame GOD, and which we expreſs by three perſons in the godhead : when the heathens come to underſtand theſe expreſſions, they
may be impreſſed upon them in our uſual myſtical terms ; but all abſtruſe fanatical formulas and creeds, ſuch as is the Athanaſian creed,
ought never to be offered to them.

The catechiſms whereby we initiate our children and the Indian
heathen into the chriſtian religion perhaps require caſtigation. That
of the church of England in its firſt queſtions ſeems very low and ſilly,
adapted to a nurſe and her child, and may give the Indians a mean
opinion of our religion doctors.

Queſtion. What is your name ?
Anſwer. A. B.
Queſtion. Who gave you this name ?
Anſwer. My godfathers and godmothers.

That of the Weſtminſter aſſembly of divines immediately enters
into the moſt abſtruſe articles of our religion.

How many perſons are there in the godhead ?
What are the decrees of God ?
Who is the redeemer of God's elect ?
What is effectual calling ?

Good works ought inceſſantly to be preached to the Indians. Free
will and predeſtination ought not raſhly to be touched upon, according to our notions of the preſcience and omniſcience of GOD. and of
the free agency of mankind which renders them accountable for their
actions ; they are ſo much in contraſt, that to reconcile them is one of
the greateſt myſteries of the chriſtian or any other religion.

Their inſtruction ought to be brief, and not verboſe ; not to meddle
with the manifold ſmall differences and controverſies among our ſec-
aries, becauſe, as the conceptions, humours, and intereſt of ſeveral
people are various, a general comprehenſion is impracticable in na-
ure. Only teach them that all religions are good which are con-
iſtent with ſociety ; that is, all religions are good, that teach men
o be good. Our attachment to peculiar ways of worſhip, is not

" the

" the difficulties of the chriftian religion were fuch as the
" Indians could not endure ; their fathers had made
" fome trial of it, but found it too hard for them,
" and therefore quitted it." The fundamental catholick articles of our religion are fhort, fimple, and eafily underftood by the meaneft capacity. 1. To adore
one fupreme being, in his agency of creating and
governing the univerfe. 2. To honour our natural
parents, and all perfons in political authority (parents
of the country) over us. 3. To love our neighbours
as ourfelves. 4. To be merciful, even to brute beafts.
Whatever is inconfiftent with any of thefe, is irreli-
gion. " What doth the Lord require of thee, but
" to do juftly, and to love mercy, and to walk

from any light within us ; but is inculcated in our tender flexible
years, by our parents, nurfes, preceptors, priefts, and laws of our
country. Orthodoxy in religion is ambulatory ; upon a revolution,
the party that prevails is the orthodox.

All bigots or uncharitable idle fectaries are difturbers of fociety,
(fuch are the Roman catholicks, the high-fliers of the church of England, the covenanters or Cameronians of the kirk of Scotland, &c.)
and their ringleaders fall under the infpection of civil authority, and
may without any imputation of perfecution upon account of religion,
by way of a falutary civil remedy, be fent to a mad-houfe or work-
houfe, to bring them to a right mind.

Some proper degree of learning or literature, adminiftred to the
Indians, is requifite, not only to civilize them, bring them to our language and manners, but to render them lefs fubject to credulity and
francticknefs in their devotions. The Roman catholick tenet of ignorance being the mother of devotion, is meant only of a fuperftitious
devotion, not of a proper decent mode of worfhip.——I do not join
avowedly with the free-thinkers, who from the maxim of Fruftra fit
per plura fay, that the intricate method of our redemption from
damnation and hellifh everlafting penances, by the omnipotent God
might in a peremptory manner have been done by a fiat.

Myfteries, are properly deviations from the ordinary laws of nature or providence : myfteries in moft fchemes of religion are unneceffary, and too much multiplied : the ftanding maxim ought to be
Nec Deus interfit, nifi dignus vindice nodus. Human laws and fanc-
tions cannot extend to numberlefs human vices and wickedneffes
therefore divine rewards and punifhments of a God who knows
fecret ought to be inculcated.

" humbl

" humbly with God." The few credenda, or articles of
faith in any fcheme of practical religion; the lefs intricate,
more comprehenfive, and confequently not fubject to
fplit into fectaries: all enthufiaftical or juggling fchemes
of devotion are a nufance; the Wh—ld (an infignificant
perfon, but a happy dramatick actor of enthufiafm) new-
lights, pretend to know one another at firft fight as
much as if they were of the order of free-mafons.

In former times, before hired miffionaries from incorporate focieties took place, the voluntier provincial
miffionaries, viz. Mr. Elliot, Mr. Mayhew, &c. of New-
England, who believed what they taught, were of exemplary good life, and fpared no fatigue, and were of great
fervice in civilizing our intermixed Indians, though their
faith was not ftrong enough to carry them out among
the tribes of our adjacent wildernefs Indians. We have
fcarce any account to give of the late miffionaries from
the three feveral focieties now fubfifting for propagating
of chriftian knowledge amongft the wild Indians, or
men of the woods, as the French call them. The Albany
church of England miffionary fometimes vifits the adjacent tribe of Mohawk Indians of the Iroquois nation.
The congregationalift miffionaries from the New-England fociety in London upon the New-England frontiers
at Gorges, Richmond and Fort-Dummer, act only as
chaplains to thefe fmall garrifons of ten or a dozen men
each. Mr. [b] Brainerd, a late miffionary upon the fron-

[b] The rev. Mr. Brainerd, a miffionary from the Scot's fociety
to the Indians upon the rivers of Delaware and Sefquahanna, was a
true and zealous miffionary, giving allowances for his weak enthufiaftick turn of mind. In his printed book, Philadelphia 1745, concerning the Indian converfions, " at a diftance with my bible in my
" hand, I was refolved if poffible, to fpoil their fpirit of Powowing,
" and prevent their receiving an anfwer from the infernal world." In
the year 1744, he rode about 4000 miles to and fro among the Indians, fometimes five or fix weeks together, without feeing a white
man; he had three houfes of refidence at diftances in the Indian countries. Is there any miffionary from any of the focieties for propagating
the gofpel in foreign parts, that has reported the like?

I 3   tiers

tiers' of the Jerfics and Penfylvania upon the exhibition of the Scot's fociety for propagating chriftian know-ledge, feems to have been the only minifter who faith-fully performed the fervice of an Indian miffionary.

In all royal charters, and proprietary grants of colonies in Britifh North-America, one of the principal defigns is faid, to be the converfion of the Indians by good inftruc-tion and an exemplary good life : the miffionaries from the fociety do not in the leaft attempt the converfion of the Indians, becaufe it requires travel, labour, and hard-fhips ; and the Britifh people in general, inftead of chrif-tian virtues, teach them European vices: for inftance, by introducing the ufe of intoxicating liquors, for private profit, they difpenfe more ftrong liquor than gofpel to the Indians ; and thus have deftroyed, and continue to deftroy perhaps more Indians, than formerly the Spa-niards did, by their inhuman and execrable cruelties, under the name of converfions ; the Spaniards deftroyed only their bodies, we deftroy body and mind. Mr. Mayhew in his journals writes, that the Indians told him, that, " they could not obferve the benefit of chrif-" tianity, becaufe the Englifh chriftians cheated them of " their lands, &c. and the ufe of books made them " more cunning in cheating." In his Indian itineraries, he " defired of Ninicroft, fachem of the Narraganfet " Indians, leave to preach to his people ; Ninicroft bid

Enthufiam in the Roman Catholick miffionaries is encouraged by their church and ftates; it prompts them (fome as merit, fome as penance) to endure all manner of hardfhips towards promoting, not only their religion, but alfo their trade and national intereft with the Indians. Religious fuperftitions, by falling in with the weak and en-thufiaftick natural propenfities of mankind, are very powerful; but in time ought to be rectified, as reafon gets the better of thefe human infirmities. As ftrong reafoning is not accommodated to the bulk of mankind, credulity or revelation is a more eafy poffeffion of the mind; without revelation a man is quite at a lofs, from whence he came, for what purpofe he exifts, and where he is to go when he ceafes to live : there is a ftrong propenfity in human nature to reli-gion ; fome abandoned politicians make a wrong ufe of this, to pro-mote their wicked defigns, ambitions, and interefts.

" him

" him go and make the Englifh good firft, and chid
" Mr. Mayhew [*i*] for hindering him from his bufinefs
" and labour;" in another place Mr. Mayhew writes,
" the Mohog Indians told him, that they did believe in
" God, and worfhip him, but as feveral nations had their
" diftinct ways of worfhip, they had theirs, which they
" thought a good way." The Indians were entirely
wanting in any fet form of religious devotional worfhip.

Seeing the religion miffionaries neglect the converfion
of the Indians, and take no further care than with relation to their falaries or livings, and of being ftationed
in the moft opulent towns, which have no more communication with the favage Indians, than the city [*k*] of
London has ; the refpective governments upon the
continent of America ought to contrive fome method of
civilizing the Indians, which will be attended with
many confiderable advantages. 1. Our own trahquillity.
2. Our Indian fkin and fur trade.   3. By rendering
them ferviceable to us in our agriculture and navigation ;
thus a too great importation of foreigners may be
avoided. In Penfylvania has been a vaft importation
of Palatines, Saltfburghers, and other foreigners. By
a late letter from a gentleman of Philadelphia, a man
of veracity, penetration, and authority in the province of Penfylvania, I am informed ; (this I publifh
with relation to thofe gentlemen, who feem inadver-

[*i*] This faying of Ninicroft's was very applicable to Mr. Wh—ld,
a late vagrant dramatick enthufiaft in North-America : H—ly of the
oratory, fo called in London ; an ecclefiaftical mountebank ; and fuch
like impoftors, ought to be animadverted upon ; they are a fcandal
and reproach to the chriftian religion.

[*k*] As to the converfion of Indians, they make it a fine-cure, or only
a name or free gift, and may be enjoyed any where to the fame advantage. As an hiftorian upon the place of obfervation, I could not
avoid (without fufpicion of partiality) reprefenting thefe mifapplications in a true and proper light, being a publick affair ; I do not
meddle with the perfonal character of any miffionary ; if the bifhop's
commiffary has any authority, it is his office and care ; I avoid being
officious.

tently

tently to infiſt upon the introducing of floods of foreigners among us :)

" That the Germans in all probability, allowing for
" progreſs of time, will be poſſeſſed of the chiefeſt and
" moſt valuable of our lands ; by their induſtry and
" penurious way of living, get rich where others ſtarve.
" The Iriſh were ſettled this ſide of Seſquahanna river
" many years before the Dutch (meaning the high Dutch
" or Germans) came among us, and wherever they had
" a good plantation, the Dutch bought it from them.
" At preſent the Iriſh families are but here and there on
" this ſide of the ſaid river ; they move to the weſtward
" of the river ; the Dutch follow them, and by offering
" high prices for their lands, the Iriſh quit, and go far-
" ther ; the Dutch by their ſuperior induſtry and fruga-
" lity may out the Britiſh people from the province."
This province by importation of foreigners does at preſent, in fencible Men, very near equal all the Engliſh or
Britiſh militia, in the Engliſh or Britiſh continent of
America ; in caſe of a French or Dutch war, theſe Dutch
or German foreigners by herding or ſettling together,
retaining and propagating the language and differences
in religious worſhip ; upon a diſcontent or diſaffection
(better we never had one foreign family ſettled among us)
may become not only a uſeleſs, but a pernicious body.

The miſſionaries from the ſociety in London for propagating the goſpel, &c. call all diſſenters, the ſeparation : Mr. Hobart, [*l*] a late noted congregational writer,
ſays, this ſociety and their miſſionaries are epiſcopal ſe-
paratiſts ; both ſides are notoriouſly in the error. William
George, D. D. dean of Lincoln, in his late ſermon before the ſociety for propagating the goſpel, &c. ſays,
" Circumſtances in worſhip, in their nature variable,
" are left to be determined by the diſcretion of thoſe,

[*l*] Mr. Hobart (perhaps from party-prejudice) a gentleman of
learning and application, has fallen into a very groſs miſtake, viz.
That the church of England is a ſeparation of New-England. Before
the union of the two kingdoms of Great-Britain 1707, the eccleſiaſ-
" whoſe

' whofe bufinefs it is to fee that all things be done
 ' decently and in order."

There are in Great-Britain three incorporated pious
focieties [*m*] for propagating chriftian knowledge. I fhall
here give fome account of them, with relation to the
Britifh North-America fettlements.

I. Anno 1659, the parliament of England encouraged
the propagation of the gofpel among the Indians in New-
England and parts adjacent ; and enacted a corporation,
confifting of a prefident, treafurer and fourteen affiftants,
called, The prefident and fociety for propagating the gofpel in New-England and parts adjacent ; that the commiffioners for the united colonies of New-England for
the time being, fhall have power to difpofe of the faid
monies of the corporation. By a collection in virtue of
an act of parliament, in all the parifhes of England, was
collected a confiderable fum, which purchafed a confide-
able land eftate. Upon the reftoration, their charter
was deemed void, and col. Beddingfield, a Roman catho-
ick military officer, who had fold lands to this fociety,

cal conftitution of the Englifh American plantations, was (Roman
catholicks excepted) a general toleration of all chriftian profeffions
without any preference. In the treaty for this union, it was naturally
agreed by the commiffioners, and afterwards confirmed in perpetuity, .
by acts of both parliaments ; viz. that the church of England was to be
deemed the eftablifhed church, with the eftablifhed toleration, in all
the formerly Englifh colonies, by this expreffion, " and territories
thereto (to England) belonging." I cannot account for the reverend
Mr. Hobart's lapfe into that fophiftical fchool-boy evafion, that the
territories thereto belonging, is meant of the Jerfey iflands only. but
not of the plantations ; the act of uniformity, 1558, 1. Eliz. is out
of the queftion, becaufe at that time we had no plantations, therefore
fhall not adduce it. In the ftrict act of uniformity 14 Carol. II ;
here is no addition of territories thereto belonging, (the Jerfey iflands
at that time belonged to England) all the charter and proprietary
grants had a claufe of a general liberty of confcience (Roman catholicks excepted) in their colonies, to encourage fettlers of all fectaries ;
becaufe an exclufive uniformity occafions much diftraction and confufion among the good chriftians of feveral denominations, and might
have been an obftruction to the fettlements.

[*m*] See vol. I. p. 231.   was

was adviſed to ſeize them as being an illegal purchaſe and under value. The members of the ſociety ſollicited K. Charles II. for a new charter, which they obtained dated Fabruary 7, 14 Carol. II; ordaining that for eve hereafter within the kingdom of England, there ſhall b a ſociety or company, for propagation of the goſpel in New-England and the parts adjacent in America. Th firſt nominated members were of the higheſt rank and ſtations at court; their ſucceſſors to be choſen by the ſo ciety, but never to exceed the number of forty five. In chancery they recovered Mr. Beddingfield's land. Ro bert Boyle, Eſq. was appointed the firſt governor; upon his deceaſe, Robert Thompſon was elected; and upon his death Sir William Aſhurſt of London, alderman The preſent governor is Sir Samuel Clark, baronet, wh ſucceeds his father Sir Robert Clark, baronet. Th whole revenue of the corporation is 500 l. to 600. l. ſterl per ann. at preſent they exhibit ſmall but well placed ſa laries to ſeveral miſſionaries Engliſh and Indians; an appoint commiſſioners in New-England to manage thi charity. There was a benefaction of the good an honourable Robert Boyle, Eſq. of 90 l. ſterl. per ann to this corporation; another of Dr. Daniel Williams, diſſenting miniſter of London; he left to the corporatio the reverſion of a real eſtate upwards of 100 l. ſterl. pe ann. which fell to them 1746; the clauſe of his wi concerning it is:

" I give to Mr. Joſeph Thompſon and the reſt of th
" ſociety for New-England, my eſtate in Eſſex, called
" Tolſhent, Becknam Mannor, or by any other nam
" which I bought of Mrs. Hannah Fox, alias Bradle
" with all the profits and advantages, belonging to n
" after the death of the ſaid Fox, now Brandley, as lo
" as the ſaid ſociety or corporation ſhall continue; up
" condition, that 60 l. per ann. ſhall be allowed betwe
" two well qualified perſons, as to piety and prudence,
" be nominated ſucceſſively by my truſtees, to preach
" itinera

" itinerants in the Englifh plantations in the Weft-Indies,
" and for the good of what pagans and blacks lie neglec-
" ted there.   And the remainder to be paid yearly to the
" college of Cambridge in New-England, or fuch as are
" ufually employed to manage the blefled work of con-
" verting the poor Indians there ; to promote which, I
" defign this part of my gift.   But if my truftees be
" hindered from nominating the faid itinerants, under
" pretence of any ftatute in New-England, or elfewhere,
" I give the faid 60 l. per ann. to the faid college in
" New-England, to encourage and make them capable
" to get conftantly fome learned profeffor out of Europe
" to refide there, and fhall be of their own nomination,
" in concurrence with the minifter of the town of Bofton,
" in the faid New-England.

" And if the aforefaid fociety or corporation fhall
" happen to be diffolved, or be deprived of their prefent
" privilege ; my will is, and I hereby give the faid man-
" nor, with all the profits and advantages, to the faid
" town of Bofton, with the minifters thereof, to benefit
" the faid college, as above, and to promote the conver-
" fion of the poor Indians."

II. The ftate of the fociety in Scotland for propagating
chriftian knowledge.   This fociety began 1700 ; by
queen Anne's letter patent 1709 they were incorporated :
by donations at prefent, 1750, they are enabled to maintain 136 fchools, in which are educated above 7000
children of both fexes ; and from its firft erection to this
time, it has been the means of inftructing about 50,000
children of both fexes.   This fociety by a new patent,
1738, are allowed to inftruct their chidren in hufbandry
and handicrafts.—By their firft patent they were allowed
to extend their care to places abroad, particularly to the
Indians on the borders of New-York, New-Jerfeys, and
Penfylvania ; the New-England fociety were fuppofed
to have the miffionary charge of New-England.   They
have contributed to a college lately erected in the New-
Jerfeys.   III. June

III. June 16, 1701, King William incorporated ſociety with perpetual ſucceſſion, by the name of th ſociety for propagating the goſpel in foreign parts, to b accountable annually to the lord high chancellor, lor chief juſtice of the king's bench, and lord chief juſtice o the common pleas. Every year ſome new members ar admitted, to aſſiſt the ſociety with their good counſel and ſubſcriptions ; the preſent members are about 230

The miſſions with the reſpective ſalaries at this time, ar

NEWFOUNDLAND.		1. School-master	1(?)
Trinity-Bay	50	Fairfield	5(
St. John's	50	New-London	6(
School-master	10	Groton school	(
		Newton	5(
MASSACHUSETTS-BAY.		Simſbury	3(
Boſton	70	Norwalk	2(
Newbury	60	Darby	2(
Marblehead	60	New-England Itinerant	7(
Salem	40		
Braintree	60	**NEW-YORK.**	
Scituate	40	New-Cheſter	5(
Hopkinton	60	School-master	1(
		New-York school-master	15
NEW-HAMPSHIRE.		Jamaica	5(
Portſmouth and Kittery	75	Hampſtead	5(
		Catechiſt	1(
RHODE-ISLAND.		School-master	1(
Newport and Catechiſt	80	New-Rochelle	5(
Narraganſet & Warwick	100	Rye	5(
Providence	60	School-master	1(
School-master	10	Oyſter-Bay schoolmaster	1(
Briſtol	60	Brook-haven	5(
		Staten-Iſland	5(
CONNECTICUT.		School-master	1(
Stratford	70	New-Windſor	3(
Catechiſt	10	Albany and Mohawk	5(

NEW

New-Jersey.	l.	North-Carolina.	
Elizabeth town	50	Itinerant north diſtrict	50
Catechiſt	10	ſouth diſtrict	50
Amboy	60		
Burlington	60	South-Carolina.	
Monmouth county	60	St. Thomas	30
Salem	60	St. Andrew's	50
Shrewſbury ſchool	10	St. George's	30
Newark	50	St. Paul's	30
		St. Helen's	30
Pensylvania.		St. John's	30
New-caſtle	70	St. James	30
Lewis	60	St. Bartholomew	30
Apaquiminick	60	Prince Frederick	30
Cheſter	60	Chriſt's church	30
Schoolmaſter	10		
Oxford	60	Georgia.	
Periquihame	60	Savannah	50
Kent county	60		
Itinerant of Penſylvania and		Bahamas.	
Jerſey	50	Providence.	60

Salaries to miſſionaries, catechiſts, ſchool-maſters, and officers of the ſociety, are an annual expence of about 3540 l. ſterl. Part of the fund for this, is yearly, by benefactions, legacies, and entrances (at five guineas each) of new members   1600 l.

Yearly payments of ſubſcribers   600

Rents of lands, and dividends in the ſtocks   317

Ten pounds ſterling in books are allowed to each miſſionary as a library ; and five pounds in devotional books and tracts to be diſtributed, ſuch as bibles, common-prayers, whole duty of man, &c.

This ſociety have the direction of two other ſeparate charitable funds. 1. The negroe fund, which at preſent may amount to 3000 l. ſterl. principal in old S. S. annuities ; their yearly donations are very inconſiderable.
                                There

There are two miſſionaries as catechiſts of negroes, one at New-York 50 l. ſterl. per ann. another at Philadelphia at 50 l. ſterl. per ann.   2. The Barbadoes eſtate, which is appropriated to particular uſes mentioned in general Codrington's will ; ſuch as, a catechiſt to the negroes in the ſociety's plantations in Barbadoes, 70 l. ſterl.   Sundries for a college in Barbadoes, called Codrington's college, a ſchool-maſter, an uſher, a profeſſor of philoſophy and mathematicks, &c.

Towards the new ſettlement of Nova-Scotia, the ſociety reſolve to ſend over ſix miſſionaries and ſix ſchoolmaſters, to prevent the new ſettlers being perverted to popery, by the preſent French popiſh ſettlers.   Our new ſettlers have not the leaſt communication with the French ſettlers ; and perhaps in the town of Halifax and Garriſon, there are no profeſſed papiſts to be found ; a parochial miniſter, with the chaplains belonging to the troops, and the congregational miniſter from New-England for the uſe of the New-England emigrants, may be ſufficient.

The ſociety for propagating the goſpel in foreign parts is a very good, pious, and moſt laudable deſign ; but the execution thereof in Britiſh North-America is much faulted [*n*].

[*n*] It is a profane ſaying of ſome ; "he who meddles with the clergy, puts his hand into a neſt of waſps or hornets :" but as this ſociety in their yearly abſtracts, requeſt that people in America, who upon the ſpot have opportunities of obſerving what relates to the execution of this pious chriſtian exhibition, may repreſent : as it falls in the courſe of this American hiſtory, without being reckoned officious or preſuming, I may be allowed to make theſe remarks.---In ſhort, the civilizing and chriſtianizing of the heathens, which with us are the aboriginal American Indians, and the imported negroe ſlaves, ſeems naturally to be the principal care of miſſionaries ; the quakers obſerve, that good ſalaries called livings, in a ſort of *ſine-cure*, is the principal concern of the miſſionaries ; itinerancies and converſions of the heathen is too laborious, and does not anſwer their intention.

Dr. Liſle, biſhop of St. Aſaph, in his ſermon February 19, 1747-8, before the ſociety, ſpeaking of Romiſh Portugal miſſionaries in Aſia,

1. Any indifferent man could not avoid imagining that by propagating the gospel in foreign parts, was meant, the conversion of natives of such parts as the royal charters and proprietary grants of our plantations, enjoin the civilizing and conversion of the Indians by doctrine and example. It is astonishing to hear some of these missionaries and their friends, indiscreetly affirm, that this was no part of the design, because not expressed in strong terms in their charter. King William, the granter of the charter, cannot be imagined to have meant, that the expulsion or elbowing out sober orthodox dissenters was the principal intention thereof, though at present, their chief practice ; there is not one missionary (the Albany and Mohawk missionary excepted) that takes the least notice of the Indians ; the society, sensible of this neglect, in their latest mission, that of Mr. Price for Hopkinton about 30 miles inland from Boston, is particularly instructed, to endeavour the propagation of the christian religion among the neighbouring Indians.

The practice of the present missionaries, is to obtain a mission to our most civilized and richest towns where are no Indians, no want of an orthodox christian ministry, and no Roman catholicks, the three principal intentions

from a society called *de propaganda fide*, says, "They settle themselves in nations which are christians already, and under pretence "of converting the infidels, which are among them, their chief "business seems to be, the perverting of christians themselves from "their ancient faith, and to draw them over." N. B. No presbyterian or congregationalist could have wrote in stronger terms, with regard to our present missionaries.—As to the conversion of the Indians not being their care, we find it not so understood in the excellent sermons preached before the society from time to time ; in many of their anniversary sermons, the preacher says, that the direct aim of the society, is the propagation of christianity abroad, among the barbarous nations of America.—In such parts of the world, as have not yet been enlightened by the gospel, or are in danger of having this light extinguished.

In the charter from the parliament of England 1659, the first president of the corporation was judge Steel, and the first treasurer was Mr. Henry Ashurst, which should have been mentioned before.

of their miffion. They feem abfurdly to value themfelves
upon the diverfion (I do not fay perverfion) of the prefbyterians and congregationalifts. All men have a laudable
veneration for the religion of their anceftors, and the
prejudices of education are hardly to be overcome;
why then fhould a perfon who peaceably follows the
orthodox allowed or tolerated way of his forefathers,
be over-perfuaded to relinquifh it, confidering that by an
interceding wavering, the man may be overfet and fink
into infidelity ? They feem to value themfelves more
upon this, than upon the converfion of a heathen to our
civil national intereft, and to chriftianity, or the reformation of a Roman catholick, as is much wanted in
Maryland ; or preferving the Britifh extract from running into infidelity, as in North-Carolina.

2. In their charter it is faid, that in feveral of the
colonies and factories beyond the feas, the provifion is
very mean in fome, and in many others none at all for
the maintenance of orthodox minifters; therefore the fociety is eftablifhed for the management of fuch charities
as fhall be received for this ufe. So it is, their miffionaries are not ftationed in fuch poor out towns, but in
the moft opulent, beft civilized and chriftian towns of the
provinces; that is, in all the metropolis towns of the
colonies, and other rich and flourifhing towns, well
able to fupport, and in fact do fupport orthodox minifters.

In all our colonies (Rhode-Ifland excepted) there is a
parochial provifion for an orthodox gofpel miniftry:
Dr. Bray, a very zealous promoter of this fociety, writes,
that in the colonies of Maffachufetts and Connecticut,
there was no need at all of miffionaries.

In the latter years of queen Anne's adminiftration,
perhaps, the defign of this charity was perverted from
the original defign of converting the heathens, preferving
of religion among our out plantations, not able to maintain a gofpel miniftry, and preventing a popifh influence:

it

it was converted to a defign of withdrawing the tolerated fober religious diffenters to a conformity with the (then) high church [*o*] ; a manuduction to popery, and the introduction of a popifh pretender to the crown : but as by the happy fucceffion of the prefent proteftant family, all hopes of this kind are vanifhed ; it is in vain and will anfwer no end, for any party of men to foment divifions among good chriftians. I have a very great regard for all good minifters of the chriftian gofpel, and have no private or particular refentment againft any miffionary ; but as an impartial hiftorian, I could not avoid relating matters of fact for the information of perfons concerned, who by reafon of diftance and other bufinefs, cannot be otherways informed.

In the charter, the propagation of the church of England is not mentioned ; the expreffions are general [*p*]. " An orthodox clergy,—Propagation of the chriftian " religion or gofpel in foreign parts." Therefore the miffionaries ought to be men of moderation, that is, of general charity and benevolence, confidering alfo that many diffenters have contributed to this charity, and are worthy members of the fociety. Fiery zealots [*q*] are a detriment to the defign of the fociety.

[*o*] Whigs and tories or high-church originally were only diverfities of fentiments concerning the hierarchy or government of the church : afterwards by defigning men, they were ufed to influence political affairs : the popifh and Jacobitely inclined ranged themfelves with the tories or high-church ; the true proteftant fober moderate revolutioners, jealous of a French influence, were called whigs.

[*p*] Becaufe at that time all orthodox proteftant ways of worfhip, were equally tolerated. In their abftract publifhed Feb. 1749-50, p. 43. concerning Connecticut, (it is the fame in all the charter and proprietary grants of colonies) it is faid. " That by charter there is a general toleration of chriftians of all denominations, except papifts, without an eftablifhment of any one fort."

[*q*] Zealots of all denominations, as it is obferved, if among the common people, are of the meaneft knowledge, that is, they are the weakeft of men, and the weaker fex or women in general ; if among politicians, they are of the deepeft wicked defigns. I cannot avoid inftancing the adminiftration in the laft years of queen Anne's reign,

By grofs impofitions upon the worthy and laudabl society, their charity and chriftian benevolence is egre gioufly perverted. I fhall mention a few inftances. In the large and not well civilized province of North Carolina, that country being poor and unhealthful, mif fionaries were not fond of being fent thither, though for many years they had no gofpel minifter of any deno mination amongft them, and did degenerate apace to wards heathenifm [*r*]; when at the fame time the wel civilized and chriftianized colonies of New-England wen crouded with miffionaries. Lately two miffionaries (no

they paffed an act for building fifty additional churches in London In all countries where liberty of confcience is amicably tolerated (tha is without an idle curfing and damning, from their pulpits, all tole rated diffenters,) the eftablifhed church will filently and graduall fwallow up all fectaries; the young people or rifing generation wil chufe to be in the fafhionable or eftablifhed way; their elders, am bitious of pofts and honours, will conform; this, is a natural converfio to the church eftablifhed. Many miffionaries, fettled among fober or thodox diffenters, by their immoderate indifcreet zeal for their own way, inftead of fmoothing by brotherly love, by a diabolical rancou eftrange them from the eftablifhed church: I gave one inftance of thi vol. I. p. 2:8. concerning a miffionary advancing the invalidity o all baptifms adminiftred by perfons not epifcopally ordained I fha here bring another inftance, from a miffionary fome years fince, wh occafionally preaching in the king's chapel of Bofton, faid, that he woul rather chufe to err with the church as it was 200 years ago (times o high popery) than &c. In a fubfequent fermon by the ingenious an worthy Mr. Harris, king's chaplain, he was chaftifed.

[*r*] Not many years fince, fome loofe clergymen of the neighbourin province of Virginia, at times, in a frolick, made a tour in North-C rolina, and chriftened people of all ages at ——— per head, and made profitable trip of it, as they expreffed it.

Mr. Hall, lately appointed miffionary for the north diftrict, write that anno 1749, he baptized 1282 perfons. Mr. Moir of the fou diftrict, cannot give an exact account of all the perfons he hath ba tized in his journies, for want of a perfon to count them (fee abftr for 1749, p, 48.) who have, he thinks, fometimes amounted to mo than 100 perfons in one day. Thefe two miffionaries were with fo difficulty obtained by the folicitation of the prefent governor of Nor Carolina; he wrote, " That they had no minifters or teachers of a " denomination, and without fome due care be taken, the very fo " fteps of religion will in a fhort time be wore out there."

mor

more) have been fent to North-Carolina; one to itine-
rate on the fouth fide of Neufe river, the other on the
north fide of that river. 2. One claufe in their charter is,
" for the inftruction of thofe who are in danger of being
" perverted by Roman priefts and jefuits to their fu-
" perftition;" this is in no refpect the cafe in the colonies of New-England, the moft crouded with thefe
miffionaries.   Maryland is our only continent colony,
affected with popery, and where the parochial minifters
feem not to attend their converfion or reformation; thus
the papifts and difloyal are indulged or overlooked, and
one would imagine that the principal defign has been
to pervert the proteftant loyal diffenters, confidering
that the miffionaries with the largeft falaries generally
ftationed in the very loyal, the beft civilized and moft
opulent towns of the colonies, are well able and
in fact do fufficiently fupport a proteftant orthodox gofpel miniftry.   I fhall only inftance the town of Bofton,
the place of my refidence, the metropolis of all the Britifh American colonies; in Bofton are many congregations of fober good orthodox chriftians of feveral denominations, particularly two congregations of the church
of England; their rectors very good men and well endowed by their refpective congregations, befides a king's
chaplain, fo called, with a falary of 100 *l.* fterl. per ann.
from Great Britain : a fuperb coftly church equal to
many [*s*] cathedrals, is now building by the church

[*s*] Extract from the Bofton Independent Advertifer, N°. 85.
Laft Friday being the 11th day of Auguft 1749, the N. E. corner
ftone of the king's chapel in this town, now re-building, was con-
fecrated and laid with great ecclefiaftical pomp and folemnity, and at
about eleven the proceffion began from the province houfe. —— Firft,
his ex—l—cy our go——or, with the rev. Mr. C—r at his right
hand, and the rev. Mr Br—k—ell at his left hand preceeded, then
the church wardens, and veftry, followed by about twenty-five
couple of the principal friends of the church; when the proceffion
came to the church-yard, his ex—l—cy, fupported by two chaplains,
defcended the trench where the ftone which was dedicated to G O D
was laying at the north-eaft corner. —— On this ftone the go——or
knocked three or four times with a mafon's trowel, (juft the number

K 2   of

of England men: yet, notwithftanding, this mo[t]
excellent and laudable charity is mifapplied [*t*] b
ftationing in Bofton a fuperfluous miffionary at th
charge of feventy pounds fterling, per annum, be
fides the allowance from his congregation. Th
bifhop of St. David's in his fermon before the focie[t]

of raps archbifhop Laud gave to the door of St. Catherine's cree
church at his memorable confecration of it) fome devout expreffion
were then dropt by the chaplain. The go——or then afcended th
ladder with the two clergymen; and this part of the ceremony bein[g]
ended, his ex—l—cy and the reft of the company in the fame manne
they walked from the province-houfe, entered the king's chapel
where was a fermon, very properly adapted to fuch an occafion, deli
vered by the rev. Mr. C—r, from the fecond chapter of Nehemiah an[d]
the twentieth verfe, thofe words of the verfe, " The God of heaven
" he will profper us, therefore we his fervants, will arife and build"—
The words that follow the text are—" But you have no portion, no
" right, nor memorial in Jerufalem." A hymn of praife conclude[s]
the folemnity—The Latin infcription upon the corner ftone is as follow[s]

Quod felix fauftumq; fit
Ecclefiæ et reipublicæ
Hunc lapidem DEO facrum,
Regiæ capellæ
Apud Boftonium Maffachufettenfium
Reftauratæ atque auctæ fundamentum
Pofuit, Gulielmus Shirley,
Provinciæ præfectus,
Augufti 11mo, anno falutis 1749.

Some Zoilus, in contraft, has produced a couplet from our Englif[h]
poet Mr. Pope:-

Who builds a church to God, and not to fame,
Will never mark the marble with his name.

[*t*] Well may the fociety complain of their funds being infufficient
I do not fay, that fuch mifapplications may in part be the occafion, th[at]
laft year, the benefactions and legacies amounted to no more tha[n]
731 *l*, fterl. whereas formerly they amounted from 2000 to 3000 *l*
fterl. per ann, even in years when they had no royal briefs: if th[e]
number of miffionaries are leffened, fee abftract 1749, and properl[y]
ftationed, there will be no reafon for complaint; I heartily wifh thi
good fociety may go on and profper, and not be impofed upon b[y]
their miffionaries; it is not at prefent rich enough to beftow fin[e]
cures.

4   ii

in Feb. 1749-50, in a few words expresses the original
defign of the fociety, " An opportunity is prefented
" both among the plain and fimple Indians, and among
" the unhappy negro flaves—an utter extinction (mean-
" ing in North-Carolina) of chriftianity was no abfurd
" or groundlefs apprehenfion [*u*]."

[*u*] Confidering the flow advances which the proteftant religion, and
a fpirit of induftry had made among the common people of Ireland,
and parochial minifters or clergy not anfwering ; by charter Feb. 6,
1731, a fociety was incorporated for erecting proteftant working fchools
in feveral parts of Ireland, the popifh children to be kept apart from
their popifh parents, and fubfifted in victuals and cloathing : not to be
admitted under 6 æt. or above 10 æt. From 1731 to 1748 have been
admitted 88ς children, whereof 5c9 have been apprenticed. In purfuance of this charity, 1749, the fchools already opened were thirty,
in building eleven ; more projected three. The annual expence of
maintaining near 900 children their prefent complement, including falaries to mafters, miftreffes, and other incident charges, is only 4,435*l.*
fterl. which effectually refcues fo many of the rifing generation from beg-
gary, and popery, our civil as well as religious locuft or caterpillar, confequently is an acceffion to the proteftant intereft, and of wealth to the
nation by their being fkilled, and habituated to labour. The annual
benefactions towards the reading and working fchools of the two incorporated focieties of Scotland and Ireland grow very faft ; the prefent members of the Irifh fociety are about 900. The laft abftract (for
1749) of the fociety for propagating the gofpel in foreign parts, hints,
that they muft be obliged to withdraw fome of their miffionaries, if their
charity does not take a better turn : the reafon is natural, the good
effects of the charity for working fchools is confpicuous, that for
miffionaries is not fo ; this will more and more difpofe people of a
charitable fpirit, to vent their charities rather upon fchools than upon
miffions. This fort of a fociety *de propaganda fide,* has at prefent upwards of feventy miffions (including catechifts and fchool-mafters) in
North-America, and is of about fifty years growth ; if it produce any
fruit it will be of the tardy kind, and perhaps not profitable ; their
accounts fent to the fociety generally mention only the numbers by
them baptized and admitted to the lord's fupper ; which if adminiftered
by any orthodox minifter is equally valid in the opinion of the fober
and moderate of the church of England : They do not enumerate the
Indians by them converted, the Roman catholicks brought over to the
proteftant religion, methodifts or enthufiafts reduced to a fober mind,
and the like, as if thefe were not in the defign of their miffion. Their
chief cure or care feems to be a good eafy living, and the occafioning
of divifions and ftrife among tolerated diffenters (I ufe the expreffion
tolerated diffenters) becaufe by act of Union the church of England

Connecticut

Connecticut, a small colony, the most prudent and industrious of all our colonies, in which are no waste lands remaining, supplied with orthodox ministers well qualified and well paid, from misrepresentations of neighbouring missionaries, is crouded with the greatest numbers of missionaries in proportion to their extent; and in the society's last abstract is accused of a PERSE-CUTING SPIRIT, because three or four mean persons were prosecuted according to law, for not paying their township rates, in which might have been included their proportion towards the supporting of a gospel ministry as endowed by a legal town-meeting. So far is New-England at present from a persecuting spirit, that in the provinces of Massachusetts and Connecticut, upon a representation home of this nature, there were acts of assembly made, " That all such professed mem-" bers of the church of England, shall be entirely ex-" cused from paying any taxes towards the settlements " of any minister or building any meeting-house," that

is beyond dispute the established way; in the published opinion of this society, there is NO EXCLUSIVE PREFERENCE (as in mercantile affairs, there are exclusive and not exclusive charters) and the withdrawing of wild youth, from the orthodox tolerated way of their forefathers, to a more fashionable and less rigorous way, occasions divisions and disaffections in families. Upon the decease of a congregationalist incumbent, in a new choice some in their nature and humours do not concur, and in resentment, perhaps by the advice of a missionary, go over to the church of England.

I shall here by way of amusement, intimate, that if this society were to relinquish their present charter, and be favoured with a new charter, for propagating of christian knowledge, working schools, and other articles of industry; to each school there may be a missionary catechist, in church of England orders, of moderation, and qualified in their working as well as devotional business; one or two acres for the site of the school, lodgings, and other conveniencies; and some adjacent small farm hired at an easy and long lease, for the improvement of the boys in husbandry, and for the profit of the school: the children to be instructed in the principles of the christian reformed religion, reading, writing, arithmetick, husbandry, and manufactures or handicrafts. In Ireland, in some schools the master has the profit of the land or farm cultivated by the boys, in lieu of his salary, and forty shillings per ann. for the support of each child.

the

the taxes of perfons attending the church of England, be paid to their church of England minifter. By acts 1728 and 1729, Anabaptifts and Quakers are exempted from paying to the parifh or townfhip miniftry, I never heard of any perfecuting fpirit in Connecticut; in this they are egregioufly afperfed: it is true, that a few years fince they made fome acts againft fome frantick preachers and exhorters, called methodifts, intruding (without confent) into the pulpits of eftablifhed minifters. In Bofton of Maffachufetts, May 25, 1743, at an annual voluntary friendly convention of the congregational minifters of the province, they entered and afterwards printed their teftimony againft the methodifts. 1. For their errors in doctrine, antinomial and familiftical. 2. Following impulfes of a diftempered imagination, rather than the written word of our bible. 3. Allowing perfons of no learning or difcretion to pray and teach in publick. 4. Intruding into the pulpit of fettled minifters, endeavouring to withdraw the affections of people from their good and orderly minifters. 5. Ordaining minifters at large without any parochial charge. 6. Endeavouring to excite in their weak hearers, ungoverned paffions, extacies, and unfeemly behaviour, acting like Bacchantes. 7. By calling poor people (whofe time is their only eftate) unfeafonably from their bufinefs and labour, to a habit of idlenefs and vagrancy. I cannot fay, that the miffionaries were very ftrenuous againft thefe irregularities, with much impropriety called Methodism, becaufe they might find fome intereft in feparations amongft the diffenting orthodox people; *divide et impera*: I find in feveral accounts of fome miffionaries fent home from time to time to the fociety, (perhaps that they may have fome pretext of doing bufinefs) complaints of infidelity and methodifm prevailing in their diftricts; at the fame time here upon the fpot, we are not much fenfible of their reclaiming the one, or their oppofing the other by word or writing.

K 4   I muft

I must again observe, that there was not any pretex for sending missionaries into the province of Massachu setts-Bay of New-England: they had a well regulatec and well provided for orthodox clergy, as appears by the laws or acts of assembly anno 1692, the first year of the present new charter. The quarter sessions are to take care, that no town be destitute of a minister, that there be a suitable provision for the minister, and that any per son to be ordained, shall be recommended by three or more ordained ministers. The missionaries from the society de *propaganda fide* of Rome, are instructed to en deavour to convert the infidel and heretical parts of the world: our missionaries cannot with any propriety or face, esteem the orthodox tolerated clergy of New-England, as hereticks; because in the published opinion of the society, in our plantations all orthodox clergy are upon the same footing, that is, no preference as to the exercise or practical part of their devotions; see the society's abstract in February 1749-50. To jostle people from one mode of christianity to another may produce free-thinking and libertinism, where there are no essential differences in doctrine, but only in the varia ble vestments and modes of worship.

Some of the missionaries in their accounts sent home, value themselves upon the bringing over some people to the observance of the festivals of the church of England. These licenced idle frolicking days are a nusance, in settling new plantations, which require six labouring days (in the express injunction of our fourth commandment) in the week. The last account of the charter protestant working schools in Ireland, well observes, " That the progress of these schools, in its natural " course, must gradually abolish the great number of " popish holy days, by means of which some hundred " thousand working hands are kept idle, the labour and " profit of them lost to the publick—p. 41. This da " mage is an astonishing drawback from the wealth and " strength of the nation."

I shall

I fhall conclude this miffionary article with a few obfervations. It is a lamentable affair, that fcarce any of
our publick charity charters are fo contrived as to prevent mifapplications.

I. The fcheme propofed, vol. II. p. 134, was the
converting of the prefent idle miffions into county working fchools, with a church of England miffionary cate-
chift of moderation, qualified in the working as well as
devotional articles ; thus the charge of our prefent feventy miffionaries will maintain and [*x*] educate about
one thoufand working children : if the prefent miffions
are continued, the miffionaries may be under the infpection and direction of a committee of fuch members of
the fociety as refide in America, or under a miffionary
general, or under the fuperintendency of the fuffragan
bifhop, when fuch is appointed for Britifh North-America, that the miffions may be ambulatory, that is [*y*],
removable to places where they are moft wanted.

[*x*] The project of initiating white and Indian children into this
mode of the church of England by church of England working fchools,
quo femel eft imbuta recens, would be more effectual than the prefent
miffionary method ; the bringing over of adults is more difficult, and
when brought over they foon die, and their influence is loft ; in the incorporated charitable focieties of Scotland and Ireland, they only regard the rifing generation, where, without any ftrained allegory, it
may be called the fowing of the feeds of chriftianity, loyalty, and induftry. The former too large charity endowments to idle clergy miffions,
to colleges, and to charity fchools, require to be qualified and reformed ;
that of working fchools has lately been attended with great fuccefs and
benefit to the countries ; that is, reading and writing being acquired,
the boys are fent to fea, to hufbandry, and other laborious trades ; the
girls to fpinning and other fervices with fome peculiar reftrictions. Sir
Richard Cox in a late piece concerning the linen manufacture, writes,
' Numerous holy-days are the bane of all induftry, and the ruin of
' every country where they are permitted : and indeed there are too
' many allowed by law.''

[*y*] This method has had a good effect in Scotland. In Scotland the
pope has two vicars apoftolical, one for the lowlands, and the other
in the highlands, with many inferior miffionaries ; anno 1740, thefe
popifh miffionaries were twenty-five ; anno 1747, they dwindled away
to eleven ; the prefbyterian Scots itinerant miffionaries are well fub-

II. If

II. If the present incumbent missionaries are
dulged with their livings or salaries for their own nat
ral life; upon their decease the respective missions m
cease (as a mission is no inheritance, it is no hardf
upon their families) and be cantoned along our inla
frontiers to keep morality and christianity among t
poor new settlers, and to convert the neighbouring I
dians to civility and some of our orthodox professions
religion [z].

III. As this is formed with the design of a very exte
sive charity, the supporting of learned and orthod
ministers or teachers, without being confined to t
mode of the church of England; why may not t
charity be extended to ministers of any orthodox p
suasion, who will declare themselves willing to serve
mission among the Indians, as also to the orthodox r
nisters of the poor out towns? At present, it is cc
fined towards promoting uniformity to the discipl
and worship of the church of England; not among t
heathen who never heard of christianity, nor in po
out-townships, but among the sober-minded, christ
only educated, and loyaly tolerated protestant dissente
in the most opulent and best civilized townships.
strict exclusive uniformity (a few Lutherans excepted
practised only in popish sovereignties.

IV. Though the members at present are about 2
any seven members with the president or a vice-pr
dent may do business; thus four or five zealots, such

sisted by many large benefactions and subscriptions; the king all
1000*l* sterl. per ann.

[g] Our young missionaries may procure a perpetual alliance
commercial advantages with the Indians, which the Roman cathe
clergy cannot do, because they are forbid to marry, I mean.
missionaries may intermarry with the daughters of the sachems,
other considerable Indians, and their progeny will for ever be a
tain cement between us and the Indians.

the high-church, or friends to a foliciting perfon, may at pleafure pervert this charity. This perhaps has been the cafe for fome years, in appointing fo many idle miffions, and many who inftead of promoting charity (the nexus of human fociety) that is, love among neighbours; as bigots or religionifts, they act the reverfe.

V. The miffionaries in their accounts fent to the fociety, ought to keep ftrictly to the truth, and not impofe upon the world; I fhall mention two or three inftances. 1. The ftory of the regular difcipline of catechumens white and black in New-York, is not known here, though in the neigbourhood. 2. A chriftian congregation of more than 500 Mohawk Indians; the whole tribe does not exceed 160 men living in a difperfed [*a*] manner. 3. A fpirit of perfecution now in the colony of Connecticut; whereas there are fundry laws [*b*] of many years ftanding in that colony, exempting church of England, Anabaptifts and Quakers from contributing towards building townfhip meetinghoufes, and from the fupport of townfhip congregational minifters.

VI. As the fociety complain of the infufficiency of their funds certain and cafual, to keep up the falaries of their too much multiplied miffionaries; they are become more circumfpect and frugal, and inftead of a full living or miffion, confidering that they confine their miffion to one parifh, they only make a fmall addition of twenty to thirty pound fterl. in the S. W. part of Connecticut colony; the miffions in South-Carolina are reduced from fifty pound to thirty pound fterling per ann. and perhaps in all large falary miffions, without any injury to the incubent, a deduction may be made equal to the allowance from the congregation:

[*a*] This refembles the legendary ftory of St. Francis, at one time converting fome thoufands of people in a defert.
[*b*] See the laft edition of Connecticut law-book, p. 169, 170, 171.

this

this will be a confiderable faving, and as the parifh
or townfhips grow, their allowance will efface t
miffionary allowance; this will be a total faving, a
naturally anfwers that of the defign of the charity
affift thefe places that are not able to fubfift a gofp
miniftry [c].

I am now got into a maze or labyrinth; to clafs tl
various fectaries in religious affairs, is an intricate l
bour : the New-England fynod, anno 1637, condemn
eighty-two errors. I muft in general obferve, that,
As to the fearing or rather loving of GOD, the beft ev
dence is the working of righteoufnefs. 2. What is gen
rally called confcience, is private opinion. 3. They wl
have no remorfe of confcience, who do not believe
future rewards and punifhments, and who do not pr
vide for their houfholds or pofterity, are infidels,
worfe than infidels. 4. They who affert that the chur(
is independent of the civil power, and juftification l
faith without good works; fuch belief is worfe than l
religion, being inconfiftent with political fociety.

In concluding this article of miffionaries, I muft ol
ferve, that if what I have wrote is difagreeable to fom
it is not from any perfonal refentment; feveral of tl
miffionaries are my friendly acquaintances; but *amic*
—— *amicus.*——*fed magis amica veritas.* The origin
defign of this fociety, was moft humane and pious; mo
than 120,000 bibles, common prayers, and other bool
of devotion, with an incredible quantity of pious fm:
tracts, have been difperfed in foreign parts. They a
by charter allowed to purchafe real eftates to the val
of 2000 *l.* fterl. per ann. and other eftates to any valu
to meet once a month to tranfact bufinefs, or oftener
need be; but no act to be valid, unlefs the majori

[c] Can Bofton, e. g. be faid, not able to fupport a gofpel miniftr
The intereft of the money, which by eftimation the church of Engla
now building may coft, is fufficient to maintain half a dozen chu:
of England rectors at a comfortable allowance.

of seven members (a quorum) with the president or a vice-president concur. There is a circumstance, which has not always been attended to by the society; appointing of missionaries, faulted as to morality, benevolence, and moderation, called high-flyers, younger sisters of popery.

I shall clafs the religious opinions which have appeared in our colonies under three general heads, the merely speculative, the antiquated obsolete or out-of-fashion opinions, and the professions or sectaries which at present subsist and are likely to continue.

1. Speculative private opinions are of no consequence in a state, until the opinionists form themselves into separate large society meetings; I shall enumerate a few. The ANTINOMIANS [d] affert that the laws of Moses are

[d] See vol. I. p. 444.
This error was become obsolete, and remained only with a very few ignorant or vicious people until lately broached here by the vagrant Mr. W——ld, an insignificant person, of no general learning, void of common prudence; his journals are a rhapsody of scripture texts, and of his own cant expressions. In his epistle to the inhabitants of Maryland he writes, " considering what usage your slaves commonly " meet with, I wondered they did not put an end to their own lives or " yours, rather than bear such usage;" thus in a most execrable manner he might have promoted *felo de se* among the slaves, and insurrections against their masters; the two great inconveniencies which our plantations are exposed to. I never could account (perhaps it was only frantick, and not to be accounted for) for his repeated vagrancies, or strolling over England, Scotland, Ireland, and our American colonies: he was no popish missionary, because, being young, he never had the opportunities of being abroad in popish seminaries or conventuals: he was no itinerant missionary (for some short time he had a mission for Georgia) of our society for propagating the gospel in foreign parts; because when he effectually acted one part towards an uniformity to the church of England, by occasioning separations and animofities among the orthodox dissenters, at the same time he found much fault with the present constitution of the church of England: he was no ministerial or court tool, as was the famous Sacheverel in the jacobite part of queen Anne's reign, because the government at present have no occasion for such: he did not travel as a naturalist or as an historian for observation, by the perquisites of preaching to defray his charges; because he had no genius nor application for such studies. Here we may observe, what trivial things may

vacated,

vacated, as being only temporary and local, that national or municipal, therefore not obligatory w chriftian nations ; that good works do not forward, r bad works hinder falvation.

In general, people ought to entertain a laudable i ligious charity towards one another, feeing they worfl the fame GOD, though in different modes : particular. to make veftments and other fanciful ecclefiaftical dec rations a matter of controverfy, is very abfurd [e]; fu indifferent trivial circumftances may be adapted to t tafte of the vulgar : the Greek and Armenian church in the Levant preferve the mode of their religion l pageantries. The Jews had a fuperb magnificent ten ple, a numerous train of gaudy officers, very expenfi facrifices. Simplicity and frugality in all affairs of life at prefent thought to be moft natural, and is general practifed : even in religion thefe things have fuffen fucceffive reformations ; the church of England is le expenfive than that of Rome ; the three licenfed diffen ing worfhips in England are lefs expenfive than the [j church of England, and the Quakers have reduced r ligion to no expence.

be great incentives to devotion, fuch as vociferation (the ftrength of l arguments lay in his lungs,) a vehement frequent ufe of cant devotion words, a dramatick genius peculiarly adapted to act the enthufiaft, pr per veftiments or drefs and action; in diffenting congregations he a fected the church of England drefs, and Paul Rubens' preaching poft in the cartoons of Hampton-Court. He and his difciples feemed be great promoters of impulfes, extacies, and wantonnefs between t fexes. Hypocritical profeffions, vociferations, and itinerancies, a devotional quackery.

[e] La Voltaire in his letters, writes, that the difputes among t capuchins, concerning the mode of the fleeves and cowl, were mc them any among the philofophers.

[f] It would be of great benefit to our out fettlers if they could i into fome fuch method, feeing the fociety for propagating, &c. t no care of them; they are not able to build publick places of worfh and fupport a gofpel miniftry, and when they endeavour it, the e pence retards their fettlements ; a great detriment to the colonies general.

The Familists [g] family, or houfe of love, was of the anabaptift tribe in Germany, and fufpected to be more addicted to carnal than to fpiritual love ; they held all pleafures and dalliances among themfelves lawful ; they were much tranfported with impulfes and other frantick notions ; they perfuaded themfelves that they were the only elect of God, and that all others were reprobates, and that they might deceive any perfon who was not of their community, magiftrates not excepted, even with an oath.   They agreed with the Antinomians in many articles.

The Mugletonians [b] are extinct.

The Gortonians of Warwick in the colony of Rhode-Ifland, were of fo fhort duration, they are not to be mentioned ; fee the fection of Rhode-Ifland.

The rigid Brownists [i] are relaxed into independents and congregationalifts.

The Independents in all our colonies, have fuffered fome reformation, and are at prefent called congregationalifts.

Puritans were for reforming the reformed religions to greater abfolute purity ; that appellation is now obfolete.

Seekers waited for new apoftles to reftore chriftianity ; thefe have quite difappeared.

Remonstrants and Contra-remonstrants [k], or predeftinarians and free-will men.   The remonftrants

---

[g] The father of this family, was Henry Nicols, born at Munfter in Weftphalia, and had refided fome time in Holland ; he firft appeared about 1540, and pretended to be greater tnan Mofes or Christ : as Mofes had taught Mankind to hope, Chrift to believe, he taught love, which is the greateft ; and that he himfelf was not like John the baptift, a fore-runner of Chrift, but Chrift was rather a type of him, and that the kingdom of Ifrael was to be eftablifhe i in the time of his miniftry : what he wrote was mean and incoherent, full of vain boafting and profane applications of the prophecies, relating to Chrift to his own perfon.

[h] See Summary, vol. I. p. 447.

[i] See vol. I. p. 443.

[k] See vol. I. p. 227.

are

are alfo called Arminians [*l*]. It is not a doctrine of a national church or embodied communion; there : fome perfons of this private opinion, among all t fectaries. Their diftinguifhing tenets, are, univer redemption, an indemnity or act of grace to all ma kind, who by a good life accept thereof, being e dued with a free will to act at liberty what is good: evil.

Concerning the fectaries in our colonies which now fubf and are likely to continue.

I do not mean a church hiftory of North-Americ: bifhop Burnet well obferves, that ecclefiaftical hiftorie are only hiftories of the vices of the bifhops and oth clergy.

Moft fectaries in religion have been occafioned I vulgar people not capable of giving allowances for tl allegories, fables, and idioms of expreffion ufed the Levant, from whence we had our fcriptural book but taking them in a literal and vernacular fenf whereas the prophets generally ufed lofty figurative e: preffions.

In our North-America colonies there are none pr: perly to be called feparatifts, Roman catholicks e: cepted (in Maryland, and by the proprietary chart: of Penfylvania, Roman catholicks are not excepted but by the act of union (territories thereto belonging the church of England is the eftablifhed church, thoug only nominal, in all our colonies and plantations. Tl denomination of whigs and tories [*m*] (*Deo gratias*)

[*l*] So called from Arminius their leader, who was fome time pr feffor of divinity at Leyden in Holland; they were alfo called R monftrants, from their remonftrating, 1618, againft fome articles the fynod of Dort concerning predeftination, election, reprobatio and the like; thus the adherents to the princes of Germany, who pr tefted againft fome proceedings at the diet of Spire in Germany 152 were called Proteftants.

[*m*] Tory, originally was a name given to the wild Irifh popifh ro bers, who favoured the maffacre of the proteftants in Ireland 164

loft: there is no general church government [*n*] ; by
the articles of union, that of the church of England is
eftablifhed in perpetuity ; but hitherto in favour to the
good confcientious diffenters of many denominations,
the colonies are not quartered upon by the regular ec-
clefiaftick troops under the direction of their proper
officers, archbifhops, bifhops, deans, archdeacons,
prebends, canons, and other fubaltern officers: the
church of England exercifes no jurifdiction (the office of
the bifhop's commiffaries is only nominal) no more than
the county affociations of minifters in Connecticut,
or the volunteers prefbyters (in imitation of the claffical kirk jurifdictions of Scotland) in feveral of our
colonies.

I fhall not here delineate or defcribe the papiftical
church of Rome, the epifcopal church of England, and
the prefbyterian kirk of Scotland ; they are generally
well known.

The papifts are of no note or notice [*o*] excepting in
Penfylvania and Maryland ; in Penfylvania by their new
charter 1701 from their proprietary and governor

and afterwards applied to all enormous high-fliers of the church.
Whig was a ludicrous name, firft given to the country field devotion
meetings, whofe ordinary drink was the WHIG or whey of coagulated
four milk, and afterwards applied to thofe who were againft the court
intereft in the reigns of Charles II, and James II. and for the court in
the reigns of king William and king George.

[*n*] Church governments may be various, and all equally allowable
by prefcription; as in the civil governments of various nations there
are monarchy, ariftocracy, democracy, and compofitions of thefe,
which in general alliances, treaties of peace, and other tranfactions
among fovereignties, are equally admitted

[*o*] Not many years fince, in Bofton were fome popifh emiffaries; but
finding only fome poor wild Irifh carters and porters of the perfuafion,
they foon relinquifhed their miffion and difappeared.

As the grants of Maryland and Penfylvania do actually tolerate the
publick exercife of the Roman catholick religion ; and as that religion
is pernicious to human fociety in general, and tends to fubvert our
prefent happy conftitution; why may it not be fuppreffed as to publick worfhip, by an act of the Britifh parliament, without giving any
umbrage to the other good grants and charters at home, and in the
plantations?

William Penn, the claufe of liberı
ñot exclude Roman catholicks, "
" acknowledge one almighty G
" under the civil government, fh
" lefted." In Philadelphia there
chapel, frequented by a poor lo
priefts are always England or M
and generally of good conduct and
jefuit is never fent. In Maryland
tholicks, their original proptietary
there may be ten or a dozen puı
father Molineux of Port Tobacco
vicar.

LUTHERANS [*p*] are to be foun(
of New-York and Penfylvania.
from the Roman catholicks princi
in both kinds, bread and wine.
the vulgar tongue. 3. Indulginı
with matrimonial pleafures. Some
fudicroufly have obferved, that
owing to his indulgence of wine a
ternity of clergy, as king Henry '
England was owing to fome petti
may obferve, that from very trivi
and good revolutions have procee
New-York there is one Lutheran
of the province of New-York feveı
by the importation of foreigneı
queen Anne's reign. In Penfylvan
a church in Philadelphia, and fev
There is one Swedifh Lutheran chu
one or two more in the country

[*p*] Luther born 1483, at Mansfield in ı
guftin monk or friar, preached againft ind
municated by the pope; he with Melanéton
ment, and afterward 1534 the whole bible
married 1524, and died 1548; the duke of

are fupplied once in feven years from Sweden, and generally with good men.

PRESBYTERIANS, church of England, and congregationalifts are the fame in all effential articles of chriftian doctrine, and their laity are all of the fame faith; the proper diftinctions are only with regard to their diftinct clergy in forms of church government, difcipline, modes of publick worfhip, and veftments. The prefbyterians in our colonies are of two forts, 1. Thofe who follow the manner of the church of Scotland as eftablifhed in Scotland by act of union: all diffenters from the church of England, (Anabaptifts, Quakers, and Moravians excepted) fouth of New-England, are called prefbyterians, the congregationals not excepted; thus the diffenting congregation in the city of New-York, though under a congregational minifter from Bofton, is called prefbyterian. The Scots prefbyterians are modelled according to a directory firft agreed upon by an affembly of divines at Weftminfter in the time of the civil war, and appointed by the general affembly of the kirk of Scotland 1647; they ufe no liturgy. 2. Thefe are properly called Calvinifts [q], and follow the confeffion of Heidelberg (in the palatinate of Germany) fuch are the church of Geneva, feveral churches in Germany, fuch are the church of Holland, and the huguenots of France; they ufe not only a liturgy or common prayer, but alfo an eftablifhed form of pfalmody. A calvinift French church fubfifted may years in Bofton, and is lately dropt, there being no French new comers, and the children of the late generations underftand Englifh better than

[q] Calvin was born in Picardy in France 1509, a man of general learning; he began his reformation at Geneva; died 1564, æt. 56; he was a voluminous writer; his inftitutions are a mafter-piece of elegant Roman Latin.

It is a common miftake, that by Calvinifts are underftood predeftinarians; before Calvin's time there were many predeftinarians; the Mahometan predeftinarians are not Calvinifts; fome predeftinarians as well as free-will men are now called Armenians, becaufe private opinions, are to be found among all fectaries.

L 2 French.

French.   There are several calvinist churches in the pi
vinces of New-York and Pensylvania

CONGREGATIONALISTS is the religious mode of Ne
England, (some church of England, Anabaptists, a
Quakers excepted) the presbyterians are only speculati
because by act of union they can have no ecclesiasti
classical jurisdiction in the colonies, and therefore are oi
congregational, but less rigid and narrow in admission
church members, and in discipline. The New-Engla
congregationals may be called independents [r] refori
ed, as not exactly the same with the independen
one of the three licensed dissenting professions in En
land, but formed according to a platform (so they c
it) of their own scheming; this platform was by a resol
of the general assembly recommended to the churche
but never enacted.

At present, anno 1750, the general method of t
New-England congregationalists [s] is, when a gosp
minister is wanted, the devout elderly men of the pr
cinct invite sundry preachers to officiate; these are call
candidates. In the next step, the church members
communicants (all males, even the poorest upon t
publick charity, and negroes) at an appointed meetin
by a majority, vote for one of these candidates, and gi
him a formal call. The following step, is a gener
meeting of the men of the congregation, who p
ministerial rates, and are qualified as town voters,
approve or disapprove of the above choice; if any dif
culty happens, a council of delegates from the neig
bouring churches is called for advice, but their opinic
is only of advice, but not absolutely obligatory. Th
council when they attend the ordination, are called t

[r] The name of Independent is quite extinct in our American co
nies.

[s] In the second session of a synod appointed by the civil legislan
at Boston in May 1680, a platform and confession of faith was agre
upon, much the same with that of the independents in England, Oc
ber 1658, called the Savoy confession of faith.

See vol. I. p. 428, &c. and other occasional hints.

ordinatic

ordination council. Upon any occasional difference in a church, a like council of advice is called, but not obligatory, and issues in a vote of the church communicants or general congregation.

The congregationalists of Connecticut are regulated by a platform or confession of their own (scarce differing from that of Massachusetts Bay) presented to their general assembly by the ministers and other delegates Sept. 9, 1707; the general assembly or legislature ordained, that all churches [*t*] conforming thereto shall be deemed established by law; but no society or church, who soberly dissent from the said united churches, shall be hindered from their worship according to their consciences.

There are several congregational churches who vary in some trifles; for instance, the rev. Mr. Colman, afterwards D. D. from one of the universities of Scotland, though frequently in mixed conversation he declared his dissent from the presbyterian church government, anno 1699, perhaps in humour and singularity, set up as a separatist from the generally received congregational mode, and perhaps with a design to allure some inclined to the manner of the church of England, to contribute towards his church; his separation was only in trifles, viz. using the Lord's prayer, reading of lessons in the bible, the hatband and rose of the church of Enlgand clergy, a freer admission to the sacraments of baptism and the Lord's supper; his successor the rev. Samuel Cooper is a good man.

1722, there was a considerable falling off or secessus from the congregational mode by Mr. Cutler, president of Yale college in Connecticut, and some of his former pupils. In consequence of their scheme, they went to

[*t*] In many respects I admire the prudence and œconomy of this government, but here I cannot avoid observing a seeming inadvertency, and afterwards not rectified, because by act of union May 1, 1707, the church of England exclusively was the only church established by law in all our plantations; this act perhaps was the occasion of Mr. Hobart's calling the church of England Separatists.

England,

England, obtained epifcopal ordi
of miffionaries; their godlinefs w
. ANABAPTISTS. See vol. I. p.
and diftinguifhing doctrine is wit
they baptize adults only, and t
dipping. This formerly was a
therefore run into many fubdivif
merated: I am well informed, tl
vania there are fixteen or feven
Anabaptifts, Englifh and Germa
of their fubdivifions. 1. Englif
nerally good people; German A
people: the German Anabaptift
publick places of worfhip in Phil
the country, and generally refuf
one of their branchings are callec
meeting in Philadelphia, but are a
people in the country, and foll
ftinction is wearing long beards,
ment oaths. The dumplers are a f
about fifty, from Philadelphia, 1
fing continency, and living in fep
men wear a monkifh habit, with
chins, but lighter cloth; as to o
with the Quakers and Moravians
people, they have a very decent
men, they are very ingenious;
have a grift mill, a faw-mill, a p
and a mill for pearl barley, all
brings them in confiderable profi
lifh Anabaptift meeting in Philac
country. 2. Firft day baptifts,
is the Sunday, as in ufe with all o
day baptifts, on the feventh day

[*u*] Not long fince the vagrant Mr. W
in the Bofton Anabaptift church; the Sep
care of a leather breeches maker; they
f ore pernicious in fociety.

I

meet for publick worfhip, and abftain from common
labour, but labour, &c. on the Sunday or firft day of
the week ; of thofe there is a congregation in Newport
and in Wefterly of Rhode-Ifland colony, and feveral in
the country of Penfylvania. 3. The firft day baptifts
are fubdivided into thofe who ufe finging [*x*] in their
publick worfhip as the generality of chriftians do ; and
baptifts who do not admit of finging in publick worfhip ;
they alledge that there muft be a great deal of hypo-
crify in promifcuous finging, as it cannot be imagined
that every one of the congregation is in the humour of
finging at the fame time.

QUAKERS, fee vol. I. p. 447. As they are not under
the confinement of creeds, confeffions of faith, plat-
forms, canons, articles, formulas, and the like, they
cannot poffibly break loofe into fectary [*y*] fubdivifions.
Their principal doctrines are to be inveftigated from
their practice, (it is to be wifhed that it were fo in all
profeffions of religion), their induftry, frugality, mutual
benevolence or friendfhip [*z*]. The external part of a
Quaker's religion confifts only in trivial matters, the

[*x*] The Quakers, and not finging baptifts, are defervedly faulted,
becaufe finging of pfalms incites and heightens devotion.

[*y*] Anno 1642 or 1644, in time of the civil wars of England, George
Fox of Leicefterfhire, æt. 25, fet up for a religionary exhorter or
teacher; he exclaimed againft the eftablifhed clergy, fome of Cromwell's
foldiers became his profelytes and would not fight; in courfe the prifons
were crouded. In K. Charles II. adminiftration they were frequently
prefented for refufing to pay tythes, and for not taking government
oaths. Robert Barclay of Scotland wrote an apology for the Quakers 1675,
and dedicated it to the king, which abated that perfecution. William
Penn, fon of vice-admiral Penn, became a Quaker, æt. 22, and with
Fox went upon a miffion into foreign countries, but from Holland they
foon returned home ; this Penn was proprietary and governor of Penfylvania ; he wrote two folio volumes in favour of the Quakers.

Benjamin Holmes lately wrote in favour of quakerifm ; his book was
firft publifhed in Amfterdam 1723.

[*z*] I know of no differences among them, only fome are more demure, fome lefs demure or precife in the antiquated habit and mode of
fpeech, that is, more jovial and debonnaire.

Not only in the neighbourhood, but by annual or periodical itinerancies of their fpeakers or exhorters, and alfo of their moft noted men.

antiqua-

antiquated modes of speech, thee, thou, thy, &c
and an antiquated dress of a plain coat without plaits, o
buttons on the pockets and sleeves, beaver like hat
with horizontal brims as is generally worn by the church
of England clergy: the pusillanimous doctrine of not de
fending themselves by force against an invading enem
is very absurd: PRO PATRIA is not only a law of na
tions, but of nature. They say that a regular clerg
with benefices are hirelings, and, like mercenary troops
do duty only for sake of their pay, and are not to be so
much depended upon as the militia or voluntary consci
entious exhorters.

Quakers hold all swearing and paying of tythes un
lawful; they do not find fault with the various forms o
civil government, but give obedience to any established
government; all who have the gift of the light within
them, men or women, are sufficiently ordained to
preach the gospel without any commission from a
church, or assistance from human learning; all praying
and preaching premeditated or extempore without the
spirit, are superstitious will-worship and idolatry; they
use neither baptism nor the Lord's supper.

Unjustly they are said not to regard the scriptures,
whereas in their exhortations, writings, and defences of
their orthodoxy, no sect use scripture phrases and quo-
tations [a] more than they do. Their affirmation in-

[a] I shall here give a few instances of their establishing some of their
tenets by scripture. 1. They seem to be generally Arminian, James ii.
20. " But wilt thou know, O vain man! that faith without works is
" dead." Acts x. 34. " God is no respecter of persons, he that fears
" God and works righteousness is accepted of him." 1 John ii. 2.
" And he is the propitiation for our sins, and not for us only, but for
" the sins of the WHOLE world.' They cannot believe that God has
fore-ordained a certain part of mankind to perish, and a certain part
to be saved; because in such a belief there is no need to take care of
salvation or good morals; this is execrably pernicious, and void all
doctrines, religious or moral. 2. All mankind have an innate divine
light, which if attended to, directs them into a good and holy life, and
averts them from sin and passions; " This is the light (John i.)
" which lighteth every man that cometh into the world." 3. Water
stead

tead of an oath, is not to be faulted, becauſe it is equally
ᵇinding, and falſifying is ſubjected to the ſame penalty
ᵃs perjury; government oaths are become ſo common,
ʰey have almoſt loſt their ſolemnity. They uſe the
ⁱame ſubterfuge with our more illiterate teachers and
ᵉxhorters, 1 Corinth. i. 26, &c. " Not many wiſe after
" the fleſh, not many mighty, not many noble are
" called; but God hath choſen the fooliſh things of the
" world, to confound the wiſe," &c. Their ſilent
ʷaiting upon the Lord in their publick places of de-
ᵛotion, is faulted by many, but they ſay, at that time,
ʰey have a divine teacher in their own heart. They
ᵇelieve a reſurrection of the juſt and unjuſt, and that
ᴳod will give a reward to every man according to his
ʷorks, whether they be good or evil; but as to the
ⁿature and manner of the reſurrection they are ſilent,
ᵗhey only ſay, that it is not ſafe to be too inquiſitive,
ʰow the dead ſhall be raiſed, and with what bodies.
ᶦ Corinth. xv. 44. " There is a natural body, and
" there is a ſpiritual body;" the apoſtle Paul ſaith,
" Fleſh and blood cannot inherit the kingdom of God,
" neither doth corruption inherit incorruption."

baptiſm is not eſſential to chriſtianity, it muſt be of the ſpirit, Acts
ᵡi 16. " John indeed baptized with water, but ye ſhall be baptized
" with the holy ghoſt;" as Chriſt was born under the law, he fulfilled
the law and was circumciſed: " in Chriſt Jeſus, neither circumciſion
" nor uncircumciſion availeth any thing, but a new creature:" as they
have charity for thoſe who uſe water baptiſm conſcientiouſly, and who
uſe bread and wine, ſo they ought to have charity for us if we diſuſe
them, becauſe we believe they are ceaſed in point of obligation. 4. In
anſwer to 1 Tim. ii. 12. " But ſuffer not a woman to teach, nor to
" uſurp authority over the man, but to be in ſilence;" they produce tho
apoſtle Paul, Rom. xvi. who adviſes to help thoſe women which la-
boured with him in the goſpel: in our bible we are told of many women that propheſied, Acts ii. 18, " And on my ſervants, and on
" my handmaidens, I will pour out in thoſe days of my ſpirit, and
" they ſhall propheſy." 5. As to their not bearing of arms, Mat. v.
44 " Love your enemies, bleſs them that curſe you, do good to
" them that hate you." 6. Their refuſing of government oaths, James
v. 12. " But above all things, my brethren, ſwear not, neither by hea-
" ven, neither by the earth, neither by any other oath, but let your
" yea be yea, and your nay nay, leſt you fall into condemnation."

Mora-

MORAVIANS, Some have tranfported themfelves
Penfylvania. In a late act of the Britifh parliamer
1749, in favour of their affirmation inftead of an oat
they are called an ancient proteftant epifcopal churc
they call themfelves Unitas fratrum or united brethre
as the Quakers with very good propriety call themfeh
Friends:

The Moravians publifh no creed or confeffion
faith, and can be characterifed only from their mann
and preaching in a whining canting enthufiaftical ftrai
in church government they are epifcopal, but refi
taking oaths as do the Menenifts in Holland, and t
Englifh Quakers; they refufe carrying arms, b
willingly contribute towards the pecuniary charge of
war, which Quakers refufe; they ufe inftrumental m
fick in their worfhip; in Philadelphia they have a ch
pel with a fmall organ, and in the country at Bethlehe
their grand fettlement about fifty or fixty miles fro
Philadelphia, at their folemn feftivals, befides t
organ they ufe violins, hautbois, and French horn
they poffefs 7000 or 8000 acres of land, and make co
fiderable fettlements; they are very zealous towar
converting the Indians; fome Indians have joined th
fociety and live with them; they fend miffionaries abro
almoft every where, even to Greenland, or Davis's ftrait
beginning of June 1749, there arrived in Philadelpl
three natives of Greenland, two young men and
young woman converted in their own country by Mor
vian miffionaries; they came in a fhip belonging to t
fociety which had carried thither two years fince a rea
framed church [b] to be erected there; thefe Gree
landers [c] in this fhip had vifited the brethren in fev

[b] Thefe high latitudes produce no timber or other wood.

[c] Here we may tranfiently obferve, that at this cafual congrefs
Indians from lat. 5, lat. 40, and lat. 65, their hair, eyes and co
plexions were the fame; only, the farther north, the complexions w
a fmall matter paler: but their languages were entirely diftinct. T

ral parts of Europe, in England, Holland, and Germany, and returned from Philadelphia in the same ship to Greenland. The Moravians have a mission at Barbice in Surinam, and two Indian converts from thence, with the Greenland converts, and some converts of the Delaware Indians, met at Bethlehem.

1. The Moravians [d] have among them in Pensylvania some men of letters; Mr. Spenenbergh was a professor of some science in Germany at Halle; but they chiefly consist of handicrafts, by which they carry on their improvements cheap. They encourage marriage amongst their young people; but to marry by casting of lots to preserve an equality among themselves, which they affect very much is not natural. By a late act of parliament they are indulged with an affirmation instead of an oath in these words, " I A. B. do declare in the " presence of Almighty God, the witness of the truth " I say;" but if convicted of wilful and false affirming, shall incur the same pains and penalties as are enacted by law against wilful and corrupt perjury; but shall not by their affirmation be qualified to give evidence in criminal cases (Quakers affirmation is good both in criminal and civil cases) and not to serve in juries.

After the general description of our plantation sectaries, these in each colony should have been enumerated; but by anticipation they are generally to be found, 1. Those of the four colonies of New-England are at full length. 2. In the province of New-York, besides the church of England, there are the mode of the kirk of Scotland, Dutch Calvinists, and some Lutherans of the confession of Augsburgh in Suabia of Germany, 3. In the Jerseys there are the church of England missions, the

Greenland or Davis's Straits converts were clad in seal skins, hair on, but in general were a nasty sort of christians.

[d] So called from Moravia, a country adjacent to Bohemia; they seem to be a sprout from the old stock of the Hussites; the Hussites; disciples of Huss and Jerome of Bohemia, followed the tenets of the Waldenses who appeared about 1310, and of Wickliffe an English Lollard, middle of 14th century.

Scots

Scots presbyterians and quakers rule the roast. 4. Beside
the church of England missionaries in the country o
Pensylvania, there is one English church in Philadelphi,
a very large congregation. In Philadelphia (and man
in the country) there are two presbyterian meetings, on
called new light of Whitefield's institution, the other ac
cording to the Scots presbyterian mode; and besides a
a great distance in the country there is a congregatio
of Cameronians or covenanters, who renew the solem
league often, and deny all submission to magistrates fror
the sovereign to the constable, because at the revolu
tion the king by law assumed to be head of the church
and contrary to their covenant, in England establishe
prelacy instead of presbytery. The Quakers have tw
large meetings in Philadelphia. and a meeting almost ii
every township of the three first settled counties
in the other three counties they do not prevail; bu
every where preserve power by their two irresistibl
maxims of riches and unity; they have the secret o
keeping their young people up to these, and let them
think and talk otherwise as they please. 5. In Marylanc
there are several parishes according to the way of the
church of England, and the most beneficial of any ir
our plantations, because as the number of taxables o
congregation increases, being taxed at so much tobacc
per head, the value of their livings grows: whereas ir
Virginia the parsons are fixed at a certain salary o
16,000 wt. of tobacco per ann. without any regard to
the increase of the congregation: in Maryland are ter
or a dozen publick Roman catholick chapels, many pref
byterians, and some Quakers. 6. In Virginia there ar
no dissenters from the church of England, a few Qua
kers excepted, their clergy are not noted for their piet
and morality or exemplary life, and require missionar
reformers more than the congregationalists of New-Eng
land; it is said that many of them are a scandal to th
profession of the church of England. 7. In North-Ca
rolina scarce any religion; there are two missionarie

and a few Quakers. In South-Carolina there are church of England miffionaries, and the progeny of fome Scots prefbyterians. 9. In Georgia DE NIHILO NIHIL.

A few Mifcellany Obfervations.

All charities, excepting to poor orphans, other impotent poor, and children of indigent parents, are charities ill applied; charities towards converting people from one mode of religion to another, where both are confiftent with fociety, are not laudable.

By a general naturalization, foreigners may be imported to all our colonies; but to be intermixed with the Britifh fettlers, their publick worfhip of any denomination, and fchooling to be in Englifh [e]; thus in a few years, they will not differ from the Britifh only in family names.

In New-England the congregationalifts at firft acted with too much feverity, which occafioned fome inhabitants of Bofton to petition K. Charles II. anno 1679, for a church of England, modeftly called the king's chapel, (thus it is with ambaffadors chapels,) fignifying not an eftablifhed, but tolerated or privileged place of worfhip.

The clamours concerning the perfecutions of diffenters from the congregational way were very ill founded; for inftance, 1725, the affeffors of Tiverton and Dartmouth were by a proper warrant from the province treafurer committed to jail for not affeffing the townfhip towards common rates.

[e] A late propofal in Penfylvania of erecting German fchools was moft abfurd.

S E C T.   XI.

Concerning the colony of Connecticut.

THIS is the laft of the four colonies former
called, The dominions of New-England. It is
plantation of induftrious fagacious hufbandmen, no
withftanding that fome of the meaner fort are villain
corruptio optimi peffima, efpecially in not paying the
juft debts to the inhabitants or dealers of the neighbou
ing colonies; in all their elections of governor, cou
fellors, reprefentatives, judges, and other publick of
cers, by cuftom, they generally prefer the moft worth
Their eaftern townfhips have been tainted by the adj;
cent paper-money-making colonies of Maffachufett
Bay and Rhode-Ifland, and followed that fraud inftea
of going into the better currency of their weftern a
joining province of New-York; the Connecticut adm
niftration are at prefent fenfible of this error, and ha
reduced all their publick fees and fines to proclamatic
money.—I could not avoid this preamble, by way
eulogy upon the prefent adminiftration in their exen
plary jurifdiction. They have fubfifted as a gover
ment about ninety years, and from œconomical expei
ence, have formed a body of laws lately revifed ar
publifhed anno 1750, in a fmall folio of 258 pages,
the moft natural, equitable, plain and concife laws f
plantations, hitherto extant.

This colony at prefent is by royal charter, a coa
tion of two diftinct voluntary focieties, formed fro
articles by fubfcription of many planters, then call
Hartford and New-Haven colonies. That of Hartfo
was from an emigration of fome difcontented rigids
fome townfhips adjoining to Bofton (fee vol. I. p. 44
they went weft fouthwardly, and planted the lands n
called Springfield, Suffield, Enfield, Windfor, Ha

1, &c. fome of thefe were within the
fdiction : thofe who were without the
bfcription of articles formed them-
odel of Maffachufetts-Bay into a vo-
zal jurifdiction. Their firft election of
>36; 1637 people from England un-
of Mr. Eaton, Mr. Davenport, &c.
Indians, and began another, diftinct
ion upon Long-Ifland found called the
iven, and continued one of the [f]
New-England until the reftoration of
ind was then with the faid colony of
charter incorporated into the prefent
icut.

1, fon of John Winthrop, governor
lay, as agent from the lords Say and
fort Saybrook 1635, and was after-
rnor of Hartford colony. Upon the
Charles II. he went home and ob-
:er incorporating Hartford and New-
o one united colony; he was fourteen
his united colony [g].

eer governor of Hartford colony was
born in England 1600, a Turky
on; he returned to England, was in
, and died in London 1657. After-
r. Hains was chofen governor. After

nies of New-England from 1643 to 1663, were
nouth, Hartford, and New-Haven.
; or civil war in England, the colonies in Ame-
l acted at pleafure.
formerly governor of Connecticut, died in
æt. 73, eldeft fon of Mr. Winthorp, governor
lied March 26, 1649.
to experimental philofophy and medicine; fe-
ill ufed by that family in charity to the poor;
be found amongft the firft philofophical tranf-
oyal fociety; he was a great admirer of Van
:h in antimonials.

them

them George Willis, Thomas Wells, and John Webſ
were choſen governors.

Mr. Eaton, an eaſt country merchant of Londɩ
one of the patentees of Maſſachuſetts colony, with
parcel of planters 1637 ſettled at New-Haven. Aſ
being for many ſucceſſive years governor, he died 16ſ
to him ſucceeded Francis Newman, he continued thɩ
or four years governor and died.   Mr. Leet, a lawy
ſucceeded and continued governor until Hartford a
New-Haven were by royal charter united into one co
ny, and was their deputy governor under Mr. Winthr
while he lived, and after Mr. Winthrop's death con
nued ten years governor till his own death.

We ſhould have mentioned that Robert, earl of W
wick, having obtained a grant 1630 from the council
Plymouth, procured a patent from king Charles I.
lands in New-England from Narraganſet river, as ɩ
ſea coaſt runs towards Virginia forty leagues, and ɛ
and weſt from ſea to ſea or to Maſſachuſett ſouth liɩ
this was made over to William viſcount Say and Sɛ
Robert lord Brook, and company; they built a fort
the mouth of Connecticut river, and called it Say-Broo
but finding no profit to accrue, they ſold it to the ſ
tlers 1644.

The preſent boundaries of Connecticut colony ɩ
its north [b] line upon Maſſachuſetts-Bay province
about ſeventy-two miles, ſettled 1713; its [i] eaſte
line upon the colony of Rhode-Iſland of about for
five miles, ſettled 1728; its ſoutherly line is uɩ
Long-Iſland ſound, being a ſea line of about ninɩ
miles in a direct W. ſoutherly courſe from the mouth
Pakatuke river to the mouth of Byram river; its weſt
line as finally ſettled with New-York, and by a deed

[b] See vol. I. p. 416. by miſtake it was ſaid to have been conſin
by the king in council.
[i] See vol. II. p. 93.

furrender from the colony of Connecticut to the king, May 14, 1731, is as follows.

This weft line was regulated thus, beginning at twenty miles eaft from Courtland's point [*k*] of Hudfon's river; N. 12 d. 30 m. E. fifty-two and half miles to a continuation of the Maffachufetts and Connecticut divifional line in N. lat. 42 d. 2 m. [*l*] From the abovefaid projection from Courtland's point run S. 24 d. 30 m. eaft, feven and one quarter miles, then W. S. W. thirteen miles fixty-four rod, then S. S. E. eight miles to the mouth of Byram river. A line parallel with the firft two lines at the diftance of one mile three quarters of a mile and twenty rod eaftward is the prefent boundary between Connecticut and New-York, and the land comprehended by thefe parallel lines is called the Oblong granted by Connecticut to New-York as an equivalent for fome lands upon the Sound, fettled by, but not originally belonging to, Connecticut; this was confirmed by the king in council. The Oblong contains about 69,000 acres, whereof 50,000 acres is in difpute, the property being claimed by Eyles and company, alfo by Hanly and company [*m*]; it remains a place of refuge for the mifcreants from New-England and New-York.

The partition line between New-York and Connecticut as eftablifhed December 1, 1664, runs from the mouth of Memoroncok river (a little weft from Byram river) N. N. W. and was the ancient eafterly bounds of New-York till Nov. 23, 1683, the line was run nearly the fame as it is now fettled.

Duke of Hamilton's grant took in part of the prefent colony of Connecticut; this grant was from Narraganfet-

[*k*] Courtland's point is computed to be forty miles as the river runs from the city of New-York.

[*l*] This N. W. corner of Connecticut colony is twenty and three quarter miles from Hudfon's river, about nine miles above Kingfton, one mile below the mouth of Efopus river, and about fifty miles below Albany.

[*m*] See New-York fection.

Bay to Connecticut river, and back into the coun
until it met with Maſſachuſetts ſouth line; but as
was never purchaſed of the native Indians, and ne
ſettled, it may be deemed as obſolete; there have b
ſome attempts to revive this claim, but never pre
cuted.

The Indians almoſt extinct; they have a ſmall reſe
upon the eaſt ſide of Connecticut river at Piſtol poin
Weathersfield; a very ſmall parcel of Nianticks ab
five or ſix miles weſt from New-London; there is
Indian reſerve of —— acres upon New-London rivel
the northern parts of that townſhip called Mohegins.

In Connecticut are eight convenient ſhipping pe
for ſmall craft, but all maſters enter and clear at
port of New-London, a good harbour five miles wit
land, and deep water. Here they build large ſhips, t
their timber is ſpungy, and not durable; it ſplits
rives well into ſtaves; ſmall veſſels are built at Saybro
Killingſworth, New-Haven or Wallingsford river, &
In the Sound the tide flows from ſix to eight feet, t
deep water is upon the Long-iſland ſide.

Foreign veſſels entered and cleared in the port of Ne
London from the 25th of March 1748 to the 25th
March 1749; ſcarce any regiſtered more than eigl
tons, and generally are Weſt-India traders.

Entered inwards.		Cleared outwards.
Brigantines	3	Brigantines
Sloops	30	Sloops
Schooners	4	Schooners
	37	

Here, as in all other Britiſh colonies, the collector
other cuſtom-houſe officers, are by warrant from
commiſſioners of the cuſtoms in conſequence of an or
from the treaſury; the commiſſioners of the treaſury
rect all officers of the revenue.

In Connecticut the government is in the hands of the representative of the freemen or people [*u*], as was also the property; but at present no colony or general lands remain (so it is in Rhode-Island) excepting some Indian reserves.

In the reigns of Charles II. and James II. the colony of Connecticut (as also of Rhode-Island) in the case of their charter, did not stand a law suit at home, as did Massachusetts-Bay, but tacitly dropt their charter or jurisdiction, and upon the happy revolution tacitly reassumed their jurisdiction, which was deemed good, and subsists to this day.

This colony (before a charter granted them, by the two distinct appellations of Hartford and New-Haven) was two of the four associated colonies of New-England; Old Massachusetts and Old Plymouth were the other two; the quota of charges of the two Connecticut colonies of Hartford and New-Haven was equal to that of the old colony of Massachusetts Bay.

As to their wars or rather bickerings with the Canada French and their Indians, as also with our intermixed Indians in their insurrections, they were in common with Massachusetts-Bay colony and province; we refer to the section concerning Massachusetts-Bay. What happened prior to the Connecticut royal charter, see vol. I. p.

[*n*] Our colonies are of various natures. 1. In some the government and property are in the crown; South-Carolina, North-Carolina excepting the property of the earl of Granville's one eighth share; Virginia, excepting the property of the north neck which belongs to lord Fairfax; New York, New-Hampshire, Nova-Scotia, and Newfoundland. 2. In some, both government and property are in the proprietaries, such as Maryland, and Pensylvania. 3. In some the government and property is in the representatives of the people, e. g. Connecticut and Rhode-Island. 4. In others, the government is in the king, but the property is in the representatives of the people, as in Massachusetts-Bay. 5. Government in the king, and property in a certain body of proprietors, as in the New Jerseys. 6. Georgia may be said not digested.

1893 their fhare in the reducing of Port-Royal, n
Annapolis, 1710, fee vol. I. p. 308 ; their fhare in
fham expedition 1711 (the nation was at that time, a
by management, frequently the dupe of the minift
againft Canada, fee vol. I. p. 312 ; their quota in tl
unaccountably rafh, but by divine providence extraor
nary fuccefsful, expedition againft Louifbourg of Ca
Breton, fee vol. I. p. 350 ; the affair of the projec
but abortive expedition 1746 againft Canada, fee vol
p. 315.

Abftract of the Connecticut CHARTER.

" Connecticut colony was incorporated, April 2
" 1662, by charter of K. Charles II. from the huml
" petition of nineteen gentlemen principal propriet
" in the faid colony, partly by purchafe for valuat
" confiderations, and partly gained by a conqueft; a
" living remote from other Englifh plantations : the
" gentlemen's names are — John Winthrop, Hen
" Clarke, Nathan Gold, Henry Wolcot, John Ogde
" John Clarke, John Mafon, Matthew Allyn, Richa
" Treat, John Talcott, Thomas Welles, Antho.
" Hawkins, Samuel Willis, John Tapping, Richa
" Lord, Daniel Clarke, Obadiah Brown, John Demin
" Matthew Chamfield, with all others who fhall be ma
" free of the company, are incorporated by the name
" THE GOVERNOR AND COMPANY OF THE ENGLISH (
" LONY OF CONNECTICUT IN NEW-ENGLAND IN AM
" RICA, with perpetual fucceffion, to purchafe la
" and chattels, and them to leafe or alien as corporatic
" in England may do, with a common feal; and th
" fhall be elected out of the freemen one governor, (
" deputy governor, and twelve affiftants, viz. the f
" governor John Winthrop, firft deputy governor Jo
" Mafon, the firft twelve affiftants Samuel Willis, M
" thew Allyn, Nathan Gold, Henry Clarke, Rich
" Treat, John Ogden, John Tapping, John Talc
" Thon

" Thomas Welles, Henry Wolcott, Richard Lord, and
" Daniel Clarke ; the governor may at any time call an
" assembly ; to have two annual assemblies, viz. second
" Thursday in October, and second Thursday of May to
" consist of the assistants and deputies, not exceeding
" two from one place, chosen by the freemen of each
" place to be a general assembly, whereof the governor
" and deputy governor, and six of the assistants at least
" to be seven. This general assembly may change the
" times of their meeting and elections ; to admit freemen,
" and constitute such officers as they should think fit ;
" and once every year on the second Thursday of May,
" the governor, deputy governor, assistants, and other
" officers, shall be in the said general court newly chosen
" for the year ensuing, and to take their respective corpo-
" ral oaths for the due performance of their offices before
" two assistants ; the first nominated governor to take
" his oath before a master in chancery. The inhabitants
" to have a power to import inhabitants and goods into
" the colony, paying the usual duties. All our subjects
" inhabitants born there, or at sea, coming to or going
" from thence, to be deemed natural born subjects. The
" general assembly to erect judicatories, and to make
" reasonable laws, not contrary to the laws of England,
" and to settle forms of magistracy and magistrates, and
" to impose lawful fines and other penalties ; and in ge-
" neral, that our said people may be so religiously,
" peaceably, and civily governed ; as that their good life
" and orderly conversation, may win and invite the na-
" tives of the country to the knowledge and obedience of
" the only true God and Saviour of mankind ; this with
" the adventurers free profession, is the only and prin-
" cipal end of this plantation. A power martial to raise
" forces for their own defence, to kill or otherways de-
" stroy by all fitting ways any who attempt the detri-
" ment of the colony, and upon occasion to use law
" martial ; and upon just causes to invade and destroy
" the natives or other enemies of the said colony. Li-

" berty

" berty is referved to all his majefty's fubjeĉts to :
—" to build wharfs and ftages upon wafte lands—
" colony is bounded eaft by the Narraganfet river, c
" monly called Narraganfet-Bay, where the faid r
" falleth into the fea; and on the north by the line of
" Maffachufetts plantation, and on the fouth by the
" and from the faid Narraganfet-Bay on the eaft to
" South-Sea on the weft part. To be holden in free
" common foccage as of our manor of Eaft-Greenw
" paying only the fifth part of all the ore of gold anc
" ver that may be difcovered there.

    " By writ of privy-feal,   HowAF

    Their prefent enaĉting ftile is, " Be it enaĉted by
" governor, council and reprefentatives, in general c
" affembled, and by the authority of the fame."

The prefent counties and towns are

HARTFORD county.	* Berkamftead
Hartford	* Colebrook
Windfor	* Gofhen
Weathersfield	* Norfolk
Middletown	* Cornwall
Farmington	* Canaan
Symfbury	* Kent
Haddam	NEW-HAVEN count
Eaft-Haddam	Milford
Colchefter	Guilford
Hebron	Brentford
Glaffenbury	Wallingford
Bolton	Darby
Willington	Waterbury
* Stafford	New-Milford
Toland	Durham
Litchfield	* Sharon
* Harwinton	* Salifbury
* Hartland	NEW-LONDON cour
* Winchefter	New-London
* New-Hartford	Norwich
* Torrington	Saybrook
	Stonin

Stonington
Killingworth
Lyme
Groton
Prefton

FAIRFIELD county.

Fairfield
Stratford
Norwalk
Stanford
Greenwich
Woodbury
Danbury
New-Town
Ridgefield
* New-Fairfield

WINDHAM county.

Windham
Lebanon
Plainfield
Canterbury
Mansfield
Coventry
Pomfret
* Morthlake
Killingley
Afhford
Volentown
* Union
Being in all about a hundred reprefentatives.

Every townfhip fends two reprefentatives excepting thofe marked * which are new or poor townfhips, pay no colony rates, and confequently fend no reprefentatives to the general affembly or legiflature: Haddam and Eaft Haddam fend only one reprefentative each.

The freemen of each town fhall in September meet to chufe reprefentatives for the general affembly, and twenty perfons in nomination for the next May general election. In April the twelve affiftants to be chofen by the freemen of each town out of the twenty nominated perfons, to be fent fealed up to the general affembly, with the votes for the governor, deputy governor, fecretary and treafurer; as alfo votes for the reprefentatives for the May affembly called proxies, returned by the conftable of each town.

The affiftants and the reprefentatives are paid out of the colony treafury.

Annually two general courts; the firft at Hartford, called the court of election, held on the fecond Thurfday in May, where the freemen fhall elect a governor, deputy governor, twelve affiftants, treafurer and fecretary; the

M 4   fecond

fecond at New-Haven, fecond Thurfday in October : in
the general court fhall fubfift the power of making
laws, granting levies, difpofing of colony lands, erecting of judicatories and officers, granting releafe in criminal or capital cafes, diffolving and proroguing o
themfelves. The governor, deputy governor, or fecretary may call a general court upon emergencies. No
member of the general court during its feffions, to be
arrefted, except for treafon or felony. Every town may
fend one or two deputies. Previous to all other bufinefs
the houfe of reprefentatives or deputies are to chufe a
fpeaker and clerk. They are the only judges concerning
their own election. Every day's abfence, fine ten fhillings, to be paid to the colony treafurer. In an equivote
the governor in the upper houfe, and fpeaker in the
lower houfe, fhall have a cafting vote.

Courts of judicature.

All cafes exceeding the value of forty fhillings fhall
be determined by a jury of twelve men in common
law.

Annually in January at a town meeting there fhall
be chofen jury-men to ferve in the feveral courts, qualification fifty fhillings at leaft freehold, rated in the general lift ; the names of the jury-men fo chofen fhall be
put in a box with a lock, and when any number o
jury-men are fummoned to ferve at any court, the town
conftable fhall at random draw fo many out of the box
as is required from that town ; any juror fo drawn, but
not appearing at the court, penalty ten fhillings, and
deficiencies in juries to be filled *de talibus circumftantibus*
The number of jury-men to be annually chofen in each
town.

In HARTFORD county.			
Hartford	20	Symfbury	1
Wethersfield	20	Glaffenbury	1
Windfor	20	Hebron	1
Farmington	20		—
Middletown	20		13
			NEW

New-Haven county.		Fairfield county.	
New-Haven	20	Fairfield	20
Milford	12	Stratford	20
Wallingford	15	Norwalk	20
Brentford	10	Stanford	12
Guilford	12	Danbury	12
Durham	6	New-Town	12
Darby	6	Ridgefield	6
Waterbury	6	Greenwich	10
	87		112

New-London county.		Windham county.	
New-London	15	Windham	12
Norwich	15	Lebanon	12
Preston	15	Coventry	12
Stonington	15	Plainfield	12
Groton	15	Canterbury	12
Lyme	15	Pomfret	12
Saybrook	15	Volentown	12
Killingworth	15	Ashford	12
	120	Mansfield	12
			108

N. B. I cannot account, why Haddam and East-Haddam, Colchester, Bolton, Willington, Toland, and Litchfield, in the county of Hartford; New-Milford, and Durham, in the county of New-Haven; Woodbury in the county of Fairfield; and Killingley in the county of Windham, which send representatives to the general court or assembly, do not send jurors to the courts below.

All judges and justices are appointed by the general assembly, and commissioned by the governor with the province seal; the governor, deputy governor, and assistants, are justices *ex officio*.

As

As to the courts, where though the case may be
confiderable value, no jury is required: there is

1. The court of probates.

2. Court of vice-admiralty are the fame officers as
New-York.

3. Jufticiary court of admiralty ; fome of the jud
are from New-York,

There fhall be a fuperior court of judicature, am
latory from county to county ; this court to confift
one chief judge and four other judges (whereof thre
quorum) and fhall have cognizance of all pleas of
crown that relate to life, limb, or banifhment; of
vorce; of all pleas, real, perfonal, or mixt; the f
to try by a jury or otherways, proceed to judgm
and award execution.   This court to be held in
county twice annually.   The chief judge, or in his
fence, any three of the judges, may call a fpecial c
upon extraordinary occafions.   Any one judge
open and adjourn the court, and where no judge pref
the fheriff may adjourn the court to next day,
judges to appoint and fwear their own clerk.

An inferior court of judicature to be held in
county twice a year, by a judge with two or more juft
of the quorum commiffioned for that purpofe; to de
mine by a jury or otherways all civil caufes, real,
fonal, or mixt, as alfo all criminal matters, not
tending to life, limb, banifhment, or divorce.   I
power to levy a county tax.

A fpecial county court may be called upon any e:
ordinary occafion, and may adjourn themfelves to
diftant time to appoint and fwear their own clerk:
county treafurer.   Every chief judge or prefiden
moderator in any civil court fhall have a cafting vo

A court of probate confifting of one judge and a
by him to be appointed, to be held in each of the fo
ing diftricts, called the diftrict of Hartford, New-H:
New-London, Fairfield, Windham, Plainfield, Guil
Wood!

Woodbury, Stanford, Eaft-Hadham, Litchfield, Danbury, and Norwich.   In difficult cafes may call in two or three juftices of the quorum.   Any perfon aggrieved may appeal and review to the next fuperior court of the county.

The judges of probates to enquire after all efcheats, and give notice to the colony treafurer, who is to make fale by publick vendue of all efcheats for the benefit of the colony; but if afterward any juft title of an heir appear, it fhall upon reafonable terms be reftored.

Executors after two months probate, neglecting to regifter an inventory of the deceafed's eftate, fhall forfeit five pound per month.   Executors refufing to accept, adminiftration fhall be granted to the next of kin, or principal creditors.   Executors neglecting to prove a will after thirty days, fhall forfeit five pound per month. Adminiftration upon inteftate eftates, to the widow or next of kin, at the difcretion of the judge of probates. The diftribution of inteftate eftates to be, one third of the perfonal eftate to the widow for ever, and her dower of one third of the real eftate for life; the remainder to be equally divided among the children, but the eldeft fon to have a double fhare; and if all daughters, they fhall inherit as copartners; the divifion of the eftate to be by three fufficient freeholders upon oath appointed by the judge of probates.   The portion of any child dying before of age or married, fhall be divided among the furvivors. No reprefentatives to be admitted among collaterals after brothers and fifters children.   Where no legal reprefentatives, the widow fhall be allowed one moiety of the perfonal eftate for ever, and one third of the real eftate for life.   All fales of lands made by adminiftrators fhall be void.

Marriages.   No perfon to be married unlefs publifhed in fome congregation, or publickly pofted up eight days before fuch marriage. No perfon to join people in marriage, befides a juftice in the county or an ordained minifter of the parifh where the parties
dwell.

dwell.   Any juftice or minifter marrying perfons wit
out publication, and certificate of the confent of the p
rents or guardians, penalty twenty pound.   Any man e
deavouring to obtain the affections of a maid, witho
liberty of courtfhip from the parents or guardians, f
the firft offence five pound, &c.——Degrees of kindr
forbidding marriage, are according to the Levitical la
and fuch marriages are declared to be null and void, a
to fit upon the gallows with a rope about their nec
and ftripes not exceeding forty, and to wear the letter
on their arm or back.   If any perfons within the fa
degrees do marry or cohabit, or perfons cohabiting aft
divorce, penalty as adultery ; excepting cafes of al
fence, as the law directs, where the fuperior court m
grant liberty to marry again.

A man found abed with another man's wife, bo
to be whipt not exceeding thirty ftripes.   Men or wc
men wearing contrary apparels, fine not exceeding fi
pound.

The age of confent for marriage is to the man fourtee
æt. to the women twelve æt.   No perfon unmarried fha
keep houfe of himfelf, without confent of the town, p
nalty twenty fhillings per week.   Contracts of perfon
under parents, guardians, or mafters, are not valid
The felect men and overfeers of the poor, with the affen
of the next juftices, may bind out poor idle childrer
boys to twenty-one æt. girls to eighteen æt.

The dower for widows where no jointure was mad
before marriage, is one third of the perfonal eftate with
out limitation, and one third of the income of the re
eftate for life, but to keep it in good repair.

All perfons of right underftanding æt. twenty-one (
upwards, though excommunicated; by deed or will
feventeen æt. and upwards, may difpofe of perfon
eftate.   The age for chufing of guardians fhall be fou
teen æt. for males, and twelve æt. for females.

Where parents or mafters neglect children under the
care, the felect-men may bind them out, boys to twent
one æt. girls to eighteen æt.   Idiot

Idiots, impotent and diſtracted, ſhall be under the direction of the county courts, to be provided for by the following degrees of kindred; father or mother, grand-father or grand-mother, children or grand-children, if able.   The eſtates of ſuch (if any) by a proper order may be ſold for their maintenance.   Where no ſufficient relations or eſtate does appear, they ſhall be ſupported at the charge of the town where they live. The ſelect-men are to appoint them guardians.

Idle perſons and drunkards, by warrant to be brought before a juſtice; the goods of ſuch perſons ſhall be under the management of the ſelect-men, who may ſell all or part (not real, without an order of the general aſſembly) of their eſtates, and on deficiency, diſpoſe of their perſon to ſervice for a certain time, to pay their juſt debts. May appeal from the ſelect-men to the county court.   All ſuch perſons are diſabled from making of contracts.

In this colony is no particular court of chancery; in ſome caſes the general court act as a court of chancery or equity.

Juſticiary courts of oyer and terminer, called aſſizes and general goal delivery, is the ſame with the ſuperior court.

The court of vice-admiralty, the ſame judge and other officers of that court, which ſerve for the province of New-York, ſerve alſo for the colony of Connecticut.

The juſticiary court of admiralty for trial of crimes committed at ſea conſiſts of judges, ſome from the colony of Connecticut, and ſome from the province of New-York, purſuant to the inſtructions from home.

A juſtice may determine in any caſe not exceeding forty ſhillings, if land is not concerned; if the judges find that the jury have not attended to the evidence, they may cauſe them to return to a ſecond and third conſideration, but no more. The judges to determine in caſes of law, where the jury brings in a non liquet or

i   ſpecial

fpecial verdict, viv. " If the law be fo in fuch a poir
" then we find for the plaintiff, but if the law be othe
" ways, then we find for the defendant." May appe
from a juftice to the county court, and from then
may review to the next county court, or appeal to tl
next fuperior court ; from the review to the feco
county court, may appeal to the next fuperior cou
but without any review in the fuperior court ; but
from the firft county court he appeal to the fuperi
court, he is admitted to review in the next fuperi
court. In a debt upon bond, bill, or note, for a val
not exceeding forty fhillings, no appeal to be allowe
and if not exceeding ten pound, no appeal is allow
from a county court.

No appeals are allowed to the king in council. Sor
have gone home by way of complaint at a confiderab
charge, but no relief, excepting the cafe of Jol
Winthrop, Efq. who procured a declaration of tl
king in council, " That their law concerning dividi
" land inheritance of an inteftate was contrary to the la
" of England, and void :" but in fubfequent cafes tl
colony have no regard to the declaration.

The general affembly hear writs of error againft pr
ceedings of the fuperior court ; and in fome inftances a
as a court of chancery.

Where any other court exceeds their jurifdictic
the judges of the fuperior court may grant a pi
hibition with the fame power, as the king's bench
England.

Sheriffs to be appointed by the governor and cour
called affiftants, giving fecurity ; in cafe of riots or gr
oppofitions in his office, may raife the militia of
county, and to be under his command.

Each county appoints one king's attorney.

In cafes of account, the court may appoint three
ditors.

In cafes of abatement of a writ, the plaintiff upon
paying to the defendant his cofts to that time, may am

the defect and proceed. No writ shall abate for a circumstantial miftake.

In all actions before a justice; fix days warning is required; before a county or superior court, twelve days.

Any defendant upon default, paying down to the adverfe party cofts, may be admitted to the tryal.

All titles of lands to be tried in the county where the land lies.

No perfon to be kept in prifon, where fufficient eftate does appear; where no eftate appears, the debtor fhall fatisfy the debt by fervice.

Fees. For attending the general court, per diem, to an affiftant fix fhillings, to a reprefentative four fhillings and four pence, per mile, travelling out; chief juftice of the fuperior court twelve fhillings; affiftant judges nine fhillings; county courts chief judge feven fhillings; juftices of the quorum five fhillings; licence to a tavern keeper three fhillings; acknowledging any inftrument fixpence; to the fecretary for the colony feal one fhilling; to the general affembly for every petition one pound; attornies fees, fuperior court eight fhillings; inferior or county court four fhillings; goalers fees, commitment and difcharge two fhillings; for dieting each prifoner per week two fhillings; to a county furveyor of lands and for his houfe, befides expences, four fhillings per diem. *N. B.* Thefe fees feem to be in the bills of the emiffion equal to three and half old ten. of New-England common currency.

Publick houfes of entertainment for each town to be nominated in January annually by the magiftrates, felectmen, conftables, and grand jury-men, be approved of by the next county court, and licenfed by them: the houfe-keeper not to fuffer fons not of age, or fervants, to fit tipling, fine fix fhillings; ftrangers and foreigners excepted: none to keep company in publick houfes evening next following the Lord's day, or days of faft; any perfon found in a tavern (fome exceptions) the night before and the night after the Lord's day, or after nine
o'clock

o'clock in any other night, fine three shillings; b)
special warrant, houses may be broke open in search
after persons in taverns; inhabitants not to sit in a
vern drinking above one hour at a time, excepting up
extraordinary occasions, fine six shillings; tavern hunt
to be posted up at the tavern doors with a prohibit
of entertaining them upon penalty of three pound;
tavern-keeper to bring an action for drink, sold after (
days; none but licensed houses to sell strong liquor
quantities exceeding one quart of wine or spirits, or (
gallon of any other liquor, fine three pound first offer
six pound second offence, and so doubled every offen
if not able to pay, to be whipt not less than ten, and
exceeding fifteen stripes every offence.

In Connecticut (and all over New-England every (
stituted township is a CORPORATION;) the qualificat
for a voter or freeman is twenty one æt. and upwa:
with a freehold rated in the common list at fifty shillir
or personal estate rated at forty pound besides his po:
person. Township meetings or assemblies may m
prudential laws or orders, penalty of transgression
to exceed twenty shillings. Township officers to
chosen annually in December, viz. select-men not exce
ing seven, listers (assessors) not exceeding nine, &c.
elections to be by a major part of 'the qualified vo:
Town clerks to register marriages, births, and burial
No person to be admitted an inhabitant of a town,
by consent of the select-men; no stranger to reside
ceeding—days without liberty from the select-men,
the entertainer finable. A stranger continuing after b(
warned out, fine ten shillings per week, or whipt
exceeding ten stripes. One year's residence qualif
person for an inhabitant. A stranger entertained al
four days, the entertainer shall be at the charge if t
sick. Vagrants to be ordered from constable to cons
back to the place they came from; if they return,
be toties quoties whipt not exceeding ten stripes.

Annt

Annually on the firſt Monday of March the proprietor-ſhips not conſtituted into townſhips, are to meet and chuſe a moderator, clerk, treaſurer, and a committée to ma-nage affairs in the intervals of their general meetings. By a major vote computed by intereſt, they are to be choſen, and may levy taxes as may be needed. Suffi-cient partition fences to be five feet, if rails or wooden fences; ſtone fence four feet high; or hedges, brooks, ditches, creeks, rivers, in the judgement of the fence-viewers, equivalent thereto. No perſon to feed his cat-tle in his neighbour's land, as if common field, without leave, from 10th April, to 10th October.

Taxes conſiſt in the articles of rates, impoſt, and ex-ciſe.

Rates comprehend the poll-tax. Every perſon an-nually, at or before September 10, to give in a liſt of his polls and rateable eſtate: thoſe liſts to be returned to the general court in October: perſons to be four-folded who leave out part of the eſtate, or who give in no eſtate; the liſters may relieve people overcharged, may appeal to a juſtice, and to the ſelect-men of the town.——Every male perſon from ſixteen to ſeventy æt. to be ſet in the liſt at 18 l. (governor, deputy governor, aſſiſtants, mi-niſters of the goſpel, preſident and tutors of the colle-giate ſchool, ſtudents there, ſchool-maſters, and infirm perſons are excuſed) every ox at 4 l; each ſteer, cow, or heifer of three years and upwards at 3 l; ſteer or heifer of two years at 40 s; each ſteer or heifer of one year 20 s. Each horſe or mare of three years old and upwards at 3 l. of two years old 40 s. of one year old 20 s. Every ſwine one year old and upwards 20 s. Each dwelling-houſe with adjoining land 20 s. per acre; plow and mow-ing land in ſome countries 15 s. in others 10 s. in others, 7 s. 6 d. per acre; boggy mowing meadow land 5 s. per acre; all upland paſture or mowing 8 s. per acre. Pe-culiars to be aſſeſſed by the neareſt town. Veſſels at 15 s. per tun. The preſident of Yale college, and all mini-

sters of the gospel, their estates in the towns where th
live are exempted.   All allowed attornies at law, so
their faculty ; and others higher in proportion to the
business.   All traders, &c. to be rated for their faculti
at the discretion of the listers.

RATES.   In our American colonies, in affessing
rates, real estate is generally valued at seven years in
come, which is favourable.   In Great-Britain, lands ai
sold at twenty or thirty years purchase.

In Connecticut 1 d. rate, produces from 4000 l. t
5000 l. currency.

IMPOST.   There is a high duty upon the exportatio
of all timber and lumber to the neighbouring govern
ments of Maffachusetts, New-York, Rhode-Island, an
New-Hampshire; this is designed in lieu of a prohib
tion, that after some years the colony may not be dest
tute of those materials.   The impost upon rum is p
gallon 1 d. if imported directly from the West-Indies c
sugar islands, and 2 d. from all other parts; a drawbac
is allowed upon its exportation.

All foreign trading veffels not owned in the colony a
clearing, to pay ——— powder money to the nav
officer.

The governor with advice of the council, upon oc
casion, by proclamation may for a time prohibit th
exportation of grain and other provisions ; delinquent
forfeit these goods by an order obtained from a speci
county court.

EXCISE 3 d. per gallon on all wine and diftilled li
quors ; this is applied to defray county charges.   Th
county courts to appoint receivers of the excise, fees 2 s
in the pound.   Receivers may agree with the public
houses by the year.

The act regulating maritime affairs extending fron
p. 147, to p. 152, in twenty-seven sections in their la
book; does not contain any thing peculiar.

B

By the act for forming and regulating the militia, the governor to be captain general, the deputy governor, lieutenant general: the military companies of the several townships to be formed into thirteen regiments of foot, and to each regiment of foot, one troop of horse of sixty-four men, officers included. These field officers of each regiment, colonel, lieutenant colonel, and major, to be appointed by the general assembly, and commissioned by the governor. Once in four years to be called together for regimental exercise. All male persons from sixteen to fifty æt. to attend military musters, excepting Indians and negroes, secretary, justices, church officers, members of the collegiate school, allowed physicians and surgeons, representatives, school-masters, attornies at law, a miller to each grist mill, ferry men, constant herds-men, constant mariners, sheriffs, constables, and impotent persons. All militia listed soldiers to be provided, besides their accoutrements, with on epound of good powder, four pound of bullets, and twelve flints. In each company of sixty-four soldiers, besides officers, there shall be a capt. a lieut. and four serjeants; where thirty-two soldiers, there shall be a lieut. ensign, and two serjeants; where but twenty-four soldiers, there shall be two serjeants. The companies to be trained four times a year, every soldier for not appearing to pay three shillings.

The arms and ammunition of all persons in the government to be viewed on the first Monday of May annually. Each trooping horse freed from rates and impresses. Disorders on training days, may be punished by laying neck and heel, riding the wooden horse, or fifteen shillings. The fines to be applied for colours, drummers, halberts, banners, trumpets, trumpeters, and other charges of the company. The colony to provide a magazine of powder and shot, and the select men of each town to provide military stores for their towns.

The select men may appoint watches and wards in their several towns.

Any

Any perfons may form themfelves into artillery com
panies fo called, for promoting military exercifes.

Deferter from the king's fervice, fea or land, fir
twenty pounds, and half a year's imprifonment.

The training militia of this colony, may confift (
about 15,000 men. 1740, at a great ftruggle in th
election of a governor, there were about 4000 freeme
voters. [o]

No impreffes of perfons or cattle, but by warran
with a reafonable allowance for fervice, and for damag
if any happen.

[o] In the houfe of reprefentatives of Maffachufetts-Bay, in th
journal, June 3. 1748, they declare that Connecticut is two thirds
big (meaning in perfons and eftates, but not in extent of territor
Plymouth, and province of Maine included) as the province of Maf
chufetts-Bay. With fubmiffion, I find Connecticut not half fo big
numbers and eftates as Maffachufetts-Bay. At times by the prud
adminiftration of the jurifdiction of Connecticut colony, their tax
were only from 4000 l. to 5000 l. currency per ann. whereas the po
and rates of the Maffachufetts-Bay, were at the fame time per a
about 400,000 currency.

1742, By the valuation on Maffachufetts-Bay, were 41,000 wh
males taxable for polls; allowing for concealments they may be ef
mated at 50,000 fencibles; which multiplied by four according
Dr. Halley's rules, makes 200,000 men, women, and children; a
in Connecticut about 100,000 people. In general, the neareft ef
gate that can be made of the people in New-England, is

Maffachufetts-Bay	200,000
Connecticut	100,000
Rhode-Ifland	30,000
New-Hampfhire	24,000

354,000

One fourth part of thefe are 90,000 fencible men, one fifth is 70,0
fencible marching men, fufficient to fwallow up the French of Ca
da, and Cape-Breton iflands at a few meals or encounters

In political balances, the number of inhabitants is a grand arti
In Great-Britain and Ireland are about ten millions of people, in Fra
about double that number, in Spain about five millions, according
the duke de Riperda's eftimate, in the feveral United provinces cal
Holland, about three millions; but the produce of trade called r
ney, fometimes implies the inferiority of fencible men; thus the
neral balance of trade being in favour of Holland, it becomes
center of exchange for all Europe.

Their produce, manufacture, trade and navigation.

Connecticut ufes fcarce any foreign trade; lately they fend fome fmall craft to the Weft-India iflands; they vent their produce in the neighbouring continent colonies, viz. wheat, Indian corn, beaver, pork, butter, horfes, and flax. For fome years they have been endeavouring to raife hemp and flax; flax may fucceed, but hemp feems to require a ftronger foil and warmer climate; it thrives better farther fouth, as in Penfylvania; that from the northen parts, does not drefs fo kindly, nor whiten fo well. The Ruffia hemp exported from the northern parts of Archangel, Narva, Revel, and Riga, is brought down from the fouthern parts of Ruffia.

Wool, hemp, flax, and iron, are the general materials of all our manufactures. The raifing and manufacturing of hemp, flax, or any other herba into cordage, canvas, and other linen, is a general and great advantage without any detriment to our mother country; it may be fome difadvantage to our traders to Ruffia, Germany, and Holland; but private lucration ought to give way to a publick good. The linen bufinefs employs variety of people, pulling the flax, watering of it, breaking, fwingling, hackling, fpinning, weaving, &c.

Some years fince, the government of Connecticut eftablifhed a corporation for commerce, called the New-London fociety; but in the fraudulent humour of thefe times, contrary to the defign of their inftitution, they foon began to manufacture printed fociety notes to be impofed as a currency: the government in their wonted prudence declared it a nufance; thefe bills were forbid a currency, and called in at the charge of the fociety.

In all countries, the inhabitants may be reduced to three claffes, 1. Villenage or coatters. 2. Yeomanry or farmers who improve their own freeholds; and 3. Gentry who live by the rents of their eftates farmed to others; the fecond fort is generally our cafe.

Irifh

Irifh potatoes or folanum efculentum tuberofum C.B.]
is much planted in New England, thrives well, and is
good ufe; varieties here, are the rough coat, red coat, fl
white, and long white: my tafte prefers the rough coa

[*p*] There is copper ore in Simfbury hills, about a de
zen miles weft of Connecticut river; it has been wrough
but did not turn to account; at prefent it lies dormant.

For their wheat and Indian corn; fee elfewhere, a
alfo for their merchantable falt pork.

Ship building and ftaves are their chief lumber expor

[*p*] I learned from Mr. Baden, as was hinted before, an ingeniou
miner and effay fent from London a few years fince by a company of
gentlemen, to explore New-England for metallick ores and minerals
he found. 1. Bog and rock iron ore plenty, but not profitabl
2 Some lead ore, but fo intermixed with rock and fpar, as not t
turn to any account. 1. In Simfbury near Connecticut river, ther
were three different companies wrought for copper ore; Mr. Belche
and Cafwell, they alfo erected a fmelting houfe in Bofton; thof
turned to no account, and the affair dropt. 2. Some affociated mei
chants of Bofton, got a leafe of fome adjacent copper mine lands
they carried it on with vigour, and fent quantities of their ore to Eng
land; the company found the fcheme turn to no advantage, and de
fifted. 3. A company of bites, rented fome adjoining lands; the
pretended to find fome fhoades, a good fymptom for veins; they pu
fome of thefe pretended rich fhoades aboard of a fmall floop; thi
floop perhaps by contrivance funk in Connecticut river; the owner
did not find it advifeable to weigh the ore, left the fallacy of th
fhoades might be difcovered. Schaylers rich copper mines in the Jei
feys, are not much wrought; the owners keep them depofited as of
gold. There are fome fymptoms of copper ore in Attleborough, bi
not explored. In Attleborough, there is a magnetick iron ore;
yields a red fhot iron, not good, (fee vol. I. p. 540.) In Attle
borough Gore is fome copper ore, but fo intermixed with the iron roc
ore, as to render both unprofitable.

Mr. Baden found fome allum flate or ftone; but no vitriol ftone
pyrites, fuch as is found on both fides of the river Thames in Englan
along the Kentifh and Effex fhores; no falt fprings; we have ruddl
which ferves to. mark fheep, and may ferve as a ground colour f
priming, as Spanifh brown, and black lead in Brimfield; thefe aren
metallick ores, but boles or terras; of ochres, there are none of a
value; fome yellow ochre.

In New-England, they do not forge bar iron fufficient for the
home comfumption, by bloomeries and refineries; they import fro
England, New-York, the Jerfeys, Penfylvania, and Maryland.

[*p*] Wo

[q] Wool not fufficient for the houfe confumption of the colony.

A very confiderable produce in the colony of Connecticut is a feminary of learning, or fchola illuftris, called a collegiate college, and when profeffors in feveral fciences are endowed, it will be called an univerfity; this plant is vigorous and thriving, under the cultivation of the prefent prefident, the worthy reverend Mr. Clap.

Some account of Connecticut college, called Yale college in New-Haven.

Anno 1636, the general affembly of Maffachufetts-Bay (fee vol. I. p. 543.) granted fome money towards erecting a college or collegiate fchool in Cambridge near Bofton; the people of Connecticut contributed fome fmall matter, and after fome years, becaufe of the diftance and charge, their minifters, and fome in civil authority prefented, 1701, a memorial to the general affembly, defiring that a collegiate fchool might be erected and endowed, and propofed ten minifters of forty æt. and upwards, as truftees for ordering the fame; furvivors to fupply vacancies, feven to be a quorum: accordingly a charter [r] for this purpofe was granted October 1701, to appoint officers, make laws, but not repugnant to the laws of the civil government; to give degrees, poffefs lands not exceeding the yearly value of 500 l. and other eftates, and to receive yearly out of the publick treafury, 100 l. currency [s]; Saybrook was refolved upon as a proper place, and the truftees chofe Mr.

[q] England is always jealous of our exporting fheers wool to foreign markets, but it may be depended upon, that our New-England wool is not fufficient for home confumption, and we import many woullens from Great-Britain. Some years fince, but not at prefent, fome was fhipped from Nantucket to France; very fmall quantities.

[r] This charter was drawn up by Mr. fecretary Addington of Maffachufetts-Bay.

[s] Equal at that time to about 70 l. fterl.

Pierfon

Pierfon minifter of Killingworth for rector; [t] and ur
til a place could be fitted up in Seabrook, the fchola
were to meet at the rector's houfe in Killingworth, whe
they continued till the rector's death, 1707. Mr. Hen
mingway, fince minifter of Eafthaven, was the fir
fcholar, and folus about half a year. Several of th
truftees gave books out of their own libraries to begin
library for the college; Mr. Lynde of Saybrook, gave
houfe and land; major James Fitch of Norwich, ga'
land in Killingley, which were afterwards, 1730, coi
verted into 628 acres in Salifbury. There was a gener
contribution throughout the colony.

Upon rector Pierfon's death, Mr. Andrews of Milfo
was chofen pro tempore, until they could procure a re
dent rector, and the fenior clafs was removed to Milfo
the bthers to Saybrook, under the care of two tutor
they boarded at private houfes, and went to fchool
their tutors chambers under the infpection of Mr. Buc
ingham of Seabrook, one of the truftees, and continu
in this ftate about feven years. In this fpace of time, fu
dry donations of valuable books were made to the librar
particularly by Sir John Davie of Groton, upon his rec
very of the family honours and eftate in England. Th
greateft donation of books, was from the generofity ai
procurement of Jeremiah Dummer, Efq. agent in Lo
don, ann. 1714, he fent over above 800 volumes of v
luable books, whereof about 120 volumes at his ov
coft, and the reft by procurements from Sir Ifaac Ne
ton, Sir Richard Blackmore, Sir Richard Steel, I
Burnet, Dr. Woodward, Dr. Halley, Dr. Bentley, I
Kennet, Dr. Calamy, Dr. Edwards, Mr. Henry, N
Whifton, &c. Governor Yale of the Eaft-India co
pany, fent 300 volumes, but a great part of this
luable library was loft in a tumult upon the removal
the library from Seabrook.

[t] The rector, and ten truftees conftituted the coporation.

There were divisions concerning a fixed situation for the college, and in the mean while, 1718, it was agreed that the students might go where they saw cause to be instructed : the greater part went to Wethersfield, under the instruction of Mr. Elisha Williams, afterwards rector ; some remained at Seabrook, under the tuition of Mr. Hart, and Mr. Russel.

1716, The majority of the trustees voted a convenient college, and rector's house to be erected in New-Haven, which was effected accordingly, but with much opposition and confusion from the northern and eastern parts of the colony ; [*u*] the trustees notwithstanding held their first commencement at New-Haven in September 1717.

The foresaid Elihu Yale, Esq. an East-India merchant, from his correspondence with Mr. Saltonstal governor of Connecticut, bestowed in the whole, 100 l. sterl. in three hundred volumes of books, and about 400 l. sterl. in effects, and by will designed 500 l. sterl. more, but this was never accomplished ; 1718, Mr. Dummer sent more books value 30 l. and Jahaleal Brenton, Esq. of Newport, Rhode-Island, gave 50 l. sterl. The college building was raised October 3, 1717, 170 feet long, 21 feet wide, and three stories high ; cost about 1030 l. sterl. contained above fifty studies, besides the hall, library, and kitchen. September 12, 1718, there was a splendid commencement, and the trustees gave it the name of Yale college, and sent a letter of thanks to Mr. Yale for his generosity to the colony, and letters of thanks to Mr. Drummer, and general Nicholson, for their donations of books. In December following, upon removing of the books from Saybrook, there happened a tumult ; about 250 of the most valuable books, and sundry papers of

[*u*] The affair was referred to the general assembly 1717 ; the upper and lower house differed, and the reference dropt. N. B. last year there were scholars residing at New-Haven thirteen ; at Wethersfield fourteen ; at Saybrook, only four.

impor-

importance, were conveyed away by unknown hand and never could be recoved.

1719, The truftees chofe Mr. Cutler, minifter of Stratford, to be a refident rector, and for his accommo dation, a rector's houfe was built 1722 ; coft by fubfcrip tion, 35 l. by impoft upon rum, 115 l. and fome pa out of Mr. Yale's donations by fale of lands 120 l. an by a general contribution 55 l.

1722, At the commencement he declared himfelf to t of the church of England, and defigned for epifcopal o ders, which by going to England, he obtained with a D I At prefent he is a miffionary in Bofton. The college con tinued without a refident rector four years ; the forefai Mr. Andrews performed this office at their commenc ments.

1723, The general affembly gave to the college a additional explanatory charter, [x] viz. that a trufte might refign at pleafure, that feven truftees fhould be quorum, and to act by a majority ; that a minifter of 3 æt. might be chofen a truftee, and that the rector fhoul be a truftee ex officio.

Mr. Daniel Turner of London, fent them a collectio of valuable books, 28 volumes in phyfick and furgery the college conferred upon him a diploma of M. D.

1725, September 29, the truftees chofe Mr. Elift Williams, minifter of Newington parifh in Wethersfie as rector, and upon giving his confent to the confeffion faith and rules of church difcipline agreed upon by tl churches of the colony of Connecticut, he was inftalle rector by the truftees ; he reformed the college ve much, and advanced ufeful and polite literature.

In October, 1732, the general affembly granted the college 1500 acres of land, being 300 acres in each

---

(x) It is faid to be drawn up by governor Saltonftal.

At the firft founding of this college, it was ordered, that where fpecial provifion was made by the truftees, the laws of Hartford c lege, in the province of Maffachufetts Bay fhould be their rule.

the new towns of Norfolk, Canaan, Goshen, Cornwal, and Kent : which after some years may be valuable.

1732, The rev. Dr. George Berkley dean of Derry, (late) bishop of Cloyne in Ireland, came over to found an episcopal college in the continent of North-America, or the British West-India islands ; he resided some time at Newport of Rhode-Island, and purchased a country seat with about ninety-six acres of land.   For certain reasons, he gave over his design of erecting an episcopal college, and returned to England. Although there was something peculiar in his manner, he was a gentleman of general learning, and of a generous disposition to propagate the same among mankind ; he was a good judge of the world, and of all our colonies and seminaries of learning; (the episcopal college of Williamsburg in Virginia not excepted,) he gave the preference to the college of Connecticut, a laudable colony; he gave his farm in Rhode-Island to this college, the income to be premiums from time to time, for the best Greek and Latin scholars in the judgment of the president and senior episcopal missionary of the colony; this has been some incitement to excel in the classicks. He gave them a fine collection of books of near 1000 volumes, whereof 260 were folio's, 400 l. sterl. value.   These donations were made partly out of the dean's own estate, but principally out of the monies put into his hands for founding the episcopal college.

Rector Williams, by reason of indispositions, October 31, 1739, resigned, returned to his own estate in Wethersfield, and was employed in a civil and military capacity. The reverend, learned, worthy, and mathematically ingenious Mr. Thomas Clap, minister of Windham, succeeded ; and in April 1740, gave his assent to the Seabrook articles 1708, of faith and discipline ; he had been fourteen years minister of Windham, he was installed rector : his first essay was to form a new body of laws, and to place the books of the library in a proper distinct order, to be with facility to come at ; this catalogue is printed.

1742,

1742, The general affembly augmented the annu
grant to the college, whereby they were enabled to fu
port three tutors and a rector, (formerly one tutor carri
on two claffes) The prefident requires confiderable enco
ragement, as he is obliged to perform the office of pre
dent, profeffor of divinity, profeffor of mathematick
and of a tutor in ordinary.

1744, Anthony Nougier of Fairfield, by will left
the college 27 l. fterl. to be put to intereft.

The affembly was petitioned by the truftees, for
new and more perfect charter, whereby the college w
to be incorporated by the name of the prefident ai
fellows (not truftees) of Yale college in New-Have
This was approved of by the name of an act for t
more full and compleat eftablifhment of Yale colleg
&c. dated May 9, 1745. It is ordained, 1. That [
Thomas Clap, Samuel Whitman, Jared Eliot, Ebenez
Williams, Jonathan Marfh, Samuel Cooke, Samu
Whitlefey, Jofeph Noyes, Anthony Stoddard, Benjam
Lord, and Daniel Wadfworth, are a body corporate ai
politick by the name of the prefident and fellows of Ya
college in New-Haven, with fucceffion. 2. All form
donations to this collegiate fchool, though in various e:
preffions, are confirmed and vefted in the faid prefide
and fellows, with fucceffion. 3. That the forefaid pre:
dent and fellows fhall continue during life, or until th
refign, or are difplaced. 4. There fhall be a genei
meeting of the prefident and fellows annually on the fecoi
Wednefday of September ; the major vote of the mer
bers prefent fhall be definitive ; in cafe of an equivo
the prefident fhall have a cafting vote. 5. The prefide
and fellows, fix at leaft, concurring, may remove a

---

[y] This is an ingenious gentleman, mathematically learned ;
this time, 1750, contriving fome compendiums and other impro
ments in aftronomical calculations. Many of the ftudents (ftudent
college about eighty) are expert in aftronomical calculations, from
folid good tuition and inftruction of the worthy Mr. Clap, a credit
the colony.

appoint in their room, a prefident and fellows, a clerk, a treafurer, tutors, profeffors, fteward, and other neceffary fervants.   6. That the prefident, fellows, tutors, profeffors, and all other officers, before they enter upon the execution of their office, fhall publickly take the oaths, and fubfcribe the declaration appointed, 1 Georgii I. 7. The corporation may appoint from time to time regulations not repugnant to the laws of England or of the colony, but may be difallowed by the general affembly. 8. The corporation may confer degrees as in other colleges. 9. All eftates belonging to the college, (if real, not exceeding the value of 500 l. fterl. per ann.) all members and refident officers of the college, tutors and ftudents, are exempted from rates, military fervice, working upon the high ways, &c. 10. A grant of 100 l. proclamation money annually during the pleafure of the affembly.

1745, Philip Livingfton, Efq. of the king's council of New-York, as he had four fons educated in this college, gave 200 l. currency, to begin a foundation for a profeffor of divinity, to be called the Livingftonian profeffor of divinity.

1746, Mr. Samuel Lambert of New-London, merchant or dealer, left fome lands to the college, but from fome intricacies in his affairs, they turned to no great account, excepting about 100 acres in Wallingford, and fixty-two acres in New-Haven.

There were a great many fmaller donations from time to time, which in a fummary are not to be enumerated, and for the fame reafons I am obliged to omit the lifts, from the foundation to this time, of the fucceffive rectors or prefidents, truftees, treafurers and tutors.

1748, Upon a motion of the prefident, the general affembly ordered a new college to be built at a publick colony charge, 100 feet long, and forty feet wide, eight rooms on a floor, three ftories high, befides garrets and cellars.

The

The regulations as to the degrees of batchelors an
masters, are the same as in Hartford college of the pr
vince of Massachusetts-Bay, see vol. II. p. 546.

This college at New-Haven thrives much ; in Se;
1749, there commenced eleven masters, and twenty-thr
batchelors ; at Cambridge in Massachusetts-Bay, Ju
1749, there commenced only nine masters, and twent
two batchelors, though a college of much longer stan
ing, and in a large goverment : at that time it was o
served by many, that every thing in the province
Massachusetts-Bay was upon the decline, attributed
the late bad civil administration.

Mountains and Rivers.

Connecticut is generally broken land, that is, hills an
dales, but well watered.   Simsbury, or the copper mir
hills, are their highest lands, but not fertile, as it is sa
of all metallick ore hills.

The noted rivers and runs of water in Connectic
are, 1. Those which fall into Thames river or Nev
London long creek. 2. Connecticut river with its branche
3. Housatonick river with its branches, which, at Stra
ford, falls into Long-Island sound. Paukatuke river whic
divides Rhode-Island colony, from Connecticut colon
and Byram river which divides Connecticut colony fro
the province of New-York, are of no consideration.
Upon the Long-Island sound is a range of townships.

1. Thames river is a long navigable creek of abo
fourteen miles, the head of it is in Norwich ; this is th
barcadier for the easterly parts of Connecticut, and
time may be the principal trading place of the colon;
at present the township of Norwich pays the highest t
of any township in the colony, and consists of five
six parishes.   From Connecticut river to the easte
boundary of the colony, is an extraordinary well water
countı

country, confifting of two principal rivers and their branches, which fall into the bottom of this creek in Norwich; thefe two rivers are Satucket and higher Wilemantick, and Quenebaug. Quenebaug rifes in Brimfield, paffes through Stourbridge, and Dudley in the province of Maffachufetts-Bay, thence in the colony of Connecticut, it divides Pomfret from Killingley, Canterbury from Plainfield, and in Norwich falls into Sakatuke river which difcharges into Thames river or creek. This river from Brimfield of Maffachufetts-Bay, in its courfe in Thompfon parifh of Killingley of Connecticut, receives French river from Leicefter and Oxford, and further in Killingley receives Five Mile river, whereof Honeycomb Brook comes from Douglafs, and Muddy Brook from Woodftock, next Nathomy brook from Pomfret, Moufafhop river from Valington, Rowland's brook in Canterbury, and many other runs of water too minute to be mentioned : Quenebaug river falls into Satucket river a few miles before it difcharges into the creek. Satucket river where it originates in Brimfield, is called Willemantick river, and in Stafford of Connecticut receives feveral fmall runs of water ; it divides Toland from Willington, and Coventry from Mansfield ; in Windham (where it is called Windham river) it receives in its weftern fide Scagungamog river and Hope river; on its weftern fide, it receives Manchoag river which had received Fenton river, and higher had received in Afhford Bigelow river, Still river and Bungea river from Union and Woodftock ; in Norwich, it received Quenebaug river, as above.

2. Connecticut river with its branches and townfhips upon the river, its branches are enumerated, vol. I. p. 459, &c. in the fection of Maffachufetts-Bay.

3. Houfatonick, Weftenhock, or Stratford river, fee vol. I. p. 456.

4. Upon the Long-Ifland found, is a delightful and profitable range of good townfhips, the glory of all our
American

American plantations, Stonington, Groton, New-L
ñon, Lyme, Saybrook, Killingſworth, Guilford, Bro
ford, New-Haven, Milford, Stratford, Fairfield, N
walk, Stamford, and Greenwich.

As the governors are annually elective, that is, v
variable, I ſhall not mention ſuch temporary matte
only obſerve, that the Winthrop family has for m:
years been the moſt noted in New-England: Mr. W
throp was the firſt reſident governor of Maſſachuſetts-B
his ſon John Winthrop, Eſq. procured the preſent ch
ter of Connecticut colony, and was their charter or I
governor, and afterwards their elective governor for m:
years paſt; this man's ſon John was ſucceſſively gover
for many years; he died æt. 69, November 27, 17
was born in Ipſwich of New-England, 1638; Gur
Saltonſtal, a worthy man, a congregationaliſt preach
was elected in his room, and was with good content t
ceſſive governor, elected for many years till death; Oc
ber 1724, was ſucceded by Joſeph Talcot, Eſq. &c.

Currencies, I refer to the Appendix; at preſent o
obſerve, that the 28,000 l. ſterl. reimburſement,
rates of ſeven pence per annum, will cancel all their
per currency, in two or three years [z].

[z] In New-England, we are ſtill in confuſion as to our paper cu
cies; governor Sh---y's precipitate ſcheme of 1749, has had a
effect, nothing could be raſher excepting the Cape-Breton expedi
where the chance againſt us was vaſtly great, but beyond all ht
probability ſucceſsful; the unexpected intervention of ſome B
men of war under the direction of Mr. Warren, alleviates the t
unloatneſs of the affair; it peculated and depopulated New-Eng
occaſioned near one million ſterling additional national debt tc
kingdom of Great-Britain, and finally was reſtored to the Frencl
better ſtate than ſtatu quo. Perhaps the Ch---ﬅo ſettlement in N
Scotia as a barrier againſt the Canada and Cape-Breton French
their Indians, at preſent carried on with much vigour, may turn t
ſame bad account as G-- gia (which GOD forbid) ſaid to be a b
againſt our ſouthern enemies the Spaniards, and their Indians.
ſteries of ſtate I do not pretend to explore or explain; quæ ſupr:
non ad nos; the ſoil adjacent to Ch---ﬅo is ſo irrecoverably bad, i
never be a PLANTATION; it may anſwer as a good fiſhing villag
may, as a place of arms, be ſupported at a great charge: I do n

I

I fhall here infert abftracts of fome of their laws exemplary, natural, plain, and concife, adapted to plantations.

In the late authoritative revifal (1750) of their municipal laws; the introductory law or act, is, in the manner of a magna charta, fecuring the general privileges of his majefty's fubjects in the colony, in thefe words, " Be it enacted, &c. that no man's life fhall be taken away; no man's honour or good name fhall be ftained ; no man's perfon fhall be arrefted, reftrained, banifhed, difmembered, or otherwife punifhed ; no man fhall be deprived of his wife and children; no man's goods or eftate fhall be taken away from him, nor any ways indamaged under the colour of law, or countenance of authority; unlefs it be by virtue or equity of fome exprefs law of the colony warranting the fame, eftablifhed by the general court, and fuffi-

this was a political amufement, to divert people (by giving them fomething to play with in their imaginations) from canvaffing the furrender of Cape-Breton without any equivalent to the Britifh nation, not fo much as an explicit confirmation of the ceffion of Nova-Scotia, or L'Acadie.

That New-England is ftill in confufion, appears, 1. By the affembly of Maffachufetts-Bay being perhaps obliged to difpenfe with an act of their own, confirmed by the king in council, and to prolong the time for cancelling their province bills : the generality of the refponfible merchants of Rhode-Ifland, though they have always declared againft multiplying of a depreciating currency, in a memorial to the general affembly of Rhode-Ifland, fay, though the act December 1748 of Maffachufetts-Bay for drawing in their publick bills of credit, was in a too violent and hafty manner. 2. The colony of Rhode-Ifland this fpring, 1751, have emitted 100,000 l. currency with a greater intereft and to be cancelled after ten years ; this is a ftep towards reformation.

Connecticut continues honeft. New-Hampfhire, always inclinable to a depreciating fraudulent paper currency, from a difference between their governor and houfe of reprefentatives, formerly mentioned vol. II. p. 34, have had no legiflative capacity for fome time, and confequently incapable of augmenting their paper currency, much to the detriment of their governor, who by confenting to fuch emiffions, might have obtained an addition to his falary.

ciently publifhed: In cafe of defeft of fuch laws
any particular cafe, by fome clear and plain rule w:
ranted by the word of God.

All his majefty's fubjects within this colony, whetl
they be inhabitants or not, fhall enjoy the fame juft
and law, that is general for the colony, in all cafes pi
per for civil authority, and courts of judicature in t
fame; and that without partiality or delay.

That no man's perfon fhall be reftrained or imprifon
by any authority whatfoever, before the law hath fe
tenced him thereunto; if he can and will give or put
fufficient fecurity, bail or mainprize for his appearan
and good behaviour in the mean time, unlefs it be f
capital crimes, contempt in open court, or in fuch cal
where fome exprefs law doth allow or order the fame.

No perfon, except in his own cafe, other than a qu
lified attorney, is allowed to plead at the bar: in ca
not exceeding five pound, one attorney only is allowe
in larger cafes two attornies and no more.

Each town fhall have a peculiar brand for their hor
on the near or left fhoulder.

All cafks fhall be of the London affize, viz. bui
126 gallons; puncheons, eighty-four gallons; ho
fheads, fixty-three gallons; tierces, forty-two gallo
barrels, thirty-one gallons and a half.

Miller's allowance for grinding per bufhel, three qu
Indian corn, two quarts other grain, one quart malt.

Every town to have a fealer of weights and meafur

In Conneéticut, as generally among the congre
tionalifts of New-England, according to the Je
manner, they begin and end the Lord's day at the
ting of the fun.

Here are about 150 eftablifhed minifters called pre
terians, congregationalifts, and confociated; be
confcientious diffenters, faid not to be eftablifhed
                                                        toler;

tolerated. In fome townfhips are many parifhes or precincts.

In all our colonies voluntary affociations (moft of which may afterwards be confirmed or incorporated by provincial or colony charters) towards academies and libraries, ought to be encouraged.

The civilizing and chriftianizing of the Indians was one great and profeffed condition in all our royal grants.

I do not endeavour a ftrict pedantick narration; but though in a common place manner, I fhall obferve fome method.

Common intereft is fix per cent per ann. letting of cattle and maritime affairs excepted.

In all our plantations, colonies, and provinces, they abound with civil and military titles of judges, fquires, colonels, majors, and captains; gratifications for being of a governor's party, or by a pecuniary intereft.

By an act of the affembly of Connecticut, in building of veffels, no timbers or plank to be allowed other than white oak and rock oak, except for the deck and ceiling.

In New-England, particularly in Maffachufetts-Bay, it is not only the depreciating of the currencies by enormous paper credit emiffions called money, but the fcarcity of labourers from vaft expeditions unprofitable and ruinous to the colonies. In manufactures, our labour is fo dear, that we cannot afford our goods any where at market, fo cheap as other plantations or countries may. It is not fcarcity of provifion or depreciations only, but chiefly fcarcity of labourers and confequently advance of labour: to inftance only, that in bricks, where the difference is only in labour, about forty years fince they were fold at one piece of eight per thoufand, at prefent they are fold at three pieces of eight.

Concerning the TENURE OF LANDS. All grants of colony lands by the general affembly fhall be according

to

to the moſt free tenure of Eaſt-Greenwich in the county of Kent in England, conform to our charter grant. All townſhips and farms, to particular perſons, ſhall be from the general aſſembly by patent ſigned by the governor and ſecretary with the colony ſeal. Title of lands to be tried in the county where the lands lay. All eſtates for miniſtry, ſchools, and charitable uſes, are free from payment of rates.

Three freeholders appointed by the court of probates to divide real eſtate among legatees or heirs of inteſtates. No Indian title without the approbation of the general aſſembly to be pleadable. Proprietors having loſt their bounds, three freeholders appointed and ſworn by a juſtice of the peace, may ſet up and fix the bounds, but with appeal. In deviſe of real eſtate, wills to be witneſſed by three perſons in the preſence of the teſtators. Guardians to minors with ſome perſons appointed by the court of probate may divide lands with the ſurviving partners. Lands held in partnerſhip to be divided by writ of partition. Perſons preſuming to ſell Indian rights of lands not confirmed by the general court, fine fifty pound, and the perſons wronged by ſuch ſales to recover treble damages. All grants and diviſions of lands heretofore made by ancient cuſtom of town-meetings ſhall be good and valid though without conſent of the proprietors act May 9, 1723. Hereafter undivided common lands ſhall belong to the proprietors excluſive of other inhabitants, which proprietors may have their own meetings to manage ſuch undivided lands. Sales of lands deviſed to be ſold by executors, ſhall be good and valid, though ſome of the executors do not join in the ſale. Five proprietors of undivided lands may obtain a meeting to be called by a juſtice's warrant. All eſtates though accruing by wife, formerly ſold by the huſband alone, (act bears date Oct. 10, 1723) the deeds ſhall be valid, but for the future no ſuch deed ſhall be valid without the wife's conſent by hand and ſeal. Proprietors of land in common, may make rates to defray neceſſary

charges

charges.   By an act of parliament 1732, in any actions
in the plantations, when one of the parties plaintiff or
defendant refides in Great-Britain, evidences to prove
any matter or thing, may be taken in Great-Britain
before any chief magiftrates where the party refides,
which certified and tranfmitted, fhall be good as if done
viva voce in open court in the plantations ; and all
houfes, lands, negroes, and other hereditaments, as by
the laws of England, fhall in the plantations be liable to
fatisfy debts : where an adminiftrator makes it appear,
that the deceafed's perfonal eftate is not fufficient to fatisfy the debts, the affembly may direct his real eftate to
be fold towards paying of his debts.   Partition of lands
not to be valid till furveyed and recorded.   No deed of
real eftate is complete until it be figned, fealed, witneffed,
acknowledged and recorded.

No lands to be bought of Indians without confent of
the general affembly [*a*]. No Indian to be fued for debt.
No indenture for fervice made by an Indian, fhall be
valid, unlefs acknowledged before authority.

Debtors.   Any book debt not accounted for with the
original debtor in feven years, fhall not be pleadable
after the debtor's death.
Upon execution iffued, the fheriff fhall at the ufual
place of the debtor's abode demand the debt ; upon non-
payment he fhall levy the execution upon the moveables
(neceffary apparel, houfhold ftuff, tools, and arms excepted) and fet up a lift of the faid goods upon the town
poft, to be fold by out-cry after twenty days.   In want
of goods, and upon the creditor's refufing lands, the
debtor's body may be feized.   May levy execution up-

[*a*] The affembly 1722, confirmed a purchafe made fix or feven
years fince from the Mohagan Indians upon the Mohagan hills, part of
their referved lands, to governor Saltonftal, major Livingfton, Dennie,
Rogers, and Bradfhaw ; this was conftituted the north parifh of New-
London.

on real estate valued by appraisers. All executions are returnable in sixty days, or to the next court.

Debtors committed to jail, swearing that they have not estate to the value of five pounds, shall be subsisted by the creditors at a certain rate. Debtors and felons to be kept separate. The county sheriffs to have the custody of the jails.

As to absent or absconding debtors, if no estate is to be found, the debtor's agent, or usual place of abode, may be served with a writ; if no debtor nor agent appear, the writ may be continued to the next court, and if need be to one court further, and then judgment to be rendered for the plaintiff, and execution granted upon the debtor's effects wherever found : persons concealing the goods of absconding or absent debtors, are liable to satisfy the debt sued for.

No writ of error shall be brought for the reversal of any judgment after the space of three years, and no review upon a writ of error.

The estates of deceased insolvent debtors to be distributed in equal proportions to the creditors; debts to the government, sickness, and general charges being first paid; saving to the widow (if any) her houshold goods and dower during her life, and upon her death to be distributed among the creditors. A certain time allowed for receiving claims, the commissioners to be appointed by the judge of probates : creditors not bringing in their claims during that certain time allowed, are for ever excluded.

No action to be brought for bill, bond, or note, but within the space of seventeen years. No action of trespass or defamation (fine for defamation not to exceed ten pounds) but within three years.

Any debtor in a debt not exceeding twenty pound, may confess judgment before a single justice.

Criminal affairs. The governor, deputy governor, or
three

three affiftants, may reprieve a condemned malefactor to the next general court or affembly.

The capital crimes are confpiracy againft the colony, rape, beftiality, fodomy, falfe witnefs in cafes of life and death, wilfully firing houfes, disfiguring, or dif-membering the private parts, wilful murder, and blaf-phemy.   Deifm, firft offence incapacity of any employ-ment, fecond offence outlawed.

All complaints and prefentments, to be made within one year after the offence is committed, excepting in capital crimes; difmembering is banifhment, and theft, exceeding ten fhillings.

All fines impofed by the general court or affembly, and by the fuperior court, belong to the colony trea-fury; impofed by the county court, belong to the county treafury; impofed by an affiftant or juftice, be-longing to the townfhip treafuries.

Tavern offences. See the paragraph of excife.

A bill of divorce and liberty to marry again, may be granted by the fuperior courts, in cafes of adultery, fraudulent contract, wilful defertion for three years, or feven years abfence not heard of.

Single perfons committing fornication to be fined thirty-three fhillings or whipped, not exceeding ten ftripes; anti nuptial fornication only half penalty.

Every perfon playing at dice, cards, or tables, fine twenty fhillings.

Forgery. Three days publick pillory, double dama-ges to the injured party, and incapable of being an evi-dence in law.   The form of their oath is, You fwear by the name of the ever-living God.

All kind of delinquents to pay the charge of prefen-tation, guilty or not guilty.

Perjury twenty pound fine, and fix months imprifon-ment; if unable to pay his fine, fhall fit in the pillory with both ears nailed, and incapable of giving evidence.

Lord's day, penalties: neglecting of the publick worſhip, working or playing on the Lord's day, ten ſhillings; rude behaviour, diſturbing the publick worſhip, forty ſhillings; travelling, twenty ſhillings; going abroad excepting to publick worſhip, five ſhillings; no veſſels to ſail excepting upon extraordinary occaſions, thirty ſhillings; and ſeveral other particulars: refuſing to pay ſhall be publickly whipped.

Theft, to forfeit threefold, and a diſcretionary fine, not exceeding forty ſhillings, and if the value amount to twenty ſhillings and upwards, ſhall alſo be whipped not exceeding ten ſtripes; if the offender cannot pay, the perſon may be ſold for a certain term of years ſervice: penalty for receiving or concealing ſtolen goods, is the ſame; buying goods of ſlaves, penalty is treble value, ſervice or whipping.

Riots. [b] Three or more perſons aſſembled together, to do an unlawful act; if they obſtruct the proclama-

[b] About thirty years ſince, there was a riot act made in New-Hampſhire.

In the province of Maſſachuſetts-Bay, the violent, haſty, and raſh manner of calling in all their publick credit bills in the ſpace of one year by act of aſſembly, which had been gradually emitted in the courſe of fifty years, was found impracticable, and was like to have produced a general tumult: this occaſioned the making of a riot act, February 14, 1750-1, to be in force for three years, viz. where any perſons to the number of twelve, armed with clubs, or other weapons, or any number of perſons conſiſting of men, armed or not armed, ſhall be unlawfully riotouſly aſſembled; any juſtice of peace, field officer, or captain of the militia, ſheriff, under ſheriff, or conſtable, ſhall make proclamation to diſperſe; if they do not diſperſe within an hour, every ſuch officer with aſſiſtance, may carry them before a juſtice, and if in reſiſting any perſon is hurt, or killed, the officers and aſſiſtants are indemnified: perſons not diſperſing in the ſpace of one hour, ſhall forfeit to the king all his lands and chattels, or ſuch part thereof at the diſcretion of the juſtice for the uſe of the province, and be whipped thirty-nine ſtripes, one year's impriſonment, and receive the ſame number of ſtripes once every three months during his impriſonment. Demoliſhing houſes the ſame puniſhment or penalty. This act to be read every general ſeſſions of the peace, and anniverſary meeting of each town; no

tion in reading, or do not difperfe after proclamation made by a proper officer, fhall be punifhed by fine not exceeding ten pound for each perfon, and imprifonment not exceeding fix months, or by whipping not exceeding forty ftripes : if any rioter is killed or hurt by any perfon of the poffe, fuch perfon is indemnified. The profecution muft be within twelve months. The fheriff, f need be, may raife the militia in his aid.

Manflaughter (without premeditated malice) but wilful, penalty, forfeiture of goods, burnt in the hand with the letter M, whipped, and difabled from being evidence in law.

Lafcivious carriage may be punifhed at difcretion by the county court, by fine, houfe of correction, or corporal punifhment.

Burglary or robbery ; penalty is branding, ears cut off, and whipping : third offence is death.

Counterfeiting or altering publick bills of credit of this or of the neighbouring colonies ; penalty, cutting off ears, branding, and work-houfe for life, eftates forfeited, and to be debarred of all trade. Any fociety prefuming to emit bills of credit to be ufed in trade, to be punifhed as in cafe of counterfeiting ; the utterer to orfeit double the fame.

Criminal perfons making their efcape from the authority of other provincial governments to this government, may be remanded back to the place of perpetration.

The colony acts relating to the religious obfervation of the firft day of the week, Sunday, fabbath-day or Lord's-day, perhaps are too puritanical ; they feem to droop gradually, I fhall not revive them.

profecution after twelve months ; the judges may abate the whole or any part of the whipping.

In the colony of Rhode-Ifland, there are no riot acts, becaufe, as generally fuppofed, they are inconfiftent with their conftitution.

Any

Any perfon of the age of difcretion (which is fourteen æt.) publifhing a lie to the prejudice of the common-wealth, or damage of private perfons, to be fined, ftocks, or whipping.

Apprentices and fervants æt. fifteen or upwards, ab-fconding from their mafter's fervice, fhall ferve three times of their abfence. Servants or apprentices flying from the cruelty of their mafters, may be protected by a magiftrate and difcharged from their fervice.

A woman delivered of a child, afterwards found dead, if fhe cannot prove, at leaft by one witnefs, that fuch child was born dead, the mother fhall be accounted guilty of murder.

Any flave or Indian ftriking a white man, penalty whipping, not exceeding thirty ftripes.

Penalty for perfons who refift, or abufe any king's officer, fine not exceeding ten pound.

Curfing or fwearing; penalty fix fhillings, or the ftocks. Every houfholder to have at leaft one bible, or-thodox catechifm, and other books of practical godlinefs.

A houfe of correction to be eftablifhed in each county, two thirds of their earnings towards their fupport, and one third for other charges.

Penalty for felling ftrong liquor to an Indian ten fhil-lings per pint; drunkennefs and idlenefs are the general vices of Indians. An Indian convicted of drunkennefs, penalty five fhillings or ten lafhes. All the Indians in a townfhip fhall be muftered once a year, and the requifite laws read to them. All Englifh families taking Indian children into their families, fhall teach them to read Englifh, and inftruct them in the principles of the chriftian religion; for every three months neglect, a dif-cretionary fine not exceeding thirty fhillings.

The laws relating to the obfervation of the fabbath day and regulation of publick worfhip are fevere; and too many to be inferted here; thefe are under the infpec-tion of the grand jury, tything men, and conftables.

Private

Private lotteries, and wagers to vend goods, forfeiture is the value of the goods.

Parish churches of the established religions (presbyterians, congregationalifts, and confociated minifters) are under the direction of the county courts; tolerated diffenters from thofe profeffions are left at large.

Any Indian, molatto, or negroe travelling without a pafs, may be feized as a runaway.

Schools are well regulated, and have a colony allowance. Every ecclefiaftical fociety of feventy families or upwards, fhall have a fchool for the inftruction of children to read and write. A grammar fchool to every head or county town. One college or *fchola illuftris* in the colony.

There are fevere penalties for cutting down of trees, or firing of woods and lands; the accufed, where there is no proof, muft exculpate himfelf by oath.

A Digreffion, concerning North-America *grain and grazing, with a few occafional remarks relating to natural biftory, efpecially as to the feafons, winds, and weather, in a loofe mifcellany common place manner.*

Connecticut is a good country as to climate and foil; and is valuable for grain and pafture. Any country is happy, where the meaner inhabitants are plentifully and wholfomely fed; warmly and decently cloathed: thus it is in Connecticut.

Upon the firft arrival of Europeans in America, the Indians bread kind were only the maize or Indian corn of the cerealia or grain, and the phafeolus or kidney beans called Indian or French beans of the legumina or pulfe kind [c]. Befides they eat earth nuts of feveral kinds, berries of many kinds, and variety of maft [d], too nume-

[c] The Indians upon the fhore, ufed the pifum maritimum fpontaneum perenne humile repens; beach peafe; flowers end of May; it refembles that of marifon. H. Ox. 2. 43.

[d] Mafts, from mafticare, are feveral forts of foreft-nuts, cheftnut, walnut, hazle-nut, and the like.

rous

rous to be enumerated and deſcribed in a ſummary. As
alſo their hunting of ſundry kinds of quadrupeds or
beaſts, mooſe, deer, &c. their fowling, eſpecially of
birds, webfooted; their catching of river, pond, and
ſea fiſh, eſpecially of the teſtaceous.

As the frumentum Indicum, or Indian corn, was their
principal ſubſiſtence, though not ſpontaneous, but cultivated, I cannot avoid giving ſome particular deſcription and account of it; hitherto it has not been minutely
deſcribed. It has with much impropriety been called
frumentum Saracenicum; properly, frumentum Saracenicum (from the Saracens country in Barbary) is buck-
wheat, and at preſent is cultivated by the Dutch in the
government of New-York for haſty pudding, and as
provender for horſes.

Its moſt profitable culture is in light ſandy land, with
a ſmall intermixture of loom; it requires ſand heat, ſuch
as is that of pitch pine or huckle-berry lands. Though
a hungry grain, it requires much and repeated labour.
It is firſt plowed, then croſs plowed, next harrowed all
ſmooth, then furrowed and croſs furrowed; at proper
diſtances of about four feet at the interſections in hollows
are dropt five or ſix ſeed grains (a peck ſows or plants
one acre) and by the hoe covered with earth the end
of April and beginning of May; ſoon after its firſt appearance, it is plowed two furrows lengthways between
each row of grain, and by the hoe the weeds are brought
towards the grain; this is called the firſt weeding:
after ſome time it is croſs plowed two furrows between
each planted row, and by the hoe the earth and weeds
are brought to the corn, this is called half-hilling; next
it is plowed lengthways, as before, two furrows, and by
the hoe the earth is brought to the roots, and forms a
hill to prevent the winds eradicating of it; ſometimes
it is hoed a fourth time: in the middle of Auguſt the
grain becomes mellow fit for roaſting, a ſort of delicacy
in the ſugar iſlands, called mutton: it emits its coma,
plume,

plume, or blooms, end of June; then they cut off the top
of the ftalks, that the grain may receive the more nou-
rifhment [*e*]. A wet fummer makes it run too much into
ftalks and leaves, which ftarves the ears. End of September and beginning of October the ears are hand gathered,
the tops are very agreeable to cattle for fodder. The ears
have eight, ten, twelve, fourteen rows of grain, the more,
rows, the better is the grain; fome fay there has been
eighteen rows, but none under eight rows.

Indian corn does not weigh fo heavy as New-England
wheat; their Indian corn at a medium is in weight forty
five pound, their wheat fifty-five pound, per bufhel.
The Virginia Indian corn is white and flat, yielding a
better or whiter meal; the New-England corn is of a
pale yellow, fmaller but thicker, and anfwers better in
fatning of beeves, hogs, and other ftock; Virginia corn
is planted at greater diftances, being of greater growth,
and is all white; in New-England and Canada it is generally of a pale yellow, does not bear fo many ears as that
of Virginia, it is of a leffer habit and quicker growth.
The Indian corn of New-England at a medium produces
twenty-five bufhels per acre, and ripens in a fhorter
time [*f*]; (this a providence in nature, becaufe their
hot feafons are fhorter) the Virginia feed in New-England does not ripen into grain, as requiring a longer
growth than the New-England feafons do allow. The
Weft-India or fugar iflands have per ann. two crops of

[*e*] Here the farina fecundans of vegetables feems to be evinced:
this plume or flower, if cut off before its maturity, the maize bears no
ear or grain. In New-England where the grain is of various colours
(white, yellow, reds of feveral fhades, blues of feveral fhades, marbled,
and mixtures of thefe in the fame ears) the grains planted of various colours, and in the neighbourhood receive alterations in their colours or
fhades by the various impregnations: this is obfervable alfo in other vegetables, beets, carrots, &c.

[*f*] Thus in Lapland and the northern parts of Sweden, barley from
fowing ripens two weeks fooner than at Stockholm; and in New-England, Indian corn ripens in fewer days from planting or fowing than in
Virginia.

4   Indian

Indian corn planted May and September: in our continent we have only one crop planted in May. Capt. Hill
of Douglaſs by way of experiment planted Indian corn,
middle of June, it was ripe middle of Auguſt in a hot
ſeaſon. End of April they begin to plow; Indian corn
harveſt is the beginning of October; when it begins to
be in the ear, rain or drizzle occaſions a ſmut.

The phaſeolus; which we call Indian beans or
French beans, becauſe the French from the Canada Indians were the firſt in propagating them [g]. It is the
phaſeolus Indicus fructu tumidiore minore niveus et verſicolor.
Moriſon, tab. iv. ſect. 2. They are generally white, and
there is an indefinite number of ſimple colours and va-
riegations or marblings.

In New-England (ſome parts of Connecticut excepted)
the general ſubſiſtence of the poorer people (which con-
tributes much towards their endemial pſorick diſorders)
is ſalt pork and Indian beans, with bread of Indian corn
meal, and pottage of this meal with milk for breakfaſt
and ſupper.

For the varieties of *phaſeolus* called Indian beans, calavances and bonaviſt, ſee vol. I. p. 122, and the ſections
farther ſouth.

Connecticut wheat is full of cockle [b]. Twenty
buſhels per acre is a good crop. It is ſaid, in Canada
they ſow no winter grain. New-England wheat is ſubject to blaſt; ſome think that it proceeds from the *farina
fecundans* of adjacent barberry buſhes [i].

---

[g] When Engliſh peaſe (piſum majus flore fructu albo. C. B. P.)
ſell at three, theſe Indian beans ſell in proportion at two; they are
more colicky than peaſe; the tribe of the phaſeolus is very large; ſome
years ſince, Peter Coelart in Holland cultivated above 100 diſtinct ſpecies. The cow itch, as we pronounce it, is the cow-hege of Zura in
the Eaſt-Indies: phaſeolus ſiliquis hirſutis, pilis pungentibus.

[b] Lychnis ſegetum major. C. B. P.

[i] Barberis latiſſimo folio Canadenſis. H. R. P. it is plenty all
over North-America, it is of a larger habit than that of Europe, is from
ten to twelve feet high; it is uſed as hedges, but ſpreads too much into
Our

Our beft wheat is from Virginia and Maryland; next beft is from Penfylvania, fifty-five pound to fixty pound per bufhel, and cafts whiter than the Engl fh wheat; the farther north the flour cafts the darker; Nova-Scotia wheat cafts almoft as dark as rye. Some years fince in a fcarcity of wheat in New-England, fome was imported from England; from the long weft-ward paffages it became mufty, caft dark, and did not anfwer.

In New-England the allowance to a baker of fhip-bifcuit is three bufhels and a quarter wheat for 112 pound weight of bifcuit, befides——per ct. weight for baking

Herrings [*k*] have formerly been taken notice of.

In New-England fome oxen of eighteen ct. wt. and hogs of twenty-five fcore have been killed; Connecticut falt pork is the beft of America; they finifh the fatning of their hogs with Indian meal.

In New-England their barley is a hungry lean grain, and affords no good malt liquor; molaffes is the prin-cipal ingredient in all their buvrage. Their barley of four rows called French barley is not fo good as that of two rows called Englifh barley. Their oats are lean, chaffy, and of a dark colour.

In New-England they fow their winter grain the third and fourth weeks of Auguft.

In New-England, after gathering in their common grain, flax, &c. the firft natural appearance of indi-

fuckers. There is a law in Connecticut, p. 13. for deftroying thefe bufhes, they are thought " to be very hurtful by occafioning, or at leaft increafing the blafting of Englifh grain."

[*k*] Upon the coaft of Great-Britain, the herring fifhery begins a little before midfummer; they emerge or make their firft appearance off Crane-head in Braffa-Sound N. Lat. 61 and half d. from thence gradually proceed fouth to Dogger-Bank, where that fummer fifhery ends: the winter fifhery begins off Yarmouth, and continues about feventy days, they proceed fouthward, and are caught in plenty about the Thames mouth until the latter end of January.

genous

genous plants is *panicum non criftatum-fpica multiplici,*
ambrofia, and *virga aurea annua Virginiana Zanoni.* Near
Bofton and other great towns, fome field plants which
accidentally have been imported from Europe, fpread
much, and are a great nufance in paftures, fuch as *ra-*
nunculus pratenfis repens hirfutus, C B. P. Butter cups,
bellis major, I. B. the greater wild white daify, *dens leonis.*
Ger. dandelyon, &c. at prefent they have fpread inland
from Bofton abot thirty miles.

Great-Britain and New-England, though differing a-
bout 10 d. in lat. feem to be of the fame temperature:
New-England is fomewhat colder in winter and warmer
in fummer, from the vaft land continent N. W. of it,
which receives and communicates continually (therefore
with intenfenefs,) by the lambent air thefe different
temperatures of the feafons. N. W. is our general
or natural wind. 1. After ftorms or perturbations of
our ambient air from any point of the compafs, being
expended, the wind fettles N. W. 2. All our fpring
and fummer fea breezes, return to the N. W. 3. In
the middle of February 1731-2, called the cold Tuefday (the moft intenfe infupportable cold I ever felt) the
wind was at N. W. It is not eafily accounted for, that
in different countries though the temperature of the air
be nearly the fame, the natural growth of plants differs
much, v. g. the *bellis minor* or leffer wild daify, a native
of Great-Britain, abounds there from fifty degrees to
fixty degrees of lat. but will not grow in North-America. All of the cucurbitaceous kind, pompions, &c.
(Mr. H—y an ecclefiaftical mountebank, in his farces
called oratory, calls the New-England people pom-
pionites) by cultivation without the force of hot beds
grow well, but in Great-Britain requires force.

In a new country there may be a tax upon improved
lands, as a fund for premiums to encourage the clearing
and planting of wildernefs lands for the firft year; the
fecond and third year are the next profitable for produce,
and

and requires no bounty, and afterwards, efpecially in New-England, it ought to be fmoothed and lie for pafturage.

In New-England, two acres cow-pen land, may raife about a tun of hemp, but is foon exhaufted.

Locufts, called grafhoppers, and a fpecies of caterpillars, fome years are very noxious to our paftures; in the fummer 1759, a fmall locuft, with a drought, deftroyed our herbage; they generally prevail June and July.

Lands in New-England, which yield at a medium 20 ct. wt. of hay, are the beft, if 40 ct. wt. the hay is rank and four; fome frefh meadows, if mowed more than once, yield greater quantities. In mowing lands, an uniformity of grafs ought to be attended to and endeavoured, becaufe fome graffes ripen foon, and are upon the decline before others attain a perfection for mowing. End of June and beginning of July, the height of upland or Englifh hay harveft is over; third and fourth weeks of Auguft they mow their falt-meadow hay. Salt-hay is from falt or fpring tide marfhes; frefh hay is the natural growth of inland marfhes; Englifh or upland hay, is the herbage imported from Europe. [*l*] New-England crops or produce are very uncertain; for inftance of hay, in the fpring 1750, it fold for 4 l. New-England currency; in the fpring 1751, it fells for 15 s. per ct. wt. Two acres, if good, is a cowland.

Cyder is a confiderable produce for confumption and exportation; when diftilled, it does not yield above one twelfth fpirit; end of Auguft they begin to make a mean fort of cyder from the windfalls.

Turneps fowed in any latitude thrive, even in Davis's-Straits or Weft-Greenland; our beft New-England turneps, are from new lands N. E. from Bofton.

[*l*] In hot countries they make no hay; it dries too quick, dry rots, and turns to duft. In fome parts of North-America, the winters are too long and cold, and in other parts too hot for grafs; confequently can afford no quantity of provender for cattle, and will never be beef countries.

Some remarks relating to the natural history of New-England.

The seasons from year to year are better determined by some passenger birds and fish, than by the blossoming of trees, and flowering of some inferior vegetables; for instance, swallows constantly arrive from the southward in the second week of April, with a latitude of only two or three days; peaches sometimes blossom beginning of April, in some years not till the beginning of May, a latitude of thirty days. Anno 1735, last day of December, first and second of January, fell about twenty inches of light snow, wind N. W. northerly, followed by a very hard frost, and peaches did not begin to blossom till May 7. Anno 1719, the beginning of winter was very severe; peaches did not blossom the spring following.

End of autumn, and beginning of winter, if dry, follows a mild winter; but if falling weather, rain, or snow (freezing inland is a basis for snow to lodge and chill the winds from N. to W.) produces hard freezing in our plantations, which are to leeward. 1731-2, Feb. 14 and 15, tinctura sacra froze, the coldest weather I ever felt; after a flight of hail and snow, the wind from S, came suddenly to the N. W. 1732, April 5, wind N. E. northerly falls about fourteen inches snow, soon dissolved, a great storm at sea; 1751, April 6, all day a heavy fleaky snow, but soon dissolved. Travelling in Connecticut from Pensylvania, 1716, June 26, finger cold, roads froze, ice thick as a crown-piece, Indian corn beginning to bloom is hurt [*m*].

[*m*] The northerly and N. E. snows, as being from the sea, are softer and milder, than those from the north westerly land continent. Great snows lodged in the woods westward, covered from the dissolving influence of the sun, by their chill retard our springs; it is a vulgar error, that the snows lodged upon the ice of our western great lakes is the occasion; from the observation of a curious gentleman, an officer

Mackarel

Mackarel [*n*] fet in fecond week of May, lean, and feem to eat muddy. Some are caught all fummer; there is a fecond fetting in for autumn, fat and delicious eating; they are a N. lat. fifh, and are not to be found fouth of New-England; beginning of July, for a fhort time they difappear or will not take the bait.

Herrings (a bad kind) fet in middle of May, they feem to be whimfical or variable as to their ground.

Frogs feem to be dormant, as are fnakes in the winter or very cold feafon; we have three fpecies of frogs, rana viridis arborea, the green-tree frog; the rana terreftris et aquatica; the rana maxima Americana aquatica, the bull frog.

1719-20, January 7, the coldeft of days, wind at N. W. fnow lying about one foot deep; Charles-Town ferry (tide runs four or five knots) froze over in twenty-four hours, paffable on the ice (no weather, it is faid, fo cold, fince winter 1697) continued extreme cold to the fourteenth. This year the peaches did not bloffom.

Wild geefe fly to the fouthward middle of September, and return beginning of March; a wild goofe may yield half lb. feathers; fix brants yield 1 lb. feathers. Cuckows return beginning of April. [*o*]

In the winter feafon, we have from fifteen to twenty days, at times, a froft fo fevere, as in chambers to freeze the ink.

In maritime places, as are all our North-America colonies, the weather is variable, according as the wind

belonging to the four independent companies ftationed in the province of New-York, who commanded the garrifon at Ofwego upon the lake Ontario about three years, I find that the great lakes are never frozen over, and confequently cannot lodge fnow.

[*n*] Hook mackarel for a market, are preferable to thofe caught by feins which bruife one another.

[*o*] In Europe, the cuckows, paffenger birds, arrive generally beginning of April, therefore the firft day of April is called fools day; this bird is fo foolifh as not to have any exclufive neft; hence filly married men, whofe wives are not exclufive but common, are called cuckold, knockoock, or cocu.

blows

blows from the fea or inland ; in iflands it is more conftant, becaufe all winds come from the fea; as alfo
inland countries, as is Canada, their winds are all from
the land, and confequently of the fame nature.

The New England winters generally fet in end of
October, and beginning of November, and are over
middle of March; the extreme frofts are from Chriftmas
to middle of February ; the very hot weather is in the
firft weeks of July.

Early winters are generally fevere and long. 1732,
The rivers froze up middle of November, and continued
froze until end of March, many cattle die for want of
provender.

Mr. Thomas Robie, a fellow in Cambridge college
of New-England, an ingenious accurate obferver, com-
paring with Mr. Derham's obfervations at Upminfter in
England, found that winds continuing long in one
quarter, efpecially if ftrong, were nearly the fame in
both places, allowing fome days for their paffage from
one place to the other.

Salmon are a high latitude fifh, they are not to be
found fouth of New-England; the farther fouth, the
later they fet in, and continue a fhorter time; for inftance, in Connecticut river they fet in the beginning of
May, and continue only about three weeks ; in Merrimack
river they fet in, beginning of April, to fpawn, and lie
in the deep cold brooks until September and October,
then filently (fo as not to be obferved) and with difpatch,
they return to the fea; in Chebucto, Cape-Breton, and
Newfoundland, they continue the greateft part of the
year. The people living upon the banks of Merrimack
river in Maffachufetts-Bay of New-England, obferve,
that feveral fpecies of fifh, particularly falmon, fhad,
and alewives, are not fo plenty in the feafons as formerly;
perhaps from difturbances or fome other difguft, as it
happens with herrings in the feveral friths of Scotland.

Smelts, a high latitude fifh, fet in to Bofton wharfs
middle of September and take the hook; beginning of
February,

February, they go up to fpawn in the frefhes; no fmelts
fouth of New-England; tom-cod goes up to fpawn end
of November.

We reckon it a good paffage for trading veffels, from
New-England to London in four weeks, and from London to New-England in fix weeks.

In New-England, generally the falling weather is from
N. E. to S. E. In winter, if the wind is N. of E. fnow;
if S. of E. rain. The N. E. ftorms are of the greateft
continuance, the S. E. ftorms are the moft violent.
1716-17, February 20 to 22, wind at N. E. northerly,
fell a very deep fnow upwards of three feet upon a level.
N. W. freezing wind backing to the S. W. if reverberated, proves the moft intenfe cold weather; thus chemical reverberated heats are the ftrongeft.

Trees generally lofe their leaves middle of October.
The button tree, or platanus occidentalis, is of a fine pa-
rabolick form fit for avenues, but its verdure is of fhort
continuance, and the tree is not long lived; it is not full
in leaf till middle of May, and its leaves begin to fade
end of July.

Our great rains are in Auguft about two months after
the fummer folftice, and our great fnows in February,
two months after the winter folftice; the greateft
fnow in my remembrance was 1716-17, third week of
February.

In falling weather, wind, the farther north from the
eaft, the finer and dryer is the fnow; the farther fouth
from the eaft, the more flaky and humid is the fnow;
when the wind comes fouth of the S. E. it turns to
rain.

The winds from the W. S. W. to the N. N. W. are
dry winds, fit for dry curing of falt-fifh; farther north,
they are damp and foft as coming from the ocean; farther fouth are from the hot latitudes, and fun-burn the
fifh.

Early fprings accelerate the buds and bloffoms of
trees, and frequently a fubfequent eafterly chill blafts

or pinches them ; but are advantageous for hay, becaufe a late fpring is too foon fucceeded by the fummer, and the grafs before it becomes thick, runs into ftalks, ftraw or ftubble, and feed : Indian corn require early fprings, becaufe, if too late, it is in danger of autumnal frofts.

In extreme freezing weather, the infenfible perfpiration or vapours from the harbour, houfe pumps, &c. becomes a fenfible perfpiration, being by the cold condenfed in form of fmoke.

1732-3, The winter was very fevere and long with gufts of wind : fifty to fixty veffels bound to New-England, could not hover upon the coaft to wait a favourable fpurt of wind and weather for pufhing in ; but were obliged to bear away to Bermudas, South-Carolina, and the Weft-India iflands : peaches were not generally in bloffom till middle of May : thefe effects of a fevere winter did not reach South-Carolina.

Oats, barley and rice, are ripe middle of July.

No herrings (alewives, the fame fpecies) appear fouth of Great-Britain, and none fouth of New-England, which makes a difference of 10 d. in lat. but not in temperature ; therefore the temperature muft be nearly the fame, though differing in latitude : this is alfo obfervable in falmon.

We have natural pacers of horfes, which at a cow run, (a gait which they acquire by pafturing, when colts, with the cows) will pace three miles in feven minutes.

1719, October 14, hard froft as if mid-winter, robins difappear. This winter I walked round Bofton Peninfula at a quick pace upon the ice, without all the wharfs, in one hour feven minutes.

End of February arrive wild geefe, brants and teal.

Our intenfe hot days are with the wind from S. to W. S. W. From N. to E. N. E. is our moft chilly weather. The dry winds are from W. to N. N. W. All other winds carry more or lefs damp ; this is manifeft in the drying of falt cod-fifh. Our dry winds with continuance, are from the continent N. N. W. to W. S. W.

Our

Our falling weather, is from the ocean, wind N. N. E. to E. S. E. The other winds are variable, and partake of both. From middle of October to middle of April requires chamber fires. Long winters are bad for neat cattle, becaufe without fufficiency of grafs or hay, fubfifting only by grain, they lofe their cud. Our feafons as to temper of the weather may be reckoned, winter from the winter folftice to the fpring equinox, fpring from faid equinox to fummer folftice, fummer from faid folftice to autumn equinox, and autumn from thence to winter folftice.

End of Auguft the fymptoms of approaching winter begin to appear, we call it the fall (autumn) of the year; the leaves of maple turn red, the leaves of birch turn yellow. The alnus or alder holds its leaf, and the verdure of its leaf the longeft; it is a conifer: the betulo, though a conifer, lofes its leaf foon. Some afters are the lateft of our wildernefs flowers. We have fcarce any winter flowering fhrubs. Auguft fometimes is a very hot month; 1719, Auguft 15, fo hot that fome men and cattle die in travelling the road (the fucceeding winter was very cold and long) fome boys faint away at fchool; ftrong wind S. W. foutherly, dufky morning.

In fome very fevere winters, fuch as 1732, lumps of ice fettle upon the oyfter banks, and kill the oyfters.

When tides fet in higher than ufual for the feafon and time of the moon, it is a fign of eafterly winds at fea, and veffels from Europe have fhort paffages.

Early winters are generally fevere and long.

The New-England earthquake of November 5, 1732; an undulatory motion was felt the fame day and hour at Montreal in Canada, but more violent; this was not fo violent as that of 1727, October 29. ten and half in the night; a vibrating motion was felt at Barbadoes the preceding day.

In hot countries, the birds have gay plumage, and fing but little; their flowers have beautiful mixtures of colours, but little or no fragancy. In hot countries no

good

good wines; extreme heats or colds do not agree with wines.

Where there is a hollow sea, land is at a great distance: certain kinds of fish and fowl are symptoms of land.

The quality of lands in New-England is known by the produce; in the best lands are chestnuts and walnuts, next is beech and white oak, lower is fir, then pitch pines, then whortles or huckle-berry plains, lastly, some marshy shrubs, low and imperfect, being the lowest degree of suffrutex vegetation.

We have a few winter birds of passage, which arrive in autumn when the summer passenger birds depart, and go off in the spring when the summer passage birds return, e. g. the snow bird or passer nivalis. Some passengers remain only a few days, some a few weeks, others for some months.

In New-England are some pretty little quadrupedes: putorius Americanus striatus, the pol cat or skrunk; Sciuri or squirrels of several kinds, the black, the grey fox squirrel, the ferret squirrel, &c. I seem to forget that a place is reserved in the Appendix for some things relating to natural history. [p]

[p] My summary design does not allow of botanick excursions. I shall only observe, 1. that in the country near Boston, I have collected and described about eleven hundred indigenous species of plants, perhaps a few of them might be casually imported from Europe. Ray in his synopsis of British plants, enumerates about 1400 distinct species. Tournefort, in his Histoire des plantes des environs de Paris, enumerates and describes about 1037 species. 2. New-England, perhaps all North-America, seems mostly to abound with plants, flore composito, flore apetalo, capillares, musei, lichenes and mushrooms. Between the tropicks, they are generally anomalous, monopetalous and polypetalous, not reducible to our European tribes, and require a botanical addition of more tribes; Tournefort in his Appendix, and corollary has no new genius of verticillatæ umbelliferæ, cariophylei, and very few of the papilionacei. 3. The marine plants seem to be the same all over the earth, perhaps from the communications of the seas: the maritime plants differ much. 4. The farther south, the timber and other wood rivels better into staves and the like, but does not yield much

Goose-

Goofeberries, rafpberries, and ftrawberries are fpontaneous in all our North-America fettlements.

The clearing and cultivating of wildernefs lands, is a very laborious and tedious affair.

Between the tropics, winds are generally eafterly, called trade winds; from the tropics to the high latitudes, they are variable, but moftly wefterly, being an eddy of the trade winds: in the north high latitudes, the winds are froze N. E. to N. W. [*q*]

The great import of moloffes into New-England, hinders the cultivation and malting of barley and other grain; therefore ought to be charged with a high duty, equivalent to a prohibition.

Hunting and other fports of the field are little ufed in America.

The difcovery and fubfequent poffeffion of American lands, gave the Englifh an exclufive right againft all other people, the native Indians excepted. Grants of lands to particular perfons, or to companies and corporations by the crown, notwithftanding other purchafers from the Indians, fixes the tenures of the lands in the crown, by fome fmall quit-rent. The Indians of the N. E. parts of America feem to be the leaft improved of human kind; they are ftrangers to religion, policy, and arts.

crooked timber, being fpungy; in the intermediate latitudes, from the alternate variable hot and cold weather, it is not durable; in very hot countries their wood is hard and ponderous.

[*q*] Our intenfe heats are many weeks after the fummer folftice, in the firft half of July; our intenfe colds are in January. Thus it is in all phænomena of nature where there is a reciprocation of caufes and effects; the intenfenefs of the effects are fome time after the efficient caufes have paffed their height; e g. the ofcillation of the ocean in tides, the tides are not the higheft until the third or fourth tide after new and full moon; in fummer the hotteft time of the day is about two or three hours P. M. and in winter the coldeft time of the day is generally about the fame hours; our cold weather is protracted into the fpring feafon of the year, and occafions fhort fprings; our warm weather is protracted alfo, and occafions long autumn weather.

In

In New-England, idleneſs prevails too much; they obſerve religiouſly that article in the fourth commandment, Reſted the ſeventh day, but neglect a very eſſential article, Six days ſhalt thou labour; when wages are high and proviſions cheap, they do not labour half their time.

Wild pigeons, palumbus torquatus migratorius, ſee vol. I. p. 126, in their paſſage northward, begin to appear in New-England end of February and beginning of March, but not in large numbers, becauſe they travel more inland for the benefit of laſt autumn berries of ſeveral ſorts in the wilderneſs; they return in their paſſage ſouthward, in large quantities, end of Auguſt, and ſome years ſince have been ſold at four-pence currency per dozen; they at that ſeaſon keep towards the plantations for the benefit of their harveſt. They are of great advantage in their ſeaſons towards victualling our plantations; the country people feed ſome of them (they are catched alive in nets or ſnares) for ſome time with Indian corn, and brought to market, and are good delicate eating; cumin ſeed, or its oil, are found by experience the beſt lure to induce the pigeons to their nets. The ſpring flights 1751, were very large, like thunder ſhower clouds, but ſoon over.

Cuckows, as above, come in fourth week of March, and beginning of April; black-birds arrive from the ſouthward about the ſame time with the ſwallows; ſecond week of April.

Mackarel. See above.

Brants arrive middle of February, very lean and of ſhort continuance; they return in autumn fat, and in October proceed ſouthward.

Cateſby, a late aſſiduous naturaliſt, enumerates 113 diſtinct ſpecies of birds from 50 to 45 d. N. lat. in North-America, and obſerves, that animals, particularly birds, diminiſh in number of ſpecies as we raiſe the degrees of northern latitudes. He obſerved about eighteen ſorts of ſerpents; whereof only four are of the viper kind,

kind, and of thefe the rattle-fnake, viper caudifona Americana, is the moft pernicious.

A frofty winter produces a dry fummer; a mild winter produces a wet fummer.

Rains and fogs are more common on the fhore, and in foundings than in deep water at fea.

In Canada, the winds are more uniform and intenfely cold than in New-England, becaufe the bleak damp eafterly winds from the ocean do not reach fo far; the Canada fprings are fometimes more early than the fprings in New-England; in Canada the fnows fall early before the frofts enter the ground deep, therefore fo foon as the fnows diffolve, the fun fooner enters the ground, than in a frozen foil.

Forefts cover and retain the fnow long in the fpring, and occafion late fprings by their chill; when cleared, we fhall have better feafons.

In a mifcellany or loofe article, I may be allowed to infert any thing for information or amufement, if not too foreign to the propofed fubject. 1. Our Indians formerly accounted by fingle wampum, by ftrings of wampum, and by belts of wampum; in the fame manner as the Englifh account by the denominations of pence, fhillings, and pounds. 2. An Indian preacher, *pavement*, or naturally, in the introduction to his fermon, faid, " Brethren, little I know, and little I fhall fay ;" though generally the lefs a preacher knows, the more tedious are his fermons. And in the old manner of fingle, faid, " God does not require of us to part with our fons, as he did of Abraham of old, but to part with our fins." 3. Clergy, though by fome faid to be of human inftitution, are defigned as of good ufe to perfuade people into civility and good manners, and feem to be effential to fociety; but their bad examples of immorality, and paffionate condemning of all who do not follow their not effential mode or whims, renders them more hurtful than beneficial to fociety.

SECT.

SECT. XII.

Concerning the Province of New-York.

TO deduce this colony and any other of the British colonies in America, ab origine, as it were, with their progreffive improvements and viciffitudes, fee vol. I. fect. 2. article 3 giving fome account of the difcoveries and firft fettlements in America from Europe:—and fect. 4. general remarks concerning the Britifh colonies in America,—and particularly p. 204. concerning New Netherlands, comprehending the prefent Britifh provinces of New York, New-Jerfeys, and fome part of Penfylvania. In a fummary, references are more proper and confonant, than recapitulations.

As New-Jerfeys,and part of Penfylvania, were formerly with New-York called the Dutch colony of New-Netherlands, or Nova Belgia ; I cannot here avoid by anticipation mentioning fome things concerning them. In thofe times all the country from Maryland to New-England was called Nova-Belgia, or New-Netherlands.

King James I. by letters patent, April 10, 1606, in one patent incorporated two diftinct companies or colonies. 1. The firft colony to Sir Thomas Gates, Sir George Summers, Richard Hackluit prebend at Weftminfter, and Edward Maria Wingfield, Efq. adventurers of the city of London with their affociates ; from 34 d. to 41 d. of northern latitude, including all the lands within an hundred miles directly over-againft the fea coaft, and back into the main land one hundred miles from the fea coaft, and each plantation or fettlement to extend 100 miles along the fea coaft. 2. The fecond colony to Thomas Hanham, Raleigh Gilbert, William Parker, and George Popham, Efqrs. of the town of Plymouth, with their affociates ; liberty to begin their firft plantation and feat, at any place upon the coaft of

'irginia, where they fhould think fit, between the de-
rees of 38 and 45 of northern latitude; with the like
iberties and bounds at the firft colony, provided they
eated within a hundred miles of them.

What relates to Virginia is referred to the fection of
Virginia. Anno 1610, my lord Delaware was fent governor to Virginia by the South Virginia company; falling in with the land about two degrees to the northward
of the capes of Virginia, difcovered a fine large bay, in
compliment to his lordfhip, called Delaware-Bay.

The Swedes and Finns feem to have been the firft oc-
cupiers of fome parts of that large country, afterwards
called by the Dutch, Nᴇᴡ Nᴇᴛʜᴇʀʟᴀɴᴅꜱ; they made
fettlements both fides of Delaware river, and began feveral towns and forts, Elfenburgh, Cafimier, now called
New-Caftle, &c. The Dutch traded thither and foon became more powerful and rich than the Swedes; the
Swedes and Finns followed hufbandry only, and being in
conftant fears from their neighbouring numerous Indians,
put themfelves under protection of the Dutch 1655, and
John Kizeing the Swedifh governor, made a formal furrender of that country to Peter Stuyvefant, governor for
the ftates of Holland. Whereupon all the tract of land
in North-America from the latitude of about 38 D. to
the latitude of about 41 D. in Connecticut, was called
New-Netherlands by all people, except the Englifh, who
ftill claimed it as part of New-England: in fact, governor
Argol of Virginia had feveral bickerings with the Dutch,
particularly 1618, in the bay of Delaware, and with others
elfewhere, in the affair of the Englifh exclufive trade
and property in thofe parts; but in the fcene of the dole-
ful civil wars in England under various forms of adminiftrations, finding intricate labour enough at home,
neglected the American plantations; and their neighbouring European fettlements at full eafe, were much increafed to our prejudice. The progeny of the banditti
Swedes, who firft fettled Delaware river, ftill live in a
feparate manner; they have at times preachers and
took

books of devotion from Sweden, but do not hold their
lands of the Penns, becaufe the royal grant of Penn
exempts lands then fettled by any chriftians ; but they
are as to jurifdiction under the government of Penfylvania.

New-York and New-Jerfeys at firft were traded to,
and fome fettlements made there, by the Englifh and
Dutch : the Dutch placed a governor there, of which
the court of England complained to the ftates of Holland ; the ftates difowned it, and faid, that it was only a
private undertaking of an Amfterdam Weft-India company, and K. James I. commiffioned Edward Langdon
as governor, and called the country New-Albion; the
Dutch fubmitted to the Englifh government. During the
civil troubles in England in the adminiftration of King
Charles I. and of the republican party, the Dutch again
eftablifhed a government there, till it was reduced by
England 1664. When this reduction was upon the anvil,
K. Charles II. made a previous grant of that country,
called by the Dutch, NEW-NETHERLANDS, March 12,
1663-4, of property and government to his brother the
duke of York.   Duke of York, June 24, 1664, made a
grant of that portion now called New-Jerfey, (fo called,
in compliment to Sir George Carteret a Jerfey-man)
jointly to lord Berkley of Straton, and to Sir George
Carteret vice chamberlain, and of the privy council; a
further account of this belongs to the fection of New-
Jerfeys.

K. Charles II. anno 1664, fitted out an expedition for
the reduction or recovery of New-Netherlands, fo called
by the Dutch, confifting of a fquadron of fhips commanded by Sir Robert Carr, and fome land forces aboard
under the command of col. Richard Nicols. Upon their
arrival at New-Amfterdam, fince called New-York, the
Dutch after fome fhew of refiftance, but much terrified,
upon the offers of protection for their perfons and properties, and liberty to remove with all their effects, if
they faw fit, fubmited to the Englifh ; articles were drawn
up,

up, figned and exchanged in September 1664 : the Englifh poffeffed of New-Amfterdam, called it New-York :
in a fhort time thereafter, the Englifh fquadron entered
Delaware bay and river, and all the fettlements there,
followed the example of the Dutch capital New-Amfterdam, and poffeffion of all New-Netherland was taken
for, and in the name of, the duke of York, to whom K.
Charles his brother had previoufly given it by a royal
patent; and all manner of jurifdiction, as well civil as
military, was exercifed throughout the whole country,
excepting in the Jerfeys, which the duke of York had difpofed of to Berkley and Carteret, by the fole appointment of the duke and his deputies.

By the third article of the peace of Breda figned July
21, 1667, between England and the United Provinces,
the Englifh were to remain in poffeffion of that whole
country, in exchange for the country of Surinam, which
the Dutch had taken from the Englifh. King Charles in
the beginning of 1672, having declared war againft the
United Provinces, the Dutch fent a fquadron of fhips to
New-York, which they foon reduced with the reft of
the country; but by a peace concluded at Weftminfter,
February 9, 1673-4, in the fixth article it was again reftored to England in general terms, "that whatfoever
country, iflands, towns, ports, caftles, or forts have or
fhall be taken on both fides, fince the time that the
late unhappy war broke out, either in Europe or elfewhere, fhall be reftored to the former lord and proprietor, in the fame condition they fhall be in when the
peace itfelf fhall be proclaimed ; after which time there
fhall be no fpoil nor plunder of the inhabitants, nor demolition of fortifications, nor carrying away of guns,
powder, or other military ftores which belonged to any
caftle or fort at the time when it was taken."

This tract of land, as it had been taken and poffeft
by a foreign power, though afterwards delivered or furrendered back by treaty, to obviate or remove all difputes
concerning the validity of former grants, King Charles
4   was

was advifed to make a new grant of that country to his brother the duke of York by letters patent, bearing date, June 29, 1674.

Let us now proceed more particularly to the province of New-York, the fubject of this fection.

Anno 1664, K. Charles II. appointed commiffioners to fettle the boundaries of the feveral colonies: [r] from mifinformation they fettled the line between New-York and Connecticut by a N. N. W. line, as is mentioned in our vol. II, p. 161 ; they were made to believe that this N. N. W. line would leave twenty miles to New-York on the eaft fide of Hudfon's river; whereas it foon crof-fed Hudfon's river, and left many of the Dutch fettle-ments upon Hudfon's river, to the colonies of Maffa-chufetts-Bay, and Connecticut, but thefe colonies never took poffeffion thereof. This line is upon record in New-York and Connecticut.

The partition line of New-York with Connecticut was run February 14, 1684, by commiffioners of both colo-nies, and figned at the town of Milford in Connecticut by col. Thomas Dongan governor of New-York, and by Robert Treat, Efq. governor of Connecticut, and con-firmed by king William in council, March 28, 1700 ; but as this line was not well marked, diftinguifhed, or afcertained, efpecially as to the equivalent lands; not long fince, by both parties, it was finally run, well marked out, and afcertained, and confirmed by the king in council, as related in our vol. II. p. 161. in the fec-tion of Connecticut.

As to the eaftern boundary of the province of New-York ; New-York hint at claiming fo far eaft as Con-necticut river, becaufe 1. By ancient Dutch maps pub-lifhed before the Englifh royal grants of the colonies of

[r] We formerly mentioned, their fettling of the boundaries between the colonies of Maffachufetts-Bay and Rhode-Ifland.

Maffachu-

Maffachufetts-Bay and Connecticut, the Dutch had actually a fort at the mouth of Connecticut river, as appears by records [s]. 2. That part of New-Netherlands in the duke of York's grant, is described, " and also " all that ifland or iflands, commonly called by the fe- " veral name or names of Mattowacks or Long-Ifland, " fituate, lying, and being towards the weft of Cape- " Cod and the narrow Highganfets, abutting upon the " main land between two rivers, there called and known " by the feveral names of Connecticut and Hudfon's ri- " vers, and all the lands from the weft fide of Connecti- " cut river, to the eaft fide of Delaware-Bay." 3. This ifland, now called Long-Ifland, remains with the province of New-York, by a mutual tacit confent of both colonies.   In anfwer to thefe allegations it is obvious, 1. That the line lately fettled between New-York and Connecticut, and confirmed or ratified by the king in council, is at twenty miles eaft of Hudfon's river, and cuts off all their claims of this nature upon Connecticut. 2. By the like parity of reafon, and precedent, the New-York claim to that part of Maffachufetts-Bay, which lies weft of Connecticut river, is cut off; moreover the Dutch never traded or fettled fo high upon Connecticut river. 3. Therefore in equity, New-York is bounded north of Connecticut N. W. corner, by a line parallel to and at twenty miles diftant eaft of Hudfon's river, to over-againft the great crook [t], elbow, or great falls of Hudfon's river, and thence in a due north line to the fouth

[s] The children of William Brown, Efq. of Salem in New-England, are great-grand-children of a grand-daughter of mynheer Provoft, at that time governor of this fort.

[t] Great crooks of boundary rivers not well difcovered and defcribed at the times of granting and bounding colonies, are now conftrued as a termination of fuch lines; thus it was lately by determination of the king in council, with refpect to the line between the provinces of Maffachufetts-Bay and New-Hampfhire at Pantucket falls of Merrimack river, fee vol. I. p. 423.

boundary line of the French Canada country ; [*u*] this line with other difputable claims is now in agitation at Paris by Britifh and French commiffaries.

Unlefs there be fome general, but definitive articles of agreement, fee vol. I. p. 13, with the French, concerning boundaries, we ought to have continued refidence of commiffaries at Paris or elfewhere ; if the prefent commiffaries are fo happy as to fettle the boundary lines, between Canada on the French fide, and Nova-Scotia, New England, and New-York on the Britifh

[*u*] The various difputes between the courts of Great-Britain and France (I muft once and again beg pardon for meddling in ftate affairs, or arcana imperii, by chance they fall in my way, and in fome manner I fcramble over them) concerning the national properties and jurifdictions of fome difputable countries in America, which perhaps might have been fettled in the late definitive (fo called) treaty of Aix la Chapelle, more expeditioufly and with better effect, confidering 1. That by meer dint of good fortune, providence feemed to be of our fide, and gave us poffeffion of Louifbourg at the mouth or entrance of St. Laurence or Canada great river, the French Dunkirk of North America. 2. By our natural fuperiority at fea, we had entirely obftructed the French plantation American trade, which might have induced or forced the French to make us fome favourable conceffions ; than by tedious and generally ineffective fubfequent treaties by commiffaries, which frequently terminate only in a neutrality till next general rupture, or in fome mutual conceffions by way of equivalents detrimental to that fide who may have lately received the law ; thus for inftance, if the court of Great-Britain at this juncture fhould quit claim the neutral iflands in the Weft-Indies to the French, as an equivalent for fome conceffions to be made in Nova-Scotia by the court of France to the Britifh.

At prefent, 1751, the French with a confiderable military force, make a ftand on the north fide of Chicanecto-bay and river in about 25 d. 25 m. The parallel of 45 d. is the northern extent of king James I. grant 1606 to the North-Virginia company ; this is perhaps the foundation of the French claim. If the partition line with France or Canada is to be fettled at 45 d. north lat. continued, it will fall in with St. Laurence or Ontario river, a little above Montreal ; including the greateft part of Champlain or Corlaers lake with the formerly Dutch country adjoining. If the fouth limits of Canada are thus fettled, New-York weft line will begin at this determination, and pafs along Ontario river to Ontario lake, along Ontario lake, and its communicating run of water to the lake Erie, till it meets with Penfylvania north line.

fide,

fide, there will ftill remain further lines to be fettled, of which I can give fome inftances, which may occafion great contention, the fymptoms whereof appear already ; but as thefe things at prefent are in embrio, I fhall touch upon them only by way of annotational amufement. [*x*]

[*x*] There is a tract of valuable land weft foutherly from Penfylvania: Penfylvania in the grant extends 5 d. W. from Delaware river, and takes in a confiderable fhare of lake Erie, and within which bounds fince the late peace the French have erected a fortification with a view of claiming that country, as formerly they built a fort at Crown-point, to fix a claim to the country of lake Champlain. Our Indian traders inform us, that below lake Erie, upon the river Ohio, called by the French La Belle Riviere, and the great river Ouabache, which jointly fall into the grand river of Miffiffippi, are the moft valuable lands in all America, and extend from 500 to 600 miles in a level, rich foil. Luckily for us, the French, laft war, not being capable of fupplying the Indians of thofe rivers with goods fufficient, thefe Indians dealt with our traders, and a number of them came to Philadelphia to treat with the Englifh ; hitherto they have faithfully obferved their new alliance : thefe Indians are called the Twichetwhees, a large nation, much fuperior in numbers to all our Six nations, and independent of them. This gave the government of Canada much uneafinefs, that fo confiderable a body of Indians with their territory, trade, and inlet into the Miffiffippi, fhould be lopt from them ; accordingly the governor of Canada in the autumn 1750, wrote to the governors of New-York and Penfylvania, acquainting them, that our Indian traders had encroached fo far on their territories by trading with their Indians ; that if they did not defift, he fhould be obliged to apprehend them, wherever they fhould be found within thefe bounds ; accordingly in the fpring 1751, fome French parties with their Indians, feized three of our traders, and confined them in Montreal or Quebeck : the Twichetwhees, our late allies, refented this, and immediately rendezvoufed to the number of from 500 to 600, and fcoured the woods till they found three French traders, and delivered them up to the government of Penfylvania. Here the matter refts, and waits for an accommodation betwixt our governor and the French governor, as to exchange of prifoners ; and as to the main point of the queftion, in fuch cafes the French never cede till drubbed into it by a war, and confirmed by a fubfequent peace. However it is probable, that in a few years our fettlements, if well attended to, will be carried thither, if, with the protection of the Indians of that nation, they are countenanced by our governments. With this view the governor of Penfylvania is labouring with the affembly to have

The

The north and south boundaries in North-America
dominions, belonging or claimed by different foviereign-
ties, and of feparate colonies under the fame fovereign,
are beft determined by parallels of latitude which may
be fuppofed invariable; thus the boundary of Hudfon's-
Bay company by the treaty of Utrecht is well fixed at
49 d. N. lat. perhaps that of Canada with Nova-Scotia, New-England and New-York, may be fettled at
45 d. In New-England that of Maffachufetts-Bay with
New-Hampfhire, by the king in council is fixed at a
parallel of about 42 d. 50 m. Maffachufetts-Bay with
Rhode-Ifland and Connecticut is in 42 d. 2 m. New-
York and Penfylvania is 42 d. compleated, or the be-
ginning of the 43 d. which is twenty miles north of
New-York ftation point with the Jerfies; Virginia with
the Carolinas as fettled, 1739, is in about 36 d. 40 m.
Some colonies are only bounded by rivers, the river
Powtomack bounds Virginia from Maryland, the river
Savannah divides South-Carolina from Georgia.

In all affairs, the French act the huckfters; at firft
make great demands, but afterwards gradually recede.
It is faid, that as the French are now in poffeffion of
Crown-Point fort and fettlement near lake Champlain in
about 44 d. N. lat. their firft demand of boundaries was
a parallel of 44 d. lat. which cuts off from us part of
New-York and New-Hampfhire, almoft the whole of

---

fome place of ftrength, fecurity, or retreat for our Indian traders,
under the name of a trading or truck-houfe; the Indians have given
their confent to this fcheme, which they never granted to the French;
it will be a difficult matter to perfuade a quaker affembly into any
thing, where a military ftrength or fecurity is implied.

We may obferve, that fome part of thefe Indian lands W. foutherly of Penfylvania, to the quantity of 600,000 acres, have a year
or two ago, been granted by the crown to a company of gentlemen in Virginia, free of quit-rent for twenty-one years; in the prayer
of their petition, they propofe the fettling and cultivating the fame,
as well as to carry on trade with the Indians. The whole of this affair is now reprefented at home to the miniftry, by the governor of
Penfylvania.

the

the province of Maine, all the good country upon Que-
nebeck river, all Sagadahock, or the late property of the
duke of York, almoft the whole of Nova-Scotia, including Anopolis-Royal in 44 d. 40 m. and Chebucto
in 44 d. 10 m. and Canfo; the French court are fince
faid to have ceded, and propofed to make a ceffion of
one degree of latitude; that is, their bounding parallel
of latitude fhall be 45 d. as the grant of K. James I.
anno 1606, to the North-Virginia company extended
no further; and moreover, that the French governor
Champlain had taken poffeffion of the gulph and river
of St. Laurence before this, and before the Dutch occupied the New-York fettlement.   This parallel of
45 d. in favour of the French, includes all the Canfo
iflands with the northern parts of the bay of Fundy:
and the good country upon St. John's river; leaving
to Great-Britain the peninfula of Nova-Scotia, Crown-
Point, and the greateft part of the country upon lake
Champlain or the Dutch Corlaers lake; [y] the ceffion
of Nova-Scotia to Great-Britain by the treaty of Utrecht,
was underftood by the nation or people of Great-Britain, to be according to the extent of the French commiffion fo far as Cape-Rofiers, to Mr. Subercaffe, their
laft] governor, of L'Acadie; but by a parallel of 45 d.
in the meridian of Cape-Rofiers, in lat. of 50 d. 30 m.
we give up 5 d. 30 m. of latitude; in the meridian of
Quebeck in lat. 46 d. 55 m. we give up about 1 d.
55 m. of latitude; in the meridian of Montreal, a very
fmall matter.   Thus the French explain the loofe treaty of Utrecht, to our very great difadvantage, as if
they gave the law, and were fupreme judges thereof; O
tempora!

[y] This Corlaer was a principal man amongft the Dutch fettlers,
and this lake was called by his name; the French call it lake Champlain, and it generally has obtained that name; Champlain was the
firft governor of Canada.

- The north boundary of the province of New-York, may be the fouth line of Canada when fettled; probably it will begin at a point in a meridian twenty miles eaft of the crook or great falls of Hudfon's river, and running weft will crofs lake Champlain, and terminate in Cataraqui river.

Its W. line runs up Cataraqui river, and lake called generally lake Ontario, and terminates on lake Erie in north lat. 42 d. complete. From Ofwego upon lake Ontario, may be reckoned the width of the government of New-York, 220 miles, viz. due W. from the lake, 200 miles to Albany or Hudfon's river; and from Albany twenty miles due W. to the weft line of Maffachufetts-Bay province.

The fourhern line of the province of New-York is in feveral directions or flexures. 1. From lake Erie along the north or head line of Penfylvania in lat. 42. to Delaware river. 2. Thence twenty miles down faid river to the north divifional point of New-York and New-Jerfies on faid river in lat. 41 d. 40 m. 3. Thence in a ftraight line E. 42 d. to 41 d. lat. on Hudfon's river. 4. Thence twelve miles down Hudfon's river to north end of the ifland of New-York, then down faid Hudfon's river on the W. fide of New-York ifland to Sandy-point, the entrance of New-York road and harbour about thirty miles. 5. Thence along the fouthern fhore of Long-Ifland, round the E. end of Long-Ifland, including Fifher's ifland and Gardner's ifland, which lie near the entrance of New-London harbour in Thames river of Connecticut colony; then along the northern fhore of Long-Ifland found, to over-againft the mouth of Byram river, where the weftern divifional line between New-York and Connecticut begins.

The eaftern line is from the mouth of Byram river, along the Oblong as defcribed in the fection of Connecticut, vol. II. p. 161, to the N. W. corner of Connecticut colony, or S. W. corner of the province of Maffachufetts-Bay, about eighty miles: thence in a parallel with

I

Hudfon's

Hudfon's river at twenty miles diftance E. from Hudfon's river, along the weftern line of Maffachufetts-
Bay, about forty-feven miles to the N. W. corner of
Maffachufetts-Bay, which is the S. W. corner of lands
lately annexed, or crown lands put under the jurifdiction of the province of New-Hampfhire pro tempore ;
thence in a like parallel from Hudfon's river, about
forty miles upon the weftern line of New-Hampfhire,
to the latitudes of the great falls or crook of Hudfon's
river ; thence in a due meridian line on the weft line of
the crown lands, [z] at prefent in the jurifdiction of
New-Hampfhire, to the fouth boundary line of Canada,
when by. much protracted, and finally perhaps difad-
vantageous negotiations it fhall be determined.   The
reader may obferve, that I have neither inclination nor
intereft to be of any fide, other than folicitous for a national concern.

We may obferve, that as the dividing line between
New-York and New-Jerfies in duke of York's grant of
1664, to lord Berkley, and Sir George Carteret, is from
the N. latitude of 41 d. on Hudfon's river, to the lat.
of 41 d. 40 m. on the northermoft branch of Delaware
river ; fo that the fixing of the two latitudes, and running of the line between them, was all that was required
for the fettling of that line: accordingly, 1719, by act
of the general affemblies of both provinces, commiffioners and furveyors were appointed : after many obferva-

[z] In a late final fettlement of the north boundary of the province
of Maffachufetts-Bay, if the adminiftration at home, for the intereft
of our mother country and its plantations, had been advifed by gentlemen intelligent in the affair, the lands north of that line, being
crown lands, might have been annexed to the province of Maffachufetts-Bay, though not property, yet in jurifdiction, as are the
lands of Sagadahock: the infignificant impotent fmall province of
New-Hampfhire can never be capable of cultivating and defending it
againft the Canada French and their Indians ; fo large a tract of wildernefs lands as this, is, leaving a vaft country uncultivated, or to the
ufe and improvement of the French.

tions, the latitude of 41 d. 40 m. on the northermoft branch of Delaware river was fettled, and executed by indentures under hands and feals; and to commemorate the fame, thefe indentures were recorded at Perth-Amboy in New-Jerfey, lib. D. No. 2. p. 280, &c. and in New-York, in a book of entries beginning of Auguft 1739, p. 168, &c. then a ftraight line was run by the faid commiffioners and furveyors to Hudfon's river, and the furveyors made many obfervations there, of the meridional altitudes of the fun and proper ftars, to difcover the proper latitude on Hudfon's river; but the commiffioners never met afterwards to fix that point; therefore it remains undetermined to this day, though frequently demanded by the Eaft-Jerfies.

The deed of the equivalent lands, (fee vol. II. p. 161) called the Oblong from Connecticut to New-York in the king's name, was not fealed or delivered until May 14, the grant of the greateft part of thefe lands to Sir Jofeph Eyles, and company was next day after, being the 15th of May, and not put upon record till fome time thereafter. The controverfy between Eyles and company, and Hauly and company, concerning the property of thefe lands, is ftill fubfifting: the contracted nature of a fummary does not allow us to infert it at large; only we obferve, [a] that Sir Jofeph Eyles and company, March 10, 1730-1, prefented a petition to the king in council for this land, by the name of " a cer-
" tain tract of land in your majefty's province of New-
" York in America, &c." computed at 62,000 acres; on the fame day it was referred to a committee of the privy council, and 24th of that month, they refer it to the lords commiffioners of trade and plantations; the lords of trade made their report to the lords of the committee. " We think it for his majefty's fervice to

[a] This I infert in fo minute a manner, by way of information, how plantation affairs are managed at the feveral boards in Great-Britain.

grant

grant to them, their heirs and affigns, the lands they petition for," &c. and on the 30th March 1731, the lords of the committee make their report to the king in council, " apprehending that all reafonable encouragement ought to be given for the fettling of lands in your majefty's plantations, do agree with the opinion of the faid lords commiffioners for trade, &c. and that it may be advifable for your majefty to grant to the petitioners the faid lands in the manner above propofed." April 8, 1731, the king in counfel approves of the report of thofe lords of the committee, and orders a grant accordingly, by ordering the lords commiffioners of his majefty's treafury to prepare a warrant for paffing it, and on the 4th of May, 1731, the lords commiffioners of the treafury directed the warrant for the grant to the attorney and folicitor general; the grant itfelf, under the great feal of Great-Britain, is dated May 15, 1731; after reciting the words of the petition, " are gracioufly pleafed to gratify the petitioners of their requeft: know ye," &c. [*b*]—About the fame time the governor and council of New-York granted, by virtue of their royal inftruction for granting of province lands, to Hauly and company the fame lands; which of thefe grants fhall take place, is not as yet decided; it is certain, that the deed of thefe equivalent lands, from Connecticut to his majefty, was not fealed and delivered until May 14, 1731, yet at the diftance of 1000 leagues was granted next day to Eyles, &c.

The extent of the province government or jurifdiction of New-York is as follows; from N. to S. that is, from Sandy-Hook in lat. 40 d. 30 m. to the fuppofed Canada line in the parallel of 45 d. lat. are 313 Englifh miles; the extent from W. to E. is various. 1. From the E.

[*b*] There feems to be fome impofition in the petition of Sir Jofeph Eyles and company, reprefenting thefe lands, as productive of pitch, tar, other naval ftores, mines, and furs.

southerly

foutherly termination of the boundary line between the
Jerfies and New-York, in lat. 41 d. upon Hudfon's river to Byram river, where the colony of Connecticut begins, are ten miles. 2. From the W. northerly termination of the faid boundary line between Jerfey and
New-York on the north branch of Delaware river in lat.
41 d. 4 m. to Connecticut W. line, including the Oblong,
are eighty-two miles, whereof about fixty miles from
Delaware river to Hudfon's river, and twenty-two miles
from Hudfon's river to the prefent Connecticut W. line,
Oblong included. 3. From 41d. 40 m. on Delaware
river, New-York runs twenty miles higher on Delaware
river to the parallel of 42 d. lat. which by Penfylvania
royal grant divides New-York from the province of Penfylvania; upon this parallel New-York is fuppofed to
extend weft to the lake Erie; and from thence along
lake Erie, and along the communicating great run of
water [c] from the lake Erie to the lake Ontario or Cataraqui, and along lake Cataraqui, and its difcharge Cataraqui river to the aforefaid Canada, fuppofed line with
the Britifh colonies; we fhall inftance the breadth of
New-York province from Ofwego; [d] as being a me-

[c] In this run of water or communicating river, are the noted
great Niagara falls frequently mentioned, and a French pafs to keep
up the communication between Canada and Mififfippi, called fort
Denonville.

[d] Ofwego, formerly mentioned, is a fort, and Indian trading
place in times of peace, with a garrifon of twenty-four foldiers from
the four independent regular companies, to prevent any diforders in
trade, this being in the feafon a kind of Indian fair: laft French
war the garrifon confifted of 200 men of regular troops and militia,
and the French did not find it convenient to moleft them. Our traders with the Indians fit out from Albany, and pay a certain duty upon what they vend and buy at Ofwego: their rout is, from Albany
to Schenectady town, or corporation upon Mowhawks river, fixteen
miles land carriage; thence up Mohawks river; in this river is only
one fhort carrying place at a fall in that river; from Mohawks river
a carrying place of three to five miles according to the feafons, here
are convenient Dutch land carriages to be hired, to a river which falls
into the Oneidas lake; then from this lake down Onondagues river
dium

dium in this line.   Ofwego fort and tracing place with
many nations of Indians upon the lake Ontario, Cataraqui or Ofwego, in lat. 43 d. 33 m. lies weſt northerly
from Albany about 200 miles, and twenty miles from
Albany to the weſt line of the province of Maſſachuſetts-
Bay, in all about 220 miles.   Montreal lies N. by E. of
Albany above 220 miles.

Beſides the main land country of New-York, there are
ſome iſlands belonging to it.   1. Long-Iſland, called by
the Indians Matowacks, and by the Dutch, Naſſau; it lies

to Ofwego trading place upon lake Ontario ; there is a ſhort fall in
Onondagues river.   Almoſt the whole of the eaſt ſide of the Ontario
lake lies in the Onondagues country.   From Ofwego fort to Niagara,
falls on French fort Dononville are about 160 miles, and from Ofwego fort fixty miles to fort Frontenac, alſo called Cataraqui fort,
where the lake vents by Cataraqui river, which with the Outawae
river makes St. Laurence river called the great river of Canada ;
this fort Frontanac is about 200 miles down that rocky river to Montreal.

By conjecture of the French Coureurs des bois in round numbers,
the circumference of the five great lakes or inland ſeas of North-
America, are, Ontario, 200 leagues, Erio, 200 leagues, Hurons 300
leagues, Mihagan, 300 leagues, and the upper lake 500 leagues.

As I do not write this, as a rigidly connected piece, I mention
ſeveral things as they occur, but without any conſiderable deviation.
1; The Mohawk nation of our allied New-York Indians live on the
ſouth ſide of a branch of Hudſon's river called Mohawks river, but
not on the north ſide thereof, as is repreſented in the French maps.
2. The Oneidas nation lie about 100 miles W. from Albany, near
the head of the Mohawks river.   3. The Onondagues lie about 130
miles weſt from Albany.   4. The Tuſcaroras, an adventitious or ſixth
nation (in former times they were called the Five nations) live partly
with the Oneidas, and partly with the Onondagues.   5. The Cayugas
about 160 miles weſt from Albany.   6. The Senecas who live upon
the frontiers of Penſylvania are about 140 miles weſt from Albany.
A French noted writer M. de Liſle calls theſe Five nations by the
name of Iroquois.

Formerly the French had popiſh miſſionaries with the Oneides,
Onondagues, and Cayugas, and endeavoured to keep them in their
intereſt.

There is ſcarce any beaver in the country of the Five nations ;
therefore their hunting at a great diſtance from home, occaſions frequent jarrings with other Indian nations; this trains them up by
practice, to be better warriors than the other Indian nations.

in

in length from E. to W. about 120 miles, and at a medium is about ten miles broad; its east shore is a sandy flat, as is all the E. shore of North-America from Cape-Cod of New-England in N. lat. 42 d. 10 m. to Cape-Florida in about 25 d. N. lat. Upon the shore of Long-Island are very few inlets, and these very shallow: its north side is good water, there being a sound between it and the main land of Connecticut; the widest part of this near New-Haven of Connecticut does not exceed eight leagues. Two thirds of this island is a barren sandy soil. The eastern parts were settled from New-England, and retain their customs; the western parts were settled by the Dutch, where many families to this day understand no other language but the Dutch. It is divided into three counties, Queen's county, King's county and Suffolk county, and pays considerably above one fourth of the taxes or charges of the goverment of the province. Hell-Gate, where is the confluence or meeting of the E. and W. tide in Long-Island found, is about twelve miles from the city of New-York. 2. Staten-Island at its E. end, has a ferry of three miles to the W. end of Long-Island; at its W. end is a ferry of one mile to Perth-Amboy of East-Jersies; it is divided from East-Jersies by a creek; is in length about twelves miles, and about six miles broad, and makes one county, called Richmond, which pays scarce one in one and twenty of the provincial tax; it is all in one parish, but several congregations, viz. an English, Dutch, and French congregation; the inhabitants are mostly English; only one considerable village, called Cuckold's-town. 3. Nantucket, Martha's vineyard and Elizabeth islands were formerly under the jurisdiction of New-York; but upon the revolution they were annexed by the new charter of Massachusetts-Bay, to the jurisdiction of Massachusett's-Bay; not many years since, some of the freeholders of these islands when occasionally in New-York, were arrested for the arrears of the general quit-rents of these islands. 4. Manhatans, the Indian name, New-Amsterdam the Dutch name, or New-York the English name, may be called an island, though it has

a coma communication with the main land, by King's-bridge, the whole island being about fourteen miles long, but very narrow, is all in the jurisdiction of the city of New-York; it lies on the mouth of Hudson's river.

In the province of New-York are four incorporated towns, who hold courts within themselves, send representatives to the general assembly or legislature, with sundry exclusive privileges.   1. The city of New-York and its territory, formerly established by col. Dongan, sends four representatives.   2. The city of Albany probably had their charter also from col. Dongan, and is nearly the same with that of New-York; sends two representatives.   3. The borough of West-Chester; and 4. The township of Schenectady; it seems these two corporations had their charters before the revolution, and each of them send one representative to the general assembly.

As a specimen of town corporation charters, in the plantations, I shall insert an extract of the charter of the city of New-York; it is the fullest and the most exclusive of any of them.   It begins by mentioning or reciting several grants of privileges which they have enjoyed by patents and charters.   " Whereas the city of New-
" York is an ancient city, and the citizens anciently a
" body politick with sundry rights, privileges, &c. as well
" by prescription as by charters, letters patent, grants and
" confirmations, not only of divers governors and com-
" manders in chief in the said province, but also of seve-
" ral governors, directors, generals, and commanders in
" chief of the Nether Dutch nation, whilst the same was
" or has been under their power and subjection. That Tho-
" mas Dongan, Esq. lieutenant governor of New-York,
" under king James II. August 27, 1686, by a charter
" confirmed all their former grants not repugnant to the
" laws of England and province of New-York, with some
" additions, granting to them all the unappropriated lands
" to low-water mark in Manhatan's island, under the year-
" ly quit-rent of one beaver skin, or the value thereof;
" their jurisdiction to extend all over the island, &c." That
this charter was confirmed by a subsequent charter from
                                                    lord

lord Cornbury governor, April 19, 1708, with some additions granted to them the ferries, &c. That as some questioned the validity of their former charters, because they were in the governor's name only, and not in the name of their kings and queens, they petition governor Montgomery for a new charter, confirming all their former privileges, with some additions; granting to them four hundred feet below low-water mark in Hudson's river, &c.

Governor Montgomery's charter by which they now hold, is dated January 15, 1730, and afterwards confirmed or corroborated by an act of the provincial assembly or legislature of New-York, and declared to be a publick act, relating to the whole colony. The substance of this charter is as follows:

" They are incorporated by the name of the mayor, al-
" dermen and commonalty of the city of New-York.—
" The city to be divided into seven wards, viz. west-ward,
" south-ward, duck-ward, east-ward, north-ward, Mont-
" gomery-ward, and the out-ward divided into the Bowry
" division and Harlem division.—The corporation to con-
" sist of one mayor, one recorder, and seven aldermen,
" seven assistants, one sheriff, one coroner, one com-
" mon clerk, one chamberlain or treasurer, one high con-
" stable, sixteen assessors, seven collectors, sixteen con-
" stables, and one marshal. The mayor with consent of
" the governor, may appoint one of his aldermen his de-
" puty. The governor yearly to appoint the mayor, she-
" riff, and coroner, and the freeholders and freemen in
" their respective wards to chuse the other officers, ex-
" cepting the chamberlain, who is to be appointed in coun-
" cil by the mayor, four or more aldermen, and four or
" more assistants. The mayor to appoint the high con-
" stable; all officers to take the proper oaths, and to con-
" tinue in office till others have been chosen in their
" room; when any officer dies, the ward is to chuse an-
" other; upon refusal to serve in office, the common
" council may impose a fine not exceeding 15 l. for the
" use of the corporation. The mayor or recorder, and
" four

" four or more aldermen, with four or more affiftants, to
" be a common council to make by-laws, to regulate the
" freemen, to leafe lands and tenements, &c. but to do
" nothing inconfiftent with the laws of Great-Britain or
" of this province; fuch laws and orders not to continue
" in force exceeding twelve months, unlefs confirmed by
" the governor and council. May punifh by disfranchifing,
" or fines for the ufe of the corporation. The common
" council fhall decide in all controverted elections of offi-
" cers. The common council may be called by the mayor,
" or in his abfence by the recorder; fine of a member for
" non-attendance not exceeding 20 s. for the ufe of the
" corporation. The corporation may eftablifh as many
" ferries as they may fee fit, and let the fame. To hold a
" market at five or more different places every day of the
" week, excepting Sunday; to fix the affize of bread,
" wine, &c. The mayor with four or more aldermen
" may make freemen, fees not to exceed 5 l. none but
" freemen fhall retail goods or exercife any trade, penalty
" 5 l. no aliens to be made free. To commit common
" vagabonds, erect work-houfes, goals, and alms-houfes.
" The mayor to appoint the clerk of the market, and
" water bailiff; to licence carmen, porters, cryers, fca-
" vengers, and the like; to give licence to taverns and
" retailers of ftrong drink for one year, not exceeding
" 30 s. per licence; felling without licence 5 l. current
" money toties quoties. The mayor, deputy mayor, re-
" corder, and aldermen for the time being, to be juftices
" of the peace. The mayor, deputy mayor, and recor-
" der, or any of them, with three or more of the alder-
" men, fhall hold quarter feffions, not to fit exceeding
" four days. Moreover, recorder, and aldermen, to be
" named in all commiffions of oyer and terminer, and
" goal delivery. The mayor, deputy mayor, recorder,
" or any one of them, with three or more of the aldermen,
" fhall and may hold every Tuefday a court of record, to
" try all civil caufes real, perfonal, or mixt, within the
" city and county. May adjourn the mayor's court to any
" time not exceeding 28 days. The corporation to have a
" common

"common clerk, who shall be also clerk of the court of
"record, and sessions of the peace, to be appointed dur-
"ing his good behaviour, by the governor; eight attor-
"nies in the beginning, but as they drop, only six to be
"allowed, during their good behaviour, for the mayor's
"court; the mayor's court to have the direction and
"cognizance of the attornies, who, upon a vacancy shall
"recommend one to the governor for his approbation.
"The mayor, recorder, or any alderman, may with or
"without a jury determine in cases not exceeding 40 s.
"value. No freeman inhabitant shall be obliged to serve
"in any office out of the city. A grant and confirmation
"to all the inhabitants of their hereditaments, &c. paying
"the quit-rent reserved by their grants. The corpora-
"tion may purchase and hold hereditaments, &c. so as
"the clear yearly value exceed not 3000 l. sterl. and the
"same to dispose of at pleasure. To pay a quit-rent of
"30 s. proclamation money per ann. besides the beaver
"skin, and 5 s. current money in former charters re-
"quired. No action to be allowed against the corporation
"for any matters or cause whatsoever prior to this char-
"ter. A pardon of all prosecutions, forfeitures, &c.
"prior to this charter. This grant or the inrolment there-
"of (record) shall be valid in law, notwithstanding of
"imperfections, the imperfections may in time coming
"be rectified at the charge of the corporation."

As I am now to relate the French and Indian wars
which concern the British province of New-York, with
their other Indian affairs; as also some account of the
successions of governors and governments in the colony
of New-York; instead of summary references, as we
proposed, for the ease of the reader I shall use a connected and fluent short recapitulation, which will point
out sundry of our claims in North-America.

French and Indian wars, with other Indian affairs.

Sebastian Cabot, a subject of England, employed by K.
Henry VII. to discover a N. W. passage to China, ann.
1496

1496, touched at all the confiderable inlets on the eaftern coaft of North America from Cape-Florida in N. lat. 25 d. to N. lat. 67 and half d. and took a NO-MINAL poffeffion of the whole for the crown of England (fee vol. I. p. 273) but making no fettlements, he made no title by occupancy, or purchafe from the Indians.

Sir Walter Raleigh, a native of England, anno 1584, with people fettlers, landed at Roanoak in the prefent North-Carolina, fettled and took poffeffion for queen Elizabeth, and called all the North-America coaft by the name of Virginia [*e*], in honour of the virgin queen Elizabeth. After fundry fmall adventures of Virginia in general, April 10, 1606, two companies were incorporated in one letter patent by K. James I. called the South and North Virginia companies. The South-Virginia company began a fettlement in Chefepeak-Bay 1607; the North-Virginia company carried on (but in feparate adventures) fome fmall trade in fifh and fur, but made no fettlement with continuance till 1620 [*f*] when they began to fettle Plymouth in New-England; being late in the feafon, the weather obliged the defigned fettlers to put up with the firft land or harbours; accordingly they landed in Plymouth-Bay of Maffachuetts, and have continued there ever fince.

Capt. Henry Hudfon [*g*] in fome Dutch company's

[*e*] Some pedantick criticks, in imitation of fome annotators upon the Greek and Roman clafficks, imagine that he meant a young virgin country, never before occupied by the Europeans.

[*f*] The defigned fettlers had made a fort of contract with the council of Plymouth or North-Virginia company, for a territory upon Hudfon's river: this evinces that in thefe times, the Dutch or any other European nation by prior difcovery, occupancy, prefcription, or any other claim, had no equitable right to that country

[*g*] This Hudfon was a great enthufiaftick projector of N. E and N. W. paffages, and gave name to Hudfon's Bay, and Hudfon's river of New-York; he perifhed in one of his paffage adventures, being never heard of more.

It is faid by the French, that Canada was firft fettled by the French under Champlain their firft governor 1603, being five years before Hudfon took poffeffion of New-Netherlands for the Dutch.

service, but an Englishman, anno 1608, came to the mouth of Hudson's river (as it is since called) though in the limits of both the said corporations or companies, and without licence from the king of England, purchased (as it is said) of the Indians that certain territory, and disposed of his rights to the Dutch West India company, or rather to some merchants of Amsterdam; and the Dutch made some imperfect irregular settlements there. Sir Samuel Argol governor for the South-Virginia company 1618 drove the Dutch from their usurped settlement: however, the Dutch obtained 1620 of that pacifick easy prince K. James I. leave to make a small settlement there for wooding and watering of their Brazil fleets, and 1623 the Dutch made a regular colony of it, and their commander in chief was called director general of the New Netherlands.

Carr, a sea commander, and Nichols a land commander, arrived before New-Amsterdam, since called New York, with an armed force August 20, 1664, and summoned the Dutch governor to surrender; accordingly the 27th following, articles were agreed upon; New-Netherlands was surrendered to England, and col. Richard Nichols was appointed lieut. governor by the duke of York, who had obtained a previous grant thereof from his brother K. Charles II. New-Netherlands was confirmed to England by the treaty of Breda 1667: but as England, March 17, 1671-2 proelaimed war against the Dutch, the Dutch easily reconquered it from the English 1673, col. Lovelace governor; but afterwards by the treaty of London 1673-4, the Dutch made an absolute cession thereof to England; and in consequence thereof as New-Netherlands had been conquered since the first grant, to prevent difficulties in titles, K. Charles II. made a second grant, June 29, 1674, to his brother the duke of York, with the right of government to him, his heirs and assigns. I shall not anticipate what matters of this grant belong to the sections of the Jerseys and Pensylvania.. Governor Andros by letters of October

31, 1674,

31, 1674, acquaints the neighbouring governors, that he had received poffeffion of New-York, &c. No act of government appears upon record from July 19, 1673, to November 6, 1674; then were publifhed the fecond royal letters patent to the duke of York of New-York and the Jerfeys, dated June 29, 1674.

The Dutch interlopers at their firft arrival in this country 1608, entered into alliance with the Five Nations called by the French Iroquois; it continued without interruption, and remains to this day a firm alliance with the Englifh [b] who fucceeded the Dutch in the European jurifdiction of thefe countries.

Thefe five tribes of Indians are called nations, though properly all of one nation; they are diftinguifhed by the names of Mohawks, Oneidas, Onondagas, Cayugas, and Senecas. In the North-Carolina war with the Tufcarora Indians 1711, many of thefe Tufcaroras were obliged to fly their country, and fettled with the Onondagas and Cayugas, and are now called the fixth nation. The feveral fmall villages of Sefquahanna and Delaware river Indians, are under the protection of the Senecas; the Senecas are by far the largeft of the Six nations, and lie upon the frontiers of Penfylvania. Several of the renegadoes of the Five nations have fettled above Montreal, and are called Cohunagos or praying Indians.

Why do we not fend military officers amongft the Indians to inftruct them in the European arts of war. The French with good fuccefs follow this practice. Some fay that the officers of the four independent companies of fufileers [i] in New-York live like military monks in idlenefs and luxury.

[b] The reader may excufe my frequent inadvertent impropriety of writing in times fince the union, Englifh inftead of Britifh; it is the common fpeech expreffion, but very improper.

[i] Fufileers are fo called, becaufe they are fuppofed to be armed with light mufquets called fufees.

The. French ufe an argument with the Indians to be of their fide, viz. that they do not covet their lands, as the Englifh do.

During K. William's war, the inhabitants of Canada lived in continual fears of thefe Five Indian nations ; their feed time and harveft were much neglected. Canada is a tyrannical government and barren foil. Their lands fcarce produce fufficient for the fuftenance of the inhabitants.

We may obferve, that amongft the abovefaid Six Indian nations or tribes, the Onondagas refemble that canton, where the deputies of the feveral Swifs cantons meet upon affairs of great concern. The Onondagas, Oneidas, and Cayugas, have frequently been in the French intereft, by the management of the French miffionary priefts. Our miffionary priefts, inftead of this laborious, but vaftly ufeful publick duty, are indulged in a fort of fine-cures, in our moft opulent and well provided fettlements ; they labour only in confounding the fober and induftrious well-meaning prefbyterians, congregationalifts, &c. to the great detriment of the publick good; a new regulation amongft our miffionaries is much wanted.

1665, Sept. Courfal arrived governor of Canada; next fpring with twenty-eight companies of regular troops, and all the marching pofte of Canada that could be fpared, marched perhaps 250 leagues into the country of the Five-nations ; they did little or no execution ; and 1667 a peace was concluded between the French and their Indians, and the province of New-York with their Five nations of Indians : this peace continued till 1683.

1684, De la Barre governor of Canada, with all the pofte of Canada, marched and rendezvouzed at Cataraqui fort [k], while at the fame time he was only amufing

---

[k] It is now called fort Frontenac, being built by count de Frontenac governor of Canada, on Cataraqui lake, near the mouth of Cataraqui

the

the government of New-York, with !some trifling complaints againft the Five Indian Nations, to lull them
afleep. 1684, in July, lord Howard of Effingham, governor of Virginia, and col. Dongan, lieut. governor of
New-York, had an interview with the Five Indian nations at New-York.

1685, Marquis de Nonville, who fucceeded the governor general de la Barre, with 1500 men, regular troops,
Canada militia, and Indians, rendezvouzed at fort Frontenac or Cataraqui, defigned againft the Five Indian
nations; they did no execution.

1687, Governor general Nonville with 1500 French
and Indians infulted the Seneca nation. In return for
this, the Five Iroquois nations to the number of 1200
men, July 26, 1688, invaded the ifland of Montreal;
the governor general with his court, were there at that
time; they ravaged the country, killed many people,
and carried off captives; the Mohawks loft only three
men; the French abandoned their fort upon Cataraqui
lake, and left twenty-fix barrels of gun-powder.

In February 1689-90, the French, confifting of 500
Coureurs des bois (in New-England they are called
Swampiers,) with as many Indians or favages, made
incurfions upon the province of New-York; they burnt
Corlaer's village called Schenectady, and murdered fixty-
three perfons.

In the memory of man the Mohawks never received
fuch a blow as in the winter 1692-3; col. Fletcher with
300 volunteers marched to Albany, and the French with
their Indians returned home.

---

river, which runs to Montreal, and with the Ouatawaes river forms the
great river of Canada called the river of St. Laurence.

M. de la Salle upon Cataraqui lake built a bark of fixty tons, but the
neighbouring Indians in jealoufy foon burnt her.

For the Indian nations where the Englifh and French have particular
concerns, fee vol. I. p. 179.

For the Iroquois or Six nations of Mohawk Indians, fee vol. I. p.
185; they may confift of about 1500 marching men.

In 1696, The French with a large force made an incursion upon the New-York Indians, with a defign to deftroy the fettlements of Albany and Schenectady, but were repulfed by governor Fletcher.

During queen Anne's war, the Five Indian nations had a neutrality with the Canada French and their Indians, and by this means the province of New-York carried on a continued advantageous trade with Canada.

New-York had no concern in the New-England Indian war 1722 to 1725.

The French had lately erected a fort at Crown-Point near the lake Champlain upon the frontiers of New-York government. During the late French war from 1744 to 1747 inclufive, Crown-Point was the rendezvouz of the Canada French and their Indians, confequently their onfets were moftly upon the province of New-York and the N. W. corner of the province of Maffachufetts-Bay: 1745 from Crown-Point they deftroyed Saratoga fettlement, about thirty miles above Albany. The New-York frontier places where militia were pofted, are Schenectady, Albany, and Kinderhoek. Anno 1745, 1746, and 1747, the French and their Indians, above Albany, killed and captivated above 320 of our people.

Toward that chargeable amufement, called the intended expedition againft Canada of 1746, New-York province contributed fifteen companies of 100 men per company; the fix pound New-York currency in levy money, and victualling for fixteen or feventeen months, was a confiderable load.

The four independent regular companies of one hundred men each, ftationed at New-York many years, are an advantage to the country; they draw from Great-Britain, about 7,500 pound fterling, per annum.

Succeffion

Succession of governors in the province of New-York.

I shall not enumerate the commanders in chief; during the possession and jurisdiction of the Dutch, they were stiled variously, viz. directors, generals, governors, &c. The present stile of the British governor, is, " Captain general, and governor in chief in and over the province or colony of New York, and territories thereon " depending, and vice-admiral of the same." Before the revolution, the commanders in chief had only the title of lieutenant governor under the duke of York, as he was principal governor by patent. Upon K. James II. abdication, the property and government of the colony of New-York, and the territory of Saradahock in New-England, reverted to the crown.

The first English governor was col. Richard Nichols, his commission bore date April 2, 1664. He was commander of the land forces in the reduction of New-Netherlands, and one of the commissioners for settling the boundaries of our colonies in North-America. He continued governor to 1683, and was succeeded by

Sir Edmond Andros [*l*]; he was governor only for a short time, and was removed to the government of New-England; the several charter colonies of New-England having, from the iniquity of the times, either by a course in law had their charters taken from them, or tacitly dropt; he arrived in Boston in December 1686 with lieut. governor Nicholson and two independent companies of soldiers. See vol. I. p. 413. In April 1689, by a revolution in New-England, in consequence of the general revolution at home, he was disqualified and went home; excepting his bigotry [*m*] to popery and the arbi-

[*l*] Sir Edmond Andros 1672 had some command in New-York, and after him col. Lovelace.

[*m*] The Roman catholick religion or popery seems to be requisite where an arbitrary power in the king and his ministry are endeavoured after. An enthusiastick implicit faith as to religion in the pope and his clergy, is in a political way, a natural introduction of a passive obedience

trary.

trary power of his prince, he was a good moral man. He was appointed governor of Virginia 1692; he died in London 1714, of a good old age.

Andros was fucceeded by col. Dongan 1684; he was a Roman catholick, but much of a gentleman and patriot; he was irreconcilable to a French intereft; upon the revolution, being a papift, he was in confequence difmiffed from his government; but as a reward for his merits, he was created earl of Limerick. He made feveral grants of lands in Sagadahock, the duke of York's property, at prefent under the jurifdiction of the province of Maffachufetts-Bay; thefe grants in time, when claims are to be fettled, may occafion much confufion.

Upon the revolution, col. Benjamin Fletcher was appointed; he came over 1692 with fome regular troops, and was very induftrious in repulfing the Canada French and their Indians. In his time, 1696, the church of England in New-York (called Trinity church) was built; it is the only church of England upon the ifland.

After this col. Leflie ufurped the government (as his partifans faid, for a publick good) for which he and his friend Milburn fuffered as traitors, having held out for fome time the fort againft col. Slaughter, who was appointed governor by the king, and upon this kind of interregnum, fucceeded Slaughter; he died foon in New-York.

Col. Dudley, as prefident, fucceeded in the chief command of the province; he was afterwards governor of the province of Maffachufetts-Bay for many years, fee vol. I. p. 478. He was a cunning man, and fome fay, a notorious time-ferver.

in civil affairs, to the king and his miniftry; and perhaps in all politias. An enthufiaftick (man is an enthufiaftick animal) fuperftitious deference for the clergy is a fine qua non in civil government; therefore the clergy ought to be facred, and not ridiculed by the inconfiderate wits of the age; the famous Dr. Swift is here much to be faulted, his fort was in this fort of ridicule. The devotion we pay to the clergy introduces a proper fubmiffion to civil authority; and it is the clergy's bufinefs to labour this point.

Lord

Lord Bellomont was appointed governor 1697; in his very late paffage to his government of New-York, the fhip by ftrefs of weather was obliged to bear away to Barbadoes, and did not arrive in New-York till May 1698. He was at the fame time governor of New-York, Maffachufetts-Bay and New-Hampfhire: he did not proceed to Bofton till June 1699, and after obtaining a generous allowance of 1000 *l.* and a gratuity of 500 *l.* from the affembly, he returned to New York. In New-York he was allowed 1500 *l.* currency yearly falary, and the lieut. governor capt. Nanfon was allowed 500 *l.* lord Bellomont died in New-York, February 1700-1.

Lord Cornbury, fon to the earl of Clarendon, fucceeded; he arrived in New-York 1701: upon the proprietors of the Jerfeys refigning the government into the hands of queen Anne, he was likewife 1702 appointed governor of the Jerfeys. Earl of Clarendon, formerly lord Cornbury, went home by way of Virginia, and was fucceeded by

Lord Lovelace; he arrived November 13, 1708, and died in May 1709.

1710, April, col. Ingolfby, capt. of one of the independent companies, by a letter from the queen to the council of New-York, was difmiffed from being lieut. governor of New-York and Jerfeys.

1710, June 14, arrives col. Robert Hunter with 2700 Palatines to fettle in the province of New-York; thefe Palatines were allowed only ten acres of land to one family, therefore they generally removed to Penfylvania, where they had better encouragement. 1707, col. Hunter had been appointed lieut. governor of Virginia, but was taken by the French in his voyage thither. From New-York he went for England 1719 [n]. Upon K. George II. acceffion, he was continued governor of New-York and the Jerfeys. Upon account of his health, he obtained the government of Jamaica; he arrived in

[n] His wife, lady Hay, died Auguft 1716.

Jamaica,

Jamaica, February 1727-8; by this advice of his phyficians he certainly obtained a reprieve of his life for
fome years.

Col. Hunter was fucceeded in the government of
New-York by William Burnet, Efq a worthy fon of
the celebrated bifhop Burnet [*o*]; he arrived in autumn 1721.

Upon the acceffion of K. George II. col. Montgomery, a favourite, was appointed governor of New-York
and Mr. Burnet was removed to the government of
Maffachufetts Bay commonly called New-England,
where he died Sept. 7; 1729. Governor Montgomery
arrived in New-York, April 28, 1728, and died there
July 1, 1731.

In January 1731-2, col. Cofby was appointed governor of New-York and the Jerfeys; after a few years he
died in New-York.

Auguft 1736, George Clarke, Efq. lieut. governor
of New-York fucceeded in the adminiftration, and continued fome years.

George Clinton, Efq. [*p*] uncle to the earl of Lincoln,
was appointed governor of New York in May 1741; he
did not arrive in his government until September 21,
1743; he continues governor at this prefent writing,
July 1751.

Concerning the legiflature and laws of New-York.

It is a fundamental in the Britifh conftitution both at
home and abroad, in all the plantations, to make no
laws, nor to raife any money without the confent of the
people.

The legiflature of the colony of New-York confifts of
three negatives.

1. The governor or commander in chief for the time
being.

[*o*] See vol. I. p. 480.
[*p*] The hon. George Clinton, Efq. is at prefent admiral of the White.

2. The

2. The council; their complement is twelve in number, appointed by the king; when by death or other circumstances they fall short of a certain number, the governor may *pro tempore* fill them up to that number.

3. The twenty-seven representatives of the people elected by themselves; they are all county representatives, excepting the representatives of four towns, and of three great manors, viz. For the county of.

Richmond	2	New-York county and city	4
King's	2	Albany city	2
Queen's	2	West-Chester borough	1
Suffolk	2	Schenectady town	1
West-Chester	2	Manor of Ranflaer	1
Orange	2	Livingston	1
Ulster	2	Courtland	1
Albany	2		

In each of our colonies there are some fundamental constitutions which may be reckoned as invariable. 1. In the charter governments, their charters are their direction. 2. In the proprietary governments of Maryland, Jerseys [*q*], and Penfylvania, there are the proprietors original conceffions to the people, not to be varied, but under certain reftrictions; for instance, in Penfylvania, no article in the law of Mr. Penn's conceffions can be altered without the confent of fix in feven of the affembly men or representatives. 3. In the royal or crown governments, the governor's commiffion with the inftructions, are the *magna charta* of the colony during that commiffion; moreover, some of the affemblies in king's government at their firft congrefs or formation, make fundamental laws for themfelves; I fhall for inftance, produce that of New-York. Amongst our colonies we have very confiderable variations in their conftitutions. In Penfylvania there are only two negatives in the legiflature, the council having no negative.

[*q*] Jerfeys ever fince 1702 is become a king's government, but they ftill obferve the conceffions of the proprietors called their law of conceffions.

In

In Virginia no bill can originate with the council. In some colonies the governor and council are the supreme court of judicature; in others they are no court of judicature.

The New-York printed law-book begins April 1691 with a *magna charta* or fundamental constitution, viz. That the kings of England only, are invested with the right to rule this colony; and that none can exercise any authority over this province, but by his immediate authority under his broad seal of the realm of England. That the supreme legislative power and authority (under the king) shall be in the governor, council, and representatives of the people in general assembly; the exercise and administration of the government shall be in the governor and council, with the consent of at least five of the council; to govern according to the laws of the province, or in defect of them, by the laws of England. Upon the death or absence of a governor, the first in nomination of the council to preside. That every year there be held an assembly, and every freeholder of forty shillings per ann. and freeman of a corporation, shall have a vote in chusing representatives; here the representatives are enumerated, and as many more as his majesty shall think fit to establish. That the representatives during their sessions, may adjourn themselves and purge their own house; no member going, coming, and during their sessions, to be arrested or sued, except for felony and treason. Their laws to continue in force till disallowed by his majesty, or till they expire. That every man shall be judged by his peers, and all trials shall be by the verdict of twelve men of the neighbourhood; that in all capital and other criminal cases there be a grand inquest to present the offender, and afterwards twelve men to try the offender. That in all cases bail by sufficient sureties be allowed, unless in case of treason, and of such felonies as are restrained from bail by the laws of England. That no tax or imposition be laid but by the general assembly. That no freeman, tavern-keepers excepted,

cepted, be compelled to entertain any foldier or mariner, unlefs in times of actual war with the province.—That all lands in this province be accounted as freehold and inheritance in free and common foccage, according to the tenure of Eaft-Greenwich in England.   That all wills attefted by three or more witneffes, and regiftered with the office of the county in a fet time, be a fufficient conveyance for lands, &c.   That any chriftian religion not difturbing the peace of the province, be freely allowed of, the Roman catholick excepted [r].   The enacting is, " By the governor, council, and general affembly " of the province of New-York."

A fummary cannot enumerate many of their municipal laws.   The juftices of each county fhall yearly fummon all the freeholders in January to chufe two church wardens and ten veftry men to affefs, and the minifter to be called, chofen and appointed by the wardens and veftry.   Elections for reprefentatives to be in the fheriff's court of the county or city, qualification for a voter forty fhillings at leaft freehold per annum improved land; no perfon to be chofen but who refides in the place.   An. 1700 there was an act to prevent all vexatious fuits or actions againft thofe who at the happy revolution in England, did here begin fuch another revolution; they appointed capt. Jacob Leyfler their commander in chief till his majefty K. William's pleafure fhould be known; and feized the perfons and goods of feveral difaffected people.   In each county or town, at the feffions of the peace. the juftices of the peace, or at leaft five of them, whereof two of the quorum, fhall appoint the rate for their county, as alfo a treafurer and collector.   All men from fixteen to fixty æt. to be lifted in fome company of militia; each footman to have a cartouch box and fix charges, the horfe twelve charges; at their habitation to keep one pound

[r] In Penfylvania and Maryland, by the royal patents, by the proprietors conceffions, and by the fubfequent provincial laws, Roman catholicks are not excepted.

of powder, three pound of bullets each foot; and two pound of powder, and fix pound of bullets each horfe.

In the province of New-York, to obtain a good title to the vacant lands, firft there muft be produced an Indian deed, which muft be approved of by the governor and council, by warrant; it is furveyed by the provincial furveyor, and patented by the governor and council: the fees are very high.

The quit-rents for lands lately taken up are two fhillings proclamation money per 100 acres. Two thirds of the government pay fmall or no quit-rents, efpecially for old grants, the larger grants on Hudfon's river called manors; their quit-rents are only a pepper-corn, buck-fkin, or the like, when demanded.

The valuations of the feveral counties may be taken from the quotas allowed each of them, in proportion to their refpective taxes, when paper money was emitted upon loan; for inftance 1738, they emitted 40,000 *l.* currency upon loan, whereof

To New-York city and county	10,000 *l.*
Albany city and county	5,000
Queen's county	6,000
King's county	2,400
Suffolk county	3,000
Richmond county	1,600
Ulfter county	4,000
Orange county	2,000
Dutchefs county	2,000
Weft-Chefter	4.000
	40,000

As to their paper currencies they are referred with other things of that nature to the Appendix. At prefent I fhall only obferve, that towards the charge of an intended expedition againft Canada, 1709, they emitted 13,000 *l.* publick bills of credit at eight fhillings currency per oz. filver, bearing intereft; in the after emiffions,

emiffions, no intereft was allowed; the contrivers of this fraudulent paper money currency, perceived that a reafonable intereft would prevent its depreciation, and obftruct the advantages which they propofed from its depreciation [s]. They plaufibly and fallacioufly alledged, that the allowing of intereft, occafioned their being hoarded up as common bonds bearing intereft, and did not ferve as a common currency. In anfwer to this, the anti-depreciators may obferve, 1. That any confiderate good man will allow, that money not payable or cancellable till after fome years, if only upon note bearing no intereft, is not fo valuable as the fame fum of money upon bond bearing intereft, payable after the fame number of years; that is, thefe bills upon note only, in the nature of things muft admit a depreciation or difcount, and ftill a greater difcount if thefe notes ftretch too much their credit: this is the genuine mercantile nature of our depreciating plantation paper currency. 2. In the beginning they were not emitted as a tender in law, or common currency; but as government bonds or debentures bearing intereft as are transferable ftocks of publick debts in Great-Britain, which by reafon of the intereft allowed, do increafe to a valuable premium upon a transfer, and cannot depreciate as the plantation publick notes of credit have done.

As the plantations are at a vaft diftance from parliamentary enquiry, fome of our colonies have from time to time been loaded with amufing feint expeditions, the original and continuing caufes of the plantation frau-

[s] This was the cafe in the enormous multiplied emiffions of paper credit or money, as it was called, in a neighbouring province; as the governor happened himfelf to be of the debtor fide of the queftion, and for valuable confiderations, as it is faid, inftead of borrowing the money already emitted, from the merchants at a reafonable intereft, which they generoufly offered, and which would have prevented further depreciating emiffions; he chofe rather, though with the confequence of involving the country in confufion and ruin, in favour of the land bank (an affumed name) and other fraudulent debtors, to depreciate the debts by vaft multiplied emiffions bearing no intereft.

dulent

dulent paper credit called paper currency; the fraudulent debtors finding their advantage in depreciations, contrived fundry methods of further paper credit emiffions : thus in Maffachufetts-Bay in the courfe of fome years in the adminiftration of governor Sh——, one fhilling was depreciated to the value of one penny fterl. New-York did reftrain itfelf from running much into a multiplied depreciating paper currency, fo that their exchange with London never did exceed 190 *l*. New-York currency for 100 *l*. fterl. *N. B.* When I any where mention exchange, I mean private punctual bills of exchange; government bills admit of a dilatory payment, and are bought cheaper; for inftance, upon the Cuba or Spanifh Weft-India expedition, government bills were fold in New-York and Eaft-Jerfey at 140 to 150; in Weft Jerfey and Penfylvania at 130 to 135; when at the fame time private punctual bills were fold at 190 in the firft, and at 180 in the other places.

The militia of the province of New-York, are nearly upon the fame regulation with the militia of New-England; befides there are four regular independent companies of fufileers, 100 private men to a company; their pay, cloathing, and accoutrements from Great-Britain, amount yearly to upwards of 7800 *l*. fterl. they are under the immediate direction of the commander in chief for the time, and are a confiderable perquifite: they are principally ftationed at the city of New-York, Albany, and Ofwego; New-York was fo called from the duke of York's Englifh title, and Albany (formerly Orange Fort, by the Dutch) by his Scots title; the battery at New-York is called Fort George.

Befides the five or fix nations of Iroquois or Mohawk Indians, there are feveral fmall parcels of Indians, upon the upper parts of Hudfon's river, called River Indians or Mohegins; this was the Indian name of the great river, now called Hudfon's river.

At

At fundry times in the city of New-York there have been negro confpiracies, more than in the other colonies; this I cannot account for; April 1712, a negro confpiracy kills many white men, and fets the town on fire.

Courts of judicature are much the fame as in New-England [*t*]. The judges of the fuperior or fupreme court are appointed by the king in council, and fometimes *pro tempore* by the governor; they are called firft, fecond, &c. judges: the firft judge is called chief juftice, and feems to have a confiderable authority or influence above the other judges. The prefent chief juftice is James Delancy, Efq. of a regular liberal education, and good eftate; he was appointed by governor Cofby, 1733, in the place of Lewis Morris, Efq. who fucceeded an eminent lawyer Roger Mompeffon, Efq. chief juftice of New-York and the Jerfeys, who furrendered that of the Jerfeys 1709.

Here is a court of chancery, a court not known in New-England; the governor is chancellor. In many of our colonies it renders the courts below of lefs authority; as it is very chargeable, and may be arbitrary; the chancellor ought to be a diftinct perfon from the governor (as are the intendants of the French colonies) and upon mifdemeanor, liable to the governor's infpection by fufpenfion or the like.

The general affembly is no court of judicature, but they examine into the erroneous proceedings of the courts of judicature, and grant re-hearings.

Concerning New-York *produce, manufactures, trade, and navigation.*

Wheat and flour are the moft confiderable articles of their produce and manufactures; fee their exports of

[*t*] This fummary if not checked, is like to become too bulky, therefore I fhall avoid repetition of things which bear a femblance to things already faid.

provisions, in the clauses of custom-house entries and clearances.

Skins and furs are a good article, but not so large as formerly.

The article of iron in pigs and bars is a growing affair.

Schuyler's copper ore is from a mine in the Jersey's, but exported from New-York, therefore it is mentioned in this section. In the beginning of its discovery it seemed to be very rich : it appears that it was formerly wrought by the Dutch, because in new working it, were found hammers, wedges, &c. it sold in Bristol the ore at forty pound sterl. per ton. The cartage to Hudson's river is short, and their first agreement with the miner, was to allow him one third of the ore for raising and laying it above ground ; it was done up in quarter barrels, whereof six made a ton. The richness of this copper mine made so much noise in the world, that, a few years since, to engross this ore for the benefit of Great-Britain, it was by act of parliament enumerated ; but lately it has not been wrought and exported, as appears by the quarterly accounts of the custom-house of New-York ; I cannot account for this.

By a late act of parliament, salt may be imported directly from any parts of Europe to New-York.

In queen Anne's reign there were three government packet boats, which alternately sailed monthly between England and New-York, to tarry fourteen days at New-York, for the plantations or colonies benefit of trade, and for the government dispatches ; these have been laid aside many years.

Governor Burnet (his head was well turned) obtained an act of assembly 1727, afterwards confirmed by the king in council, prohibiting all trade with Canada, that the French might not be supplied with goods (in one year 900 pieces of strouds have been carried from Albany to Montreal) suitable for promoting a French civil, as well as trading, interest with the Indians, and that the

Indians

Indians may be induced to go a trading to Ofwego [*u*], a late well projected and well executed Englifh mart for Indian trade; governor Burnet always and effectually minded the bufinefs of his deftination. The Indian trade is now in the hands of many; before governor Burnet's time it was engroffed by a few, and the Indians are become more dependent upon the Englifh than formerly. From Albany to Ofwego, is a much eafier conveyance, than from Montreal, 200 miles up a rapid ftony river to fort Frontenac on lake Ontario, called alfo Ofwego.

In the province of New-York there is one collection or cuftom-houfe diftrict, kept in the port of New-York; the twelve months accounts from September 29, 1749, to September 29, 1750, ftand thus :

Entered inwards.		Cleared outwards.	
Ships	23	Ships	36
Snows	22	Snows	28
Brigantines	45	Brigantines	58
Sloops	131	Sloops	150
Schooners	11	Schooners	14
	232		286

Here are included all veffels both on foreign voyages, and on coafting voyages of the neighbouring colonies; whereas in the collections of New-England the foreign voyages are only to be underftood; for inftance, Bofton cuftom-houfe from Chriftmas 1747, to Chriftmas 1748, foreign veffels cleared out 540, entered in 430; the fifhing and coafting veffels of the adjoining colonies of Maffachufetts-Bay, New-Hampfhire, Connecticut, and Rhode-Ifland, amounted to about as many, and are not included.

[*u*] The carriage or communication between Albany and Ofwego is fo commodious, that at a time in relieving the garrifon of Ofwego, forty people came in one birch canoe, forty-five feet in length, feven feet in breadth, from Ofwego to Schenectady 183 miles, carrying places included.

N. B. No

N. B. No copper ore was exported in thefe twelve months.

Entered in from Great-Britain and Ireland fixteen veffels ; cleared out for Great-Britain and Ireland twenty-one veffels; cleared out for Holland five veffels.

Cleared out 6731 ton provifions, chiefly flour; befides grain eftimated or fhipped by number of bufhels, and not by tons.

Imported about 800 pipes Madeira wines, whereof re-exported 226 pipes. The Madeira wines fhipped to New-York are reckoned better than what are fhipped to any other of our colonies, therefore fome are re-fhipped to the other colonies.

Cleared out, tar 2008 barrels, pitch 156, turpentine 20, which were imported to New-York from the Carolinas. The colony of New-York does not produce naval ftores fufficient for their own ufe.

Mountains, rivers, and fome mifcellanies.

The moft confiderable highlands are the Catkill mountains weft of Hudfon's river, and about ninety miles N. from New-York. What I mentioned vol. I. p. 454, 455, by way of annotation, concerning the runs of water from the Catkill mountains, en paffant; now in its proper place requires to be corrected, and ought to be underftood as follows. On the eaft and fouth eaft fides of the Catkill mountains, feveral ftreams run, and fall into Hudfon's river below Albany; on their N. W. fide proceeds Schorie river, and falls into the Mohawks river, a branch of Hudfon's river, at fort Hunter about thirty miles above Albany; and this Schorie river in its courfe comes within three or four miles of the main branch of Delaware river; from the S. W. fide flows a confiderable branch of Delaware river. Conajoharie river falls into the Mohawks river about ten miles above fort Hunter, and comes very near to a branch of Sefquahana river; this branch of Sefquahana is fo large, that at eighteen miles from the Mohawks river, the Indians go down in

canoes

canoes to all the Indian settlements upon Sesquahana river. From this situation of these rivers, no runs of water from the Catkill mountains can fall into lake Ontario, into the river Ohio, or into the Sesquahana river.

Excepting Long-Island and Staten-Island, the main land sea line, from Byram river to New-York island, is very short.

The only considerable river in this province is Hudson's river; from the elbow, where is the great carrying place to Wood-Creek towards Canada, to Sandyhook at its mouth, are near 200 miles; the tide way reaches upwards of 150 miles to Cohoes at the mouth of the Mohawks river, about six or seven miles above Albany church; its course is about S. twelve degrees West; the tides, that is, the floods and ebbs, are about twelve hours later at Albany than at New-York; a little above the high lands at about fifty miles above the city of New-York, the water of the river becomes fresh; at about 100 miles comes on the W. side Esopus or Soaper's river; the S. line of the province of Massachusetts-Bay continued twenty miles, strikes Hudson's river a little below the mouth of Esopus river; this Esopus river is noted for the manufactures of iron pigs and bars, flour, malt liquor, &c. a little farther on the E. side of the great river, is the camp or Palatine town in the manor of Livingston about forty miles below Albany; at 125 miles on the E. side falls in Kinderhock river after receiving Claverhock river; the great Ranslaers manor, or Ranslaer Wyk, reaches along the great river, and 20 miles each side of the river from Kinderhock manor to Mohawks river; in this manor is the city of Albany, and many peculiar tracts of land; at 150 miles as the river runs is the city of Albany; at 157 miles on the W. side is Cohoes, or the mouth of the Mohawks river; at 162 miles is Housuck river's mouth, where live a small tribe of Indians called Scatacooks; this Housuck river is on the E. side of the great river, and comes from the north west parts of Massachusetts, and the S. W. parts of

New-

New-Hampſhire; the north line of Maſſachuſetts-Bay province continued twenty miles, falls in with Hudſon's river a little below Cohoes; at 200 miles from New-York is the elbow or flexure of this great river at the great falls.   From theſe great falls the route to Montreal in Canada is ten to fifteen miles land carriage to Wood-Creek, then along the Verdronken drowned or overflowed lands to Crown-point a French fort and paſs near lake Champlain, then along this lake to Chamblais river, and a little above Chamblais [*x*], another French fort and paſs upon Chamblais river, croſs la Prairie to Montreal.   There is another route up Hudſon's river above the elbow falls, to a carrying place to lake Sacrament, and thence to the ſouth end of lake Champlain.

The city of New-York from governor Burnet's obſervations, lies in 40 d. 50 m. N. lat. 4 h. 58 m. W. long. from London.   Here the variation 1723 was 7 d 20 m. W. decreaſing.

Upon the acceſſion of a new governor, the general aſſembly of New-York generally ſettle the ſalaries and other ordinary articles in ſupport of the government, for five or more years.

For their ſectaries in religion, ſee the Rhode-Iſland ſectary, vol. II. p. 156.

As I find that the deſigned Appendix or ſupplement may prove out of proportion too large, with reſpect to the principal hiſtory, I ſhall in each ſubſequent ſection annex by way of miſcellanies ſome matters which might have been referred to the Appendix.   Theſe miſcellanies of the nature of digreſſions, and like change of

---

[*x*] As we formerly hinted, from fort Chamblais down the river of that name are ſeventeen leagues to cape Sorrel upon the great river of Canada; this fort Sorrel is fifteen leagues below Montreal, and thirty-five leagues above Quebec the capital of Canada, the ordinary reſidence of the French governor general of Canada. Quebec, from the accurate obſervations of des Hayes, is ſeventy d. W. from London. Boſton, the metropolis of Britiſh America, by the good obſervations of Mr. Robie, is ſeventy one d. thirty m. W. from London.

diet,

diet, may relieve a palled ftomach or appetite in reading.

Good iron is diftinguifhed by its ringing amongft other bars. The beft iron bars break fibrous and bearded; if they break glaffy and fhining, the iron is brittle, and not good.

The inconveniencies of fmall governments or provinces, fuch as is that of New-Hampfhire in New-England, is that perhaps they are below the notice of the miniftry and boards in Great-Britain; their governors and other officers are of little confideration, have little or nothing to lofe, and therefore act impune.

The plantation legiflatures are fo far circumfcribed, that they can make no laws inconfiftent with the laws of Great-Britain.

If the French be allowed to become mafters of the river of St. Laurence, of the great inland lakes, and of the great river Miffiffippi; they are in confequence mafters of all the inland trade of North-America; an incredible prejudice to the Britifh nation.

The back of Long-Ifland was the firft place of the Englifh whale fifhery, fmall whales affect flats; and at this time whalers make voyages upon the flats of Virginia and Carolina.

It is faid that the common laws of England extend to the plantations; that the ftatute laws made fince the plantations had a being, do not include them unlefs they are particularly mentioned in the act of parliament.

In all our colony affemblies of reprefentatives, there ought to be a limited fmall quorum of members to meet adjourn, and to fend for abfent members, and a much larger quorum to proceed upon bufinefs: this regulation may alfo take place with relation to the judges of the feveral executive courts of law.

To obviate any prejudices which a reader may entertain againft this hiftorical fummary, compofed with much labour, merely for a publick good; the writer thinks it convenient at times to explain himfelf in ge-

neral.

néral. 1. He has endeavoured a laconick ſtile, which by many is reckoned harſh, and not fluent or ſonorous; the good judges the mathematicians and merchants, uſe it as the ſtrongeſt, the moſt conciſe and expreſſive. 2. The writer is of no party, and ſubjected to no dependence; he is neither whig nor tory, a temporary courtier nor anti-courtier: a tory is for rendering that branch of the preſent legiſlature called king or monarch, ſole and independent, with a paſſive obedience and nonreſiſtance; a republican is for lowering or annihilating the prerogatives of a king, and for an unlimited extenſion of the privileges of the people in their repreſentatives; but a genuine whig is for maintaining the balance of power among the ſeveral orders or negatives of the legiſlature; I profeſs myſelf of this politia, as it is no faction; all the others are factious. 3. Religion, as it was in all times, and in all countries, deſigned for the benefit of ſociety, it naturally is ſubordinate to the civil government; and a reſident, whether native or adventitious, ought occaſionally to conform to the eſtabliſhed manner of the ſectaries tolerated by the laws of the country, though not raſhly to renounce that form of worſhip which was parental or educational, which generally tends to libertiniſm and licentiouſneſs in religion. 4. As in my courſe of the colonies I continue to increaſe my diſtances, it is not to be expected that I can be ſo particular and copious, but ſhall endeavour ſtrictly to inveſtigate the truth, though the farther from my place of reſidence my view becomes more contracted and leſs diſtinct.

In the Britiſh plantations or colonies all grants of lands made by the governor and council, are declared to be good in law, againſt his majeſty and ſucceſſors.

As the king and his miniſtry in Great-Britain, though they do not chuſe the parliament, yet have a very great influence in the choice; ſo it is with reſpect to the governors and aſſembly men in our colonies.

4

The

. The reprefentatives from the feveral counties and townfhips are not their peculiar or feparate agents, but their quota in their provincial reprefentation; hence it is that they are not under the cognizance of their county or town, but under that of the general affembly.

The North-America trade confifts in fifh, naval ftores, other timber and lumber, fkins, furs, tobacco, and rice; I do not mention copper ore though enumerated, becaufe at prefent it is not wrought or exported.

The publick taxes in our provinces, are the province and county rates; and the townfhip or parochial rates for the minifters of the gofpel, called paftors, priefts, rectors, and other denominations, as alfo for the fchool, poor, highways, and fundry other fmall articles.

By act of parliament, 1731, there may be imported from the Britifh plantations into Ireland in Britifh fhipping, all forts of plantation goods excepting thofe goods commonly called enumerated commodities, viz. fugar, tobacco, cotton, wool, indigo, ginger, fpeckled wood or Jamaica wood, fuftick or other dying woods, rice, moloffes, beaver-fkins and other furs, copper ore, pitch, tar, turpentine, mafts, yards, and bowfprits.

The fugar act (as it is called) of parliament, 1733, and fince continued, is concerning foreign plantation produce or manufacture, imported into the Britifh plantations, viz. rum, duty nine pence fterling, per gallon; moloffes or fyrups, fix pence; fugars and paneeles, five fhillings per hundred weight.

In North-America, hunting, fifhing, and fowling, with fundry berries and earth-nuts are the principal food or fubfiftence of the Indians; the more civilized, cultivate Indian corn and kidney beans, called Indian beans. The bread grain in Europe, is generally wheat, rye, oats, and barley, for baking and malting,

The

The [y] wool in our northern plantations is of as good a ftaple, but coarfer than the Englifh wool; the farther fouth in our colonies, the wool becomes coarfer, even to a *lana caprina*, as in our fugar iflands; therefore the plantations are not capable of rivalling England in fine woollens.

In our northern colonies after the middle of Sept. fcarce any fpecies of fpontaneous plants make a feafonable appearance; confequently botanick fimpling is then over.

In our new wildernefs colonies, the timber and other foreft wood of the firft clearing is generally dotted, becaufe ancient or old; the following growths are good and found.

In the price of grain and other provifions there is a fort of natural ftandard, whereby the hufbandman may have a living profit, and the labourers in manufacture, &c. may not have provifions fo cheap, that the earnings of a few days work will afford fome days of idlenefs; in this refpect our produce and manufactures have fome kind of a natural dependence.

[y] There are certain ports only, allowed in Great-Britain and Ireland, for the exportation and importation of wool and woollens. No cloths, excepting of the manufacture of Great-Britain, can be imported into any of his majefty's dominions.

The woollens from Great-Britain exported annually are computed at about three millions fterling; but being free of duty, they for fome felfifh ends are not entered exactly, therefore the value cannot be accurately afcertained.

The woollens of Great-Britain are above one third of the univerfal export. At a medium, wool manufactured is double the value of the wool itfelf, and deducting all charges, one third of the neat profit goes to the landlord.

SECT. XIII.

Concerning the province of New-Jersey *or* Nova-Cæsarea.

WE have in the section of New-York [z] given some general account of the first settlement of New-Netherlands or Nova-Belgia, which comprehended the present New-York, New-Jersey, and the three lower counties of Penfylvania upon Delaware river.

Upon a design formed by the court of England to reduce New Netherlands [a], K. Charles II. made a previous grant of the property and government of the fame to his brother the duke of York, March 12, 1663-4; it was not reduced by settled articles until September 1664, and confirmed to England by the treaty of Breda, 1667.

The duke of York by commiffion April 2, 1664, appointed Richard Nichols, Efq. deputy governor of all New-Netherlands, but did not enter upon his government, till Aug. 27, 1664, which was pofterior to the duke of York's affignment, June 24, 1664, of the property and government of New-Jersey to lord Berkley and Sir George Carteret.

The duke of York, June 24, 1664, made a joint grant of that part of New-Netherlands (now called New-Jersey) [b] to lord Berkley of Stratton, and Sir George Carteret; they appointed Philip Carteret, Efq. their lieutenant governor; he entered upon his govern-

[z] P. 220, &c.
[a] Stuyvefand was at that time Dutch governor of New-Netherlands. His commiffion from the States General was dated July 26, 1646.
[b] This grant was called New-Jersey, from the name of the ifland of Jerfey in the channel of England, the country of Sir George Carteret one of the firft affignees. It is fometimes called Nova-Cæfarea.

ment

ment in Aug, 1665, where he remained only six months, and returned to England, and back again to his government of the Jerseys. This grant of the duke of York, was from the Noorde Rivier, now called Hudson's river, to the Zuyde Rivier, now called Delaware river; and up Hudson's river to 41 d. N. lat. and up Delaware river to 41 d. 20 m. and from these two stations headed by a strait line acrofs.

By the intrigues of France, England was persuaded to proclaim war against the Dutch, March 17, 1671-2, and a Dutch expedition reconquered New-Netherlands from the English July 30, 1673. Col. Lovelace was at that time governor; by the treaty of London, February 19, 1673-4, New-Netherlands was restored by the Dutch to the crown of England, and Sir Edmond Andros appointed governor.

As New-Netherlands had been conquered, that is, alienated from England, since the crown of England's former grant to the duke of York; to obviate any difficulties in the validity of that grant, king Charles II. made a new grant of property and government to his brother the duke of York, June 29, 1674, which was published Nov. 6, following. No act of government in the Jerseys is to be found upon record from July 19, 1673, to November 1674.

Duke of York by lease and release, July 28 and 29, 1674, conveyed to Sir George Carteret the eastern division of the New-Jerseys, divided from the western division of the Jerseys by a strait line from the S. E. point of Little-Egg harbour in Barnegate creek, being about the middle between Sandy-Hook and Cape-May, to a kill or creek a little below Rencokus-Kill on Delaware river, and thence (about thirty-five miles) strait course along Delaware river up to 41 d. 40 m. N. lat. the north divisional point or station of the divisional line between New-York and the Jerseys. *N. B.* The first effort of the rioters for setting up Indian purchases against the title of the crown was 1672, to evade paying quit-rents
which

which commenced March 25, 1670; they threw off the government of the proprietors, and the people chose a governor for themselves; governor Carteret and his secretary went for England to complain, but the Dutch conquest happening soon after, governor Carteret did not return till November 1674, with new conceffions, being the third parcel of conceffions, and from that time all remained quiet, and the rules of property were well obferved until Sir Edmond Andros broke through all thefe rules; he ufurped the government of all New Jerfey 1680, and carried governor Carteret prifoner from Elizabeth town to New-York; upon complaints to the duke of York, he with refentment recalled Sir Edmond Andros, and the property and government of the Jerfey proprietors was re-eftablifhed 1683, and continued till fome months before the revolution 1688, when K. James broke through the rules of property, and alfo feized the government of New-Jerfey and of the neighbouring provinces, and put them under the command of Sir Edmond Andros; upon the revolution the proprietors re-affumed the right of government [*c*].

Upon the revolution the proprietors appointed John Totham, Efq. their lieutenant governor, and afterwards col. Dudley [*d*], but the people fcrupled to obey them, and the proprietors appointed col. Andrew Hamilton, who continued governor fome years; but by fome defigning men the people received a notion that col. Hamilton, as a Scots man, could not be governor of an Englifh colony; they difmiffed him, and conftituted Jeremiah Baffe governor 1697; but as Baffe had never been approved of by the king, the proprietors in a fhort time difmiffed him, and reinftated col. Hamilton, but he never was confirmed by the crown, and col.

[*c*] For fake of connection I continue this thread, and leave fome intervening matters to be afterwards related.

[*d*] Col. Dudley was afterwards deputy governor of the Ifle of Whight, a member of parliament of England, and governor of the provinces of Maffachufetts-Bay and New-Hampfhire in New-England.

Hamilton

Hamilton was superfeded by Mr. Baffe a fecond time, and Baffe was finally superfeded by Andrew Bowne, Efq. the laft governor for the proprietors.

The people of the Jerfeys continued for fome years fo mutinous, that the proprietors for their own eafe, by their agents, Sir Thomas Lane for Weft-Jerfey, and Mr. William Dockwra for Eaft-Jerfey, in the name of the proprietors, found it expedient by a proper inftrument, April 17, 1702, in concert, to furrender the government to the crown, referving to themfelves all their other rights, and they jointly with the crown formed fome fundamental articles by way of a *magna charta.* Lord Cornbury, governor of New-York, was by queen Anne conftituted the firft crown governor of the united Jerfeys.

Lord Berkley, fome years after his grant from the duke of York 1664, affigned his right to William Penn, Efq. Gawen Laurie of London, merchant, Nicholas Lucas, and Edward Byllyng; fhortly after this, thefe affignees agreed upon a partition with Sir George Carteret, and Sir George obtained of the duke of York, July 1674, a confirmation of this partition grant, as is above related—July 1, 1676, Sir George Carteret gave to the affignees of lord Berkley a quit-claim of the Weft-Jerfeys, as thefe affignees gave to Sir George a like quit-claim of the Eaft-Jerfeys; this partition was confirmed by an act of the general affembly of the Jerfeys, 1719.

Sir George Carteret made over the Eaft-Jerfeys to certain truftees December 5, 1678, to be fold by them after his death. After Sir George's death, the truftees affigned the Eaft-Jerfeys to twelve proprietors, February 2, 1681-2.

William Penn,	Thomas Wilcox
Robert Weft,	Ambrofe Riggs,
Thomas Rudyard,	John Hayward,
Samuel Groom,	Hugh Hartfhorn,
Thomas Hart,	Clemens Plumfted,
Richard Mew,	Thomas Cooper.

By

By an inftrument amongft themfelves, they declared that
the purchafe was equal, and no advantage fhould be
taken of furvivorfhip. Thefe firft proprietors by twelve
feparate deeds, feparately conveyed one half of their intereft to twelve other perfons feparately,

Robert Barclay,	Gawen Laurie,
Edward Byllyng,	Thomas Barker,
Robert Turner,	Thomas Warner,
James Brien,	James Earl of Perth,
Arent Soumans,	Robert Gordon,
William Gibfon.	John Drummond,

in fee fimple.   The duke of York, March 14, 1682, by
patent or grant confirmed the Eaft-Jerfeys to thofe twenty four proprietors in property and government; and
July 17 following, the famous Robert Barclay [*e*] the
quaker was agreed upon, and under him *pro tempore* Mr.
Laurie with a council. Mr. Barclay continued governor
until 1685.   He was fucceeded by lord Neal Campbell
of the Argyle family; about this time came over the
quaker fo called, George Keith [*f*].

From the duke of York's firft grant of all the Jerfeys
to lord Berkley of Stratton, and to Sir George Carteret,
knight and baronet, vice chamberlain of his majefty's
houfhold, and one of his majefty's moft honourable
privy council, jointly; Philip Carteret, Efq. was governor of their joint concern, that is, for all the Jerfeys until
1672, when the people, efpecially of Elizabeth-town,
began to mutiny upon account of the demand of quit-
rents, which according to the conceffions took place
March 25, 1670.   Thefe mutineers affumed the go-

[*e*] In king Charles II. reign there was a kind of perfecution of the
nonconformifts in religion, and Robert Barclay head of all the quakers
in Great-Britain, with his family removed to the Jerfeys; from this
perfecution the Jerfeys is fettled chiefly with Quakers, Anabaptifts, and
Prefbyterians.

[*f*] George Keith was a noted Quaker, he came over to the Jerfeys,
taught fchool, and was land furveyor general; he returned to England,
and for his conveniency, accepted of a church of England benefice, and
wrote againft the Quakers.

vernment,

vernment, and conftituted James Carteret, a diffolute fon
of Sir George Carteret, their governor; and governor
Philip Carteret was obliged to go to the court of England with complaints againft the mutineers; col. Lovelace at this time was governor of New-York; the Dutch
conqueft intervening, he did not return until 1674, when
upon a peace the Dutch refigned to the crown of England the country of New-Netherlands, and the duke
of York had made a divifional or feparate grant of Eaft-
Jerfeys to Sir George Carteret; governor Carteret brought
over fome additional conceffions, which were called the
third concoffions; as he had bought fome fhares in the
Elizabeth-town Indian purchafe, the Elizabeth-town
men gave him no uneafinefs, he refided in Elizabeth-
town till death; he made it the feat of government.
Robert Barclay the noted quaker writer, was the firft
governor for the twenty-four proprietors.

Upon the Dutch peace 1674, Sir Edmond Andros
was appointed governor of the Jerfeys, but by virtue of
the duke of York's fecond or divifional grant, Sir George
Carteret appointed Philip Carteret, Efq. his lieut. governor for the Eaft-Jerfey, in which ftation he continued
to the time of his death, November 1682; he received
fome infults from Sir Edmond Andros. From 1674, Sir
Edmond Andros was governor of the Weft-Jerfeys for
the duke of York, who had twifted the government out
of the hands of lord Berkley's affignees, and upon proper
reprefentations the duke of York quitted the government of Weft-Jerfeys to the affignees of lord Berkley,
and they appointed Edware Byllyng, one of the affignees
or proprietors, governor 1680, having obtained a new
grant of the Weft-Jerfey; at the fame time the duke
made a new grant or confirmation of Eaft-Jerfey to the
grandfon of Sir George Carteret. In the Weft-Jerfeys to
Mr. Byllyng 1690, fucceeded [g] doctor Daniel Cox of the

[g] The affairs of this colony have always been in a confufed ftate,
which occafions an unavoidable confufion in the hiftory thereof.

college

college of phyficians in London, he having purchafed the greateft part of the property of Weft-Jerfey, was governor thereof; but as his profeffional bufinefs did not allow him to leave London, he appointed a deputy governor, and at length fold his intereft to Sir Thomas Lane and others for 9000 l. fterl. a great price at that time.

The original twenty-four fhares of Eaft-Jerfey by fales of fmall parts of the fhares and fucceffion of children, became very much fubdivided; for inftance, fome proprietors had only one fortieth part, of a forty-eighth part, of a twenty-fourth fhare; Weft-Jerfey was in the fame condition. This occafioned much confufion in management amongft thefe general proprietors, particularly in appointing governors; therefore the proprietors in good prudence refigned the government to the crown, referving all their other rights as we formerly mentioned; the proprietary government continued until Auguft 14, 1703, when lord Cornbury publifhed his commiffion from the crown as governor of all the Jerfeys; thus the Eaft and Weft-Jerfeys, which had been feparate governments from 1674, to 1703, became united in one government or jurifdiction, and continued under the fame governor with the province of New-York, until 1736, when the government of New-York devolved upon lieutenant governor Clarke: as he had no command in the Jerfeys, the government of the Jerfeys devolved upon the prefident of the council, and ever fince the command in chief has been in a diftinct perfon from that of New-York.

Upon the proprietors furrendering the government to the crown, they obtained of the crown a fet of perpetual inftructions to all fubfequent governors by way of conceffions, or magna charta, for the proprietors and people, particularly in favour of the proprietors. 1. Not to confent to any tax upon unprofitable or vacant lands. 2. None but the general proprietors to purchafe any lands of the Indians. 3. To take care that all lands purchafed, be improved by the poffeffors.

After the Dutch peace there was (upon ceasing of head-land bounties) 1685, a council of proprietors appointed for the East-Jerseys; they ordered a dividend of 10,000 acres to be taken up at pleasure, to each of the twenty-four proprietorships of the East-Jerseys; there was a second division of 5000 acres to each of the twenty-four proprietorships, Feb. 21, 1698; and a division of 2500 acres, Dec. 2, 1702. To enforce the affair of a council of proprietors, there passed an act of general assembly, March 25, 1725, that a certain number of the general proprietors, or their proxies, having the value of eight whole shares in themselves, shall be a council of the proprietors of the eastern division, to divide lands, examine claims, &c. and to have two stated yearly meetings at Perth-Amboy, about the times of the sittings of the supreme court of judicature. 1737, The council of proprietors advertised, that after 1739, there should be a further dividend of 2000 acres per ann. to each of the twenty-four proprietorships, until all vacant lands shall be divided.

In the first concessions, February 10, 1664-5, the proprietors Berkley and Carteret promise to all adventurers and settlers who should plant there, sundry privileges, particularly of head-lands for each head of settlers: this promise was only designed to be of four years continuance; but from time to time was extended to January 13, 1685-6, and then ceased; the general proprietors then began to make dividends amongst themselves as above. The head-lands were to settlers, in any place exceeding ten miles from the sea, eighty acres per head, and to those who settle nearer, sixty acres.

In the beginning, the general lots were laid out, none less than 2100 acres, and none more than 21,000 acres; whereof one seventh to be reserved to the general proprietors, the remainder to persons who should come and plant the same.

In taking up lands either by purchase, and agreement with the general proprietaries as at present, or as

formerly

formerly by way of head-lands, the governor and majority of the council gave a warrant' to the surveyor general or his deputies, to survey and lay out the same; next the surveyor is to certify the survey, upon which the governor and council make a grant in the form following, " The lords proprietors of Nova-Cæsarea, or " New-Jersey, do hereby grant to A. B. of —— in the " province aforesaid, a plantation containing—— acres " English measure, to him or her, to his or her heirs or " assigns for ever; yielding and paying yearly unto the " said lord proprietors, their heirs or assigns, every 25th " day of March, according to the English account, one " half-penny, lawful money of England, for every one of " the said acres; to be holden as of the mannor of East-" Greenwich in free and common soccage; the first pay-" ment of quit-rents to begin the 25th ——Given under " the seal of the province, the—day of——in the year " of our Lord——signed by the governor and a majo-" rity of the council. N. B. One half part of the " mines of gold and silver are reserved; and if in three " years, the conditions stipulated are not fulfilled, the " grant to be void."

We may observe, that there are three sorts of proprietors in the Jerseys. 1. The general proprietors. 2. Purchasers under the general proprietors. 3. Claimers under patents for head-lands from the general proprietors on quit-rent.

A Digression concerning Indian deeds, and proprietors quit-rents in the plantations.

In our plantations the case of persons holding lands by Indian deeds only, without the approbation of the crown, or of the respective legislatures who may be deemed to have the exclusive prerogatives of granting the right of pre-emption to subjects; as also the affair of paying quit-rents to the crown, or to general proprietors grantees of the crown, as a matter of considerable

concern, feems to require a digreffionary article. As the colony of New-Jerfey is the moft noted for thefe difputes,
[*b*] we fhall here give the incidents of claims by Indian
deeds only, in Elizabeth townfhip.

In both the Jerfeys, feveral poffeffions and claims of land
are founded upon Indian deeds only ; the Indian Elizabeth-town grant is the moft noted, and has been the
moft vexatious, formerly containing upwards of 400,000
acres of the moft valuable lands in New-Jerfey, bounded
by Raritan river, Amboy-Sound, Arthur Cul-Bay, and
Paffaick river ; Daniel Pierce, and affociates, purchafed
one half of thefe lands for 80 l. fterl. and laid out the
townfhips of Woodbridge and Pifcataway, for which
they foon after obtained fufficient patents from the
rightful proprietors under the crown, at one half-penny
per ann. quit-rent, and peaceably enjoy the fame to this
day.

The firft Indian grant of thefe lands was to Auguftin
Herman, a Dutchman, in 1651 ; upon the Dutch furrender to the crown of England, he relinquifhed thefe
lands, and therefore they efcheated to that crown as de-
relicts, and confequently could not be conveyed again by
the Indians to any perfon or community.

Notwithftanding this, fix perfons with their affociates, September 26, 1664, petitioned governor Nichols
for liberty to purchafe of the Indians, and fettle certain

[*b*] Where the peace and tranquillity of a country or colony cannot
be maintained, by the civil power, which feems to have happened
at fundry times in the Jerfeys, a military force is abfolutely requifite.
Some young regiment, inftead of being in courfe difbanded in Great-
Britain or Ireland, may be fent to the feditious colony, they will foon
quell the rioters, and when the fpirit of mutiny is drove out, the regiment may be difbanded in the colony ; they will contribute towards
peopling the colony; and moreover, as being ufed to a regular and
proper fubmiffion to authority, by their example, they will teach the
fame to the people of the colony. Thus the regiment of Carignan,
fome years fince was fent over from France to Canada, and difbanded
there ; thus in the time of the government of lord Colpepper, a regiment was fent from England to Virginia, to quell the riots under
Bacon, and afterwards diffolved there.

tracts

tracts of land upon Arthur Cul-Bay, which he granted September 30, 1664; accordingly these associates made a purchase from the Indians, October 28 following, in the name of John Bailey, Daniel Denton, Luke Watson, of Long-Island, husbandmen, and their associates, of a tract of land bounded as above : the consideration was, paying to the Indians twenty fathoms of trading cloth, two made coats, two guns, two hatchets, ten bars of lead, twenty handfuls of gun-powder; and after one year's expiration, the remainder of the purchase was 400 fathoms of white wampum (value 20 l. sterl.) or 200 fathoms of black wampum : in consequence of this, governor Nichols granted to these associates a patent for said lands, with a liberty to purchase further of the Indians so far as Snake-Hill, dated December 2, 1664.

That the reader may have some conception of the dispute concerning the property and quit-rents of these lands, between the proprietors who hold of the crown, and of the people who hold by supposed Indian purchases, which has occasioned much disturbance in this government; we shall make the following observations.

1. Nichols, lieutenant governor of New-Jersey for the duke of York, being informed of the duke's assignment to lord Berkley and Sir George Carteret, suspecting that he would soon be superseded by a lieutenant governor of their own appointment, and perhaps for other considerations, September 30, 1664, gave licence to certain persons (as is above related) to purchase lands of the Indians, which they did October 25; and the 3d of December following, Nichols gave them a patent for the same, subjected to certain quit-rents. This patent, though posterior to the aforesaid assignment, was conformable to his instructions, and before any proper notice received of that assignment, [i] and therefore in equity alledged to be good,

[i] The dispute concerning the equivalent lands called the Oblong made over by the colony of Connecticut to the province of New-York, between associates who had a grant of them from the king in coun-

especially

especially confidering, 2. That Philip Carteret, Efq. lieutenant governor for the affignees, did foon after his entering upon the government of the Jerfeys, (he entered Auguft 1665.) as it is faid, under hand and feal gave licence
to a company of fundry perfons to purchafe of the Indians within his government what quantity of lands they
fhould think convenient; and accordingly, as the Elizabeth men fay, their anceftors, with advice and confent of
faid governor, made fundry purchafes of the Indians.
3. Governor Carteret for his own ufe purchafed fome of
thefe Indian grant rights, particularly that of Bailey,
May 21, 1666; only four families were fettled at Elizabeth-town (afterwards fo called) before governor Carteret's arrival; Carteret died governor of Eaft-Jerfey,
Nov. 1682; during his government the provincial general affemblies, the council, the fuperior or fupreme courts
of judicature, and general offices of the government
were kept at Elizabeth-town, which was fo called by the
name of Elizabeth, wife of Sir George Carteret; it was
the firft Englifh fettlement, and the moft ancient town
of the province.

Moreover, the proprietors who hold by Indian grants,
fay, as a precedent, although the courts at law in the
Jerfeys, May 14, 1695, gave jndgment of ejeçtment in
favour of James Fullerton, who held under the general
proprietors, againft Jeffrey Jones, who held by the Indian
grants. Upon Jone's appeal to the king in council,
the judgment was reverfed and fet afide February 25,
1696: the general proprietors fay, that the judgment
was reverfed only becaufe of fome errors in the procced-
ings. A petition or complaint of Elizabeth-town Indian grant proprietors, was read before the king in council, July 19, 1744, reprefenting the hardfhips they fuftained from the general proprietors. 1. That generally

cil, and affociates who had conformable to inftruçtions, a grant of
them from the governor and council of New-York, is of this nature
but hitherto not determined. See vol. II. p. 232.

the council and judges are interested in the general proprietors side of the question, and are therefore become judges in their own cause. 2. By act of assembly they have procured part of the county of Somerset, who are mostly of the general proprietors side, to be annexed to the county of Essex, where the lands of the proprietors grant proprietors generally lay, for the sake of having juries in their interest. For a six-penny damage, we are sometimes brought in for two or three hundred pounds proclamation money costs; and we are daily threatened with great pretended damages and heavy costs: therefore they pray, that the king would take them under his immediate protection, and either determine the affair in your majesty's most honourable privy council, or appoint disinterested commissioners out of some of the neighbouring colonies, and by a jury from thence also to be taken, to hear and finally decide in said cause; or that your majesty would be graciously pleased to appoint commissioners, to hear, enquire into, and determine said controversy; or grant such relief as to your majesty may seem meet. This was referred to the committee of council for plantation affairs. August 21, 1744, this committee refer the petition to the lords commissioners for trade and plantations, to report to the committee, what they conceive proper for his majesty to do therein. The board of trade and plantations report to the said committee of privy council, &c. &c. &c. The character of a summary obliges us to stop; and only further to observe, that this affair hitherto is not issued.

In answer, the general proprietors represent to the board of trade and plantations, 1. That they humbly conceive, the complaint is not sent from the whole body, or from any considerable number of inhabitants there, but from a few factious and mutinous people impatient of any government. 2. The rioters pretend a sole right in the Indians, but no right in the king and his grantees, with a design to deprive the proprietors of their

right

right to the foil and quit-rent, and with a defign to ftrip his majefty of his royal right to that and the other, plantations, and to render them independent of the crown.

Complaints dated April 13, 1745, were filled in chancery of the Jerfeys, againft the Elizabeth proprietors called Clinker right men, confifting of 124 folio pages; and was followed by a long bill from the council of proprietors of the Eaftern divifion of New-Jerfey, met in Perth-Amboy, March 25, 1746, in behalf of themfelves, and the reft of the general proprietors of the Eaftern divifion of New-Jerfey, whom they reprefent. In their inftruments they feem to alledge, 1. That as the Indians had granted thefe lands to Herman 1651, they could not grant them to Bailey, &c. as is above faid. 2, Confidering the long poffeffion of the Elizabeth men, and the great charge and labour in clearing thefe poffeffions, governor Nichols's patents upon Indian deeds are in equity deemed good; this does not excufe the poffeffors from paying quit-rents and other acknowledgment conformably to the grants; and that in fact, March 11, 1674-5, the Elizabeth men offering to pay to the lord proprietor 20 l. fterl. per ann. quit-rent for eight miles fquare, this offer was refufed by the governor and council infifting upon the half penny fterl. per acre per ann. 3. The riotous proceedings of the Elizabeth men and others claiming by Indian deeds, viz. goal broke open, people forceably turned out of the poffeffion of their lands; this they call clubing them out; and the officers of the government publickly infulted and beat; fome of the rioters have come fifty miles and upwards to join in a riot.

The late riots in the Jerfeys are between the proprietors who hold by a town right, and thofe who hold by patents from the general proprietors.

The general proprietors fay, that the only good title in the province is under the crown; and all pretences from Indian purchafes only are void.

The

The boundaries of New-Jerfey, *rivers, and fome diftances,*
of noted places.

It is bounded eafterly by the province of New-York
from 41 d. N. lat. on Hudfon's river to Sandyhook, about
forty miles; from Sandyhook E. foutherly upon the
ocean forty leagues to Cape-May, at the entrance of Delaware-Bay; from Cape-May it is bounded wefterly on
Penfylvania, along the various turnings of Delaware river to 41 d. 40 m. north lat. which, if in a ftraight line,
would be about 200 miles; the N. eafterly line of New-
Jerfey with New-York, was determined by the duke of
York in his grant of New-Jerfey to Berkley and Carteret, to be from a point in the main branch of Delaware
river in lat. 41 d. 40 m. to a point in Hudfon's river in
lat. 41 d. The point on Delaware river is fully agreed
upon and afcertained by both governments, the other
on Hudfon's river is not fo fully agreed upon; the line
from point to point may be about eighty miles long, E.
41 d. S.

Anno 1676, by agreement between the four affignees
of lord Berkley on the one fide, and Sir George Carteret
on the other fide, (perhaps this is the reafon of the
name quinquepartite line) New-Jerfey was divided into
two provinces, called the Eaft and Weft-Jerfey, and confirmed by the duke of York 1680, and 1682, and by
act of affembly 1719; this line as run by Mr. Laurence, November 1744, was in length 150 miles twenty
chains, N. 9 d. 19 m. W. from Little-Egg harbour in
the ocean, to 41 d. 40 m. N. lat. The S. point of this
line was fettled 1676, the north point of the line
was fettled 1719, but the line itfelf was never run till
1744, and that only by the proprietors of Eaft-Jerfey
ex parte. In this line fome errors have been difcovered
and require to be rectified. As there is a confiderable difference in the variations of the compafs, at the north
: and

and fouth terminations of this divifional line, this divifional line cannot be ftraight. The firft falls in Delaware
river in Trent town, are oppofite to the 47th mile of
this divifional line.

' In order to difcover the main branch mentioned in the
grants, and the largenefs of fome other branches of Delaware and Sefquahanna rivers, there was lately a furvey
line run nearly due weft from Minifinck ifland on Delaware river about twelve miles above the divifional line
croffing the N. E. branch of Delaware river, to Sefquahanna river for eighty-five miles, and where it fell in
with Sefquahanna, that river was about thirty chains
(four rods to a chain) wide, and near this there was a
branch which fell into the principal river of Sefquahanna
about 300 feet wide, and in the fork was an Indian village called Solochka. The weft branch of Delaware river
was only twenty-five feet wide, the N. E. branch where
the ftation point of the divifion line between New-
York and Jerfey is fixed at 41 d. 40 m. lat. is above
500 feet wide. The fork fo called of Delaware river is
about feventy miles upon a ftraight line below this ftation point: at this ftation point anno 1744, the variation of the compafs was W. 6 d. 35 m. anno 1719, it
was obferved to be about 8 d. as is before mentioned.
The ftation point at Egg-Harbour 1744, was 5 d. 25 m.
Mr. Serjeant Hook fome time fince made a purchafe
of 3750 acres upon Delaware river in the Weft-
Jerfey, and gave one tenth of it as a glebe to the
church.

The principal rivers in the province of New-Jerfey,
are the Noorde Rivier or Hudfon's river, which we have
already delineated in the fection of New-York, and
Zuide Rivier or Delaware river, which we fhall defcribe
in the fection of Penfylvania; only we fhall obferve,
that in the Jerfey fide of this river are feveral fhort
creeks. Thefe of Cohanfy, and of Salem twenty miles
higher, make one diftrict of cuftom-houfe; at Bridlington

ton twenty miles above Philadelphia is another cuftom
diftrict. Thefe two cuftom-houfe diftricts, their quarterly
entries and clearances of veffels, are generally nil, and
fcarce deferve the name of preventive creeks. The
main branch of Delaware river comes from Cat-kill
mountains, a few miles weft of the fountains of Sco-
harie river a branch of the Mohawks river. Raritan river
falls into Sandyhook-bay at Amboy point; the tide flows
twelve miles up to Brunfwick : at the mouth of this river is the only confiderable fea port and cuftom-houfe
of New-Jerfey : here is the city of Perth-Amboy, it is
the capital of the province of New-Jerfey, and here are
kept the provincial records : here is a good deep water
harbour and promifing country; but notwithftanding,
it has only the appearance of a mean village : the name
is a compound of Perth, the honorary title of the
late Drummond earl of Perth, and Amboy its Indian
name.

The fea line of New-Jerfey is Arthur Cul-Bay and
Amboy-Sound, between Staten-Ifland and the main
about twenty miles S. Thefe receive the rivulets of Hac-
kinfack, Paffaick, Bounds-creek, and Raway; from
Amboy point to Sandyhook (Sandyhook is in Eaft-
Jerfey) twelve miles E. from Sandyhook to Cape-May,
120 mile S. wefterly, is a flat double fandy fhore, having
fome inlets practicable only by fmall craft.

There are feveral chains or ridges of hills in this province, but of no confideration.

Perth-Amboy is the provincial town of Eaft-Jerfey ;
Bridlington is the province town of Weft-Jerfey, diftance fifty miles, where the general affembly of all the
Jerfeys fits alternately, and where the diftinct provincial
judicatories or fupreme courts fit refpectively. Bridlington, commonly called Burlington, is a pleafant village.
Elizabeth-town is the moft ancient corporation and confiderable town of the province. Brunfwick in Eaft-
Jerfey is nearly the center of the Eaft and Weft-Jerfeys ;

I   here

here is lately eftablished a college [k] for the inftruction of youth, by a charter from governor Belcher, October 22, 1746, with power to confer all degrees as in the univerfities of England: the prefent truftees are generally prefbyterians, a majority of feven or more truftees to have the management; each fcholar to pay 4 l. per ann. at 8 s. oz. filver; Mr. Jonathan Dickenfon was their firft prefident, Mr. Burr is their prefent prefident; in this college October 5, 1749, commenced feven batchelors of arts.

The road as in prefent ufe, from New-York city to Philadelphia, is, from New-York to Elizabeth-town feventeen miles, thence to Brunfwick twenty-two miles, thence to Trent town ferry thirty miles, thence to Philadelphia twenty miles; being in all from the city of New-York to Philadelphia 104 miles.

From Cape-May to Salem are about fixty miles, thence to Bridlington fifty miles, thence to Trent town falls fifteen miles. Thefe are the firft falls of Delaware river, and the tide flows fo high; below thefe falls when the tide is down and no land floodings in the river, the river is fordable.

In the province of the Jerfeys are five corporations with courts; whereof three are in Eaft-Jerfey, the city of Perth-Amboy, the city of New-Brunfwick, and the borough of Elizabeth-town; and two in Weft-Jerfey, the city of Bridlington, alias Burlington, and the borough of Trent town: of thefe only two, Perth-Amboy and Burlington, fend reprefentatives to the general affembly.

There is not much to be faid concerning their wars with the Indians and Canada French: the Five nations of Iroquois which we call Mohawks, have always been in our intereft; they, efpecially the large tribe of Senecas,

[k] Formerly by miftake, I wrote, that this college was by royal charter.

cover the provinces of New-Jersey, Penfylvania, Maryland, and Virginia.   Ever fince the firft fettling of this
province, the publick has never been put to one penny
charge for keeping the Indians in peace. The chain
Canada expeditions of 1709, and 1711, led this province, and all the other British provinces to the northward of it, into a pernicious paper currency, called publick bills of credit; their firft paper currency was emitted 1709 of 3000 l. to be cancelled by taxes the fame
year, and 1711 they emitted 5000 l. to be cancelled by
taxes in 1712 and 1713, and afterwards many emiffions
for charges of government [*l*] and loans amongft themfelves, but never did run fuch depreciating lengths, as
have been done in New-England.   See the article of
plantation currencies in the Appendix.

At prefent the Weft-Jerfey money or currency is in
value equal to that of the adjoining province of Penfylvania; the Eaft-Jerfey currency is the fame with the adjacent province of New-York; their refpective dealings,
being almoft folely with the refpective adjoining provinces.   Penfylvania paper currency was at firft emitted at
the value of proclamation money; which is 6 s. currency
equal in value to a heavy Spanifh piece of eight; but at
prefent a milled piece or Spanifh dollar paffes for 7 s. 6d.
currency, a heavy piftole 7 s. a guinea 34 s. and moidores 44 s.   New-York paper currency was at firft emitted at 8 s. per oz. filver: at prefent a dollar or milled
piece of eight being 7-8ths of one oz. filver, is 8 s. currency, piftoles 28 s. if not under 4 d. 6 grains wt. guineas 35 s. moidores 45 s.

Their various fectaries, not in religion, but in religious modes of worfhip, may be found in a general
article of the fection of Rhode-Ifland; we fhall only

[*l*] The forces raifed there towards the late Cuba or Spanifh Weft-
India expedition, and afterwards five companies of 100 men each,
towards a feint expedition againft Canada 1746, was a confiderable
charge to them in levying and victualling.

obferve

obferve that this colony was firft fettled by prefbyterians, anabaptifts, and quakers, who to this time ftill
prevail; notwithftanding the great charge of miffionaries from the fociety for propagating the gofpel,
who by miftake feem to embarrafs the chriftian religion in general, more than to cultivate it. Why fhould
religious, pious, and fober chriftians, induftrious, frugal, and orderly common-wealths men, be thus difturbed
and perplexed, in their legally tolerated way, differing
from the miffionary eftablifhed church, not in doctrine,
but in fome anceftorial innocent modes of worfhip:
while at the fame time the heathen Indians, the principal object of their miffions, as may well be imagined,
neither civilized nor chriftianized, are wholly neglected
by them ?

Inhabitants of the Jerfeys, men, women, and children,
are reckoned at about 50,000, whereof 10,000 may be
reckoned a training militia.

The valuation of the feveral counties, that is, their
proportions in every thoufand pound tax, a few years
fince, ftood thus,

EAST-JERSEY.	£		WEST-JERSEY.	£	
Somerfet	39		Cape-May	31	
Monmouth	169	10	Salem	144	
Middlefex	115		Gloucefter	86	
Effex	136		Burlington	123	10
Bergen	82		Hunterdon	74	
	541	10		458	10

The two new out counties of Morris, and Trent, feem
hitherto not reduced to any regulations.

Succeffion of governors in the province of New-Jerfey.

The affair of governors is above intermixed with the
hiftory of the various changes of the property and jurifdiction; we fhall now recapitulate what relates to government

vernment and governors in a connected aud concise
manner.

The duke of York had a grant of the property and
government of New-Netherlands from his brother Charles
II. March 12, 1663-4. Duke of York by commission,
April 2, 1664, appointed Richard Nichols, Efq. his
lieut. governor or deputy of the whole New-Netherlands,
but did not enter upon his government until August 27,
1664.

Upon the duke of York's affignment, June 24, 1664,
of that part called the Jerfeys to lord Berkley and Sir
George Carteret, they appointed Philip Carteret their
governor: after fix months refidence he went to England, and foon returned to his government; but 1672,
a turbulent people, to evade paying quit-rents, alledge
that they did not hold of the proprietors Berkley and
Carteret, but by Indian grants : they relinquifhed governor Carteret, and chofe a governor of their own : governor Carteret went home with complaints, and did not return till November 1674, a Dutch jurifdiction upon a re-
conqueft intervening from July 1673, to November
1674; Berkley and Carteret had a divifional feparate
grant from the duke of York 1674; and Sir George
Carteret fent over Philip Carteret, governor of Eaft-
Jerfey: the duke of York kept the jurifdiction of Weft-
Jerfeys in his own hands by deputies. Nichols and
Andros were governors of New-York and Weft-Jerfey
for the duke of York.

Becaufe of fome differences between governor Andros
of New-York, and governor Carteret of Eaft-Jerfey,
Andros ufurped the government of Eaft-Jerfey 1680;
and fent from New-York to Elizabeth-town fome foldiers ; they ufed governor Carteret rudely, they broke
open his houfe, carried him from his naked bed on
board of the floop to New-York, where he was kept
prifoner the greateft part of the year : governor Andros
favoured the Indian grant proprietors, with a defign to
foment divifions and confufion; divide et impera : upon
com-

complaints fent home to the duke of York, Andros was difmiffed from the government with a fhew of refentment, and the duke of York gave new deeds to the proprietors of the Eaft and Weft-Jerfeys, with exprefs grants of thefe powers, which Sir Edmond Andros pretended were wanting, the better to juftify his former conduct; by virtue of thefe new grants dated 1680, the proprietors were next year re-eftablifhed in the New-Jerfeys: Philip Carteret died governor of Eaft-Jerfey, November 1682. To prevent irregular purchafes of the Indians, the affembly of Eaft-Jerfey, 1683, paffed an act " forbidding the taking of any Indian deeds but in the " name of the lords proprietors, upon the pain of be-" ing profecuted as feditious perfons, and as breakers of " the king's peace, and of the publick peace and fafety " of the province;" the fame act, but fomething more fevere, was paffed in Weft-Jerfey.

In Weft-Jerfey, upon the duke of York's quitting the government to the affignees of lord Berkley, 1680, one of the affignees or proprietors was by them appointed governor, and to him, 1690, fucceeded Dr. Daniel Cox, who had purchafed the greateft part of Weft-Jerfey.

In Eaft-Jerfey upon the duke of York's new deed to the proprietors, Robert Barclay, a noted quaker writer, was made governor; fometimes he officiated by a deputy; 1684, Gawn Laurie was his deputy, and continued till 1685: foon after this, king James affumed the government, but upon the revolution, the proprietors were reftored to their former rights, and appointed John Totham, Efq. for their governor, who was fucceeded by col. Dudley; but the people fcrupled to obey them, and the proprietors appointed col. Hamilton for governor.

After fome time the people alledged, that as a Scotsman he could not be governor of an Englifh colony,
and

and a party of the proprietors appointed Mr. Baffe governor; foon after, another party of the proprietors again appointed col. Hamilton, Auguft 14, 1699, and not long after, fome of the proprietors appointed Mr. Baffe again; thefe appointments were not confirmed by the king. Mr. Bowne fuperfeded them; thefe times in the Eaft-Jerfeys were called the revolutions, [*m*] and was governor when the proprietors of both Jerfeys, becaufe of diffenfions amongft themfelves in appointing governors, and from the confufions occafioned by the Indian grants men, found it advifeable to refign the government, but no other of their rights, to the crown, 1702.

Thus both Jerfeys were united in one jurifdiction, and had for their governor the fame perfon who was governor of the province of New-York; fee the fection of New-York, vol. II. p. 249, viz. lord Cornbury, col. Hunter, [*n*] William Burnet, Efq. col. Montgomery, and col. Cofby.

Upon Cofby's death, lieut. governor Clarke, 1736, fucceeded in the command of New-York, but not in that of the Jerfeys, which in courfe fell into the hands of the prefident of the council of the Jerfeys: ever fince, the governors of New-York and of the Jerfeys have been in diftinct perfons.

[*m*] During the revolutions in the alternate adminiftrations of Hamilton and Baffe from 1698, to the refignation of the government to the crown, there were in the province continued confufions, mutual breaking of goals, refcuing of prifoners, beating and abufing of civil officers; fometimes the chief command was in the council; the refignation of thofe governments to the crown by Sir Thomas Lane knight and alderman of London, agent for Weft-Jerfey, and of William Dockwray, the famous projector of the ufeful, and to the publick revenue of Great-Britain beneficial, penny poft office, agent for Eaft-Jerfey.

[*n*] Governor Hunter was allowed by the general affembly of the Jerfeys, during his adminiftration, 500 l. per ann. currency, and 100 l. for contingencies.

Lewis Morris, Efq. formerly chief juftice of the province of New-York, was the firft diftinct governor of the Jerfeys; he died May 14, 1746; to him fucceeded.

Jonathan Belcher, Efq. formerly governor of the provinces of Maffachufett's-Bay and New-Hampfhire, fee vol. I. p. 481; was nominated by the king for governor of the Jerfeys, and arrived there foon after: he continues governor at this prefent writing, Auguft 1751. His firft meeting with the provincial affembly was Auguft 22, 1746.

The legiflature, and fome municipal laws of New-Jerfey.

The legiflature confifts of three negatives; the enacting ftile is, " Be it enacted by his excellency the governor, council, and general affembly."

The three negatives are, 1. The governor, ftiled governor in chief, vic-eadmiral, and chancellor of the province of New-Jerfey.

2. The council nominated by the king; their complement is twelve, as it generally is in all our colonies. The governor and council are a court of error and chancery.

3. The houfe of reprefentatives in this province; they are particularly called the affembly; though in propriety the governor, council, and houfe of reprefentatives of the people, met in a legiflative capacity, are the general affembly of a province or colony [o]. This houfe of reprefentatives or affembly confifts of twenty-four members, whereof twenty are reprefentatives of counties, the other four from the cities, fo called, of Perth-Amboy and Burlington, viz.

[o] I cannot account for fuch improprieties in our colonies; thus in Virginia, the houfe of reprefentatives is very improperly called the houfe of burgeffes, becaufe Virginia is reprefented by counties. In the province of North-Carolina adjoining to Virginia, they are guilty of the fame impropriety.

In

In East-Jersey.		In West-Jersey.	
From the county of		From the county of	
Bergen	2	Hunterdon	2
Essex	2	Burlington	2
Middlesex	2	Gloucester	2
Somerset	2	Salem	2
Monmouth	2	Cape-May	2
From the city of		From the city of	
Perth-Amb.	2	Burlington	2
	12		12

The new counties of Morris county, and Trent county, hitherto do not send reprefentatives.

All the acts of the affembly of New-Jerfey muft have the royal affent.

The houfe of reprefentatives is no court of judicature, but have the privilege of enquiring into the male admi- niftration of the courts of juftice.

The magna charta or fundamental conftitution of the province of New-Jerfey, confifts of three fubfequent fets of conceffions from the proprietors, and of the perpe- tual inftructions for all fucceffive crown governors as agreed upon 1702, at the proprietors refignation of the government to the crown. Thefe are reckoned of a higher nature, than the acts of their affemblies, and are termed by the affembly, the laws of conceffions. The firft conceffions were 1664, from lord Berkley and Sir George Carteret, joint proprietors of New-Jerfey by affignment from the duke of York. The fecond con- ceffions 1672, were from the faid proprietors jointly; the third conceffions were only for Eaft Jerfey by Sir George Carteret 1674, upon the duke of York's grant- ing him a divifional grant: thefe were only additional and explanatory of the firft conceffions.

The bounty lands to the firft fettlers called head-lands, being fo many acres per head of fettlers at one half penny fterl. per ann. per acre quit-rent. The quit-rents of the Jerfeys began March 25, 1670; the whole arrears of quit-rents from the beginning to 1747, did not exceed 15000 l. The bounty by the firſt conceſſions was only for heads imported in the firſt four years, but by ſubſequent conceſſions, it was continued to January 13, 1685. In other patents to purchaſers the quit-rents were various as per agreement, e. g. in Newark there are ſome patents at ſix pence ſterl. per ann. per. 100 acres.

The fundamental law of conceſſions is, that all va-cant lands are to be purchaſed only by the governor and council in the name of the proprietors; and all claims to lands otherways than by warrant of ſurvey, by the ſurvey of a ſtated ſurveyor, and patent from the governor and council are deemed void. There have been only two remarkable times of purchaſe from the Indians 1664, under governor Nichols, prior to the acts of con-ceſſions; and 1672 under governor Carteret, but ſubſe-quent and contrary to the firſt conceſſions. Several tracts of land have from time to time been purchaſed of the Indians by the general proprietors. By act of aſſembly, 1683, no perſon to contract for, or accept of, deeds of lands from the Indians, but in the name of the pro-prietors.

In the revolution times, as they were called, in New-Jerſey from 1698, to 1703, all rules of property were ſlighted, many riots and much diſorder enſued, and by remonſtrances to king William all eſtabliſhed rules of property were endeavoured to be everted, and Indian purchaſes eſtabliſhed, but in vain. Upon the reſigna-tion of the government to the crown, and by an act of aſſembly 1703, declaring all pretences by Indian purchaſes only, to be penal, (penalty 40 s. per acre) cri-minal, and void; and by an act 1713, a penalty is im-poſed of 20 s. for every tree cut by any perſon upon lands which are not his own property; order was re-ſtored to the great improvement of New-Jerſey, and which was enjoyed till 1745, when Indian purchaſes were ſet up again. Several actions of ejectment being

brought

brought by the council of general proprietors againſt the tenants, ſo called, in poſſeſſion of the Elizabeth rights, as holding only by a groundleſs right of title by Indian deeds; anno 1746, the Elizabeth men petition the general aſſembly, that a way may be made for their relief in the province, or that they may have liberty of application to the head and fountain of juſtice. Upon this enſued a ſuit in their provincial chancery, as before related.

Some articles in the conceſſions were, that the general aſſembly ſhall raiſe and pay the governor's ſalary and all charges of government; and that the quit rents ſhall be paid to the proprietors free of all charges, no quit-rents to be applied for that purpoſe.

To prevent interfering claims and fraudulent ſales, there are only two deputy ſurveyors in a county, under a general ſurveyor of the province, and all ſurveys are to be recorded as approved of by the ſurveyor general.

Titles of land are to be tried only in the ſupreme court of judicature.

Courts of judicature.

The ſeveral courts of judicature are nearly of the ſame conſtitution with the courts in the colonies already related. There is a ſupreme court (in New-England they are called ſuperior courts) for the Eaſt-Jerſey diviſion held at the city of Amboy two terms yearly, the third Tueſday in March, and ſecond Tueſday in Auguſt; each of theſe with only eight days continuance. The ſupreme court for the Weſt-Jerſey diviſion is held at Burlington the firſt Tueſday in November, and ſecond Tueſday in May, under the ſame regulations.

There are in each county once a year, a court for tryal of cauſes brought to iſſue in the ſupreme court; thoſe for Weſt-Jerſey are in the ſpring, thoſe for Eaſt-Jerſey are in the end of autumn.

U 3   In

In each county there are courts of quarter feffions, and county courts for holding pleas; in New-England they are called inferior courts for common pleas.

Produce, manufactures, trade, and navigation in New-Jerfey.

New-Jerfey is a good corn country: it raifes more wheat than any one of our colonies; but their wheat and flour is moftly fhipped off from New-York and Penfylvania; they raife fome hemp and flax.

They have not wrought their copper ore mine for fome time.

They manufacture fome iron ore into pigs and bars.

In the province of New-Jerfey there are three cuftomhoufe diftricts, whereof two are in Weft-Jerfey on Delaware river; Salem (this includes Cohanzey) about nine miles below Newcaftle: and Burlington about twenty miles above Philadelphia; thefe, as we have already obferved, are of no confideration, fcarce deferving the name of preventive creeks: the third is in Eaft-Jerfey at Perth-Amboy. The twelve months accounts of entries and clearances at the port of Perth-Amboy, from June 24, 1750, to June 24, 1751, ftand thus,

Entered inwards.		Cleared outwards.	
Ships	2	Ships	2
Snows	2	Snows	3
Brigantines	7	Brigantines	8
Sloops	18	Sloops	13
Schooners	10	Schooners	10
Shallops	2	Shallops	2
	41		38

both foreign and coafting voyages included. I fhall only mention fome of the moft confiderable articles of their exports and imports in that time.

Exported.

Exported.		Imported.	
Flour	6424 bar.	Rum	39,670 gal.
Bread	168,500 wt.	Moloffes	31,600 gal.
Beef and pork	314 barrels	Sugar	2,089 ct. wt.
Grain	17,941 bufh.	Pitch, tar, } 437 bar.	
Hemp	14,000 wt.	and turpent.	
Some firkins of butter, fome		Wines	123 pipes
hams, beer, flax-feed,		Salt	12,759 bufh.
bar-iron, fome lumber.			

Some mifcellanies on various fubjects.

The copper ore of the Jerfeys is very good, but the mine has not been wrought for fome years, the difficulty in draining requires a fire engine. The copper mines in Simfbury hills in New-England, about ninety miles N. E. from the copper mine in New-Jerfey, have been neglected for fome years, becaufe they not only dip too quick, and therefore are not eafily drained, but alfo the ore is of a hard nature not eafily fluxed; it is too much intermixed with fpar, the veins or loads very uncertain and unequal, and frequently only fhoads or fragments.

In Britifh North-America, hitherto no difcovery has been made of tin ores, nor of lapis calaminaris, very little lead ore, and that not good.

All over North-America is much iron ore, both rock and bog ore. Three tun of bog or fwamp ore gives about one tun caft iron ware, which can be afforded cheaper than that which is imported from England or Holland. The bars of bog ore have too much fcoriæ or drofs, and are much inferior to the bars refined from the pigs of rock ore.

In the American rivers there are many cataracts, precipices, pitches, or falls; generally from the river paffing over a ledge or ridge of rocks: that of Niagara, formerly mentioned, between lake Ontario and lake Erie, is the moft noted. There are fome cataracts or great

falls,

falls, not from a precipice of rocks, but from a very
narrow paſs in a tide river; that near the mouth of St.
John's river on the N. W. ſide of the bay of Fundy in
Nova-Scotia is the moſt noted: in this caſe, from the
narrowneſs of the paſs, the water not confined below
falls off faſter than the water confined above, the water
above is not only what the tide of flood brought in, but
alſo the river water dammed up.

The higher up a tide river, the duration of flood is
leſs, and that of ebb is more; for inſtance, in the great
river of Canada, or river of St. Laurence, anno 1748,
a flag of truce was ſent for exchange of priſoners from
Boſton in New-England to Quebec in Canada. In this
great river by order of the general governor of Canada
they were ſtopt at Liſle des Baſques, (five leagues below Tadouſack, and thirty-five leagues below Quebec)
where was good anchorage [*p*] in ten fathom water, the
tide flowed five hours and ebbed ſeven hours.

Amongſt the many hardſhips which the firſt ſettlers
of new raw colonies and plantations ſuffer, one of the
moſt conſiderable is, their ſitting down in wilderneſs,
foreſt, or wood lands; where by the exhalations from
the trees, there is a continual damp, which does not continuedly diſperſe, but hovers about, and may be ſaid in
ſome reſpect to ſtagnate and putrify, and conſequently
produce in theſe human bodies many kinds of putrid
diſorders, ſuch as putrid lingring fevers, putrid dyſen-
teries, all ſorts of ſcorbutick complaints, and the like
diſtemperatures. The damp or vapour from wood lands,
is much more conſiderable than from the ſame lands
when cleared of trees and ſhrubs. It is notorious in theſe
countries, that many ſtreams of water which in the beginning came from wood lands, and carried griſt mills
and ſaw mills; when theſe lands were cleared of wood,

[*p*] The French by their repreſentations of the difficult and dangerous navigation of this river, endeavour to intimidate all other nations from attempting the river; but now we find that it is ſafely
practicable.

their

their ftreams vanifhed and became dry, the mills ceafed, and in fome parts the cattle could not be conveniently watered.   In the philofophical tranfactions of the royal fociety in London, we find many obfervations and experiments made relating to this fubject; for inftance, two veffels containing each a certain equal quantity of water; in one of thefe veffels were fet fome living plants: after a certain fpace of time, the veffel containing water with plants evaporated much more of the water, than the veffel of water only.

S E C T.   XIV.

Concerning the Province of Penfylvania, *and its Territories.*

WE have already deduced thefe fettlements from their firft European difcoveries, and from their tranfition by the name of New-Netherlands under the Dutch, to the duke of York's property by patents from the crown of England.

This province and territories are by three diftinct grants.   1. The province of Penfylvania by patent from K. Charles II. dated March 4, 1680-1.   2. The duke of York, 1683, Auguft 24, fold to William Penn the elder, his heirs and affigns, the town of Newcaftle, alias Delaware, and a diftrict of twelve miles round Newcaftle. 3. Duke of York by another deed of fale Auguft 24, 1683, made over to faid William Penn, his heirs and affigns, that tract of land from twelve miles fouth of Newcaftle, to the Whore-Kills, otherwife called Cape-Henlopen, divided into the two counties of Kent and Suffex; which with Newcaftle diftrict, are commonly known by the name of the three lower counties upon Delaware river.

As

As the three lower counties or territories are by diftinct deeds or grants from that of the royal grant of the province of Penfylvania, when it was by the proprietary left to their option to be united with the jurifdiction of the province of Penfylvania, or to continue a feparate jurifdiction; they chufe to be a feparate jurifdiction, and not to be as it were annihilated by a prevailing jurifdiction : thus they continue at prefent two diftinct legiflatures, governments, or jurifdiction, under the direction of one and the fame governor ; but their municipal laws and regulations are nearly the fame.

K. CHARLES IId's patent of the province of PENSYLVANIA is dated March 4, 1680-1, of which an abftract is, " To our trufty and well beloved fubject William Penn, Efq. fon and heir of Sir William Penn deceafed, to reduce the favage nations by gentle and juft manners to the love of civil fociety and the chriftian religion (with regard to the memory and merits of his late father in divers fervices, particularly in the fea-fight againft the Dutch 1665, under the duke of York) to tranfport an ample colony towards enlarging the Englifh empire and its trade, is granted all that tract of land in America, bounded eaftward on Delaware river from twelve miles northward of Newcaftle to the 43 d. of northern lat. and to extend 5 d. in longitude from faid river ; to be bounded northerly by the beginning of the 43 d. of N. lat. and on the fouth by a circle drawn at twelve miles diftance from Newcaftle northward and weftward unto the beginning of the 40 d. of northern lat. and then by a ftrait line weftward to the limits of longitude abovementioned ; faving to us and our fucceffors the allegiance and fovereignty, to be holden as of our caftle of Windfor in the county of Berks, paying quit-rent two buck-fkins to be delivered to us yearly in our caftle of Windfor on the firft of January, and the fifth of all gold and filver ore, clear of all charges. Erected into a province and feignorie, to be called Penfylvania.

Said

Said William Penn, &c. and his lieutenants, with the
affent of a majority of the freemen or their delegates
affembled, to raife money for publick ufes, to eftablifh
judges, juftices, and other magiftrates, probat of wills
and granting of adminiftrations included; to pardon or
remit all crimes and offences committed within faid
province, treafon and wilful murder excepted, which,
however they may reprieve until the king's pleafure is
known; the judges by them conftituted to hold pleas as
well criminal as civil, perfonal, real and mixt: their
laws to be confonant to reafon, and not repugnant to
the laws of England, referving to us, &c. a power to
hear and determine upon appeals. In all matters the
laws of England to take place, where no pofitive law of
the province appears. A duplicate of all laws made in
faid province, fhall in five years be tranfmitted to the
privy council; and if within fix months, being there
received, they be deemed inconfiftent with the prerogative or laws of England, they fhall be void : Audience
for our fubjects to tranfport themfelves and families unto
the faid country. A liberty to divide the country into
towns, hundreds, and counties, to incoporate towns'
into boroughs and cities, to conftitute fairs and markets.
A liberty of trade with all our other dominions, paying the cuftomary duties. A power to conftitute fea
ports. and keys, but to admit of fuch officers as fhall
from time to time be appointed by the commiffioners of
our cuftoms. The proprietors may receive fuch impofitions upon goods as the affembly fhall enact. The proprietors to appoint an agent or attorney to refide near
the court in London to anfwer for the default of the
proprietors, and where damages are afcertained by any
of our courts, if thefe damages are not made good
within the fpace of one year, the crown may refume the
government until fuch damages and penalties are fatif-
fied, but without any detriment to the particular owners
or adventurers in the province. To maintain no corre-
fpondence with our enemies... A power to purfue ene-

mies

mies and robbers even to death. May transfer property.
To erect manors, that may hold courts baron. That
the crown fhall make no taxation or impofition in faid
province without confent of the proprietary, or affembly, or by act of parliament in England. Any inhabitants, to the number of twenty, may by writing apply
to the bifhop of London for a preacher or preachers."

An abftract of Mr. Penn's charter of liberties and
privileges to the people, 25th day of the fecond month,
vulgarly called April, 1682. "The government fhall be
in a provincial general affembly compofed of the governor and reprefentatives of the freemen, to make
laws, raife taxes, conftitute courts and offices, &c.
The freemen of the province fhall meet on the twentieth
day of the twelfth month, 1682, to elect feventy-two
perfons for a council, whereof twenty-four fhall fall off
yearly, and another twenty-four be elected in their room,
that many perfons may have experience in government;
in matters of confequence two thirds to be a quorum,
and the confent of the two thirds of fuch quorum is requifite; in affairs of leffer moment twenty-four members fhall be a quorum, and a majority of thefe fhall
determine: the governor or his deputy to prefide and
• have a treble vote. This council is to prepare and de-
liberate upon bills to be paffed into laws by the general
affembly, to erect courts of juftice with their officers,
to judge criminals, to have the executive power; fhall
model towns, ports, markets, publick buildings, and
highways; to infpect the management of the provincial
treafury, and order all publick fchools: this council to
be divided into four diftinct committees for diftinct
branches of bufinefs. The freemen fhall yearly chufe
reprefentatives not exceeding 200, to meet 22d day of
the fecond month (1683, for the firft time) and to continue eight days; may appoint committees to confer with
committees of the council concerning amendments of
bills, and the ninth day fhall give their affirmative or
negative

I

negative to the bills prefented; two thirds to be a quorum in paffing of laws and choice of officers; the enacting ftile to be, " By the governor, with the affent and
approbation of the freemen in provincial council and
general affembly." The firft year the general affembly
may confift of all the freemen of the province, and afterwards of 200 to be chofen annually, which as the country increafes may be enlarged, fo as never to exceed
500, at the difcretion of the legiflature. The provincial council fhall on the 13th day of the firft month
yearly, prefent to the governor or his deputy a double
number of provincial officers; and the freemen in the
county courts fhall prefent a double number to ferve for
fheriffs, juftices of the peace, and coroners for the year
next enfuing; out of each prefentment, the third day
following, the governor or his deputy fhall commiffio-
nate one; but Mr. Penn to appoint the firft officers to
continue ad vitam aut culpam. The general affembly
may be called upon by the governor and provincial
council to meet at any time. When the governor fhall
be under the age of twenty-one, and no guardians appointed by the father, the provincial council fhall appoint guardians not exceeding three, with the power of
a governor. No article in this charter to be altered
without the confent of the governor and fix parts of
feven of the freemen in provincial council and general
affembly."

Befides thefe, there were fome other fundamental laws
agreed upon in England. Every refident who pays fcot
and lot to the government, fhall be deemed a freeman
capable of electing and of being elected. The provincial
council and general affembly to be fole judges in the
elections of their refpective members. Twenty-four men
for a grand jury of inqueft, and twelve for a petty jury,
to be returned by the fheriff. All perfons wrongfully
imprifoned or profecuted at law, fhall have double damages againft the informer or profecutor. Seven years
poffeffion

poffeffion fhall give an unqueftionable right, excepting in cafes of lunaticks, infants, married women, and perfons beyond the feas. A publick regifter eftablifhed. The charter granted by William Penn to the inhabitants is confirmed. All who acknowledge one almighty GOD, fhall not be molefted in their religious perfuafions in matters of faith and worfhip, and fhall not be compelled to maintain or frequent any religious miniftry. Every firft day of the week fhall be a day of Reft. None of thofe articles fhall be altered without confent of the governor or his deputy, and fix parts in feven of the freemen met in provincial council and general affembly. This was figned and fealed by the governor and freemen or adventurers in London the fifth day of the third month called May, 1682.

There were certain conditions agreed upon by the proprietor, and the adventurers and purchafers, July 11, 1681; for inftance, convenient roads and highways be laid out before the dividend of acres to the purchafers; land fhall be laid out to the purchafers and adventurers by lot. Every thoufand acres fhall fettle one family. All dealings with the Indians fhall be in publick market.

All differences between the planters and native Indians fhall be ended by fix planters and fix natives. Laws relating to immorality fhall be the fame as in England. In clearing of land, one acre of trees fhall be left for every five acres, to preferve oak and mulberries for fhiping and filk.

None to leave the province, without publication thereof in the market-place three weeks before.

By a new charter from the proprietary fecond day of the fecond month, 1683, there are fome alterations made in his firft charter, principally as to the numbers of the provincial council and affembly; that is, the provincial council fhall confift of eighteen perfons, whereof three from each of the fix counties; the affembly to confift of
thirty-

thirty-six, that is, six from each county ; as the country increases, the provincial council may be increased to any number not exceeding seventy-two; and the assembly may be increased to any number not exceeding 200; the other articles are much the same as in the first charter : the enacting stile to be, "By the governor, with the approbation of the freemen in provincial council and assembly met;" and the general assembly shall be called, " The meeting, sessions and proceedings of the general assembly of the province of Pensylvania, and the territories thereunto belonging." Nothing in this charter to be altered, but by consent of the governor and six 7ths of the provincial council and assembly.

This charter of 1683, as inconvenient, was surrendered to Mr. Penn in the third month of 1700 by six 7ths of the freemen of the province and territories, and a new charter granted ; as this is now their standing charter, we shall be more particular. The preamble runs thus, " Whereas K. Charles II. granted to William Penn the property and government of the province of Pensylvania, March 4, 1680; and the duke of York granted to said Penn the property and government of a tract of land now called the territories of Pensylvania, August 24, 1683: and whereas the said William Penn for the encouragement of the settlers, did, anno 1683, grant and confirm to the freemen by an instrument intitled, The frame of the government, &c. which charter or frame being found, in some parts of it, not so suitable to the present circumstances of the inhabitants, was delivered up as above; and at the request of the assembly another was granted by the proprietary Mr. Penn, in pursuance of the rights and powers granted him by the crown, confirming to all the inhabitants their former liberties and privileges, so far as in him lieth. 1. No persons who believe in one almighty GOD, and live peaceably under the civil government, shall be molested in their religious persuasions, nor compelled to frequent or main-

tain

tain any religious worfhip contrary to their mind. That all perfons who profefs to believe in JESUS CHRIST, are capable of ferving the government in any capacity; they folemnly promifing, when required, allegiance to the crown, and fidelity to the proprietor and governor. 2. That annually upon the firft day of October for ever, there fhall an affembly be chofen, to fit the fourteenth day of the fame month, viz. four perfons out of each county, or a greater number, as the governor and affembly may from time to time agree, with all the powers and privileges of an affembly as is ufual in any of the king's plantations in America; two thirds of the whole number that ought to meet fhall be a quorum; to fit upon their own adjournments. 3. The freemen at their meeting for electing reprefentatives to chufe fheriffs and coroners; the juftices in the refpective counties to nominate clerks of the peace. 4. The laws of the government fhall be in this ftile, " By the governor, with the confent and approbation of the freemen in general affembly met." 5. No perfon to be licenfed by the governor to keep an ordinary or tavern but fuch as are recommended by the juftices of the county. 6. No alteration to be made in this charter without the confent of the governor and fix parts of feven of the affembly met. Signed William Penn at Philadelphia in Penfylvania, October 28, 1701, and the twenty-firft year of my government." Notwithftanding any thing formerly alledging the province and territories to join together in legiflation, Mr. Penn hereby declares, that if at any time hereafter within three years, their refpective affemblies fhall not agree to join in legiflation, and fhall fignify the fame to me; in fuch cafe the inhabitants of each of the three counties of the province fhall not have lefs than eight reprefentatives, and the town of Philadelphia when incoporated, fhall have two reprefentatives. The inhabitants of each county in the territories fhall have as many perfons to reprefent them in a diftinct affembly for the territories, as be by them requefted.

Province

Province and territories shall enjoy the same charter, liberties and privileges. This charter of privileges was thankfully received the same day by the assembly, and signed by their order; and signed by a number of the proprietary and governor's council.

The report is probable, that Mr. Penn, besides his royal grant of the province of Pensylvania, had moreover a grant of the same from the duke of York, to obviate any pretence, that the province was comprehended in a former royal grant of New-Netherlands to the duke of York.

Mr. Penn's first charter concessions, or form of government to the settlers, seems Utopian and whimsical; constituting a legislature of three negatives, viz. the governor, and two distinct houses of representatives chosen by the freemen; one called the provincial council of seventy-two members, the other was called the provincial assembly of 200 members; the council had an exorbitant power of exclusive deliberating upon and preparing all bills for the provincial assembly; the executive part of the government was entirely with them. The provincial assembly, in the bills to be enacted, had no deliberative privilege, only a yes or no; these numbers of provincial council and provincial assembly seem to be extravagantly large for an infant colony: perhaps he was of opinion with some good politicians, that there can be no general model of civil government; the humours or inclinations, and numbers of various societies must be consulted and variously settled: a small society naturally requires the deliberation and general consent of their freemen for taxation and legislature; when the society becomes too numerous for such universal meetings, a representation or deputation from several districts is a more convenient and easy administration. His last and present standing charter to the inhabitants of the province and territories of Pensylvania, Oct. 28, 1701, runs into the other extreme; the council have no negative in the legislature, and only serve as the

proprietary's council of advice to the proprietary's governor: 1746, by act of parliament, the negative of the
board of aldermen in London, for certain reasons was
abrogated. A council chosen by the people, to negative natives of representatives also appointed by the
people, seems to be a wheel within a wheel, and incon-
gruous: but a council appointed by the court of Great-
Britain as a negative, seems to be a good policy, by way
of controul upon the excesses of the governor on the one
hand, and of the people by their representatives on the
other hand.

The province of Penfylvania fome years since was
mortgaged to Mr. Gee, and others, for 6,600 *l.* sterl.
In the year 1713, Mr. Penn by agreement made over
all his rights in Penfylvania to the crown, in consideration of 12.000 *l.* sterl. but before the instrument of surrender was executed, he died apoplectick, and Penfylvania still remains with the family of Penns.

Upon the first settlement of Penfylvania, Mr. Penn
stipulated with the aboriginal natives the Indians, that
they should sell no lands to any person but to himself or
his agents ; this was confirmed by subfequent province
laws: on the other side, Mr. Penn's agents were not to
occupy or make grants of any lands, but what were
fairly purchased of the Indians ; for inftance, a few years
ago, the delegates of the Six nations of Iroquois, for a
certain confideration in goods, releafed their claims to
all lands both fides of the river Sefquahanna, fo far
fouth as the province of Penfylvania reaches, and fo far
north as the Blue or Kittatinny mountains, and received pay in part. Beginning of July, 1742, the
Six nations had a congrefs with governor Thomas
and eight of his council at Philadelphia, to receive
the other moiety as per agreement ; we shall take
this opportunity of prefenting this as a fpecimen of an
affortment of goods in demand with the Indians.

24 guns

24 guns	60 ruffled ſhirts	8 doz: gimblets
600 lb. powder	25 hats	2 doz. tob. tongs
600 lb. lead	1000 flints	25 pair ſhoes
25 pieces ſtrouds	50 hoes	25 pair ſtockings
90 pieces duffils	50 hatchets	25 pair buckles
30 blankets	5 lb. vermilion	
62 yar. ha. thick	10 doz. knives	

The ſtory of William Penn's obtaining the grant of Penſylvania is in this manner. Admiral Penn and general Venables were ſent 1655 by Oliver Cromwell with a conſiderable ſea and land force to reduce Hiſpaniola in the Spaniſh Weſt-Indies, which they did not effect, but reduced the Spaniſh iſland now called Jamaica, which remains in poſſeſſion of the crown of Great-Britain to this day. Admiral Penn upon the reſtoration became a royaliſt, was knighted, and commanded the Engliſh fleet under the duke of York againſt the Dutch, commanded by admiral Opdam 1665. Admiral Penn's ſon, William Penn, perhaps in ſome whim, put himſelf at the head of the quakers, and upon his petition to the king, in conſideration of his father's ſervices, and arrears due from the crown, he obtained a royal patent for the province of Penſylvania, and a grant from the duke of York, of the three lower counties on the weſt ſide of Delaware bay and river, being part of New-Netherlands by royal grant to the duke of York, his heirs and aſſigns. This William Penn was much in favour with king James II, as being head of a conſiderable body of ſectaries called Quakers ; by reaſon of this particular countenance, Mr. Penn was ſuſpected to be a papiſt, and a jeſuit in the diſguiſe of a quaker. At the revolution, upon ſuſpicion, king William deprived Mr. Penn of the privilege of appointing a governor for Penſylvania, and col. Fletcher was appointed by the crown ; but upon Mr. Penn's vindication of himſelf, he was reſtored to his right of government and continued to appoint lieutenant governors or deputies as formerly.

X 2

The

The boundaries of the province and territories of Penfylvania, *rivers, and diftances of fome noted places.*

The northern boundary of the province is in forty-two degrees parallel of latitude, from Delaware river (about twenty miles above the ftation point on Delaware river, where the north eafterly divifional line between the provinces of New York and New-Jerfey begins) weft, to the extent of five degrees in longitude, being about 250 Englifh ftatute miles ; thence in a line parallel with the river of Delaware at five degrees longitude weft from the faid river, to a parallel of latitude fifteen miles fouth of the moft fouthern part of Philadelphia, being about 153 miles ftrait courfe ; along this parallel fifteen miles fouth of Philadelphia to the river Delaware——miles : thence up along Delaware river to forty-two degrees north latitude, which in a ftrait line may be about 153 miles.

The territories of Penfylvania called the three lower counties upon Delaware river are bounded eaftwardly by Delaware river, from the north part of Newcaftle territorial circle, to cape Henlpen at the entrance of Delaware-Bay, about eighty miles ftrait, but much more as the fhore or country roads run : fouthwardly and weftwardly they are bounded as per agreement between lord Baltimore of Maryland, and the Penns of Penfylvania, 1732, and confirmed in the chancery of England, 1750, in thefe words, " That a due eaft and weft line be run
" from cape Henlopen to the middle of the peninfula,
" and the faid ftrait line to run from the weftward
" point thereof, northwards up the faid peninfula (and
" above the faid peninfula, if it required) till it touch-
" ed, or made a tangent, to the weftern part of the
" periphery of the faid twelve miles circle, and the faid
" due fouth and north line to run from fuch tangent, till
" it meets with the upper or more northern eaft and
" weft line, and the faid upper eaft and weft line to
" begin

" begin from the northern point or end of the said south
" and north line, and to run due westward, (*N. B.* [q]
" this is a delineation of the south line of the province
" of Pensylvania) at present cross Sesquahanna river,
" and twenty-five English statute miles at least; on the
" western side of the said river, and to be fifteen English
" statute miles south of the latitude of the most
" southern part of the said city of Philadelphia, were,
" and shall, and should at all times for ever hereafter be
" allowed and esteemed to be the true and exact limits
" and bounds, between the said province of Maryland,
" and the said three lower counties of Newcastle, Kent,
" and Suffex, and between the said provinces of Mary-
" land and Pensylvania [r]."

As the controversy of a long standing, concerning
boundaries, between Lord Baltimore of Maryland, and
the Penns of Pensylvania, has made much noise; we
shall insert a short abract of the same, for the amusement of the curious.

Lord Baltimore's royal grant of Maryland was about
fifty years prior to Mr. Penn's grant of Pensylvania, but

---

[q] In the survey 1739, of the E. and W. divisional line (about
fifteen miles south of the southermost part of the city of Philadelphia)
between Pensylvania and Maryland, the surveyors allowed a variation
of 5 d. 30 m. W. and found there was about one degree variation for
every twenty late years.

[r] They mutually quit claim, viz. Charles lord Baltimore quits
claim to John Penn, Thomas Penn, and Richard Penn, and their
heirs and assigns, all his pretensions to the province of Pensylvania,
and the three lower counties of Newcastle, Kent and Suffex, to be so
bounded as aforesaid, free of all incumbrances by Cecilius baron of
Baltimore, great grand-father, Charles grand-father, Benedict father to said Charles, and by him the said Charles, his heirs and
assigns. And on the other side, John Penn, Thomas Penn, and Richard Penn, for themselves and their heirs, quit claim unto Charles
lord Baltimore and his heirs, all their pretensions to the province of
Maryland, to be so bounded as aforesaid, free of all incumbrances, by
William Penn the grand-father, William Penn the father, Springet
Penn, William Penn the son, John Penn, Thomas Penn and Richard
Penn, their heirs or assigns.

in Baltimore's grant there was an exception of lands then belonging to the Dutch, which are at prefent the three lower counties upon Delaware river; when Mr. Penn took poffeffion he found one Dutch and three Swedifh congregations.

The grand difpute was concerning the conftruction of the expreffion forty degrees of latitude; Maryland grant 1632, fays, to the forty degrees of latitude which Maryland's fide of the queftion conftrue to be to forty degrees compleat; Penfylvania grant 1782, fays, to begin at the beginning of the fortieth degree, which the Penfylvania fide conftrue to be juft after thirty-nine degrees is compleated [s]; thus there was a difpute of the extent of one degree in latitude, or fixty-nine Englifh miles.

Confidering Maryland grant was prior, and that the Maryland people had made confiderable improvements by poffeffions, within that degree of latitude; the affair was compromifed feemingly in favour of Maryland by a written agreement May 10, 1732, as is above related: and that in two calendar months from that date, each party fhall appoint commiffioners not more than feven, whereof three or more of each fide may act or mark out the boundaries aforefaid, to begin at fartheft fome time in October 1732, and to be compleated on or before the twenty-fifth of December, 1733, and when fo done a plan thereof fhall be figned, fealed, and delivered by the commiffioners and their principals, and fhall be entered in all the publick offices in the feveral provinces and counties; and to recommend to the refpective legiflatures to pafs an act for perambulating thefe boundaries at leaft once in three years.

The party defaulting, to pay the other party on demand fix thoufand pounds fterling: accordingly the commiffioners refpectively appeared, but upon fome differences in opinion, the boundaries were not made in

[s] Thus in other affairs; for inftance in political computation, after 1700, it is called the eighteenth century.

I

the

the time limited; the failure was in lord Baltimore's side, who alledged that he had been deceived in fixing cape Henlopen twenty miles south westerly of the western cape of Delaware-Bay, whereas cape Henlopen is the western cape itself; the Penns affirm, that the western cape is cape Cornelius, and cape Henlopen is about four hours southwardly of it, according to the Dutch maps and descriptions published about the time when lord Baltimore obtained his grant.

Because of nonperformance, the Penns 1735 exhibited a bill in the chancery of Great-Britain against lord Baltimore, praying that the said articles may be decreed to subsist and be carried into execution, and that any doubts arisen may be cleared by the said decree.

After tedious delays, at length May 15, 1750, lord chancellor decreed costs of suit against Baltimore, and that the articles of May 10, 1732, be carried into execution; and that before the end of three calendar months from May 15, they should execute two several proper instruments for appointing commissioners, not more than seven of a side; any three or more of a side may run and mark the boundaries, to begin some time in November next, and to be compleated on or before the last day of April 1752, to be signed, &c. recorded, &c. and enacted, &c. as per agreement of 1732 above related. Lord chancellor decreed concerning the late disputes, 1. That the center of the circle be fixed in the middle of the town of Newcastle. 2. That the said circle ought to be of a radius of twelve English miles. 3. That cape Henlopen ought to be deemed as the place laid down in the maps annexed to the articles of 1732.

The commissioners appointed by each party met at Newcastle, Nov. 15, 1750; they agreed on a center in Newcastle, from whence the twelve miles radii are to proceed; but a dispute arose concerning the mensuration of these twelve miles. Lord Baltimore's commissioners alledged, that these miles ought to be measured superficially; the Penns commissioners alledged, that

confidering the various inequalities of the ground, fuch
radii could not extend equally; confequently from them
no true arch of a circle could be formed, and infifted
upon geometrical and aftronomical menfurations. Thus
the proceedings of the commiffioners ftopt, and they
wrote to their refpective principals for further inftructions relating to that point, and adjourned to April
25, 1751.

The confiderable rivers in Penfylvania are Delaware
(Schyl-Kill river falls into Delaware at Philadelphia)
and the Sefquahana. Delaware-Bay begins at Lewis's
near cape Henlopen [*t*]; from thence with the various
turnings of the bay and river or publick road to Newcaftle are about ninety three miles; from Newcaftle to
Philadelphia are thirty-five miles; from Philadelphia to
Trent-town falls are thirty-five miles; thefe are the firft
falls in this river, and the tide reaches up fo high;
thefe falls are practicable, and the river navigable with
boats that carry nine or ten tons of iron forty miles
higher to Durham iron works; this river proceeds from
the weft fide of the Cat-kill mountains of the province of
New-York. From Trent-town falls, this river is practicable upwards of 150 miles for Indian canoe navigation, feveral fmall falls or carrying places intervening.
Mr. W——d, a late noted vagrant enthufiaftick preacher
purchafed a confiderable quantity of lands in the fork of
Delaware river, about fifty miles above Trent-town falls,
for the education and civilizing of negroes, as he pretended; but as he could not anfwer the purchafe money,
he was obliged to relinquifh it. All his fchemes were
ill projected and ill founded: his grand church or
meeting-houfe in Philadelphia, by him declared to be
free to all chriftian itinerants, as he was a man of no penetration, he was not capable of finifhing it, and it was
transferred to a fociety for propagating of literature, a

[*t*] At cape Henlopen 1748, the variation of the compafs was four
degrees weft decreafing.

much

much more laudable inftitution than that of propagating
enthufiafm, idlenefs and fanctified amours. His orphan
houfe in Georgia in South-Carolina, in a barren infalu-
brious country, his firft project, pretence for idlerant
begging, is almoft come to nothing.

The other confiderable river is part of Sefquahana;
fee vol. II. p. 282. Its main branch comes from fome
ponds a little fouth of the Mohawks river in the province of New-York ; from the head of this branch to the
falls below Wioming [u] there is no obftruction, and
good Indian canoe navigation ; and thence to Paxton
are five or fix falls which may be fhot pretty fafely with
a frefh : this river has many good branches for Indian
fkin trade, fome of thefe branches communicate with
the countries beyond the mountains. Sefquahana river
is wide but fhallow. Delaware, Sefquahana, and Potomack, are fordable by the Indian traders in the fummer feafon.

The Indian traders fet out the beginning of May, and
continue three or four months out ; they buy the fkins
not of the Indians, but of fettlers who deal with the
Indians, called by the Dutch name of handelaars or traders ; they purchafe only with gold and filver, and
carry their fkins in waggons to Philadelphia ; the road
is about twenty miles below the foot of the blue mountains. They travel from Philadelphia to Lancafter fixty
miles (Lancafter is ten miles eaft of Sefquahana river)
thence forty miles to Paxton or Harris's ferry, thence
forty miles to Shippenfburg in the province of Penfylvania; thence forty-five miles to Potomack river (the
width of Maryland is here about twenty miles) which
divides Maryland from Virginia. A few miles weft
of Potomack river in Virginia for fome years have been
ufed with good effect, by bathing and drinking, fome
tepid medicinal waters ; they have no mineral tafte,

[u] About fifty miles below Wioming is the Indian tribe of Shamokin in the fork of Sefquahana, and about fifty miles below Shamokin
is Paxton or Harris's ferry.

4

and

and do not offufcate the glafs like Briftol hot well water.

In Penfylvania there is no real fea line excepting the weft fide of Delaware bay. The navigation of Philadelphia is almoft every winter ftopt up by ice for two or three months. The coaft of New-York, Jerfeys, and Penfylvania is free from fhip-worms or teredines. Land winds blow almoft three quarters of the year.

The Blue or Kittatinny mountains begin in Penfylvania, are about 900 miles in length and from feventy to 100 miles acrofs, not in fcattered peaks, but in uniform ridges; the farther ridges are much the largeft and higheft.

Concerning Indian affairs.

I fhall here mention fome additional obfervations concerning the Indians in general, and fome of their late treaties with the Britifh governments, particularly that of Lancafter and Penfylvania, anno 1744, as confifting of the greateft variety of articles negotiated with three diftinct Britifh provinces or colonies.

When tribes or nations of Indians go to war againft one another, they feldom make it up (the Indians are the moft implacable of mankind) but by the deftruction of the one or the other fide, or by a flavifh fubmiffion. The Iroquois or Six nations of Mohawks, as we call them, have for many years been at war (thefe wars are only clandeftine incurfions with maffacres and depredations) with the Catawbas and Cherokees; the Cherokees and Six nations as being too diftant to annoy one another much, have come to fome accommodation, but the ftate of war with the Catawbas continues.

The Penfylvanians never loft one man by any French or Indian war, but in perfonal broils and encounters perfons have loft their lives on both fides.

The

The Mohawks by the Englifh give name to all the Six nations, though the fmalleft of the tribes. The Tuf-caroras are an adventitious tribe, being emigrants or profugi in the North-Carrlina wars 1712 and 1716; they were allowed to fettle by the ancient five confederate na-tions amongft them.

For fome time paft, a kind of party divifion hath fub-fifted among the Six nations: the Mohawks, Ononda-gas and Senecas formed one party; the Oneidas, Tufca-roras and Cayugas the other party.

The Six nations fay that the Delaware and Sefquahana Indians were conquered by them, and therefore have no right to difpofe of lands.

The Indian delegates at the congrefs of Lancafter well obferved to the commiffioners from Virginia, Ma-ryland, and Penfylvania; that what the Indians received of them were goods foon perifhable, but what they re-ceived of the Indians were lands which endured for ever.

The Indians are fupplied by the Englifh with provi-fions coming and going in all treaties [x]. They have their guns, hatchets, and kettles mended gratis.

In all congreffes the Indians approve of each article by a Yo hah, the Englifh ufe a huzza.

The Indians ufe peculiar appellations for the governors of the feveral provinces or colonies; for inftance, the governors of Virginia are called affaragoa; thofe of Pen-fylvania, onas; thofe of Canada, onando; and lately they have fixed the name of tocarry hogan (fignifying excellent) for the governors of Maryland.

[x] In the Appendix to a late hiftory of the Five Indian nations, we have a pleafant or ludicrous ftory of this nature, in the Lancafter con-grefs with the Indians, 174 , the commiffioners of Virginia, Mary-land, and Penfylvania, having told the Indian delegates of the Six na-tions, that the king of Great Britain had lately beat the French both by fea and land; the Indian delegates obferved, that in confequence, the Englifh muft have taken a great deal of rum from the French, therefore you can the better fpare fome of that liquor, to make us re-joice with you in thefe victories.

We

We may here obferve the great variety in the humours of diftant nations; we fhall here inftance that of their fpeech or words. In the Eaft-Indies and China, their words are generally monofyllables; in the Weft-Indies their words are generally polyfyllables of an uncouth length; thus the Six nations at the Lancafter congrefs fay, all the world knows, that they had conquered (confequently their lands at our difpofal) feveral nations on the back or weft fide of the great mountains of Virginia, viz. the Conoy-uch-fuch-roona, Coch-now-was-roonon, Tohoa-irough-roonon, and Conutfkin-ough-roonaw.

The Six nations by natural inclination are difpofed to warlike enterprizes, and are never at peace with all their neighbours. In a fpeech at a congrefs with the Englifh, they faid, that if chriftians go to war againft one another, they in time make peace together; but it is not fo with the Indians.

The Indians when they pafs by a friendly fort march in a fingle line, and falute the fort by a running fire.

Nanandagues is a fecond fettlement of deferters from the Six nations; they live near Montreal.

The Britifh northern colonies are the frontiers and defence of all other Britifh colonies, againft the warlike robuft northern Indians. Thus it has in all times been in Europe and Afia; the hardy robuft Goths, (Getæ of Afia) Vandals, &c. from the northern climates, over-run the effeminate, indolent, relaxed foutherly people if not checked; the Indians of the higher latitudes in North-America, and in Chili in South-America, make a much better ftand againft the European intrufions, than the Indians of Mexico and Peru, who live between or near the tropicks.

It is conjectured that fix hundred fighting men may be afforded by the Indian fettlements on Sefquahana river and its branches.

In all our northern colonies, there are or have been referved lands for feveral bodies or villages of intermixed Indians.

Although the northern Indian tribes as to numbers
are contemptible, when compared with the European
nations, they ought to be kept in a political awe to prevent their fkulking incurfions and depredations upon
our frontiers when pufhed on by a rival European power; this cannot be done by ridiculous feints; for inftance, when we tell the Indians in fome congrefs, as it
happened in 1746, that all the united force of our colonies with fhips of war and foldiers from Great-Britain, are to mufter to reduce Canada, but foon after
nothing is done, or fo much as attempted; thus we
lofe our credit with the Indians, and in fact, they
have impune infulted us ever fince, in Nova-Scotia
and New-England, at the inftigation of the Canada
French.

The Indians are a falfe but crafty people. In our
late war with the French nation and their American
colonies, feveral diftant tribes of Indians in expectation
of prefents, faid they would, though they really did not
defign it, relinquifh the French intereft; fuch were the
Shawanees town upon Ohio river, the Maffafegues near
Les Etroits between lake Erie and lake Huron, confifting of five caftles or villages of about 800 men; and
the Twightwees on the Oubeck river in a treaty at Lancafter, July 1748.

The moft noted congrefs with the Indian delegates
for many years, was that in June 1744, held at Lancafter in Penfylvania, confifting of commiffioners from
the three provinces of Penfylvania, Maryland, and Virginia, concerning a great variety of articles, fuch as
quit-claiming large tracts of lands to thefe governments refpectively, and receiving prefents upon their
promife to affift the Britifh intereft in the war lately
commenced againft the French.

1. They confirmed to the proprietors of Penfylvania
all the lands each fide of Sefquahana river fo far north
as the Blue mountains.   They fettled the affair of fome
                                                    Delaware

Delaware Indians killing and robbing Mr. Armſtrong, a trader, and his two ſervants.

2. The Indians complain, that the Maryland and Virginia people had ſettled ſome land back of Virginia and Maryland, without conſent of the Six nations, or of any purchaſe made from them, which lands belong to the Six nations by their conqueſt over the antient Indian poſſeſſors. Hereupon the Indians by an inſtrument in writing releaſed all their lands in Maryland [y] to the Maryland commiſſioners for 300 *l*. in goods valued in Penſylvania currency ; we ſhall here give this as an inſtance of the advance generally put by the Engliſh upon the Engliſh prime coſts of goods.

Strouds from 5 to 7 *l*.	Vermilion	9 *s*.
Shirts 6 *s*.	Flints per m.	18 *s*.
Half thicks 3 *l*. 13 *s* 4 *d*.	Jews Harps per doz. 3 *s* 10 *d*.	
Duffil blankets 7 *l*.	Boxes per doz.	1 *s*.
Guns 1 *l*. 6 *s*.	Bar lead per ct. wt	40 *s*.
Barrel gunpowder 26 *l*.	Shot	40 *s*.

3. The commiſſioners of Virginia gave the Indians 200 *l*. Penſylvania currency in goods, and 200 *l*. in gold, as a conſideration for their deed, recognizing the king of Great-Britain's right to all the lands that are or ſhall be by his majeſty's appointment in the colony of Virginia ; and the Indians deſire that they may have a further conſideration when the ſettlements increaſed much farther back, which the commiſſioners agreed to. The Six Indian nations complain, the treaty above twenty years ſince made at Albany was not obſerved, viz. the middle or ridge of the hill on the back of Virginia was fixed as a boundary between the Indians who live upon the reſerved lands in Virginia, and the Indians of the Six nations. Another article was to ſettle an Indian road to paſs ſouthward on the back of Virginia. Another article was to

[y] About 100 years ſince, the Seſquahana or Conaſtagoe Indians, by treaty granted all the land now poſſeſſed by the people of Maryland to them and their heirs from Pataxen river on the weſt ſide of Cheſepeak-Bay, and from Choptank river on the eaſt of the ſaid bay.

bury

bury in oblivion, a skirmish which happened in the back parts of Virginia, between some of the Virginia militia there, and a party of the Indian warriors of the Six nations; upon this account the commissioners of Virginia presented the Indians with goods to the value of 100 l. sterl.

4. As the French about this time were declaring war against Great-Britain; to retain the Six nations in the British interest, after a proper speech to the Indians, Pensylvania made them a present in goods to the value of 300 l. Pensylvania currency: Virginia gave them goods to the value of 100 l. sterl. and 100 l. in gold, with a desire that they would send some of their children to be educated in Virginia, who might serve as interpreters in times to come: the Indians answered, that they were not inclined to bring their children up to learning: the commissioners of Maryland presented the Indians with 100 l. in gold.

There are frequent congresses of the British provinces with their neighbouring tribes or nations of Indians, especially of the provinces of New-York and Pensylvania with the Six nations of Iroquois or Mohawks, to retain the Indians in the British interest; these have a good effect, though generally they are only a piece of formality with this conclusion, that the Indians were pleased with their presents and promised fidelity: sometimes affairs of consequence are transacted. Thus at Albany in August and September 1746, there was a treaty between governor Clinton and the council of the province of New-York, with commissioners from the province of Massachusetts-Bay, on the one part, and the Six united nations of Indians depending upon the province of New-York on the other part; to engage these Indians in the British interest, against our enemies the French, to be assisting in the expedition against Canada, to be furnished with arms, ammunition, cloathing, and provisions, and in their absence their wives and children to be

be taken care of. 1749, Middle of Auguſt, there arrived
in Philadelphia the deputies of many different nations,
in order to tranſa&ct ſome affairs with the government.
The deputies were of the Mohawks, Oneidas, Onondagas, Cayugas, Tuſcaroras, Senecas, Shawanees, Nan-
ticokes, Delawares, Mohagins, and Turlos; the whole
number of Indians arrived in Philadelphia, women and
children included, were about 260.

Concerning the city and port of Philadelphia, *the numbers of
the Inhabitants in the province and territories of* Penſylvania.

Mr. Penn's charter erecting Philadelphia (lying between Delaware and Schuyl-kill rivers,) into a corporation and city, is ſigned in Philadelphia, by William Penn,
October 25, 1701, the thirteenth year of the reign of
king William the third, and the one and twentieth year
of my government, to conſiſt of a mayor, recorder,
ſheriff, and town clerk, eight aldermen and twelve common council men, by the name of the mayor and commonalty of the city of Philadelphia; the firſt ſet to be appointed by Mr. Penn; and yearly thereafter on the firſt
day of the third week in the eighth month, the corporation to meet, the mayor or recorder preſent with five
or more of the aldermen, and nine or more of the common council, to chuſe one of the aldermen to be mayor
for that enſuing year, and to fill up vacancies of aldermen and common council; all officers to take the de-
clarations and profeſſions directed in the provincial
charter. The mayor, recorder and aldermen, to be
juſtices of the peace and of oyer and terminer; any four
or more of them (whereof the mayor and recorder to be
two) to hear all caſes capital or otherwiſe criminal, and
with the ſheriff and town clerk to hold a court of record
quarterly for determining of pleas and other matters.
The mayor and recorder ſhall be of the quorum of the
juſtices of the county courts, quarter ſeſſions, oyer and
terminer

terminer and goal delivery in the faid county of Philadelphia ; and fhall have power to take cognizance of debts
there according to the ftatute of merchants, and of
action burnel.   The mayor to appoint the clerk of the
market.   The fheriff to be the water bailiff of the province.
The corporation have power to remove any officer of their
own for mifbehaviour.   No meeting fhall be deemed a
common council unlefs the mayor, recorder, at leaft
three of the aldermen, and nine of the common council,
be prefent ; a power to admit freemen into the corporation, to make by-laws for the government of the city, to
impofe fines for the ufe of the corporation ; none to be
admitted freemen, but fuch as have been refident in the
city for two years, and fhall have an eftate of inheritance
or freehold therein worth fifty pounds in money.   To
have two market days every week, the fourth and feventh day, two yearly fairs (each to continue three days)
May 16, and November 16. Philadelphia fhall be a port
comprehending all creeks and landings of the province.

The fituation of Philadelphia is bad, being at the confluence of two large frefh water rivers, Delaware and
Schuyl-kill, which renders their people obnoxious to
pleuritick, peripneumonick, dyfenterick, and intermitting fevers ; *communibus annis,* in proportion, they bury
near double the number of people that are buried in
Bofton of New-England. It is well planned or laid out,
in a plain, confifting of eight long ftreets of two miles,
and fixteen crofs ftreets of one mile each, at right angles,
with proper fpaces for publick buildings. As we obferved
before, the long ftreets were laid out with much exact-
nefs 1682. N. 18 d. E ; and anno 1742, in fome law
controverfies, Mr. Parfons furveyor general of Penfylvania, found them to be 15 d. E. which is a difference
of three degrees in fixty years, decreafing.

Philadelphia is nearly in 40 d. N. lat. and about five
hours or 75 d. weft of London. In the fpring 1749, the
dwelling houfes in Philadelphia, in curiofity were numbered by twelve perfons, who each undertook a part ; pub-

lick buildings, ware-houfes, and out-houfes not included; in the feveral wards, they were as follows, in all 2076.

South fuburbs	150	High-ftreet ward	147
Dutch ward	245	North ward	196
Walnut ward	104	Mulberry ward	488
South ward	117	Upper Delaware ward	109
Cheftnut ward	110	Lower Delaware ward	110
Middle ward	238	North fuburbs	62

There were eleven places of publick religious worfhip, viz. one church of England, two prefbyterians, two quakers, one baptift, one Swedifh manner, one Dutch Lutheran, one Dutch Calviniſt, one Moravian, one Roman catholick.

I fhall here interfperfe fome account of a laudable academy in Philadelphia [z], with a publick-fpirited defign of encouraging literature; that is, political and natural knowledge; fome good deferving gentlemen, by voluntary fubfcriptions, promife to pay annually for five years, in proportion to each fubfcription; which fum in grofs may amount to 5000 *l.* Penfylvania currency. The fubfcribers elect out of their numbers fifteen truftees to manage the ftock, appoint mafters with their falaries, make vifitations, &c. At prefent they have three mafters and one ufher; the firſt maſter is called rector, with an ufher under him, he teaches latin in all its gradations, even from the rudiments if required, with a falary of 200 *l.* Penfylvania currency per ann. befides the perquifites from his fcholars, which is twenty fhillings entrance, and four pound per annum for each boy's fchooling: his ufher has fixty pound per ann. with fome perquifites of fchooling fees. There is an Englifh fchoolmafter at an allowance of 150 *l.* per ann. befides perquifites from his fcholars at the fame rate with the latin fchool. A mathematical and writing mafter in the fame perfon, allowed 100 *l.* per ann. with perquifites from fcholars as the other mafters have. The boys at this time (May 1751) are from fixty to feventy, increafing confi-

[z] As this is a kind of common-place, the reader may excufe my deviating from the ftrict formal ſtiff rules of fome pedantick hiftorians.

derably

derably.   The Englifh mafter teaches in fome manner grammatically to conftrue fentences, to point out the verb with its proper antecedents and relations...They have purchafed at a cheap rate, a fine commodious building; it is that meeting houfe upwards of 100 feet long and feventy feet wide, built in the enthufiaftick times of Whitefield.   The truftees at the beginning were chiefly prefbyterians of the new-light kind, but in a few years one half of them became Moravians, and a difpute arofe amongft them, which party fhould eftablifh a minifter, but as the prefbyterians had it originally, they kept it to the laft : this divifion fubfifting, and the workmen not above half paid, both fides agreed to difpofe of it for the ufe above-mentioned, and the workmen were paid off.   The fubfcribers and their truftees hope before the expiration of the five years, to fall on ways and means to render it perpetual; they have applied to the chief proprietor Thomas Penn, Efq. to render it perpetual, begging his affiftance and countenance; but it feems Mr. Thomas Penn had in view the eftablifhment of fuch a feminary, entirely on his own foundation, but not in the city; therefore its doubted whether he may ingraft his fcheme with this, or purfue his firft intentions. There is little or no hopes of receiving any encouragement from the publick legiflature, the majority of the affembly being Quakers, who have a large publick ftock of their own for fuch a purpofe, and have finifhed a good commodious houfe of their own for a fchool; the preceptor is a Quaker, with 100 l. fterl. per ann. befides fees for teaching ; he is to teach twelve of the poorer fort gratis [a].

That the reader may make fome eftimate of the proportions of the various fectaries in Philadelphia, I fhall

[a] As I formerly mentioned, vol. II. p. 283. in New-Jerfey there is a college lately erected by governor Belcher, with ample charter privileges, but without any fupport from the publick; they depend entirely on donations and benefactions, excepting that by means of a lottery they raifed from 1000 l. to 1200, to make a beginning; a fixed place has been much controverted. They have a divinity profeffor, a profeffor of natural philofophy, and a mafter of a grammar fchool, all poorly provided for.

here

here obferve that in the laft fix months of 1750, there were buried in Philadelphia,

Swedes	13	Dutch Lutherans	28
Prefbyterians	26	Dutch Calvinifts	39
Baptifts	9	Roman catholicks	15
Quakers	104		

Burials for the twelve months of 1750, Chrift church parifh, church of England 129. Negroes 84.

Anno 1751, in Philadelphia were eftimated about 11,000 whites, 600 blacks. In the province of Penfylvania and its territories, no regular eftimate can be made of the inhabitants, becaufe there is no poll tax, nor any militia lift allowed for alarums, or common trainings, as in the other colonies, to form eftimates by.

There is only one cuftom-houfe collection in the proper province of Penfylvania, called the port of Philadelphia; to form fome notion of the extent of its trade and navigation, I have inferted the following table by way of a fpecimen of what may be compofed for each cuftom-houfe port in Britifh North-America, from the cuftom-houfe quarterly account fent home.

Delaware river or the port of Philadelphia is generally frozen up, and has no navigation in the months of January and February.

The following is an account of entries and clearances of veffels at Philadelphia, *from March* 2, 1748-9, *to December* 25, 1749.

Entered inwards, from		Cleared out, for	
Antigua	12	Antigua	14
Anguilla	5	Auguftine	3
Auguftine	4	Amboy	2
Amboy	3	Anguilla	3
Barbadoes	29	Barbadoes	22
Bofton	39	Bofton	41
Briftol	1	Bermudas	7
Bermudas	11	Cadiz	2
Cadiz	5	Cape-Breton	1
Cagliaria	2	Curaçoa	6
			Chebucto

Entered inwards, from		Cleared out, for	
Curacoa	2	Chebucto	3
Cowes	21	Fiall	2
Deal	1	Ireland	19
Glafgow	1	Jamaica	22
Hifpaniola	5	Lifbon	2
Havanna	4	London	5
Ireland	17	Lewis-town	1
Jamaica	13	Madeira	15
Lifbon	5	Maryland	8
Liverpool	3	Newfoundland	5
London	9	New-York	6
Lewis-town	2	North Carolina	6
Madeira	7	Nantucket	2
Maryland	4	New-London	1
New-York	15	Providence	8
North-Carolina	5	Rotterdam	1
Nantucket	4	Rhode-Ifland	25
New-London	1	South-Carolina	23
Portfmouth	1	St. Chriftophers	8
Plymouth	1	Surinam	1
Providence	8	St. Euftatia	6
Rhode-Ifland	23	Salem	2
South-Carolina	10	Teneriffe	1
St. Chriftophers	5	Virginia	12
St. Euftatia	3	Weft-Indies	6
Salem	3	In all	291
Turks-Ifland	8	In this lift, is	
Tortola	1	Ships	64
Teneriffe	2	Brigs	68
Virginia	7	Snows	26
In all	303	Schooners	21
In the above lift, is		Sloops	112
Ships	62	Total	291
Brigs	72		
Snows	25		
Schooners	25		
Sloops	119		
Total	303		

There are now remaining in the harbour, 19 fhips, 9 fnows, 8 brigs, 2 fchooners, and 1 floop. In all 39.

Y 3

As

As in the province of Penfylvania, there is no poll tax nor any militia incorporated and regulated; we can give no eftimate of their numbers of whites and flaves by proportional calculations.

There never was any militia within this colony on a legal eftablifhment; what not long ago appeared and made fuch a fhow by their numbers, were only volunteers commiffioned by the governor. The Quakers have always been about three quarters of the affembly, though in number perhaps not exceeding one quarter of the people; the Quakers artfully perfuade the Dutch and Germans, that if they chufe others than Quakers for their reprefentatives, they would immediately have a militia law impofed on them, which would fubject them to greater flavery, than what they fuffered in their own country.

This colony by importation of foreigners and other ftrangers in very great numbers, grows prodigioufly; by their laborious and penurious manner of living, in confequence they grow rich where others ftarve, and by their fuperior induftry and frugality may in time out the Britifh people from the colony. The greateft year of importation of Germans, Irifh, a few Welfh and Scots, was from December 25, 1728, to December 25, 1729, being about 6200 perfons. In the year 1750, Germans imported into this province and territories, were 4317; Britifh and Irifh paffengers and fervants above 1000.

We omitted to obferve, that fome Palatines who came over to New-York by queen Anne's bounty, 1707, in the province of New-York, were not allowed a fufficient encouragement of quantities of land; and by encouragement of Sir William Keith governor of Penfylvania, they removed to Penfylvania.

The numbers of foreigners, principally Germans, imported into this province or colony, in the courfe of about twenty five years laft paft, has been fo exceffive; that if it is not limited by a provincial act, or by the dernier refource, an act of the Britifh parliament, the

province

province and territories of Penſylvania may ſoon degenerate into a foreign colony, endangering the quiet of
our adjacent colonies.

The legiſlature.

In the colony are only two negatives in the legiſlature,
the governor and houſe of repreſentatives, called the aſſembly. The council ſo called, is only the proprietor's
council to the proprietor's governor, but not a king's
council; they have no concern in the legiſlature otber-
ways than by adviſing the governor in his negative. The
acts of legiſlature run thus; " Be it enacted by the ho-
" nourable——— Eſq. lieutenant governor of the pro-
" vince of Penſylvania, and of the counties of Newcaſtle,
" Kent and Suſſex on Delaware river; by and with the
" conſent of the repreſentatives of the freemen of the
" ſaid province, in general aſſembly met."

The governor of Penſylvania is only the proprietary
Penn's deputy, and is ſtiled lieutenant governor and his
honour; his ſalary in late years has been per annum
1000 *l.* currency out of the exciſe duty for the province
of Penſylvania, and 200*l.* per ann. from the territories
called the three lower counties. By act of parliament,
all lieutenant governors or deputies nominated by lords
proprietors, or principal hereditary governors of Britiſh
colonies in North-America, muſt have the royal approbation.

The proper province of Penſylvania was at firſt divided into the three counties of Philadelphia, Bucks, and
Cheſter, each ſending eight repreſentatives to the aſſembly; about twenty years ſince was added the county of
Lancaſter, ſending four repreſentatives; and lately an
addition is made of two new counties back inland, by the
names of York and Cumberland; they are allowed only
two members each; with two repreſentatives from the
city of Philadelphia, making thirty-four repreſentatives,
which compoſe the houſe of aſſembly. The qualification
for an elector or elected, is a freeman reſident in the

Y 4

country

country for two years, and worth in real or perfonal estate, or both jointly, the value of fifty pounds their currency, which if required, is to be declared upon oath or affirmation.

The three lower counties on Delaware river called the territories, are a diftinct jurifdiction, and their affembly of reprefentatives confifts of fix members from New-caftle county, fix from Kent, and fix from Suffex counties, in all eighteen members.

Their general affemblies are annually elective on the firft day of the month of October. The reprefentatives are not by towns or parifh elections (Philadelphia excepted) as in New-England colonies, but by county elections. Penfylvania proper, called the province, for many years, confifted of only three counties called the upper counties, viz. Buckingham county, chief town Briftol, nearly over-againft Burlington of the Jerfeys; Philadelphia county, chief town Philadelphia, in about forty d. N. lat. and Chefter county, chief town Chefter, about fifteen miles (on the river) below Philadelphia; and a few years fince was made the inland county of Lancafter, chief town Lancafter; lying both fides of Sefquahana river; and very lately two more inland counties, York and Cumberland. The territories are called the three lower counties on Delaware river, viz. Newcaftle county, chief town Newcaftle, about thirty-five miles below Philadelphia; Kent county, chief town Dover; and Lewis county, chief town Lewis or Hore-kill, near cape Henlopen of Delaware bay.

Courts of judicature.

• Juries are all returned by the fherih, excepting in particular cafes, but not often, when there may be a ftruck jury by confent of parties, and that muft be in the prefence of one of the judges, the fheriff, and the parties.

The fheriffs and coroners are annually elected at the fame time with the reprefentatives, by a county election; the people elect two for each office, out of which the governor

vernor chufes one, who in the fame manner may be re-
elected for three years running, but after three years,
cannot be re-elected, but by the intervention of three
years out of office, and then is capable of a new election.

Juftices of the peace, are all of the governor's appointing, and fit in quarter feffions, conformable to the laws
and inftitutions of England.

The judges of the common pleas are the juftices of
the peace in each refpective county; when the quarter
feffions are finifhed, they continue to fit in quality of the
judges of common pleas by commiffion from the governor.   Their prefent times of fitting are,

For the county of Philadelphia, at Philadelphia, the
firft Monday in March, June, September, and December.

For the city of Philadelphia, the mayor's courts are
the firft Tuefday in January, April, July, and laft Tuefday in October.

For the county of Buckingham, or Bucks, at New-
Town (eleven miles weft from Briftol) on the eleventh
day following the courts of Philadelphia county.

For the county of Chefter, at Chefter, the laft Tuefday in May, Auguft, November, and February.

For the county of Lancafter, at Lancafter, firft Tuefday in February, May, Auguft, and November.

For the county of Suffex, at Lewes, the firft Tuefday
in February, May, Auguft, and November.

For the county of Kent, at Dover, the fecond Tuefday
of the laft faid months.

For the county of Newcaftle, at Newcaftle, the third
Tuefday of the faid months.

The fupreme court confifts of a chief juftice and two
affiftant judges commiffioned by the governor: they
have all the authority of the King's Bench, Common-
Pleas, and court of Exchequer in England, in the words
of the provincial law; they not only receive appeals, but
all caufes once commenced in the inferior courts, after the
firft

firft writ, may be moved thither by a habeas corpus, certiorari, writs of error, &c.

The judges of this fupreme court have alfo a ftanding and diftinct commiffion, to hold as to them fhall feem needful, courts of oyer and terminer, and general goal delivery throughout the province, and are juftices of the peace in every county.

The fupreme courts in Penfylvania are held at Philadelphia, the tenth day of April, and the twenty-fourth day of September.

There is an officer called the regifter general, for the probate of wills and granting letters of adminiftration, whofe authority extends all over the province, but executed by a deputy in each refpective county, except at Philadelphia, where he is obliged to refide himfelf. He or his deputies, in cafe of any difpute or caveat entered, may call two of the juftices of the peace to affift him in giving decifions. The authority of this officer, and of all the others abovementioned, is founded on acts of affembly, impowering the governor to commiffion and appoint fuch as feem to him qualified for that purpofe.

The court of vice-admiralty, is, as in the other colonies, by commiffion from the admiralty in England.

The jufticiary court of admiralty, is, as in the other colonies, by commiffion under the broad feal of England, fome of the neighbouring provinces being included in one and the fame commiffion; the judges are the governors, councils, captains of men of war, principal officers of the cuftoms, and fome juftices of the peace.

The prefent taxes, or provincial revenue.

This confifts of, 1. Excife, which is thirty fhilling per pipe of wine, and four pence per gallon of rum fol in publick houfes; may amount to about 3000*l*. currency it would be much more if properly collected. 2. The intereft money of their paper currency let out by the loan

loan office on land fecurity, which may be about 5000 *l.*
per ann. Thefe two articles have hitherto been fufficient
to pay the governor, and other officers of the government, to defray the charges of treaties and prefents to
the Indians, and in general for all publick charges whatfoever.

Moreover there is in each refpective county, a county
tax towards their courts of juftice, high-ways, bridges,
&c. and a poor tax. Yearly at the fame time with the
election of reprefentatives in each county, are elected
fix affeffors, and three others, called a court of delegates;
thefe delegates are to fit and receive appeals from people who think themfelves aggrieved in their affeffments.
The affeffors without any further enquiry, by the affiftance of the former year's books, make what judgment
they think proper of every man's eftate and faculty, and
rate them from two pence to three pence in the pound;
they cannot go higher by law. Here, as every where, the
affeffed are under rated; thus a perfon in truth worth
10,000 *l.* is returned upon their lift worth from 200 *l.* to
300 *l.* and to pay two pence in the pound; thus this tax
falls heavieft upon the lower fort of people.

Produce, manufactures, trade, and navigation.

Their produce is all forts of Britifh grain of the bread
kind, Indian corn, buck wheat, hemp, and flax; flax
feed is a confiderable exportation to Scotland and Ireland;
fome tobacco, and bees-wax.

This may be called a grain or corn country, and
adapted to flax and hemp.

They manufacture wheat into flour, and flour into
bifket; the largeft branch of their export is flour, which
bears a better price abroad, than that of New-York.
Five bufhels of wheat yield about one hundred and three
quarters merchantable flour; the garnel or fecond flour
pays

pays for cafk and all other charges. They manufacture
their barley into malt, and malt into beer and ale for export.

The Irifh manufacture confiderably of [*b*] linen cloth
for fale, befides for home confumption; perhaps in this
country, the farmers, that is, the hufbandmen, make
nine tenths of all their wearing apparel.

At prefent the flax-feed from Penfylvania, Jerfey,
New-York, Connecticut, and other parts of New-England, anfwers better at home, in cultivation, than what
has been imported for many years from Holland.

Befides the above-mentioned commodities of exportation, the Penfylvania Indian traders purchafe deer-fkins
and a few furs from the Indians of Delaware and Sefquahana rivers, and from the handelaars, back of Maryland and Virginia; they export confiderably iron in
pigs, bars, and pots: fhip building, but their oak is
not durable: cordage, linfeed-oil, ftarch, foap, candles;
fome beef, pork, butter, ftaves, heading and hoops,
walnut logs and plank.

[*b*] Concerning the Britifh confumption of linen cloth, we may obferve, 1. That the linen cloth ftampt in Scotland for fale is very much
upon the increafe, as appears by eftimates made in the following periods.
N. B. The cloth at a medium is valued at eight pence to eleven pence
fterl. per yard.

Years	Yards	£.
1729,	2,183,978	value 103,312 fterl.
1739,	4,801,537	196,068
1749,	7,360,286	322,045

2. Irifh linen imported into England for feven years from Chriftmas
1741, to Chriftmas 1748, as per cuftom-houfe books, at a medium, is
about fix millions of yards per ann. 3. Befides all thefe, the Britifh
demand or imports of foreign linen is about thirty millions of yards per
ann. Here is a large field of encouragement for our northern American
colonies, proper for the production of flax and hemp, to fuperfede this
large importation of German linen: this cannot be effected, but by a great
encouragement of our grain and pafture colonies to lower the too great
plantation price of labour, and the better manuring of their lands.

The

The commodities imported for confumptioh and re-exportation, are dry goods from Great-Britain; wines from Madeira, and the other wine iflands; falt from Great-Britain, France [c], Spain, Lifbon, Mediterranean, and Weft-India iflands; from the Weft-Indies or fugar iflands and other colonies, fugar, rum, molaffes, cotton, indigo, coffee, dying woods, mahogany plank, &c. from the Spanifh coaft and Carolinas, hides, rice, pitch, tar, turpentine, &c. they import many black or horned cattle far and near, from South Carolina fouthward, and from 300 miles weftward, and from the Jerfeys.

Moft of the Dutch hufbandmen have ftills, and draw a fpirit from rye malted, from apples and peaches. There may be from 7000 to 8000 Dutch waggons with four horfes each, that from time to time bring their produce and traffick to Philadelphia, from ten to 100 miles diftance.

Their navigation may be diftinguifhed into fmall craft, that keep within the capes, and only bring produce to market: as the produce of Penfylvania reaches only fifteen miles below Philadelphia, moft of this fort of trade is carried on from the three lower counties on the weft fide of the great river of Delaware, and all the Weft-Jerfeys which lie along the eaft fide of that river: thefe are not comprehended in the cuftom-houfe entries and clearances of the port of Philadelphia.

To illuftrate the gradual increafe of the trade of the port of Philadelphia, we obferve, that anno 1736, the entries were 212, clearances 215 veffels; a little before the late French war, anno 1742, entries were 230; clearances 281. The number of veffels cleared from

[c] By an act of parliament for the encouragement of the fifhery 1727, falt is allowed to be imported in Penfylvania, from any part of Europe. There is a like act of parliament for the encouragement of the curing of fifh in New-York. Though there may be a miftake in alledging the fifheries of New-York and Penfylvania, becaufe there are no fifh cured there; yet in fundry other things it may be beneficial.

that

that port for twelve months preceding March 12, 1750-1, is 358; thole that were bound to the northward of Delaware capes, viz. to New-York, Rhode-Iſland, Boſton with its out ports, Halifax, and Newfoundland, make about ninety of that number; to Virginia, Maryland, North and South-Carolina, and Georgia, about twenty-nine; the remainder fail for Europe and the Weſt-India ſugar iſlands and colonies; the craft that go to the ſouthward, Virginia, Maryland, &c. are of no great value, but thoſe which go to the northward, eſpecially to Boſton and Rhode-Iſland, are generally of more value than the veſſels that go to the Weſt-Indies, ſome of them carry from 500 to 600 barrels of bread and flour.

They build about twenty, or upwards, veſſels that go to ſea from Philadelphia.

The cuſtom-houſe officers in this colony, have the largeſt ſalaries of any in North-America: the collector of the port of Philadelphia is a patent officer; in the proper province this is the only collection; in the territories called the three lower counties are two collections, Newcaſtle and Lewes.

I cannot account for the many cuſtom-houſe collections upon the river of Delaware; there are two on the Jerſey ſide, and three on the Penſylvania ſide: excepting the cuſtom-houſe of Philadelphia, the others are nominal and fine-cures, and might have been called branches and creeks of Philadelphia: beſides uſual officers, there is on the Penſylvania ſide, an extraordinary officer who may be called a comptroller general, a riding officer to examine and ſign the accounts of the reſpective collectors.

Before any bills of publick credit were emitted, the currency of Penſylvania was proclamation money, a heavy piece of eight was ſix ſhillings in denomination; but by the emiſſions of publick credit bills [d], as in all the co-

[d] The publick bills of credit in the plantations were called a paper currency, becauſe they were transferable; and in ſeveral of the colonies enacted to be a tender in law.

lonies,

lonies, who went into a paper currency, their denominations were depreciated, and at present a dollar or weighty
piece of eight passes for seven shillings and sixpence denomination; but by the good management of their paper
loan office, the intrinsick value of their denominations, has
not been depreciated farther. The interest of this loan money produces about 5000 *l.* currency per ann. which with
the 3000 *l.* excise, defrays the charges of government.
Their first emission of a paper currency was about twenty-
seven years ago.

Religious sectaries.

The various plantation sectaries have been already mentioned, in a general digression in the section of Rhode-
Island; but as the Moravians and Dumplers are peculiar
to this colony, what is further to be observed concerning
them, is here inserted.

In vol. II. p. 155, we mentioned that the Moravians
had lately obtained a British act of parliament indulging
them in many things; particularly, that their affirmation,
quaker-like, shall be equivalent to an oath, but with some
restrictions. There are about 800 to 900 Moravians who
have already transported themselves to this colony,
and many more may be expected, because since the pas-
sing the act of parliament in their favour, the several tole-
rations they had in Germany, Holland, and Denmark,
are taken from them: the reasons for so doing, I have not
as yet learned; but by edicts, their books, hymns, and
publick worship, are ordered to be suppressed.

In vol. II. p. 150, we mentioned a branch of the German Anabaptists called Dumplers: they are generally ignorant people, but some of their heads are not so; for
instance, Peter Miller, a German, writes elegantly in
Latin upon religion and mortification: they have a
printing press, and are continually printing; they are
very curious in writing fine, and delight much in scrolls
of writing on religious subjects, stuck up in their halls
and cells; the initial letters are beautifully illuminated
with

with blue, red, and gold, such as may be seen in old monkish manuscripts.

I am again fallen into the disagreeable subject (where offence to some or many is unavoidable) of sectaries or parties in religious affairs: what here follows was designed for the Appendix; but as I now find that a long Appendix containing many loose, not connected matters, may be tedious to the reader; I shall in the several sections following, occasionally intersperse many things designed for the Appendix.

Some years since, viz. 1722, there was a considerable secession in the S. W. parts of Connecticut, of congregationalist ministers and candidates, to better themselves in livings by church of England missions: from this incident, there has lately been revived a sophistical dispute, whether the established old congregationalist ministers, or the late new converts, church of England missionaries, are to be deemed the Separatists. The decision seems to be easy, by relating only matters of fact. By a fundamental, in the articles of union, 1707, of England and Scotland, the church of England in express plain words, is declared to be established in all the English plantations; but this seems to be only as to church government, and that only amongst the people of the church of England : the other sectaries can have no ecclesiastical jurisdiction even amongst themselves, as appears by the annexed determinaton of the lords justices anno 1725; but in their various modes of worship (Roman catholicks excepted) all christian professions are tolerated in perpetuity, and in as ample manner, as if they were churches established by law. If any sects which prevail in the legislature of any colony, impose upon the other sectaries, they are checked by the king in council, all the colonies being under the immediate inspection of the king in council. We here insert the annexed case of the act of the assembly of Connecticut, against quakers, &c.

A true copy of a letter from their excellencies the lords justices, to the hon. W——— D———, Esq. *lieutenant governor of his majesty's province of the Massachusetts-Bay.*

Whitehall, October 7, 1725.

SIR,

" THE lords justices being informed from such
" good hands, as make the truth of this advice
" not to be doubted, that at a general convention of mi-
" nisters, from several parts of his majesty's province of
" the Massachusetts-Bay, at Boston, on the 27th of May
" last, a memorial and address was framed, directed to
" you as lieutenant governor and commander in chief,
" and to the council and house of representatives then
" sitting, desiring that the general assembly would call
" the several churches in this province to meet by their
" pastors and messengers, in a synod; which memorial
" and address, being accordingly presented by some of
" the said ministers, in the name, and at the desire of the
" said convention, was considered in council, the third
" of June following, and there approved; but the house
" of representatives put off the consideration of it to the
" next session, in which the council afterwards concurred.

" Their excellencies were extremely surprised, that no
" account of so extraordinary and important a transaction
" should have been transmitted by you, pursuant to an
" article in your instructions, by which you are directed
" upon all occasions, to send unto his majesty, and to
" the commissioners for trade and plantations, a particu-
" lar account of all your proceedings, and the condition
" of affairs within your government. As this matter doth
" highly concern his majesty's royal prerogative, their
" excellencies referred the consideration of it to Mr.——
" attorney and solicitor general, who, after maturede libe-
" ration, and making all proper enquiries, reported, "that

VOL. II.   Z   " from

" from the charter and laws of your colony, they cannot
" collect that there is any regular establishment of a na-
" tional or provincial church there, so as to warrant the
" holding of convocations or synods of the clergy; but
" if such synods might be holden, yet they take it to be
" clear in point of law, that his majesty's supremacy in
" ecclesiastical affairs, being a branch of his prerogative,
" does take place in the plantations, and that synods can-
" not be held, nor is it lawful for the clergy to assemble
" as in synods, without authority from his majesty: they
" conceive the above-mentioned application of the said
" ministers, not to you alone, as representing the king's
" person, but to you, and the council, and the house of
" representatives, to be a contempt of his majesty's pre-
" rogative, as it is a publick acknowledgment, that the
" power of granting what they desire resides in the legis-
" lative body of the province, which by law is vested
" only in his majesty. And the lieutenant governor,
" council, and assembly intermeddling therein, was an
" invasion of his majesty's royal authority, which it was
" your duty as lieutenant governor, to have withstood
" and rejected; and that the consent of the lieutenant
" governor, the council, and house of representatives,
" will not be sufficient authority for the holding of such
" a synod."

" Their excellencies, upon consideration of this opi-
" nion of the attorney and solicitor general, which they
" have been pleased to approve, have commanded me to
" acquaint you with, and to express to you their surprise,
" that no account of so remarkable a transaction, which
" so nearly concerns the king's prerogative, and the wel-
" fare of his majesty's province under your govern-
" ment, has been received from you, and to signify to
" you their directions, that you do put an effectual stop
" to any such proceedings; but if the consent desired
" by the ministers above-mentioned, for the holding of
" the synod, should have been obtained, and this pre-
" tended synod should be actually sitting, when you re-
" ceive

" ceive thefe their excellencie's directions, they do in
" that cafe, require and direct you, to caufe fuch their
" meeting to ceafe, acquainting them that their affembly
" is againft law, and a contempt of his majefty's prero-
" gative, and that they are forbid to meet any more ;
" but if, notwithftanding fuch fignification, they fhall
" continue to hold fuch an affembly, you are then to
" take care that the principal actors therein be profecuted
" for a mifdemeanour.   But you are to avoid doing any
" formal act to diffolve them, left it be conftrued to im-
" ply that they had a right to affemble.   This, Sir, is
" what I have in command from their excellencies to
" fignify to you.

" And I muft obferve to you, that the precedent quo-
" ted in the above-mentioned memorial of fuch a fynod,
" being held forty-five years ago, falls in with the year
" 1680, and that the former charter, upon which the
" government of your province depended, was repealed
" by *fcire facias* in the year 1684, and the new charter
" was granted in the year 1691; from whence it appears,
" that if fuch fynod was holden as is alledged, it hap-
" pened a fhort time before the repealing of the old
" charter, but none has been fince the granting the new
" one.   I am, Sir, your moft humble fervant,

CHARLES DELAFAYE.

At the court at Kenfington *the eleventh day of* October,
1705; *prefent the queen's moft excellent majefty, his royal
highnefs prince* George *of* Denmark, *lord archbifhop of*
Canterbury, *lord keeper, lord treafurer, lord prefident,
earl of* Ranelagh, *Mr.* Boyle, *Mr. fecretary* Hodges,
Mr. fecretary Harley, *lord chief juftice* Holt, *lord
chief juftice* Trevor, *duke of* Somerfet, *duke of* Or-
mond, *Mr.* Vernon, *Mr.* Earle.

" A Reprefentation from the lords commiffioners
"   of trade and plantations, being this day read
" at the board upon an act, paffed in her majefty's

" colony of Connecticut, entitled (only) HERETICKS,
" whereby it is enacted, that all who shall entertain
" any quakers, ranters, adamites, and other hereticks,
" are made liable to the penalty of five pounds, and five
" pounds per week for every town that shall so enter-
" tain them ; that all quakers shall be committed to pri-
" son, or be sent out of the colony—That whosoever
" shall hold unnecessary discourse with quakers shall for-
" feit twenty shillings ; that whosoever shall keep any
" quakers books, the governor, magistrates, and elders
" excepted, shall forfeit ten shillings, and that all such
" such books shall be suppressed ; that no masters of
" any vessel do land any quakers without carrying
" them away again, under the penalty of twenty
" pounds.

" And the said lords commissioners humbly offering,
" that the said act be repealed by her majesty, it being
" contrary to the liberty of conscience indulged to dis-
" senters by the laws of England, as also to the charter
" granted to that colony, her majesty, with the advice
" of her privy council, is pleased to declare her dis-
" allowance and disapprobation of the said act ; and,
" pursuant to her majesty's royal pleasure thereupon,
" the said act, passed in her majesty's colony of Con-
" necticut in New-England, entitled Hereticks, is here-
" by repealed, and declared null and void, and of none
" effect.

Signed JOHN POVEY.

In the sessions 1751, of the British parliament, was
passed an act extending to the American colonies, as well
as to the kingdom of Great-Britain, and its other dominions ; entitled, " an act for regulating the commence-
" ment of the year, and for correcting the calendar now
" in use". The abstract of the act runs thus—
Whereas the legal supputation of the year in that part
of Great-Britain called England, beginning the 25th of
March, has been attended with many inconveniencies,

as it differs from the usage of neighbouring nations, and the legal computation of that part of Great-Britain called Scotland, and thereby divers mistakes happened in the dates of deeds and other writings ; and our Julian calendar having been discovered to be erroneous.; that the spring equinox, which at the general council of Nice, anno dom. 325, happened about the 21st of March, now happens the ninth or tenth of the same month, which error is still increasing ; and to the end, that the several equinoxes or solstices may, for the future, fall upon the same nominal days as at the time of the said general council, and is now generally received by almost all other nations of Europe ; and to prevent disputes with foreign correspondents of almost all other nations of Europe in their letters and accounts, be it enacted, that in all his majesty's dominions in Europe, Asia, Africa, and America, the old supputation is not to be made use of, after the 31st of December 1751, and the year for the future to commence January 1st, and the days to be numbered in the same order, and the moveable feasts to be ascertained as they now are until September 2, 1752, inclusive; and the day following (that is, the 3d of Sept. 1752) to be accounted the 14th of Sept. 1752, omitting at that time the eleven intermediate nominal days. All writings after 1st of January, 1752, to be dated according to the new stile ; and all courts after Sept. 2, 1752, shall be held in the same nominal days they now are ; (courts held with fairs or marts excepted) that is, eleven days sooner than the respective day wherein the same are now kept. Every hundredth year, excepting every fourth hundred, whereof anno 1800 shall be the first, to be deemed though a leap year or bissextile consisting only of 365 days; but all other bissextile or leap years shall consist of 366 days.—And whereas the method of computing the full moons now used in the calendar of the common prayers of the church of England, to find Easter, is become considerably erroneous ; therefore the said feast of Easter, and others depending

Z 3   thereon

thereon, fhall, after the 2d of Sept. 1752, conform to
the decree of the faid general council, and the practice
of foreign countries fhall be obferved according to the
annexed table ; and the former table, in all future additions of the book of common prayer, fhall be fuppreffed ; but the courts of feffion and exchequer in Scotland, and all markets, fairs and marts, fhall be held upon the fame natural days as if this act had not been
made, that is, eleven days later than according to this
new computation, notwithftanding that by this new computation, the nominal days are anticipated or brought
forward by the fpace of eleven days, the natural days and
times for the opening and clofing of commons of pafture and the like, not to be altered by this act, that is,
eleven days later than the new fupputation. — The natural days and times of payments of rents, annuities,
fums of money, delivery of goods, commencement or
expiration of leafes, and the like, fhall not be by this
act anticipated or accelerated ; and the time of attaining
the age of twenty-one years fhall not be altered by this
act, or the determination of any apprenticefhip or
fervice [e].

[e] Julius Cæfar began this year about the hybernal or winter folftice ; (the equinoxes and folftices are proper periods in fuch matters)
the Julian or O. S. began forty-five years before CHRIST : this ftile
was reformed by pope Gregory 1582, but was not carried back to
the nativity of our Saviour, which, in church precifenefs, ought to
have been, but only to the time of the council of Nice, which was
held anno dom. 325, by Conftantine the Great, to examine and condemn the doctrines of Arius. At the time of the council of Nice,
the vernal equinox was on the 21ft of March ; but in ftrictnefs, and
according to the precifion of devotionalift obfervers of days, it fhould
have gone back fo far as the nativity or firft year of Chrift ; the vernal equinox was then on the 23d of March, but as the Gregorian
ftile is at prefent the general practice of chriftian European nations,
the Britifh legiflature in their wonted prudence have acceded thereto,
as being a convenient civil, but not a jure divino affair. Inftead of
being too minutely precife in ftriking off thirteen days, which is the
truth of the cafe in conformity to other European countries, they
only ftruck off eleven days, for the fake of mutual conveniency ; it
is more eligible to err with the generality of Europe, than affectedly

Proprietors

*Proprietors or principal governors, and their resident de-
puties or lieutenant governors.*

The first proprietor and governor was **William Penn,**
son of admiral Penn, see vol. II. p. 307; he carried over
many quakers with him to that country; his patent included that part of new Swedeland, which lies on the
west side of Delaware river, some part of the Swedish settlements lay on the east side of the river, and are part of
west New-Jersey. Mr. Penn continued two years in
Penfylvania, and upon his father's death returned to
England, and left the government in the hands of Thomas Lloyd, with a council. Mr. Penn being esteemed
a favourite of K. James II. was suspected to be a Roman catholick and jesuit in the assumed mask of a quaker, and upon the revolution K. William was advised
to suspend his privilege of appointing a deputy governor
for Pensylvania. And

The crown appointed col. Fletcher, governor of New-
York, to be also governor of Pensylvania; but upon
Mr. William Penn's vindication of himself, he was re-
stored to his privilege of government; and appointed

Mr. Blackwell, his deputy or lieut. governor. He was
succeeded as lieut. governor by Thomas Lloyd, Esq,
upon his death.

to constitute a peculiar British stile, which would be running from
one inconvenience into another; the main intention is to produce
an uniformity in the computation of time throughout the christian part of the world; the agreeing with the rest of Europe,
ought to prevail over any argument deduced from the nicety of
calculation.

Peter Deval of the Middle Temple, secretary to the royal society,
drew the bill and prepared most of the tables under direction of the
earl of Chesterfield, the first former of the design; and the whole
was carefully examined and approved of by Martin Folkes, Esq.
president of the royal society, and Dr. Bradley, his majesty's astro-
nomer at Greenwich, who computed the tables at the end of the
bill.

Mr. Penn appointed his nephew col. Markham his deputy or lieut. governor; he had the government or direction until the second arrival of Mr. Penn, 1698.

Mr. William Penn principal governor and proprietor arrived a second time in Penfylvania, 1698. He returned to England 1700, and nominated col. Andrew Hamilton for his deputy; in his adminiftration was much confufion in the province; upon his death

1704, col. John Evans was appointed lieutenant governor.

1713, died in London William Penn, the firft proprietor and principal governor, much in debt, occafioned by his whimfical difpofition; he had agreed with the crown to refign his property and government for a certain confideration (to extricate himfelf from debt) but died fuddenly before the inftrument was executed, and the government and property remains in the family to this time.

The firft principal governor and proprietor was called William Penn, the grand-father; he was fucceeded by his fon William Penn, called the father; and he was fucceeded by Springet Pen, William Penn the fon, and laftly in the three brothers, John Penn, Thomas Penn, and Richard Penn, co-heirs in the fucceffion: thefe brothers by a written agreement with lord Baltimore proprietary of Maryland, their adjoining neighbour, 1732, fettled boundaries to be afterwards confirmed in form of law; but lord Baltimore receded and occafioned a tedious controverfy in chancery, as is above related.

John, the eldeft of the three brothers, died October 28, 1746, a batchelor, and by will, October 24, 1746, left his fhare to his fecond brother Thomas, with remainders, as is expreffed in the will.

William Penn (fon to the firft proprietor) in law called the father, (the firft proprietor, in law inftruments, was called the father) died at Liege, 1720.

1708-9, In January arrived capt. Gookin, lieut. governor.

1717,

1717, May 30, arrives Sir William Keith, lieut. governor.

1726, Major Gordon superfeded Sir William Keith.

Major Gordon died in October 1736, and Mr. Logan was in course president for a short time; but was soon superfeded by col. Thomas, a planter of Antigua: Mr. Logan died much lamented, Nov. 1751. After nine years government, col. Thomas resigned 1747, and was succeeded by James Hamilton, Esq. the present lieut. governor, son of Andrew Hamilton, a noted lawyer in thefe parts.

A medical digression, concerning the personal constitutions of people born in British North-America. *Of the endemial distempers prevalent there, and of their present medical practice.*

As this digression will not be much read by ordinary capacities, where things cannot so well be expressed in vernacular words, I take the liberty of using technical or professional expressions, and some classical phrases, and generally in a concise or aphoristical loose, but practical manner.

Their children or youth are more forward [*f*] or precoce than in Great-Britain.   2. The virility of the

---

[*f*] It is observed that in the West-Indies there are no boys, all being either children or men.

Perhaps the most noted instance of forwardness in a boy, is what Montagne of Gascony in his essays 1550 writes of himself; his father educated him in his childhood in the learned languages of Greek and Latin, in the same routine that from nurses we learn our vernacular or mother tongue: we had a remarkable instance of such routines in Boston; a worthy English gentleman, Richard Dalton, Esq. a great admirer of the Greek classicks, because of the tenderness of his eyes, taught his negro boy Cæsar to read to him distinctly any Greek writer, without understanding the meaning or interpretation. Montagne with much vanity and peculiar pedantry, says, that Buchanan was afraid to accost him when only six æt in Latin, and that Buchanan copied his instruction or education of a child from his education. Buchanan was a first rate master of the Latin classicks, and preceptor to
men,

men, and fecundity of their women, or child-bearing
fex, are much the fame as in Great-Britain, their mother
country.   3. Their longevity falls much fhorter.

king James VI. of Scotland; in his travels in France, hearing of the
forwardnefs of this boy, he went to fee him.   As Montagne is a
noted writer, I fhall for amufement mention another inftance of his
Gafcon pedantry; that in his younger years he refolved not to enter
into any matrimonial partnerfhip or contract, not even with the goddefs
of wifdom, but married æt. thirty-three.

As the education of children, is not fufficiently attended to in many
of our colonies, I fhall here infert the beginning of an experiment
of this nature.   I delight in promoting of children in town and country;   accordingly I have in Bofton taken a promifing boy entirely at
my own charge of fubfiftence and education, under my fole direction,
to form a practical (not notional) fcheme of management and education, ob ovo, or rather ab utero, becaufe of fome difficulties I was
prefent at the birth; I did not allow him to be rocked in a cradle,
fufpecting that concuffions might weaken his brain, and confequently
impair his judgment; he never had a diafcordium, mithridate, or other
opiate, or ftrong drink, to compofe him to fleep; a pernicious indolent practice of nurfes and old women, becaufe thereby convulfions
may be induced, or the child rendered ftupid for life.

To accomodate his organs of fpeech while flexible, and in the par-
rot or prattle period of life, not only to the pronunciation of our
Englifh or vernacular words, but alfo to the pronunciation of other
languages; before he was full five years of age, he did diftinctly repeat and pronounce the Lord's prayer in the five languages familiar
to me, Greek, Latin, Englifh, French and Dutch : he did well exprefs and define many harfh and long foreign words, fuch as the Indian names of fome ponds, rivers, and tribes in our neighbourhood.
Chabonamungagog, a large pond joining to Douglafs, Winipifiackit,
a great pond or lake in the province of New-Hampfhire, Papaconta-
quafh or Millers river, which falls into Connecticut river on the eaft
fide a little below North-field, Arowfaguntacook, a tribe of French
Abnaquie Indians called the miffion of St. Francis, on the fouth fide
of Canada river, Miffilimakanack, a tribe of French Indians, be-
ween the great lakes Hurons and Ilinois, Tatamaganahaw, a fmall
tribe of Mikmake Indians of Nova-Scotia, in the bay Verte of the
gulph of St. Laurence; fome Dutch words, Achtentachententigh,
eighty-eight, &c. fome Latin words, Honorificabilitudinitatibus, Ho-
nourableneffes, &c.

Inftead of the abftrufely profound catechifms, which prepofteroufly
are taught children, he is initiated in things and words which are
eafily comprehended, and fubjects of common converfation, fuch as,
   Q. What is your name ?
   A. I am known by the name of William Douglafs.

The

The remote caufes or predifpofitions to moft chronical diftempers are, 1. Mala ftamina vitæ. 2. Malus

Q. Where was you born ?

A. In the town of Bofton, in the province of Maffachufetts-Bay,
in the Britifh dominions of New-England in North-America,

Q. When was you born?

A. I was born July 25, 1745 ; but how I was made, and how I
came into the world, I have forgotten, and cannot tell.

Q What is your religion ?

A. A catholick chriftian proteftant ; to fear God and keep his
commandments, to honour and obey the civil government.

Q. What is God ?

A. The fupreme being, who created and manages the univerfe,
in fome manner inconceivable to us created beings.

Q. What is civil government ?

A. The laws and cuftoms of the country I live in, as executed by
certain appointed magiftrates.

Q. Why do you every feventh day go to a place of publick worfhip ?

A. Becaufe (as my grandmother tells me,) one day in feven is by
moft civil governments found requifite to abftain from labour, for the
refrefhment of the labouring part of mankind and cattle.

Q. Why do you in ordinary attend the affembly of Mr. Welfted
and Gray ?

A. Becaufe it is the neareft, and neighbours naturally join in their
publick devotions ; thefe two minifters or paftors are exemplary in
their lives, and agreeable in their publick difcourfes.

Q. What fectary of publick worfhip do you follow ?

A. That of my father natural or adopting. My grandmother tells
me, that by law and cuftom I muft follow the example and precepts
of my father till twenty-one æt. or till affigned.

We may obferve that of all animals, mankind attain to the greateft
perfection of knowledge, but after the longeft time arrive to the full
growth of body and mind ; therefore as this boy is too exuberant in
the growth of mind, I check or retard him by allowing him more
play than fchooling, that the impreffions may not be too flight or
tranfitory ; and allow him to affociate with active wild boys, not
wicked or vicious, that by his puerile flow of fpirit, he may practife
activity of body and mind. The Dalrymples, a family in Scotland,
noted for acutenefs, wifdom, and knowledge, allowed their boys, at
a certain age, to affociate with wild, but not wicked boys, and after
fome time took them up to a regular fober education.

At times I fend him to any tolerated place of publick worfhip,
to prevent party, bigotry, and a narrow way of thinking. I afk him
his natural remarks upon the different modes of worfhip, to make
him obfervant ; I fhall give one inftance which I hope the candid
locus,

locus, that is, a bad air and foil. 3. Indolence or in-activity. 4. Intemperance. Concerning all thefe we fhall interfperfe fome aphorifms.

During the time or period of my practice in New-England, we have had no confiderable epidemics ex-cepting fmall-pox, meafles, and fome fpecies of putrid fevers and dyfenteries; the varieties in our endemials were from the viciffitudes of feafons and weather. To write a hiftory of epidemic yearly conftitutions, in Sy-denham's manner, for a continued fucceffion of years, would be writing of a novel : our chronical ails, by the practice of our common phyficians, particularly by the routine indolent palliative repetitions of V. S. and opiates, which fix all diftempers, and render their patients vale-tudinary and fhort-lived. Opiates and inebriating li-quors have the fame effects, they carry the peccant hu-mours to the nerves, from whence they are fcarce to be removed; they are flow poifons, they enfeeble both body and mind, and produce mala ftamina vitæ in the progeny.

As New-England lies in the leeward of the wefterly extended continent of North-America, the winds (being generally wefterly) gliding continuedly along this vaft tract of land much heated in fummer, and much cooled or frozen in winter, occafion the country to be much

reader will not judge ludere cum facris ; I have a great veneration for the church of England. In a common prayer day he went to a church of England, when he came home, he faid, that he obferved the mi-nifter come into the church in a black gown, and retire into a clofet (the veftry) and come out again with a clean fhirt over his gown. His grandmother as ufually afked him where the text was ; he faid that he could not tell, becaufe every body preached promifcuoufly ; men, women, and children, fpake in publick (meaning the refponfes) his grandmother told him that the quaker fectary allow their women, (but no children) to fpeak in publick, though contrary to St. Paul's admonition.

He is taught the hours of the day, the days of the week, the months in the year, the mariner's compafs or corners of the wind ; the varieties of fhipping, fchooners, floops, brigantines, fnows, and fhips ; he reads the fign pofts, and news-papers.

hotter

hotter in fummer, and much colder in winter, than in Great-Britain ; reciprocations, but not to extremes, are falutary to the conftitutions, where the tranfitions are gradual ; thus we may obferve in nature, that for the benefit of the earth's produce, there is a reciprocation of fummer and winter, day and night, &c. In countries where the feafons are upon the extremes in fummer and winter, as in New-England, conftitutions do not wear well, analogous to the timber and plank of a fhip between wind and water. Longevity appears moftly in ifland countries, where with a fmall latitude or variation the temperature of the air continues nearly the fame.

I fhall here infert a few lines concerning the conftitution and medical practice of our northern Indians. See vol. I. p. 174.

The Indians north of Canada river, the Efquimaux and Outawaways, are generally affected with pforas, fcurvy, or itch ; from the cold intemperance of the climate. As the Indian manner of life is much more fimple than that of Europeans, they are not fubject to fo many various difeafes : their modern intemperance in drinking rum and other fpirits, kills more than all their other diftemperatures.

The Indian food is from their hunting, fowling, and fifhing ; their bread-kind is from maize or Indian corn, phafeoli or kidney beans of feveral forts, tuberofe roots of feveral kinds, mafts or nuts of various forts, great variety of foreft berries.

The varieties of national conftitutions and habits are not eafily to be accounted for ; the American Indians, by keeping principally their feet warm, the Africa negroes by keeping their heads warm, without any regard to the reft of their body, preferve their health and ftrength.

The American aboriginal Indians naturally are of weak conftitutions, they are impubes et imberbes ; but by

habit

habit from their infancy, can suffer hunger and wood damps, better than Europeans of stronger constitutions: their natural temper is cruel and vindictive.

Their physicians in ordinary are the powowers clergy of conjurers, and some old women. In their medical practice they take no notice of pulse or urine, they do not use blood letting ; they chiefly use traditional herbs; blistering with punk or touchwood, and the blisters are converted into issues ; sweating in hot houses (an extemporary kind of bagnio) and immediately thereupon immersion in cold water ; this practice has killed many of them in eruptive fevers. The American Indians are noted for their traditional knowledge of poisonous herbs and antidotes ; but I do not find that our Indian venefici are so expert in the veneficium art, as the negroes of Africa, who give poisons, which in various, but certain periods, produce their mortal effects, some suddenly, some after a number of months or years.

They cure several poisons; for instance, the bite of that American viper called rattle-snake or vipera caudisona, by proper antidotes; before they produce their usual dismal effects [g].

I hope these medical observations may be of some use to our colonies ; as they are in my professional business, by some they may be thought pedantick, by others they may be called a quackish ostentation ; once for all, I de-

---

[g] May we not hope, that in future times, some epidemical contagious distempers, such as the plague, small-pox, and the like, may be prevented or extinguished in seminio by proper antidotes : time produces surprising discoveries in nature, such as the various phænomena of magnetism and electricity; in the small-pox the late improvement of conveying it by inoculation, is found more favourable than the receiving of it the chance or natural way, as fruit from trees inoculated, surpasses natural fruit : this practice of inoculating for the small-pox, was introduced in a very rash indiscreet manner, and by weak men ; we may observe that many of the juvantia or lædentia in medicine, were discovered or rather introduced by rash fools and madmen, instance, Paracelsus's mercurial remedies.

clare,

clare, that I have no lucrative views, becaufe mihi tantum fuppetit viaticæ quantum viæ.

I here infert fome remarks upon the medical practice in our colonies; as no man's name is expreffed, and fome gentlemen practitioners of candour, probity, ingenuity, and good practical knowledge are excepted, thefe reflections may be taken in good part without further apology.

In our plantations, a practitioner, bold, rafh, impudent, a lyar, bafely born and educated, has much the advantage of an honeft, cautious, modeft gentleman. In general, the phyfical practice in our colonies is fo pernicioufly bad, that excepting in furgery, and fome very acute cafes, it is better to let nature under a proper regimen take her courfe (naturæ morborum curatrices) than to truft to the honefty and fagacity of the practitioner; our American practitioners are fo rafh and officious, the faying in the apocrypha, Ecclefiafticus xxxviii. 15. may with much propriety be applied to them. "He that finneth before his maker, let him fall into the "hands of the phyfician." Frequently there is more danger from the phyfician, than from the diftemper: a country where the medical practice is very irregular, is a good fchool to learn the lædentia, a good article in practice; but fometimes notwithftanding male practice, nature gets the better of the doctor, and the patient recovers.

Our practitioners deal much in quackery, [b] and quackifh medicines, as requiring no labour of thought or

[b] I fhall mention one remarkable inftance of colony quackery, advertifed in the New-York gazette, December 16, 1751. "In July "1751, was committed to the care of doctor Peter Billing, an expe-"rienced phyfician, and man mid-wife, and formerly in the king's "fervice, the moft extraordinary and remarkable cafe that ever was "performed in the world, upon one Mrs. Mary Smith, fingle woman, "fifter to capt. Arthur Smith, on James river, in the county of "Surry in Virginia, æt. forty-fix; fhe had been upwards of eighteen "years out of her fenfes, (moft of the time raving mad) eat her own "excrements, and was compleatly cured by him in two months, con-
com-

compofition, and highly recommended in the London quack bills (in which all the reading of many of our practitioners confifts) inadvertently encouraged by patents for the benefit of certain fees to fome offices, but to the very great damage of the fubject. How difmal is it to obferve fome apothecaries fhops wainfcotted or papered with advertifments, recommending quack medicines for the profit of the fhop, but deftruction of their neighbours? this is vending of poifons for gain.

In the moft trifling cafes they ufe a routine of practice: when I firft arrived in New-England, I afked G. P. a noted facetious practitioner, what was their general method of practice; he told me their practice was very uniform, bleeding, vomiting, bliftering, purging, anodyne, &c. if the illnefs continued, there was repetendi, and finally murderandi; nature was never to be confulted, or allowed to have any concern in the affair. What Sydenham well obferves, is the cafe with our practitioners; *æger nimia medici diligentia ad plures migrat.*

Blood-letting and anodynes are the principal tools of our practitioners; thefe palliate any diftemper for a fhort time, while, at the fame time they confound the intentions of nature, and fix the malady; they follow Sydenham too much in giving paregoricks, after catharticks, which is playing faft and loofe.

" trary to the opinion of all that knew her, no doctor in the province
" daring to undertake her. N. B. The contagious diftemper fo fre-
" quently happening to the bold adventurers in the wars of Venus
" when recent, will be cured by him for three piftoles in hand, though
" the common price is five pound all over North-America. And all
" other cafes curable in phyfick and furgery, proportionable accord-
" ing to the circumftances of people." He has alfo other matters to
publifh, particularly an elegant medicine to prevent the yellow fever
and dry gripes in the Weft-Indies; this is incomparable, if we except a quack advertifement publifhed in Jamaica (immediately after
the laft great earthquake) of pills to prevent perfons or their effects
fuffering by earthquakes.

SECT

SECT. XV.

Concerning the province of Maryland.

ALthough recapitulations or repetitions are reckoned tedious and not elegant, I find that our sections or colonies may be more agreeably introduced by some general accounts or transactions with a little variation, than by an abrupt entrance into the colony affairs.

The Cabots of Venetian extract obtained 1495, a patent from king Henry VII. of England, of all lands to be by them discovered west of Europe, as to property; with a reservation of a certain royal perquisite; this king understood perquisites: the father John, and afterwards the son Sebastian, fitted out from Bristol; in their first voyage upon the discovery of a N. W. passage to China, and the East-Indies, being obstructed by the ice, the sailors mutinied and returned to England, without effecting any thing of consequence.

Anno 1498, Sebastian ranged the continent of North-America from 40 d. to 67 d. N. lat. and at several places took a nominal occupancy from discovery, without making any settlement; thus notwithstanding the discoveries, we had no possession for near a century of years.

Sir Walter Raleigh, a noted discovery projector, see vol. I. p. 111, anno 1584, March 25, obtained of queen Elizabeth a patent for discoveries 'and settlements in America. Upon the return of the vessels of the first adventure, in honour to the virgin queen Elizabeth, the name of Virginia in general was given to the North part of the continent so far as the gulph of St. Laurence north, to Florida south. In process of time the French made some small settlements in the north parts of North-America, and called them Nova Francia, or Nouvelle France; at this time known by the name of L'Accadie, (Nova-Scotia) and Canada. The Swedes, Fins and Dutch introduced by Hudfon, made fettlements upon Hudfon's or Kord rivier, and Delaware or Zuyd rivier, and called it Nova-Belgia or New-Netherlands. Thus in the beginning of the laft century the eaftern coaft of North-America was divided into, 1. Nova-Francia, 2. North-Virginia, comprehending the colonies of Nova-Scotia and New-England. 3. Nova-Belgia or New-Netherlands, at prefent known by the names of New-York, New-Jerfeys, and Penfylvania. 4. South-Virginia, which comprehends Maryland, Virginia, North-Carolina, South-Carolina, and Georgia.

Upon the new difcoveries, many feparate grants of diftrias were made to private proprietors; but afterwards for the regularity and eafe of jurifdiaion, the crown affumed the jurifdiaions, and reduced them to more comvenient models of government.

Maryland is properly a fprout from Virginia, therefore the conneaion of this fettlement with the firft difcoveries muft be referred to the feaion of Virgin'a; here we fhall only obferve how and when it did fprout. See vol. I. p. 288, the Newfoundland feaion.

Towards the end of king James I. reign, Sir George Calvert principal fecretary of ftate, afterwards lord Baltimore, obtained a patent for fome fifhing harbours in Newfoundland; by reafon of the civil troubles in England, thefe fettlements were difcontinued; being a zealous Roman catholick, with other diffenting zealots of various feaaries, he left England and retired to Virginia: as the Virginians were generally bigots to the church of England feaary, they did not ufe him fo well as he expeaed; and as the Virginians had not fettled farther north than Potomack river, lord Baltimore went home and obtained from king Charles I. a grant of all the lands from the mouth of Potomack river in about 38 d. 10 m. N. to the Swede and Finland fettlements, which were reckoned to the bottom of Chefepeik bay, in about the latitude of 39 d. 45 m. or fifteen Englifh miles fouth

4   of

of Philadelphia parallel: the account of controverfies concerning the boundaries between the properties and jurifdictions of Maryland and Penfylvania, we refer back to the fection of Penfylvania.

The banditti Dutch, Swedes, and Fins, were prior to the Englifh in their fettlements upon Delaware river and weftward inland. Upon a new royal regulation in Virginia, feveral families went over from England to fettle there ; amongft thefe was lord Baltimore, a rigid Roman catholick ; for the advantage of a more free exercife of his religion, he retired thither ; but being ill ufed by the church of England fectaries, and finding that the humour of petitioning for large tracts of land was encouraged by the court at home, and that the Virginia fettlers had not extended farther north than Potomack river, lord Baltimore petitioned for a grant of vacant lands from the north of Potomack river to the Swedifh and Finlanders fettlements between the bottom of Chefepeak bay and Delaware river, and obtained the promife of a grant for the fame ; but dying foon, his fon and heir obtained the patent, dated June 20, 1632: that part of the patent which regards the boundaries, in the Englifh tranflation from the original Latin inftrument runs thus: " Know ye " therefore that we, favouring the pious and noble pur- " pofes of the faid baron of Baltimore, of our fpecial " grace, certain knowledge, and mere motion, have " given, granted, and confirmed, and by this our pre- " fent charter for us our heirs and fucceffors do give, " grant, and confirm, unto Cecilius now baron of Bal- " timore, his heirs and affigns, all that part of a penin- " fula lying in the parts of America, between the ocean " on the eaft, and the bay or gulph of Chefepeak on the " weft, and divided from the other part thereof by a " right line drawn from the promontory or cape of land " called Watkins-point (fituate in the aforefaid bay or " gulph near the river of Wighco) on the weft, unto " the main ocean on the eaft, and between the bounds " on the fouth as far as to the æftuary of Delaware on the

" north, where it is fituate to the 40th d. of northern
" latitude from the equinoctial where New-England
" ends, and all that tract of land within the bounds un-
" derwritten, viz. paffing by the aforefaid æftuary called
" Delaware-Bay in a right line by the degree aforefaid,
" unto the true meridian of the firft fountain of the river
" Potomack, and from thence tending or paffing toward
" the fouth to the farther bank of the faid river, and fol-
" lowing the weft and fouth fide thereof unto a certain
" place called Cinquack, fituate near the mouth of the
" faid river where it falls into the aforefaid bay or gulph
" of Chefepeak, and from thence by the fhorteft line
" that can be drawn unto the aforefaid promontory or
" place called Watkins-point. So that all the tract of
" land divided by the line aforefaid, drawn between the
" main ocean and Watkins-point, unto the promontory
" called Cape-Charles, and all its appertenances, do re-
" main intirely excepted to us, our heirs and fucceffors
" for ever. We do alfo grant and confirm unto the faid
" now lord Baltimore, his heirs and affigns, all lands and
" iflets within the limits aforefaid, and all and fingular
" the iflands and iflets, which are or fhall be in the
" ocean within ten leagues from the eaftern fhore of
" the faid country towards the eaft, &c." Lord Baltimore called it Maryland, from the name of the queen
confort.

For the north bounds of this province, fee the Penfylvania fection, vol. II. p. 308, being a parallel of fifteen
Englifh miles fouth of the fouthermoft part of the
city of Philadelphia in about lat. 39 d. 45 m. Its eaft
line is the weft line of the three lower counties of Penfylvania, already delineated, to cape Henlopen, and from
cape Henlopen by the ocean to a parallel or eaft and
weft line drawn from Watkins-point near Wighco river
in Chefepeak bay in about the lat. of 38 d. 10 m:
its fouthern bound is this parallel on the eaft fide of Chefepeak bay, and farther on the weft fide of the faid bay
up Potomack river as the river runs; here are fome
                                                    difputes

difputes with lord Fairfax, proprietor of the north neck
of Virginia: its vaft line is a fmall opening between the
properties of the Penns and of lord Fairfax as fettled by
treaty with the Six nations of Indians known by the name
of Mohawks, June 29, 1744, at Lancafter in Penfylvania, viz. that the boundaries fhall be at two miles above
the uppermoft falls of Potomack river, and run from
thence in a north line to the fouth bounds of Penfylvania,
and the Indians gave a quit-claim to all the lands in Maryland eaft of that line for the confideration of 300 *l.* currency paid to them by Maryland.

Virginia and Maryland are an open country with many
navigable rivers and creeks, without any battery defence,
and the inhabitants much difperfed ; therefore much expofed to the incurfions and depredations of hoftile armed
veffels ; fcarce any towns, general harbours and barcadiers;
becaufe moft planters or traders have navigable barcadiers
of their own ; after fome time there muft be general barcadiers at the falls of the feveral rivers for the benefit of
the inland country.

Upon the grant and patent 1632, lord Baltimore had
a defign to go to Maryland in perfon, but altered his mind
and appointed his brother Leonard Calvert, Efq. to go
governor in his ftead, and joined Jeremy Hawley, Efq.
and Thomas Cornwallis, Efq. in the commiffion. The firft
colony confifted of about 200 perfons, fent by his lordfhip in the autumn 1633; they were chiefly gentlemen of
good families and Roman catholicks ; the principal were,
Leonard Calvert, governor.

Jeremy Hawley, Efq.   } Affiftants.
Thomas Cornwallis, Efq.

George Calvert, brother to | Mr. Edward Cranfield,
   the governor. | Mr. Henry Green,
Richard Gerrard, Efq. | Mr. Nicholas Fairfax,
Edward Winter, Efq. | Mr. Thomas Dorrel,
Frederick Winter, Efq. | Mr. John Medcalfe,
Henry Wifeman, Efq. | Mr. William Saire,
Mr. John Sanders, | Capt. John Hill.
Mr. John Baxter, | A a 3   They

They failed from Cowes in the ifle of Wight, November 22, 1632; after touching at Barbadoes, and St. Chriftophers, arrived in Virginia, February 24th following, and 3d of March arrived in Potomack river; after ranging the country about Potomack river, they at laft fettled with the confent of the Indians, at the Indian town called Yamaco at the mouth of the river, to which they gave the name of St. Mary's. It is faid that in the firft two years this fettlement of a colony coft lord Baltimore about 40,000 *l*. fterl. by bringing over people, provifions, and other ftores.

During the civil wars in England, lord Baltimore was deprived of the government or jurifdiction of Maryland. About the reftoration 1661, Charles lord Baltimore, fon of Cecilius, obtained a confirmation of the grant 1632, and made feveral voyages thither, but the proprietor being a Roman catholick, the crown retained the jurifdiction, and appointed the governor and all other civil officers: the prefent proprietor is a proteftant, and enjoys both government or jurifdiction and property.

In the trading road by Harris's ferry on Sefquahana river, the breadth of Maryland from Penfylvania boundary line to Potomack river does not exceed eight miles, but higher it is faid to widen again. *N. B.* Paxton on Sefquahana river, is the trading place in this road.

The lords Baltimore referve in each county fome manors not granted, as the Penns do in Penfylvania, and as proprietors of large tracts of land in New-England referve fome part to themfelves, when they fell off parcels; thefe parcels, when improved, rife the value of the referved lands.

Maryland was fo called from K. Charles I. queen Henrietta Maria, a daughter of France; it was held of the crown in common foccage as of his majefty's honour of Windfor, paying yearly two Indian arrows to the caftle of Windfor when demanded. By an act of affembly for liberty of confcience to all perfons who profefs chriftianity, proteftant diffenters, as well as

Roman

Roman catholicks, were induced to fettle there. The prior fettlement of Virginia was of great advantage to the fettling of the colony of Maryland, in fupplying them with fundry neceffaries.

In Maryland and Virginia, the publick rates or taxes for province, county, and parifh, are called levies: it is a capitation or poll tax, upon all tytheables, that is, upon all males of whites, and upon all negroes, males and females, of 16 æt. and upwards to 60 æt.

In Maryland the tax is generally from 90 lb. to 120 wt. of tobacco, according to exigencies, per ann. for each poll, whereof 40 wt. to the rector of the parifh; the reft is for the poors rate, affemblymen's wages, &c. The clergymen of Maryland are upon the moft profitable lay of all our plantation clergy; they are not confined to a fixed falary (in Virginia the parifh minifters are fixed to 16,000 lb. wt. of tobacco per ann. falary) but in this growing country as they are paid in proportion to the number of taxables, the more that the colony increafes in people, the larger is their income, until the parifhes become fo large as to require to be fubdivided: there are at prefent near 40,000 taxables in Maryland.

In Maryland the affembly at times fixes produce at a certain price as a legal tender for the year; for inftance, anno 1732, tobacco was fixed at one penny per pound weight, Indian corn at twenty pence per bufhel, wheat at three fhillings and four pence per bufhel, pork two pence per pound weight. Quit-rents and king's duties were excepted, and were payable in proclamation money, fix fhillings per heavy piece of eight, now called a Spanifh dollar.

The people of Maryland have been happy, in not being expofed to the incurfions and rapines of the outland Indians; they are covered by the neighbouring provinces; their opening between the provinces of Virginia and Penfylvania is very fmall. Anno 1677, the Indians at war with Virginia, by miftake committed

fome

fome outrages in Maryland. A few years fince, the Indians upon referved lands, principally in the county of Dorchefter, eaft of Chefepeak bay, upon fome difguft feemed to be mutinous, but being fenfible of their own inability, that humour foon fubfided. Therefore we can have no article of their wars with the French, Spaniards, and Indians.

The hiftory of the viciffitudes in grants and confequential governments or jurifdictions is of permanent ufe; but the provincial or municipal acts as to divifions of diftricts and counties, are variable and fluctuating according to the humours of the affembly men. During the civil wars, the Baltimore family were deprived of their jurifdiction in Maryland; after the reftoration 1661, they obtained a confirmation of their royal patent, but the propiictor being a Roman catholick, the court of England appointed the governor and other civil officers. Upon the revolution the crown or court of England retained the jurifdiction of the province of Maryland. The prefent lord Baltimore is of the proteftant denomination, and is vefted in the jurifdiction as well as property of Maryland.

Into Maryland and Virginia are imported about 4000 negro flaves per ann. fome planters have 500 flaves; col. Carter of Virginia is faid to have had 900, and Mr. Bennet of Maryland 1300 at one time. A peck of Indian corn and fome falt is their weekly allowance of provifion for each negro; they are reckoned to raife 1000 lb. wt. of tobacco befides fome barrels of corn per head, 6000 tobacco plants are reckoned to yield 1000 lb. wt. of tobacco. The planters by act of affembly in Virginia and Maryland, are inhibited from planting more than 6000 plants of tobacco per negro.

It is reckoned, there may be 300 to 400 felons or mifcreants imported yearly to Maryland from England; this importation of vile levies is fufficient to corrupt
any

any plantation settlement or improvement; it is expected that the government at home are contriving a more salutary method of punishing some criminals, than by sowing them in the colonies.

As the colonies or provinces of Virginia and Maryland lie in the same long bay of Chesepeak, we cannot avoid giving a joint account of them upon some occasions, principally with regard to their trade and navigation.

Rivers and mountains.

The gradual soundings in the ocean before vessels enter Chesepeak bay, render the navigation of Virginia and Maryland very safe; by the many navigable rivers, bays and creeks, which communicate with the great bay, the water carriage is very commodious. This fine bay reaches from cape Henry, at its entrance in about 37 d. lat. to the bottom of the bay where it receives the river Sesquahana in about 39 d. 45 m. lat. Virginia lies upon this bay from cape Henry in lat. 37, to the mouth of Potomack river, which divides Virginia from Maryland in lat. 38. Maryland lies upon the other part of this long bay.

Upon the east side of this great bay are many small bays, creeks, and rivers, but of short course, because the neck of land between this bay and the ocean is narrow; in the Virginia part there are no rivers; in the Maryland part there are several short navigable rivers, which generally and naturally serve as boundaries of counties, viz. Pokomoke, Witomoco, Nanticoke, Chaptank, Wye, Chester, Safaphras, Elke, and north east rivers.

Upon the west side of this long bay are many long navigable beautiful rivers; in the Virginia part are James river, York river, Rapahanock river, and the south side of Potomack river; by these the western shore of Virginia is divided into four necks of land; the

the property of three of thefe necks is in the crown; the property of the northern neck is in lord Fairfax, who married the heirefs of lord Colpepper, as fhall be related more at large in the fection of Virginia; in the Maryland part are the north fide of Potomack river, Pataxen river, South river, Severn river, Patapfco river, Gunpowder river.

The two capes of Virginia which make the entrance of the bay, are about 20 miles diftant, and were called by capt. Smith, Henry and Charles, the names of king James I. two fons; the direct courfe of the bay is N. by W. and S. by E. From Bahama landings at the bottom of the bay to Newcaftle on Delaware river, are thirty miles good travelling.

Sefquahana river, as we mentioned in the fection of Penfylvania, comes from fmall ponds a little fouth of Mohawks river in the province of New-York, croffes the province of Penfylvania, and falls into the bottom of Chefepeak bay in the northern parts of Maryland.

The other great rivers of Virginia and Maryland all lie W. fide of the bay; only James river and Potomack river reach the great Apalachian mountains, called the Blue hills. In Virginia and Maryland the tides are very fmall.

Maryland and Virginia are flat countries, excepting the Apalachian great mountains to the weftward, which begin in the province of Penfylvania, and run 900 miles S. W. at about 150 or 200 miles diftance from the eaftern fhore of the Atlantic ocean, and terminate in the bay of Apalachia near Penfacola, in the gulph of Mexico. Col. Spotfwood, lieut. governor of Virginia, was the firft who paffed the Apalachian mountains, or great Blue hills, and the gentlemen his attendants were called knights of the horfe-fhoe, having difcovered a horfe-pafs. At prefent there are two paffes crofs thefe mountains; the north pafs is in Spotfylvania, the fouth pafs is near Brunfwick. Some rivers have been difcovered on the weft fide of the Apalachian mountains,

tains, which fall into the river Ohio, which falls into the river Miſſiſſippi below the river Ilinois.

For ſome further account of the Apalachian mountains, ſee the ſection of Penſylvania, vol. II. p. 313. The Iriſh who had made ſettlements in the weſtern parts of Penſylvania, are exceeded by the Germans of late years imported into Penſylvania. Theſe Germans by a ſuperior induſtry and frugality (notwithſtanding of the north of Ireland proteſtants being noted for induſtry and frugality) have purchaſed moſt of the Iriſh ſettlements there, and the Iriſh move farther into Maryland, Virginia, and North-Carolina, along the foot of the Apalacian mountains, where the land is good and very promiſing, being the waſh of theſe hills and mountains: the Indian traders travel this road, to head many of the rivers ; here are ſeveral congregations of Iriſh preſbyterians, to be deſcribed in the ſection of Virginia.

The alarum liſt, and the training militia, are nearly in the ſame manner, and under the ſame regulations as in the colonies already mentioned.

As to the number of white and black people in the province, we may make ſome eſtimate from the polls of taxables as found 1734 upon an exact ſcrutiny, when every taxable was allowed thirty ſhillings out of a large emiſſion of paper currency ; they were at that time about 36,000 perſons of white men, ſixteen æt. and upwards, and black men and women from ſixteen æt. to ſixty æt. perhaps at preſent the taxables may be about 40,000.

The proprietor's quit rents are two ſhillings ſterl. per ann. for every 100 acres ; he in time patented vacant lands at four ſhillings per 100 acres ; lately he has endeavoured to let vacant lands ten ſhillings quit-rent per 100 acres, but it did not take ; he manages the patenting of lands, and collecting of the quit-rents, by agents. Not many years ſince, the aſſembly, with conſent of the lord proprietor, by way of experiment, during the term of three years, granted their proprietor in lieu of quit-rents,

a revenue

a revenue of three fhillings and fixpence fterl. duty per hogfhead of tobacco, to be paid by the merchant or fhipper. Thus the planters or affembly to eafe themfelves laid the burthen upon trade; this amounted to about 5000 *l.* fterl. per ann. but upon the expiration of the three year, this project was dropped, and the proprietor found it more for his intereft to revert to the revenue arifing from the quit-rents.

The governor's allowance of falary is as per agreement with the proprietor. The council are paid by the country 180 lb. tobacco per diem, which is much grumbled at, becaufe they are of his appointment, and his creatures. The reprefentatives are paid by the country, or publick revenue, 160 lb. tobacco per diem.

The proprietor has feveral referved good manors in many parts of the province, which he lets to farm. By his patent the proprietor is not obliged to tranfmit the provincial laws home for approbation.

Anno 1704, the affembly laid a duty of two fhillings per hogfhead tobacco, one half to the proprietor, the other half towards the charges of the government.

There is an impoft upon negro flaves of twenty fhillings fterl. and twenty fhillings currency.

As in other Britifh colonies, they have diftinct province, county, and parifh rates or taxes. The provincial taxes are polls of taxables at 90 lb. of tobacco per head or upwards, according to exigencies; upon the Cuba or Spanifh Weft-India expedition, it was 120 lb. impoft upon fervants, flaves, and liquors, excife, &c.

Currencies. The principal currency of Maryland and Virginia is tobacco per lb. or hundred weight, as it is ftated from time to time by acts of affembly, or tacit general confent of the people. In Maryland before 1734, the currency was reckoned at proclamation value, fix fhillings per heavy piece of eight; but that year the affembly went into the iniquitous fcheme of paper currency, which fraudulently had been practifed in many of our

our colonies; they emitted 90,000 *l.* in bills of publick
credit, whereof thirty shillings to every taxable, being
36,000 taxables, is 54,000 *l.* the remaining 36,000 *l.*
was to build a governor's house, and to be let upon loan :
the fund for calling in these bills of publick credit was a
duty upon liquors, &c. to be paid in sterling, and lodged
in the bank of England ; all these bills to be cancelled in
the space of thirty years. These bills were not (by an act
of assembly) receivable in the proprietor's quit-rents, and
sundry publick fees, because an ensuing depreciation was
obvious to people of foresight; and accordingly from
thirty-three and three quarters difference of exchange with
London, it gradually rose to one hundred and fifty
difference. Anno 1740, the Pensylvania eight shillings was
equal to twelve shillings Maryland ; but as the' fund for
cancelling these bills of credit was regularly transmitted to
the bank of England, they gradually recovered their value,
and anno 1748, 200 Maryland was equal to 100 sterl.

The first period for calling in and cancelling one third
of these bills was in September 1748 ; and by act of affembly there was allowed from September 29, 1748, to
March 29, 1749, to bring in all the bills to be burnt ;
accordingly of the 90,000 *l.* 83,962 *l.* 16 *s.* were brought
in (the remaining 6000 *l.* was supposed to be annihilated
by being torn, lost, &c.) and burnt, the poffeffors were
paid one third in bills of exchange upon the bank of England, and two thirds in new bills ; after sixteen years
more, the poffeffors of the two thirds will receive fifteen
shillings sterling, for every twenty shillings currency.

Courts legislative and executive.

The first settlement was at St. Mary's, near the mouth
of Potomack river : the legislative court or general affembly, and the provincial supreme court of judicature, were
kept there many years ; but anno 1699, for the better
conveniency of the whole province, they were removed
to Annapolis at the mouth of the river Severn, as being
nearly the center of the province.

At

At firſt the province was divided into ten counties, being five each ſide of the great bay.

St. Mary's,		Somerſet,	
Charles,		Dorceſter,	
Calvert,	weſt ſide.	Talbot,	eaſt ſide.
Anne Arundel,		Kent,	
Baltimore,		Cecil,	

Anno 1695, Prince George, an additional county, was conſtituted on the weſt ſide of the bay, and all the counties were divided into thirty pariſhes.

At preſent 1752, the province of Maryland is divided into fourteen counties, that is, ſeven counties each ſide of the great bay.

St. Mary's,		Worceſter,	
Calvert,		Somerſet,	
Prince George,		Dorcheſter,	
Charles,	weſt ſide.	Talbot,	eaſt ſide.
Anne Arundel,		Q. Anne's,	
Baltimore,		Kent,	
Frederick,		Cecil,	

Formerly in Maryland, the aſſembly or legiſlative lower houſe (the council is called the upper houſe of aſſembly) was triennial; at preſent they are called, adjourned, prorogued, and diſſolved at the governor's pleaſure; the repreſentatives are called the lower houſe of aſſembly.

In the government of Maryland, there are four negatives in the legiſlature, viz. the lower houſe or houſe of repreſentatives where all bills for acts originate, the governor's council, the governor, and lord proprietor.

Of the four negatives in the legiſlature, the proprietor may be ſaid to have three, viz. the proprietor's own negative, that of his governor or deputy, and that of the council nominated by himſelf.

The complement of the council is twelve, appointed by the governor general, principal, or proprietor; but paid by the province, 180 lb. tobacco per diem.

The

The lower houfe of affembly, or houfe of reprefentatives, confifts of four from each of the prefent fourteen
counties, and two from the metropolis or provincial town
of Annapolis, paid 160lb. tobacco per diem.

With regard to the executive courts, we may begin
with the parifh veftries, who not only manage the affairs
of the parifh church, but alfo manage the prudential matters of the diftrict, as the felect men, fo called in New-
England, manage their townfhip affairs ; they are alfo
affeffors of rates or taxes. In each parifh they are twelve
in number for life, and upon a demife, the furvivors fupply the vacancies after the manner of the Uræfchap, of
the towns in Holland.

The county courts in Maryland are held in the months
of March, June, Auguft, and November; at prefent
they are as follow,

1ft tuefday of faid mon. in	Talbot co. Baltimore St. Mary's Worcefter	2d tuefday of faid mon. in	Dorchefter co. Cecil Anne Arundel Charles
3d tuefday of faid mon. in	Kent co. Calvert Somerfet	4th tuefday of faid mon. in	Queen Anne's Pr. George's Frederick.

In the month of April and September, there is a cir-
cuit court of affizes for trying titles of land, and of criminal cafes : one diftinct court each fide of the bay confifting of a chief judge, an affiftant judge, and proper juries,
who fit in the refpective county court houfes.

From the county courts, there is appeal to the provincial court of Annapolis, which is held 3d Tuefday of
May, and 3d Tuefday of October, in perfonal debts of
fifty pound or upwards.

In the city of Annapolis are held quarterly mayors
courts, viz. laft Tuefday in January, April, July, and
October.

From the provincial courts, held at Annapolis, there
is allowed an appeal, in cafes of 300 *l.* fterl. value or
upwards,

upwards, to the king in council; the appeal is firſt brought under the deliberation (this is a regulation for all the colonies) of a committee of council called the lords of appeals, and from thence reported to the king in council for a final determination.

The commiſſary, a place of about 1000 *l.* per ann. is not a ſuperintendant of the clergy ; he is a judge concerning the probate of wills, granting of adminiſtrations, and the like.

The lieut. governor is chancellor, he grants licences for marrying, which are given out or ſold at twenty-five ſhillings, by a miniſter or parſon in each county, whereof twenty ſhillings to the governor, and five ſhillings to this parſon; he has fees for the great ſeal of the province, and ſundry other perquiſites; the ſalary allowed him by the proprietor is per agreement and ſeldom known ; the country generally gives three half-pence per hogſhead of tobacco exported.

The court of vice admiralty is of the ſame nature as in the colonies already deſcribed; as is aſſo

The juſticiary court of admiralty for trying caſes of piracy, robbery, and other felonies committed on the high ſeas, appointed by a commiſſion from queen Anne, purſuant to an act of parliament, 11 and 12 Gul. called an act for the more effectual ſuppreſſion of piracy.

The proprietors and deputy governors.

We have already hinted, vol. II. p. 355. that Sir George Calvert, afterwards lord Baltimore, obtained from king Charles I. a promiſe of a grant of theſe lands now called Maryland; and afterwards his ſon Cecilius lord Baltimore had a royal patent for the ſame, 1632.

During the civil wars in England, and the uſurpation of Oliver Cromwell, the concerns of the Baltimore family in Maryland lay dormant, the family being bigotted Roman catholicks. Soon after king Charles II. reſtoration, 1661, Charles lord Baltimore, ſon of Cecilius, obtained a royal confirmation of the 1632 grant;

grant; he went to Maryland, and continued there some time.

Notwithstanding the Baltimore family being rigid Roman Catholick zealots, K. James II. superseded their jurisdiction there; the scheme of the English court at that time was, to reduce all proprietary and charter govern-ments to the jurisdiction of the crown.

After the revolution of K. William III. the Baltimore family had better usage, and at present they are become good protestant subjects; for the succession of the lords Baltimore, see vol. II. p. 309. Charles lord Baltimore, member of the British parliament for the county of Sur-rey, died in April 1751, and was succeeded by his son Frederick lord Baltimore.

Upon the revolution, Sir Edmond Andros was ap-pointed governor of Maryland, and was superseded by col. Nicholson: Andros died in London 1714, in a great age.

Col. Nat. Blakiston, succeeded col. Nicholson [*i*].

Col. Blakiston was succeeded by col. William Seymour 1704: Seymour put into Barbadoes by stress of weather, and had an eight months voyage.

Col. Corbet succeeded as lieut. governor in the place of col. Seymour.

[*i*] Col. Nicholson was a knight errant governor; by his cursing, swearing, and hypocritical devotional exercises, he was at times made use of by the court in dirty affairs; particularly when any new encroach-ments upon the privileges of a people were designed with harsh usage; for instance 1686, he was appointed lieut. governor of the dominions of New-England under Sir Edmond Andros: 1710, upon the much faulted revolution in the ministry of queen Anne, he was sent to the northern colonies of British North-America, with an unprecedented commission as inspector general of all affairs, ecclesiastick, civil, and military; and in that capacity did much intimidate some governors and their councils; governor Hunter of New-York, a gentleman of spirit, told me, that if col. Nicholson had proceeded to New-York, and acted in the same manner as he did in the province of Massachusetts-Bay, he would at all risks have sent him home, to be tried by the judicatories there, as a disturber of the peace of the colony under pretext of an an-ticonstitutional unprecedented commission.

Col. Hunt arrives lieut. governor, and upon K. George's acceffion he was continued governor.

I fhall only mention the fucceffion of governors of note.

Benedict Leonard Calvert, Efq. homeward bound, died at fea 1732, and was fucceeded by Samuel Ogle, Efq.

1746-7 in March arrives Samuel Ogle, Efq. appointed lieut. governor of Maryland in the place of Thomas Bladen, Efq. Mr. Ogle continues lieutenant governor at this writing, 1752.

Produce and manufactures.

Thefe are nearly the fame in the provinces of Maryland and Virginia; this article may ferve for both.

Tobacco [k] is an aboriginal American plant or herb, and is faid to have been firft found among the Florida

[k] As the ufe of this plant or herb by an unaccountable whim is become the general amufement of Europe and of the European fettlements on the eaftern fide of North-America, by fmoaking, fnuffing, and chewing; and as no authors hitherto have given us an exact defcription or icon of this plant; I do here defcribe it from the life, by my own obfervations as it grows.

There are many curious Virginia gentlemen planters, who as botanifts cultivate varieties of tobacco; but as this is not a botanical effay, I muft drop them, and fhall only defcribe that fpecies which is cultivated and manufactured for exportation in trade.

Nicotiana major latifolia. C. B. P. M. H. 2, 492. Nicotiana major, five tabaccum majus. J. B. 3, 629. Hyofcyamus Peruvianus. Dod. p. 430. tobacco: the icons of John Bauhine and of Morifon are not exact. It is an annual plant; when it is at its full growth, it is about the height of an ordinary man; the ftalk is ftraight, hairy, and clammy, like that of the hyofcyamus niger vel vulgaris. C. B. P. common black henbane; the whole habit is of an obfolete yellowifh green; leaves alternate, fome of the lower leaves are a cubit long and nine inches wide entire, but waved; the lateral coftæ of the leaf arch into one another near the margin; the leaves have no pedicles (the major anguftifolia has long pedicles) and by an auriculated bafe embrace the ftalk; towards the top, the ftalk branches from the finufes of the leaves, and higher from the finus of a flender foliculum proceed fafcicles of

Indians

Indians, who fmoak to fatisfy their hunger: fome write, that it came from the ifland Tobago, one of the Weft-India iflands of nearly the fame name; but moft probably it came from Peru, becaufe in North-America it is not fpontaneous; the aboriginal Indians of North-America do not cultivate it, they purchafe it of the Englifh planters and fmoak it with pleafure. Its claffical or tribe name is Nicotiana, fo called from John Nicot, a Frenchman, embaffador to the court of Portugal; he fent fome of its feed, which he had from a Dutchman, to the court of France.

It has been faid by fome writers, that Sir Francis Drake firft brought it to England from the ifland Tobago of the Weft-Indies.   The name is Indian; we have no certain account of tobacco, till Sir Walter Raleigh's [l] arrival in England from Virginia, 1585; it was called Indian henbane: it was ufed by the aboriginal American

flowers: the flower is flender and tubulous, one and half inch long, yellowifh, with an obfolete diluted purple brim, not divided but expanded into four or five angles; the calix is tubulous of four or five narrow fegments; the piftillum which becomes the feed veffel is conoidal, five or fix lines diameter at bottom, and near an inch long, bicapfular with a middle fpungy double placenta, and contains many fmall round brownifh feeds; the feed is ripe the end of September.   In New-England it is planted in cows pens, it is hotter and does not fmoak fo agreeably as that of Virginia.

In trade there are only two fpecies of tobacco, viz. Aranokoe from Maryland, and the northern parts of Virginia, and fweet-fcented from the fouth parts of Virginia, whereof the beft kind is from James and York rivers: the firft is the ftrongeft, and is in demand in the northern markets of Europe; the other is milder and more pleafant: the difference feems to be only from the foil: fweet fcented which grows in fandy lands is beft for fmoaking when new, or only from two to three years old; that from ftiff land, if kept five or fix years, much exceeds the former.

[l] Sir Walter Raleigh upon his return from Virginia to London 1585, having practifed tobacco fmoaking, in a gay humour in his clofet, ordered his fervant to bring him fome fmall beer; in the mean time having lighted his tobacco pipe, and collected a mouthful of fmoak, let it fly in the fervant's face to furprize him; the fervant imagining that his mafter's face was on fire, threw the fmall beer in his face, and innocently returned the jeft.

Indians,

Indians, both in North and South-America, before the
Europeans arrived there.

Imported com. annis to Great Britain from Virginia
about 35,000 hogſheads of 800 lb. to 950 lb. wt.
per hogſhead; from Maryland about 30,000 hogſheads
of 700 lb. and upwards. It is an enumerated com-
modity, and cannot be exported from Britiſh America
to any ports than Great-Britain, and its plantations.
The neat duty upon tobacco imported into Great-
Britain is about 200,000 *l.* ſterl. per ann. and 14,000 *l.*
ſeizures. Anno 1733, when Sir Robert Walpole, firſt
commiſſioner of the treaſury, was projecting a reduction
of ſundry cuſtoms or impoſts upon goods to an exciſe; he
propoſed in parliament, that the duty upon tobacco, which
at that time was ſixpence one third per pound, ſhould be
only four pence three-farthings per pound, whereof four
pence was for exciſe and three farthings duty; this ſcheme
did not ſucceed [*m*].

By a convention or agreement between the courts of
Great-Britain and France, during the late war with
France, the farmers of tobacco in France did contract
with merchants in Great-Britain (Mr. Fitz-Gerald was
the general French agent in Britain,) for ſome Britiſh
tobacco ſhips with paſsports, and to return to Great-
Britain in ballaſt; the ſhipping ports in Great-Britain
were London, Briſtol, Liverpool, Whitehaven, and
Glaſgow: the delivery ports in France were Dieppe,
Havre-de-Grace, Morlaix, Bourdeaux, Bayonne, and
Marſeilles.

Virginia and Maryland ſometimes produce more tobacco than they can vent to advantage, by glutting the
markets [*n*] too much, and occaſions a mutinous diſpo-

[*m*] Sir Robert Walpole was very intenſe upon bringing moſt duties
partly into exciſe, and partly into cuſtoms, the better to multiply revenue officers, creatures of the miniſtry, towards carrying parliament
elections, &c.

[*n*] This is ſometimes the caſe with the Dutch Eaſt-India ſpices, and
the Weſt-India ſugars.

fition

fition among the planters, as happened in Bacon's rebellion in Virginia ; and at times to keep up the price of tobacco they burn a certain quantity for each taxable, as was done in Maryland upon the firft emiffion of paper money.

The tobacco is generally cultivated by negroes in fetts, feven or eight negroes with an overfeer is a fett; each working negro is reckoned one fhare ; the overfeer has one and a half or two fhares. The charge of a negro is a coarfe woollen jacket and breeches, with one pair of fhoes in winter ; victualling is one peck of Indian corn and fome falt per week. To prevent tobacco from becoming a drug, no taxable is to cultivate above fix thoufand plants of tobacco, befides grain.

The plantation duty is one penny fterl. per pound, upon tobacco exported to the other colonies, and is about 200 *l.* towards the revenue of the college of Williamfburg in Virginia.

Tobacco is not only their chief produce for trade, but may alfo be called their medium or currency ; it is received in taxes or debts : the infpector's notes for tobacco received by him, may be transferred, and upon fight of thefe notes the infpector immediately delivers to the bearer fo much tobacco.

Formerly the tobacco affair was managed by receivers at culling houfes near the fhipping places, where the planter delivered his tobacco to the merchant ; at prefent in every river there is a certain number of country ftores where the planters tobacco is lodged ; every hogfhead is branded with the marks of the planter, ftore, and river.

The common culture of tobacco is in this manner. The feed is fowed in beds of fine mould, and tranfplant. d the beginning of May ; the plants are fet at three or four feet intervals or diftances ; they are hilled and kept continually weeded ; when as many leaves are fho. out as the foil can nourifh to advantage, the plant is ftopt and

it

it grows no higher; it is wormed from time to time; the fuckers which put forth between the leaves are. taken off from time to time till the plant arrives to perfection, which is in Auguft, when the leaves begin to turn brownifh and fpot; in a dry time the plant is cut down and hanged up to dry, after being fweated in heaps for one night; when it may be handled without crumbling (tobacco is not handled but in moift weather,) the leaves are ftript off from the ftalk, tied up in little bundles and packt up in hogfheads for tranfportation. No fuckers nor ground leaves are allowed to be merchantable.

An induftrious man may manage 6000 plants of tobacco, and four acres of Indian corn.

The fmall quantity of tobacco which fome people raife in Penfylvania and North-Carolina is generally fhipt off from Maryland and Virginia.

Tobacco is injurious to the nerves, it is fomewhat [o] anodyne, and intoxicates perfons not ufed to it.

Pork, Vaft number of fwine or hogs run wild or ramble in the woods of Maryland, Virginia, and North-Carolina; they are generally fmall; falted and barrelled; they make a confiderable branch of the export of thefe colonies; they feed moftly upon nuts of all kinds, called maft; they eat oily and rank.

Maft [p] or foreft nuts of many kinds are very plenty every fecond or third year, and the following year not fo plenty; thus it is with apples and cyder in New-England; the plenty and confequently the price of pork from Maryland, Virginia, and North-Carolina, depends upon

---

[o] The Europeans ufe wine, and other fermented liquors, as alfo fpirits diftilled from them; the Turks, Perfians, and other oriental nations, ufe opium, bang, betel, &c. all which occafion a fort of indolence or relaxation of mind: thus mankind by a natural tacit confent allow, that the intenfe application of mind, the cares and inquietudes of life, require fome fuch expedients of alleviation.

[p] This word or term feems to proceed from the latin word mafticare.

the goodnefs of their mafting years; anno 1733, a good maft year, one man a planter and merchant in Virginia, falted up three thoufand barrels of pork. Next to the pork fed with Indian corn as in New-England, acorns make firmeft pork; beech nuts make fweet pork, but flabby, foft and oily. In Weftphalia, the hogs in the woods feed moftly upon cheftnuts.

Grain. Wheat in Maryland and Virginia is fubject to the weevel, a fmall infect of the fcarabeous kind, which fometimes takes to it in the ear when growing. The Maryland and Virginia wheat weighs fome 56 lb. to 60 lb. wt. per bufhel, and cafts white; that from Penfylvania does not weigh fo much; the wheat formerly imported from Nova-Scotia was light and caft dark like rye; at prefent the prairies, as they are called, or the diked in wheat lands are wore out. May the prefent political diverting publick amufement of improving Nova-Scotia, become intentionally real, towards a fifhery, a place of arms for our navies, a nurfery of hufbandmen, and a northern frontier for the protection of our Britifh colonies.

Good land in Maryland and Virginia may yield per acre 15 bufhels wheat, or 30 bufhels Indian corn, which cafts whiter than that of New-England.

Calavances are exported to feveral of the other colonies. Phafeolus erectus minor femine fphaerico albido et rubro, hilo nigro. C. B. P. white and red calavances, or Virginia peafe; they yield better than the common peafe of Europe, and are good profitable food for the poorer fort of white people, and for negro flaves.

Maize or Indian corn has been already defcribed.

They raife in the uplands, quantities of hemp and flax. Anno 1751, in October, from the back fettlements of Maryland, there came into Baltimore town near the bottom of Chefepeak bay, fixty waggons loaden with flax feed. In fome counties of Maryland are erected charity working fchools.

B b 4   Towards

Towards the mountains there are fome furnaces for running of iron ore into pigs and hollow caft ware, and forges
to refine pig iron into bars.

Timber and other wooden lumber.   Their oak is of a
ftraight grain, and eafily rives into ftaves; in building
of veffels it is not durable, they build only fmall craft;
fome years fince they built a very large fhip called the
Britifh merchant, burthen one thoufand hogfheads; with
many repairs fhe kept in the Virginia trade thirty-fix
years.

Their black walnut is in demand for cabinets, tables,
and other joiners work.

Maryland and Virginia produce large beautiful apples,
but very mealy; their peaches are plenty and good; from
thefe they diftil a fpirit, which they call cyder brandy
and peach brandy.

The Maryland affairs, concerning their cuftom houfes
and naval officers, the number of entries and clearances
of veffels, the quality and quantity of their exports and
imports, and the tribe of officers thereto belonging, are
not hitherto fully come to my knowledge: I do not chufe
to infert any thing that is not in fome regard perfect,
therefore at prefent, I fhall only copy a few lines from
the lateft prefent ftate of Great-Britain.   I obferve their
falaries are fmall.

North Potomack	A collector and to keep a boat
Patuxent	A collector and to keep a boat
Annapolis	A furveyor
Potomack	A collector and to keep a boat
Both fides of the bay	A riding furveyor
Williamftade	A furveyor
Bohama and Saffefras	A riding furveyor
Wicomoc and Munia	A furveyor
Delaware bay	A furveyor

I

MISCEL-

Miscellanies.

As many things defigned for a general appendix, muft be loofe, incoherent, and not fluent; for the eafe of common readers, we fhall annex fome part of it to each of the fubfequent fections by the name of mifcellanies, being of things omitted, or that were not come to my knowledge at the times of writing, or not reduceable to particular fections. As I have all along given it the cha-racter of common-place, the fummary in propriety may admit of this latitude.

In the Rhode-Ifland fection was omitted an authentick court paper, dated Windfor, Sept. 13, 1686, concerning the furrender of Rhode-Ifland charter. "His majefty " has gracioufly received the addrefs of the colony of " Rhode-Ifland and Providence plantations in New-Eng- " land; humbly reprefenting that upon the fignification " of a writ of quo warranto againft their charter, they " had refolved in a general affembly not to ftand fuit " with his majefty, but wholly to fubmit to his royal " pleafure themfelves and their charter wherefore his " majefty has thought fit to accept the furrender." *N. B.* As the Rhode-Ifland charter was not vacated by any procefs in the courts of law, and the voluntary fur-render not properly recorded; upon the revolution of K. William they reaffumed their charter, and their actings in purfuance of that charter are deemed good by the court of Great-Britain.

In the mifcellany article of the fection of Penfyl-vania, vol. II. p. 337, was inferted a letter from the lord juftices of Great-Britain to Mr. D. ——— com-mander in chief of the province of Maffachufetts-Bay, concerning an illegally projected fynod or confiftory of the congregational [*q*] minifters in that colony; in this

---

[*q*] Befides other inconveniencies, there feems to be an impropriety or inconfiftency in congregationalift or independent religious focie-

                                                                letter

letter Mr. D——— feems to be faulted as conniving at
fuch anti-conftitutional proceedings; as this gentleman
was noted for his fidelity to the crown, and probity towards the people under his direction, when in the adminiftration of that colony, I cannot avoid publifhing his
vindication of himfelf in a letter to the board of trade
and plantations.

" My Lords,
" By a fhip lately arrived, I received from their ex-
" cellencies, the lords juftices, an inftruction for my
" future proceedings with refpect to a fynod propofed
" to be held by the minifters of this his majefty's pro-
" vince, which fhall be punctually obeyed as there fhall
" be occafion; their lordfhips were alfo pleafed to cen-
" fure the proceedings already had in that affair. Where-
" fore I think myfelf obliged to acquaint your lord-
" fhips, that I did not pafs a confent for a fynod, but
" only to a vote of the council and affembly, referv-
" ing the confideration thereof to the next feffions,
" as you will fee by the copies of the votes of that
" feffions tranfmitted to you foon after the rifing of the
" court; and I was then of opinion it would not come
" on the carpet again, as it never did, notwithftand-
" ing the prefent feffions had been fitting for fome weeks
" before their lordfhips orders concerning the fame
" was received; neverthelefs I fhould have taken myfelf
" obliged to have afked your lordfhips directions
" therein, if I had apprehended it to be of a new and
" extraordinary nature; but I muft obferve, that a vote
" in the fame words was paffed on the like occafion
" by his majefty's council here in the year 1715, and
" never as I have heard of, cenfured by your lordfhips;
" and here I humbly take leave to fay in behalf of

ties petitioning for a fynod, or fuperior collective authority: it
feems to intimate that the fubordinate claffical way of fubordination
in church government with the prefbyterians, is natural in its ten-
dency.

" the

" the minifters of this province, that I know them to be
" a body of men moft loyal and inviolably attached to
" his majefty, and to his illuftrious houfe, and there-
" fore I did not apprehend any inconvenience could arife
" from their affembling, efpecially fince they make no
" pretences that I know of to do any acts of authority,
" in fuch meetings, though they call them by the name
" of fynod."

From the accounts we have from time to time received
from Penfylvania, of the Moravian fectary there, and of
a late act of the Britifh parliament in their favour, it was
imagined that they were inoffenfive in their devotional
way; but their late character from Germany, feems to
caution againft their proceedings.

A continuation from the Moravian affairs, vol. II.
p. 154, 335. The Moravian indifcreet zealots [r] have
been continually endeavouring to part members from all
the three eftablifhed profeffions, (Papifts, Lutherans, and
Calvinifts) in the holy Roman empire, efpecially of
tender minds. The Bohemia and Moravian brethren,
by fcandalous fongs, fermons, and writings, obtruded as
gofpel truths under the count of Zinzendorf, a new
fort of religion; not to be tolerated in the laws of the
holy Roman empire; they ufed Herenhutifh fongs,
method, and books of inftitution, count of Iffenburgh
and Badingen.

In Maryland and Virginia there is a general toleration
to legally qualified minifters, to officiate in places legally
licenfed.

Hanover is fixty miles from Williamfburg. A minifter qualified, and a meeting licenfed, may claim the

[r] The vermin in all religions, have been enthufiafts, indifcreet
zealot. or bigots, and political managers to ferve the court miniftry in
their projects.

liberties of toleration, taking the ufual government oaths, getting the meeting houfes recorded, and fubfcribing the articles of the church of England, except the 34, 35, 36, and this claufe in the 20th article, " The church hath " power to decree rites and ceremonies, and authority in " controverfies of faith." Thefe prefbyterians voluntarily put themfelves under the immediate care of the prefbytery of Newcaftle and fynod of New-York; which they may caft off at pleafure.

Mr. Davies a prefbyterian minifter came into this colony 1748, and obtained licenfes for feven meeting-houfes, an extravagant pluraliry; among thefe he divided his time, viz. three in Hanover county, one in Henrico county fouthward, one in Carolina county northward, one in Louifa county weftward, and one in Gooch land to the S. W. of Hanover; thefe affemblies are generally called new lights, and may confift of about 300 communicants. Mr. Davies wrote anno 1751; there were not ten diffenters within a hundred miles of Hanover when he arrived there.

There is an immenfe quantity of land unfettled weftward between Hanover county, and the rivers which fall into the Miffiffippi river. The three frontier counties in Virginia, of Frederick, Augufta, and Lunenburgh, are prodigioufly large, and generally fettled by Irifh prefbyterians, as is alfo Amelia and Albemarle counties. In Virginia to the weftward, they are continually making new counties, as they do new townfhips in New-England.

The county courts grant meeting-houfe licenfes, but may be negatived by the fuperior or fupreme court. Sometimes the county courts deny the granting of licenfes, and fometimes county licenfes when granted, are negatived by the council, alledging that it does not belong to a county court to proceed in fuch affairs, and that a diffenting minifter can have no legal tolerated right to more meeting-houfes than one.

The

The [*s*] frontier counties of Maryland and Virginia are generally inhabited (as I hinted before) by north of Ireland Scots prefbyterians, who landed in Penfylvania, but fold their improvements there to the more induftrious German fettlers: their pulpit difcourfes are (generally new-lights fo called) againft the modifh fyftem of Arminianifm, moral duties, and fpeculative truths: fome of them are under the care of the imaginary fynod of Philadelphia, fome belong to the fynod of New-York; but under the immediate care of the prefbytery of Newcaftle: in this prefbytery there are twelve members, and two or three candidates upon probation.

Roman [*t*] Catholicks abound in Maryland.

[*s*] Mr. D——ies, a diffenting prefbyterian minifter of Hanover county in Virginia, in a piece which he printed 1751, concerning the ftate of religion among the proteftant diffenters in Virginia, gives fome informations concerning thefe affairs, but with a new-light, or enthufiaftick turn.   He writes, that there has been a confiderable revival, or rather fettlement of religion, in Baltimore county of Maryland, which lies along Sefquahana river and borders on Penfylvania; as alfo in Kent county, and queen Anne's county between Chefepeak bay and Delaware river.   He fays, there have been in Maryland and Virginia a great number of Scots merchants, (he means merchants clerks, fuper-cargoes, and fubfuper-cargoes) who were educated in the prefbyterian way; but generally prove a fcandal to their religion and country, by their loofe principles, and immoral behaviour, and become indifferent in religious profeffions, and affect politenefs in turning deifts, or fafhionable conformifts. *N. B.* Young perfons of any nation, after being fettered with peculiar religion modes, when turned loofe, they become wanton, and indulge themfelves in irregularities.

[*t*] It is not eafily to be accounted for, that the Britifh government are not more fedulous, in purging off by lenitives, not by drafticks, the pernicious leaven of popery (their doctrine of no faith to be kept with hereticks or diffenters from them, deftroys all fociety) which prevails in Montferrat, Maryland, and Ireland. The lift of proteftants and papifts in Ireland, as computed (in all cafes, I ufe the laft computations that are in my knowledge) anno 1732 and 1733.   Proteftant families.   Popifh families.

	Proteftant families.	Popifh families.
In Ulfter	62,620 ————————	38,459
Leinfter	25,238 ————————	92,424
Munfter	13,337 ————————	106,407
Connaught	4,299 ————————	44,133
	105,494	281,423

Aa

: [*u*] An indolent way of reading their publick prayers and fermons prevails in our colonies.

The medical digreſſion continued.

The ſcience or art of medicine will ever remain weak in theory, and muſt be ſupplied by experience, and ſome ſpecificks (I do not mean quack noſtrums) whoſe ſalutary operations or effects in ſome diſeaſes have been diſcovered, not by inveſtigation but by chance; ſuch as the Peruvian bark, mercury, opium.

Experience and ſedulous obſervation are too much ne-glected by the indolent practitioners of our colonies; they chuſe to practiſe from authorities, whereas authorities muſt always give way to experience; the nature of medical affairs allow of no other demonſtration than that of good obſervation; Sydenham on the ſmall pox is reckoned his maſter-piece [*x*].

[*u*] The churches where the miniſter reads the prayers and fermons may be called reading 'houſes, and the miniſter may be called the reader, but at preſent only the aſſiſtant miniſter is called the reader and lecturer: in Scotland, and in the foreign churches of all denominations, reading of fermons and diſcourſes is not practiſed.

[*x*] From my practice relating to the ſmall-pox, which prevailed in Boſton 1721, and 1730, for the benefit of the publick, eſpecially of my neighbours or townſmen; I beg the reader's indulgence in allowing me to obſerve, that in the management of the ſpread-ing ſmall-pox, it may be adviſeable for perſons much advanced in years, and conſequently their juices rancid, and perſons infirm and of a bad habit of body, to avoid the infection by retiring into the coun-try for a few months, conſidering that the ſmall-pox does not prevail in Boſton, but after long periods; ſince the firſt ſettlement of Boſton the ſmall-pox was epidemical or popular only 1649, 1666, 1677 and 1678, 1689 and 1690, 1702, 1721, 1730, the preſent ſmall-pox 1752, per-haps may ſpread or not ſpread. All other perſons, eſpecially children, may continue in town and run the riſk in the natural way or by inocula-tion, after a previous proper regimen: this regimen, according to the beſt of my judgment, is a mercurial purge or two, a ſoft diet; avoid catching of cold, uſe no violent exerciſe of body or perturbation of mind; upon ſeizure, if the patient is plethorick, and the fever runs high, blood-letting is adviſeable (but not upon or after eruption) and gives room for nature to act her part at more liberty; in the beginning a gentle emetick or vomit is of good uſe, it renders the habit of the

.N

In

In our colonies, if we deduct persons who die of old age, of mala stamina vitæ or original bad constitutions, of intemperance, and accidents, there are more die of the practitioner than of the natural course of the distemper under proper regimen. The practitioners generally, without any considerate thought, fall into some routine of method, and medicines, such as repeated blood-lettings, opiates, emeticks, catharticks, mercurials, Peruvian bark.

In our various colonies to prevent a notorious depopulation from mal-practice in medicine or cure of diseases; there may be acts of assembly for the regulation thereof, which at present is left quite loose. A young man without any liberal education, by living a year or two in any quality with a practitioner of any sort, apothecary, cancer doctor, cutter for the stone, bone-setters, tooth-drawer, &c. with the essential fundamentals of ignorance and impudence, is esteemed to qualify himself for all the branches of the medical art, as much or more than gentlemen in Europe well born, liberally educated (and therefore modest likewise) have travelled much, attended medical professors of many denominations, frequented city hospitals, and camp infirmaries, &c. for many years.

In the expressions of Hippocrates, this is literally an ars longa; it requires long experience and observation with a peculiar sagacity; in practice a dull application (we cannot much boast of application) does not answer; there must be a suitable genius, and sometimes a particular paroxysm of imagination, as is remarkable in poets and painters, and as I have observed in myself, in the diagnostick part of our profession. Knowledge, that is, observation and sagacity are the two great requisites in a physician.

body more meable in circulation, by its shocks; during the course of this distemper, dilute plentifully, use a cool but not cold regimen; in the declension use gentle catharticks: by this management many of my small-pox patients have sustained the distemper with ease, and without decumbiture or confinement.

In

In our colonies, how can a young man of no previous liberal education, or difpofition to a peculiar knowledge in the affair, in a few years attendance in an apothecary's fhop, and a few months travel, without practical knowledge, attain to any degree of perfection in this profeffion? Thefe things are not myfteries or infpirations of particular perfons in the cafe, but an impudent delufion and fraud. I fhall not call upon any man's name in the queftion, left it fhould appear a malicious or invidious refentment for fecret injuries done, not in the way of medical practice, but in——fuch things we may in a chriftian fpirit forgive, but naturally we cannot forget.

The practice of phyfick requires much circumfpection and difcretion, only to be attained by a long and attentive practice. The conftitutions and other circumftances occafion the fame fpecies of a diftemper to appear varioufly; for inftance,

Inebriation, an illnefs very obvious and too common in our colonies : fome it renders more vigorous, in others the tongue and limbs faulter ; fome are ferious, that is, praying or crying drunk; fome are mad or furious, fome dull and fleepy; fome gay and witty, fome dull and filly. Thus it is in all diftempers, the fymptoms vary according to the conftitution, and in the general indications of cure ought to be allowed for.

In aftronomy the inequality of the motions of the feveral planets are many and various, but by indefatigable obfervations they are reduced to equations or rules; but it is to be feared that in our microcofm or animal œconomy, there are fo many inequalities as not to admit of any fixed rules, but muft be left to the fagacity of fome practitioners, and to the rafhnefs of others.

S E C T.

S E C T. XVI.

Concerning the Colony and Dominions of Virginia.

COlumbus's difcoveries of America, fet all trading or navigating nations into the humour of difcoveries weftward of Europe. The Cabots of Briftol, Italian mariners, obtained a patent from king Henry VII. (fee vol. I. p. 111.) anno 1495, for all lands they fhould difcover weft of Europe, with certain royal refervations: they ranged the eaftern fhore of North-America, and took a formal, but imaginary poffeffion without occupancy of fundry parts thereof. From that time, for near a century, that coaft was not fo much as navigated by the Englifh; until Sir Walter Raleigh obtained a patent from queen Elizabeth, March 25, 1584, for difcoveries and fettlements in America. See vol. I. p. 112. Raleigh and his affociates fitted out two veffels, in a round-about courfe by way of the Canaries and Caribbee Weft-India iflands to the coaft of Virginia, they fell in with the ifland Roanoke upon the North-Carolina fhore, at the Roanoke inlet (about 36 d. N. lat.) of Albemarle found or river.

Sir Richard Grenville, the chief of Sir Walter Raleigh's affociates, 1585, at his return to England, left 108 men upon Roanoke ifland, under Mr. Ralph Lane; from imprudent management, they were in danger of being ftarved; but Sir Francis Drake in his expedition to the Weft-Indies, had inftructions upon his return to England, to touch in there, and carried thefe miferable people home to England. At the fame time Sir Walter Raleigh in a fhip, and about a fortnight after Sir Richard Grenville with three fhips, failed thither. Sir Walter fell in with cape Hatteras a little fouthward of Roanoke; having no intelligence of the people left at Roanoke, he returned to England: Sir Richard found the ifland, but no people; he left fifty men upon the island with two years provisions, and returned to England; these fifty men were all killed by the Indians.

Next summer, 1587, three ships with men and women settlers and provisions arrived at Roanoke, and formed themselves into a government, consisting of a governor, Mr. John White, and twelve counsellors, incorporated by the name of the governor and assistants of the city of Raleigh in Virginia: this settlement when Mr. White returned to England, consisted of 115 persons.

It was two years before Mr. White could obtain the necessary recruits of supplies; after a tedious passage with three ships, he arrived at cape Hatteras, August 1590, but in a violent storm they parted from their cables, drove to sea, and returned to England, without visiting the poor settlers, to whom no visit was attempted for the sixteen following years, and perhaps cut off by the Indians, being never heard of afterwards.

In pursuance of the new-charter of 1606, capt. Newport, vice admiral, with settlers, (some Poles, and Dutch to make tar, pitch, pot-ashes and glass,) arrived at cape Henry the beginning of May 1607; he sailed up Powhatan or James river many miles, founded James-town, and at his return for England left about 200 persons there; these may properly be called the first settlers of the colony; many of them died, and were much molested by the Indians. 1619 there arrived a large supply of 1216 people, they made many settlements: and 1620 an assembly of representatives called burgesses was instituted, and in the year following courts of judicature were appointed.

We may observe, that capt. John Smith, called the traveller, designed for Roanoke where Mr. John White had left 115 persons, fell in between the capes of Virginia, the southermost he called cape Henry, the northermost cape Charles, in honour of the king's sons; the Indian name of the bay was Chesepeak; the first great river they met with was on the south side of
this

this bay, by the Indians called Powhatan, and by the English named James river, the king of England's name: about fifty miles up this river, they made a settlement upon a peninsula, being convenient for navigation, trade, and easily fortified, and called it James-town. From that time we have had an uninterrupted possession of that country.

Capt. Smith in his history relates many misadventures of the first Virginia settlers, viz. a third supply was sent from England 1609, being nine ships, and 500 people, under Sir Thomas Gates, Sir George Somers, and capt. Newport; the fleet was scattered in a storm, and only seven vessels arrived; the commission or patent was in one of the missing ships; this Virginia settlement from 500, were soon reduced to sixty persons, almost famished by mismanagement; but Sir Thomas Gates, and Sir George Somers, who saved themselves with 150 more people in Bermudas, built two small cedar barks, set out May 10, 1610, and arrived in Virginia the 20th, to the comfort of the remaining Virginia settlers; soon finding much misery, they all embark to abandon the country, but in falling down the river, they were met by lord Delaware with three ships, and all necessaries; Sir George Somers returned to Bermudas in his former cedar bark of thirty tons, to fetch provisions, and soon died there, æt. 60. Lord Delaware returned to England, and left capt. George Percy commander. 1611, May 10, arrived Sir Thomas Dale with three ships, men, cattle, and provisions: August 4, arrives Sir Thomas Gates, governor, with six tall ships, 300 men, 100 kine, and other cattle, provisions, and ammunition. 1612, arrives capt. Argol, with men and provisions [y]. 1614, Sir Thomas Gates and capt. Argol return to England, and capt. Yearly is left commander.

[y] 1613, Mr. John Rolfe married Pocahantes, daughter of Powhatan, the king of the Indians, and peace with the Indians continued

C c 2

he fell in with Penfylvania-bay, inftead of Chefepeak
or Virginia-bay, and gave name to it (this was before the Dutch fettled) which it retains to this day;
he foon returned to England. Lord Delaware in his
fecond voyage to Virginia 1618, died in the paffage; in his firft voyage he arrived in Virginia, June
9, 1610, and continued governor until March following.

1626, Becaufe of the bad conduct of the managers,
and hardfhips fuftained by the fettlers, by a quo warranto
the patent was fued out, both property and jurifdiction
became vefted in the crown, where it remains to this
day; the fettlers pay two fhillings fterling per annum
quit-rent per 100 acres, under the direction of a king's
governor and council, with an affembly or houfe of reprefentatives chofen by the people; thefe three negatives
compofe the legiflature or general court.

When capt. Smith, fome time prefident of Virginia,
wrote his hiftory 1624, within fixty miles of James-town,
the principal fettlement, there were not above 1500 fencible men, and for want of raifing provifion fufficient,
they could not upon any exigency bring above 700 men
together.

Becaufe of notorious bad management, the company
was diffolved by king Charles I. and the colony was
brought under the immediate direction of the crown as
above, and fettlers flocked over; particularly fome of
good condition to enjoy the liberty of worfhipping God
in their own manner; lord Baltimore, a Roman catholick,
retired thither, but the people of Virginia, rigid proteftants, did not ufe him well, and he was difcouraged from
continuing in Virginia, as we have more at large related
in the fection of Maryland.

The firft fettlers intent upon taking up large tracts of
land, occafioned the feveral fettlements to be difperfed at
confiderable diftances from one another, and not in towns
or villages.

At

At prefent the jurifdiction or government is bounded
fouth by a line W. by compafs (the variation there being fmall, is neglected) dividing Virginia from North-
Carolina, beginning at a certain great tree in the north
latitude of about 36 d. 40 m. (in its progrefs it in-
terfects the river Roanoke many times in its meanders,)
and continues weft indefinitely; the weftern boundary
is the South-Sea, or lands in a prior occupancy of any
chriftian prince; it is bounded northerly, on the eaft
fide of Chefepeak bay by a line running due eaft from
Watkins-Point, near Wighco river on Chefepeak in
about the latitude of 38 d. 10 m. to the ocean; on
the weft fide of Chefepeak bay it is bounded by Potomack river to a certain head thereof, and thence by a
weft line indefinitely in lat.—This Maryland line of
jurifdiction with the province of Virginia, and of property with lord Fairfax, is not hitherto finally fettled;
eaft and fouth, Virginia is bounded by the great ocean.

K. Charles II. having gratified fome noblemen with
two large grants called the northern and fouthern grants
or necks; when thefe noblemen claimed them, it gave
great uneafinefs to the fettlers, and the colony agents in
England agreed with thefe grantees of two necks, for a
fmall confideration.

Virginia is divided by the great rivers of Potomack,
Rapanahock, York, and James, into four necks, the two
counties eaft of Chefepeak bay make the fifth great divifion; the divifion between Potomack and Rapahan-
nock rivers, is called the northern neck, and is at prefent
the property of lord Fairfax of Cameron, an Englifhman
with a Scots title.

Lord Colpepper, who came over governor of Virginia
1679, was one of K. Charles II. patentees of the northern neck; having got affignments from the other patentees, 1688, 4th Jac. II. he obtained a patent for
all the northern neck; and by inveigling the tenants
to pay the quit-rents to his agents, he became poffeffed of all the quit-rents, and his heirs at prefent en-

joy them by a kind of prefcription, but without any fhare in the jurifdiction, becaufe chargeable: he relinquifhed the government thereof to the crown. Lord Colpepper of Thorfway in England died 1719, having no male heir, the heritors are extinct; his daughter and heirefs married lord Fairfax: thus Virginia confifts of two properties in one government.

Here we muft obferve, that the continuation of this hiftorical eflay was interrupted for fome months, by the unlucky incident of an epidemical diftemper: the fmall-pox, after about twenty-two years abfence, being imported, and prevailing in Bofton of New-England; the printer and his people in fear of the fmall-pox, left their printing office in Bofton, and retired into the country.

We may alfo obferve, that the writer from an entire and unavoidable avocation of mind from all other matters but thofe of his profeffion, finds the thread of his narration affected, which with the growing remotenefs of the provinces to be treated of, will render the following accounts lefs minute, but always avoiding any deviation from truth.

A Digreffion concerning the fmall-pox.

The appendix [b] according to our firft fcheme would have been out of proportion too large; therefore we fhall occafionally interfperfe fome things defigned for the appendix, more efpecially relating to diftempers at times epidemical or endemial in the Britifh North-America

[b] This hiftory or rather thefe minutes (as we have frequently hinted) were originally defigned as a common place loofely put together, but in an hiftorical manner; if they prove informing and ufeful, fome fubfequent writers may digeft them: it is as much as my leifure time does allow, to draw the plan, and lay in the materials; a good artificer may with eafe erect the edifice.

I   colonies:

colonies: as the fmall-pox has lately been epidemical or very general in Bofton of New-England, from the beginning of April, to near the end of July 1752, I fhall here infert fome particular obfervations concerning the fame, while recent in my mind.

I. There are many things infcrutable in the nature of this diftemper. ' 1. Why it did not emerge, or at leaft why it is not mentioned in hiftory fooner than the beginning of the Saracen conquefts? 2. Seeing it is univerfally agreed, that a perfon who has had the fmall pox once, is not liable to it again, the feminium thereof being fuppofed exhaufted : how is it that parents who have procreated after having had the fmall-pox, their progeny is notwithftanding liable to receive the fmall-pox infection? 3. How is it that a woman having the fmall-pox when pregnant, the foetus does not receive the fmall-pox from the mother, but may receive it many years after being born? this was the cafe of eapt. B—— doge of Salem and others in my knowledge. 4. How is it that the difpofition of the air (Sydenham calls them, various fmall-pox conftitutions) in fundry years is more or lefs conducive to propagate the fmall-pox infection, and to render that diftemper more or lefs deleterious; thus we find by the bills of mortality of London, Edinburgh, and other great towns where the fmall-pox is never abfent, that the number of fmall-pox burials in various years differs much [c], without regard to the varieties of feafons and weather, and without regard to the more or lefs pernicious modes and fafhions of managing the fmall-pox; modes or authorities of leading phyficians have from time to time pernicioufly been introduced into medicine, witnefs in the fmall-pox, Morton's alexipharmicks, Sydenham's opiates,

[c] Within the London bills of mortality there died anno 1746, of the fmall-pox 3336; anno 1751, there died of the fmall pox 998: in Edinburgh and Weft-Kirk parifh, there died anno 1743, of the fmall-pox 249; anno 1747, there died 71.

and the repeated blood-lettings of some present noted practitioners in Great-Britain. May physicians in writing avoid all fashionable whims and cant of the times; such as were formerly occult and specifick qualities, chemical reasonings, mechanical powers, and the like: they are of no use, and soon become obsolete.

II. I have been a sedulous attendant and observer of the small-pox, which in Boston happened to be epidemical anno 1721, 1730, and 1752. In the year 1721, being a sort of novice in the small-pox practice, I confided too much in the method of the celebrated Dr. Sydenham, particularly his cold regimen, and frequent use of vitriolicks and opiates, but from their bad success I gradually corrected myself: 1730 I abandoned the cold regimen, and substituted a moderately cool regimen: I laid aside the frequent use of sp. vitrioli, as occasioning nauseas in the stomach, and of opiates as a remora or clog of the course of any distemper, and as it solicits the morbid affection to the brain; with success I followed the purging method in the declension of the small-pox; I had the hint from the accidental natural purgings in that period which saved the lives of many, and was confirmed therein by the observations of Freind and Mead. 1752, I depended almost entirely upon the fund or stock of my own observations, and my principal indications were from the juvantia and lædentia [d].

[d] Where these are not followed, medicine becomes a mere whim, and a ludibrium of the people; as in the small pox, some follow a hot regimen, some a cold regimen, some use repeated blood-lettings, some a frequent use of opiates; others declare them pernicious; some keep the body costive, some use the purging method, &c. it is only the juvantia and lædentia can determine the question, as they have in the instances of Sydenham's grand mistakes of keeping the body bound, and frequent use of opiates. The mistakes of the most celebrated practitioners ought to be more canvassed, as their authorities are dangerous precedents.

III. I am

III. I am perfuaded that during the laft twenty-two years abfence of the fmall-pox in Bofton, from 1730 to 1752, if it had been allowed its free courfe, confidering that perfons when children would have been the fubjects of it, fewer would have died of it, than have died of it in a few months 1752. If it is not allowed its free courfe when it does invade Bofton epidemically, particular perfons not qualified to receive it may avoid it, by retiring into the country for a few months. The not qualified are infants, their ftamina vitæ are too tender; pregnant women; pubefcentes and for a few years after puberty, while their juices are in a juvenile fret; perfons upwards of forty-five æt. (I write from obfervation, not from abftracted imagination) becaufe their juices become rancid; and all perfons under any conftitutional or habitual diftemperature of body, particularly the fcrophulous or ftrumous, who generally fuffer much in this diftemper; we may remark that the fmall-pox fometimes leaves fcrophulous difpofitions in perfons formerly not fcrophulous. All others to render the fubfequent parts of their life more eafy, may run the rifk in the natural, that is, accidental way (by the pores of the fkin, by infpiration, deglutition, &c.) or by the more favourable way of inoculation.

IV. Before I proceed farther, I fhall give a general numerical hiftory of the Bofton New-England periods, &c. of epidemical fmall-pox. From the firft fettling of the province of Maffachufetts-Bay the fmall-pox has been epidemical in Bofton only eight times, 1649, 1666, 1678, 1689, 1702, 1721, 1730, and 1752: I fhall enumerate the periods which happened in this current century.

1702, beginning of July, the fmall-pox appeared after thirteen years abfence; the alexipharmick method and hot regimen were ufed; about 300 white people died of
this

this fmall-pox [e]; the moft burials were in the month of December, 74 [f].

1721, it was imported (from Barbadoes) by the Saltortugas fleet middle of April; it continued fkulking about until the middle of June, when the eruptions appearing in many families, the watches appointed to prevent its fpreading were difcontinued, and it was allowed to take its courfe. In the next parcel of decumbents, the eruptions appeared about the feventh or eighth of July. In the end of July it fpread much; in October was the higheft number of deaths, and about the middle of October fmall-pox burials began to decreafe. Æneas Salter, employed by the felect men of Bofton (the prudential manager of town affairs) to make a fcrutiny after the fmall-pox ceafed, by a book in feveral columns of lifts, he found that the number of perfons who continued in Bofton (many fled into the country) were 10,567, whereof about 700 efcaped; the fmall-pox decumbents had been 5989, whereof 844 died, which is nearly one in feven. ——This fmall-pox continued in Bofton eight months; about eighty died with purples and hæmorrhages, which is about one in ten of the deaths. —— In and about Bofton 286 were inoculated, whereof the inoculators acknowledge fix to have died, which is about one in forty-eight.

The fmall-pox of 1730 was imported from Ireland in the autum 1729, and was fhut up in a few families during winter; beginning of March following it fpread much, the watches were removed, and the fourth of

[e] Hitherto petechiæ (purple fpots) and hæmorrhages, of which many died, were called a mortal fcarlet fever invading the town at the fame time with the fmall-pox, but an entirely diftinct diftemper: 1721 I was the firft who in New-England introduced them as deleterious fymptoms in the fmall-pox.

[f] In the beginning of this century, the inhabitants of Bofton, blacks included, were about 6750, and the burials communibus annis about 230. Anno 1720, the inhabitants were circiter 11,000, and burials communibus annis about 350. Anno 1735, (1729 and 1730 were meafles and fmall-pox years) the inhabitants were about 15,000, and burials communibus annis 500.

March

March 1729-30 it had a free course, and inoculation was allowed. The highest number of burials after nine years abfence was in June, it ended with the month of October. The decumbents were eftimated at about 4000 (no exact fcrutiny was made) whereof about 500 died, which is nearly one in eight, and of thefe about feventy-five with purples and hæmorrhages, Of not quite 400 inoculated in Bofton twelve died, which is about one in thirty-three; the inoculated fmall-pox was not fo favourable as 1721, they were loaded, and a more protracted confinement; many of their incifions fuffered much, and required the fpecial care of a furgeon for a confiderable time; of the twelve deaths three proceeded from the incifions ulcerating and putrifying, S—ry W——d's child, col. Ch——ley's child, Mr. G——e's forman.

The fmall-pox of 1752. A fhip from London, capt. Coufins, with the fmall-pox aboard, was bulged Dec. 24, 1751, in Nahant bay near Bofton; the people of Chelfey, the adjacent town, compaffionately affifting to fave the fhip's crew, received the fmall-pox; about one in four or five died; v. f. or blood-letting was blamed, and happily loft its reputation in the fubfequent Bofton fmall-pox. It arrived in Bofton in January following, by a failor belonging to the fhip, and got into five or fix families, but did not much fpread till the twentieth of March 1752, and Monday the twenty-third, inoculation was let loofe; fome greedy practitioners indifcriminately inoculated any perfons who could be perfuaded to receive it, even pregnant women, puerpeas, old negroes, and the like; upon a fcrutiny made July twenty-fourth, by the felect men and the overfeers of the poor in the feveral wards, the felect men requeft the practitioners to inoculate no more after the twenty-feventh of July. To take at one view the ftate of the fmall-pox in Bofton from January 1752, to July 24, the following table may ferve.

Small-

	Whites	Blacks
Small-pox in the natural way	5059	485
Whereof died	452	62
By inoculation	1970	139
Whereof died	24	7
Sick in seventeen families	23	
Persons who have not received it	174	

There died of inoculation thirty-one persons, not including the dubious deaths of Mr. Coleman's son, who
died by subsequent nervous diforders and fore eyes, and
the two daughters of Mr. Goldthwait who died under
inoculation, but as it is said by the fore throat illness. The
fcrutiny reported, that the total of refidenters, fo called,
at that time were 15,734, including 1544 negroes, and
about 1800 abfentees who had fled from the fmall-pox.
Died of an inoculated fmall-pox, about one in eighty-two
whites, and one in twenty blacks.

V. The fmall-pox in cold countries is more fatal to
blacks than to whites. In the Bofton fmall-pox of 1752,
there died whites in the natural way about one in
eleven, by inoculation one in eighty; blacks in the
natural way one in eight, by inoculation one in
twenty. In hot countries it is more fatal to whites
than blacks. In Charles-town of South-Carolina, when
the fmall-pox prevailed 1738, upon a fcrutiny, it was
found that in the natural way, of 647 whites, died
157, is one in four; by inoculation of 156 whites,
died nine, is one in twenty : of 1024 blacks in the natural way there died 138, is one in feven and half; of
251 blacks by inoculation there died feven, is one in
thirty-fix.

VI. In autumn the fmall-pox is the moft deleterious;
in all autumnal fevers there is a putrid complication
from the declining and lefs vegete feafon; in winter
the feafon does not allow it to fpread; the fpring, if not

tco

too wet, and the fummer, if not too hot, are the moſt favourable feafons for the ſmall-pox.

VII. We improve in the management of the ſmall-
pox: in the natural way 1721, died about one in feven ;
1730, about one in eight; 1752, nearly one in eleven,
which may be attributed to the gradually relinquiſhing
alexipharmicks, and a hot regimen formerly recommended by many, being one extreme ; and of a cold
management the other extreme: by this Sydenham has
done much damage: as nature's helmſinen, we have varied from a more cool to a more cordial regimen, according to the conſtitutions of different patients, and the
various ſtadia, and other circumſtances of the ſame patient: v. s. or blood-letting, was feldom uſed; fcarce
any uſe of opiates ; the patient was kept in a natural temperature with a plentiful uſe of diluters ; the body kept
foluble in all the ſtadia, and when the maturation was
completed, cordial purges for two or three days.

VIII. The greater or ſmaller mortality in the ſmall-
pox is not principally owing to the feafons, regimen,
and the like ; but fomewhat infcrutable in the various
conſtitutions of families and individuals: 1721, Mr.
Bond, a carpenter, and five of his children, died with
purples and hæmorrhages in Boſton ; 1752, four children of Mr. Wier of Charles-town died, whereof one
was inoculated. The commonly received notion of the
ſmall-pox being fatal to the New-England born, is not
true and juſt, and is of bad effect in depreffing the ſpirits
of New-England men when feized abroad : 1752 of the
ſmall-pox decumbents in Boſton died about one in
eleven ; it is feldom fo favourable in any part of Great-
Britain.

The ſmall-pox is a malignant contagious eruptive puſ-
tulary fever, obferving certain ſtadia, communicable
only by perfonal infection : it is not known to be endemial

mial in any country as the plague is in Turkey; it was
not known in America until the colonies from Europe
itroduced it. In the natural way, from infection received
to the first eruptions, allowing a latitude of varieties of
ages and conftitutions, are fourteen to twenty-one days;
in the inoculated way, are feven to fourteen days; but I
fufpect thefe of fourteen days, to have received the infection in the natural way from the inoculator, or from the
effluvia of his variolated doffils. The fmall-pox generally is not infecting, until a concocted pus is formed. In
the fmall-pox time 1752, the chicken or fpurious pox
was frequent, and fometimes paffed for the fmall-pox, and
fome perfons have ineffectually been inoculated from
thence: but if there has been an apparatus of two or three
days, though the puftules are watery or ichorous with a
thin cyftis, if the bafes be red with a circular florid cuticular expanfion, we may pronounce it a genuine fmall-pox.
There are vaft varieties of the genuine fmall-pox; in general, the fooner the feveral ftadia are accomplished, the
more benign is the fmall-pox, and frequently the danger
is in proportion to the number of puftules, efpecially in
the face. In the fmall-pox natural and ingrafted, fome
patients a few days before decumbiture, have tranfient
intermitting complaints; fome after the genuine fmall-
pox poftulary eruption is completed, have eruptions of
fpurious puftules.

To form a general idea of the fmall-pox, we may
take the diftinct plump kind as a STANDARD. It begins
with the common fymptoms of a fever (in the apparatus of many, there are no chills, rigors, and hor-
ripilations perceivable; a cough is no fymptom) particularly with a pain in the head, back, and limbs;
oppreffion e regione ventriculi, naufea, or vomitings,
fore throat in general, but no dangerous fymptom, it
gradually vanifhes after maturation; nervous affections,
deliria,

deliria, phrenfies, and fometimes convulfions in children;
[g] the end of the third or beginning of the fourth day,
the fmall-pox puftules begin to appear ; in fome few, the
eruptions make their appearance without any apparatus
fymptoms ; generally, the younger the fubject, the fooner
all the ftadia of any diftemper, particularly of the fmall-
pox, are performed; the fifth day they are round and en-
large their bafes of a lively red ; the fixth day they come
to a point; the feventh day the points or apices turn
white ; the eighth they turn yellow ; the ninth there is a
laudable digefted pus ; the tenth they begin to cruft or
fcab ; the twelfth they are dry fcabs.

X. There are fo many varieties of the fmall-pox
appearances, they cannot be reduced to claffes ; we
may obferve, that the very young and very old are fcarce
fufceptible of the fmall-pox, perhaps their vis vitæ is too
feeble for bringing the variolous leaven received, to
leaven the whole lump. I fhall enumerate fome of the
moft noted varieties. 1. A diftinct dry fort, few, not
large, bafis fcarce inflamed, very fmall digeftion, being
warty or horny ; the fifth or fixth day from eruption,
they begin to dry and foon vanifh, leaving no pittings,
only freckles. 2. The diftinct plump kind as above
defcribed for a ftandard. 3. The coherent, not well
defcribed by the writers concerning the fmall-pox ; I
fuppofe they mean a frequent or cluftered fmall-pox de-
preffed, generally pitted or umbilicated in the center,
and upon the maturation frequently attended with a
fecond or fecondary fever. 4. The confluent, which
are very irregular in their firft appearances and fubfequent
ftadia ; frequently they appear eryfipelas like, and after

[g] Sydenham and fome others reckon them a good prognoftick,
whereas many fuch die in the apparatus and beginning of eruption; all
practitioners obferve that purgings and convulfions are generally the
moft fatal diftempers of children, therefore they muft be bad fymptoms
in the apparatus of their fmall-pox: I know of no diftemper where convulfions are a favourable prognoftick.

the period of maturation, they become an afh-coloured cruft or white fkin; their fecond fever frequently becomes a hectick, not mortal until after fome weeks, months or years. 5. The fmall-pox interfperfed with petechiæ, veficulæ miliares, or fmall blifters of a limpid or bluifh ferum; with purple fpots more or lefs diluted; and hæmorrhages, which are more mortal than the plague itfelf. *N. B.* In fome there is at firft, a flufh or rafh-like formidable appearance, but foon difappearing, the fmall pox looks favourable. *N. B.* A round turgid fmall-pox with florid interftices is the beft.

XI. Among the bad fymptoms in the fmall-pox, we may enumerate the following [*b*] : mild fymptoms in a fmall-pox of a bad appearance; univerfal feeblenefs or proftration of ftrength; pain from the nape of the neck all along the fpine; naufea, and averfion to any drink; fetid anhelous breathings; groans, vigiliæ, inquietudes or languid toffings, comas, a fparkling piercing bright eye threatening a phrenfy; colliquations of any kind in the eruption, fuch as profufe fweatings, many ftools, menftruatio tempore non debito, purples and hæmorrhages. A miliary eruption, or like rank meafles, or eryfipelas like; a fpanifh brown unequal eruption, a cryftaline fmall-pox: a filiquous fmall-pox, where the puftules of a cream colour run together, waved of various figures, fpungy not mellow; a feffile fmall-pox; where the confluent fort dry in the beginning of maturation; after the eruption is compleated, miliary blifters or purples appearing in the interftices containing a dark red ferum; a fudden fubfidence of the puftules and fwelling of the face; the eyes fhut up, opening fuddenly; puftules

[*b*] Excepting in bad cafes of the fmall-pox, in Europe, phyficians are feldom called upon; it is left to the management of the matrons and to nature: it is reckoned a diftemper of children, fuch as are red gum, toothing, worms, and the like; the Dutch with good propriety call it kinderen packies, but few of the adults are to receive it, becaufe when children they are allowed to have it in common courfe.

feffile

seffile dry fubfiding in the center; interftices livid or pale; in the defquamation or declenfion, where a fanious gleeting fcab returns with a tedious expectoration of vifcid phlegm, and hectick; a cold refpiration; carrion like fetid ftools; a ftrong vibration of the carotide arteries; the firft eruptions more general in the extremities than in the face and neck: fcarce any die but in the drying defquamation or declenfion period; this drying fometimes happens in the firft of maturation, or any time of the maturation protracted but not perfected; indigo coloured ftains in the puftules; fcabs or crufts of a beeswax colour are the moft laudable, the afh-coloured are bad, the black are very bad; where the puftules after maturation feem to be at a ftand, and do not fcab or corrugate, the patient is weak, and the cafe dubious.

The management of the fmall-pox in general.

To receive the fmall-pox, when expected, in the natural or inoculated way; keep an eafy undifturbed mind, avoid catching of cold, refrain from violent exercife, ufe a foft diet, take a mercurial purge or two. 1. In the beginning [i] of the apparatus fever, give a gentle vomit (a rude vomit hurts as much as does violent exercife) it not only cleans the ftomach, but by its fhocks removes obftructions, renders the œconomy meable for a regular circulation. 2. When the defign of nature is obvious, and her intentions laudable, give no difturbance by medicines, dilute plentifully becaufe of the cauftick acrimony, let nature keep its courfe; if any extraordinary fymptom happen, as is the cuftom in Great-Britain, call in the advice of a neighbouring honeft prac-

[i] When the fymptoms of the fmall-pox appear; the temper ought not to be too much lowered by a cold regimen, by v. f. or any unneceffary evacuation; occafioning a late, imperfect, unequal, fecond crop eruption, of bad confequence; neither fhould the temper be raifed by cordials and a hot regimen to force the circulating juices to a feparation of a greater load of fmall-pox than nature intended. . . .

tifing

tifing apothecary or furgeon; or rather of fome ex-
perienced difcreet phyfician. 3. During the eruption
and maturation periods, keep the belly rather foluble
than bound, (Sydenham by a grand miftake recommends
coftivenefs even to the thirteenth day) and upon maturation, a purging natural or procured, are falutary and
have faved the lives of many, particularly in rigors
and anhelous breathings. 4. In the whole courfe of
the diftemper, the patient is to be kept in a moderate
or natural temper ; an increafed heat inflames the habit,
cold depreffes the fpirits too much. 5. Give vegetable acids (mineral acids I have found too rude, and do
hurt by occafioning a naufea or vomituition) becaufe
there is a notorious animal or urinous acrimony in the
cafe. 6. When the maturation is compleated, to prevent
or alleviate a fecond fever from fome part of the variolous
pus being abforbed by the circulating fluids, give fome
cordial purges [k] for two or three days; upon any unlucky tranflation, it is eafier to folicit the inteftines to
a difcharge, (as being more under command, than
any other fecretion or evacuation) than the falivary
ducts or urinary paffages: this purging moderates the
fuppuration, and confequently prevents much pittings
and fcars; moreover it procures fleep like an anodyne,
and more benignly, becaufe opiates protract all the ftadia:
a protracted defquamation, with a fharp fanies or corrofive
ichor, gleeting from under the fcabs, occafion pittings
and fcars; fo does picking and fcratching of the fmall-
pox fcabs, before a new fcurf fkin is formed under-

[k] In the fmall-pox of 1730, I obferved fome patients with violent
fecond fever fymptoms, upon maturation compleated, feized with a
natural purging which gave great relief; but as a blind follower of
Sydenham, I checked it by opiates, which occafioned a return of the
violent threatning fymptoms; until the effect of the opiate being over,
the purging returned with great relief, and fo toties quoties: this gave
me a ftrong hint, that purging upon maturation compleated was falutary: I ufed it with fuccefs, and introduced the good opinion of it
with many practitioners, to the faving of many lives; foon after I found
this purging method recommended by Dr. Mead, Freind, and other
phyficians in England.

neath

neath to prevent the injuries from the external air. 7. Towards the end of the defquamation give a mercurial purge or two to defecate the blood and other juices [*l*].

We may further obferve, 1. That there are fuch anomalies in conftitutions, that a few extraordinary inftances proof againft all pernicious management, are by no means to be adduced as precedents for forming of a regimen: Dr. Fuller in his Exanthematologia, writes, that a fon æt. 15, of Dr. Hooper, bifhop of Bath and Wells, in a very bad fmall-pox, for twelve days when awake, every half hour drank a bumper of ftrong beer, mountain, wine, or brandy; he recovered: fome drank only cold water and did well: Sydenham's hiftory of a young man, who in the abfence of his nurfe was thought by the ftanders by to have died and was laid out on a cold board, the nurfe upon her return, perceiving fome figns of life, put him to bed and he did well. 2. Let not numbers of decumbents be put up in one clofe room; the congeries of putrid effluvia renders the ambient air a puddle of corruption, and without a proper fpring to continue the circulation of our juices, which is the life of animals. 3. Let not nature or the fpirits (this ought to be regarded in all acute diftempers) be difturbed by noife or confabulation. 4. Where medicines are required, adminifter no medicine that continues to be difagreeable to the ftomach. 5. Any violent fymptom appearing, muft be immediately obviated; delays here are dangerous. 6. Let the belly be kept foluble; formerly from an implicit faith in Sydenham, I lapfed into that error, that the belly ought not to be kept foluble, left nature fhould be confounded in her proper courfe; whereas in truth, nature is thereby alleviated. 7. Avoid grief, intenfe thinking, or the like, particularly avoid fear; they hinder perfpiration, and all other tenden-

[*l*] Sometimes a hectick fever remains to the twentieth, thirtieth, fortieth day or longer, and the patient dies hectick or confumptive; fometime a fcrophulous difpofition remains for life.

cies to the furface or ad extra of the body.   8. Upon
the maturation, where the circulation is much crowded,
the fwelling of the face and arms, a ptyalifm, a diabe-
tical profluvium are of great relief; cordial purges anfwer the fame intention, and are more at our command;
fpitting frequently begins with the eruption, and ought
not to decline until about the eleventh day of illnefs; it
gradually becomes thick and ropy and requires plentiful
diluting.   9. Purples and hæmorrhages are more mortal
than the plague itfelf.

Concerning inoculation of the fmall-pox.

The novel practice of procuring the fmall-pox by
inoculation, is a very confiderable and moft beneficial
improvement in that article of medical practice.   It
is true, the firft promoters of it were too extravagant,
and therefore fufpected in their recommendations of it;
and fome medical writers inftance fundry diforders arifing in the animal œconomy from fome foreign liquids being directly admitted into the current of blood : thefe
confiderations made me, 1721, not enter into the practice, until further trials did evince the fuccefs of it;
but now after upwards of thirty years practice of it
in Great-Britain, and the dominions thereto belonging,
we found that the fmall-pox received by cuticular incifions has a better chance for life and an eafy decumbiture; that is, the fmall pox fo received is lefs mortal,
and generally more favourable, than when received
in the accidental or natural way, by infpiration, deglutition, pores of the fkin, and the like.   We muft ftill
acknowledge, that it falls fhort of the recommendations given by its firft promoters, being no abfolute
fecurity againft death and other calamities of the
fmall-pox; it produces all the varieties as in the natural
way, from the moft favourable dry horny diftinct
kind, to the moft deleterious attended with purples and
hæmorrhages; the confequential boils and impoftuma-

I   tions

tions are more than in the natural way, besides their
incisions ulcerating and putrifying. We hinted before,
that in Boston 1730 of the twelve inoculated deaths
three were occasioned by their incisions; two in three
a few days after inoculation complain in their axiliary,
inguinal, or parotid glands [*m*], before the apparatus fever makes its appearance. We are informed that of the
first inoculations in England, nine in ten were afflicted
with sores, so as to require the immediate care of a surgeon or dresser for some time [*n*].

To alleviate the crisis and deleterious symptoms of
the small-pox, 1. We find good success in the Circassian
way of procuring it by variolous pus applied in any
manner to fresh cutaneous incisions. The manner
which I happen to use, is a small cuticular scarification
by the point of a crooked bistoury or scalpel, in the in-
side of the upper arm, and in this incision I lodge a
very small variolated dossil in the form and bigness of
a barley corn [*o*], contained or secured by some sticking
plaister for forty-eight hours, and afterwards dressed
daily with some gentle digestive. 2. More incisions than

[*m*] Where the circulation labours, the glandular parts are the most
liable to complain.

[*n*] If the small pox procured by inoculation was so favourable as at
first pretended, it would require only a barber surgeon or cupper; the
incision or scarification is done with less risk than common blood-letting,
and requires only a soft diet and short confinement under the small care
of a nurse or attendant, and a practitioner's large bill would appear ridiculous and imposing

[*o*] At present in London, they generally use a small scratch, or
scarification in one arm, and lodge therein a small bit of variolated
thread. There is no proportion or dose of variolous matter requisite for inoculation; Pylarini writes, that by pricking the skin
with needles dipt in variolous matter or pus, people have been inoculated: the variolous miasm is inconceivably subtle; 1730, I accidentally inoculated Mr. W. Phips, by using in v. f. inadvertently a
lancet (wiped clean and dry as usual) by which I had the preceding
day taken some variolous pus for inoculation; it is true I inoculated
him afterwards in the common manner, but all the stadia of the
small-pox took their date from the v. f. and the orifice festered accordingly.

one, are an unnecessary running the risk of more ulcerating incisions.   3. Hitherto we have not perceived any
difference in the small-pox received from a laudable
distinct kind, and that from a dismal confluent kind,
which some of our audacious inoculators have used in
want of a better, that they might not loose the benefit
of an inoculated patient.   Dr. Wagstaffe writes, that
the criminals in Newgate 1721, were inoculated by pus
from a fluxed sort of a person who died before the inoculations were performed.   4. The caution that persons who are to be inoculated take, not to receive at
the same time the infection in the natural way, is a
vulgar error: the receiving of infection upon infection
does not add to its intenseness, as we may observe in
persons who receive it in the natural way and are
continually exposed to repeated infections; because whatever infection first takes place, renders the subsequent infections effete or abortive; and as the inoculated small-
pox is more expeditious in its course, any other infection
would prove abortive.

The history of inoculation relating to New-England,
is briefly as follows.   The Circassians living between the
Euxine and Caspian seas, time out of mind, have carried on a considerable branch of trade with Turkey and
Persia, in selling their own children and young slaves
taken by excursions from their neighbours, but more
especially their young women; they are beautiful, and
in great request in the seraglios and harams of the
Turks and Persians: while young they give them the
small-pox by inoculation or otherwise, and they who
retain their beauties are carried to market. This Circassian traffick conveyed the practice into Turkey; the
Turks at first from their principle of predestination would
not come into it; the old women of the Greek church
practised it for some time among the meaner sort of
people; Pylarini writes, that 1701, it first began to be
used among the better sort in Constantinople.

1713,

1713, Timonius from Conftantinople fent to the royal fociety in London incredible recommendations of this practice; " that for the preceding eight years fome " thoufands had been inoculated, and none died; while at " the fame time, half of the affected in the common way " died in Conftantinople; and what is valued by the fair, " inoculation never leaves pits or fcars: children have no " convulfions." Pylarini, the Venetian conful at Conftan- tinople, 1714, fent to the royal fociety a more modeft account of the fame. " I was not an eye-witnefs to all " that I now relate; inoculation fometimes does not take " place; with fome, in the glandulous parts and emunc- " tories, abfceffes do arife after fome time." Dr. Le Duc a native of Conftantinople, and who was himfelf inocu- lated, affured Dr. Jurin, that out of many thoufands, in the fpace of about forty years paft, who had been inoculat- ed in and about Conftantinople by one Greek woman, not fo much as one perfon had mifcarried.

1721, I lent thefe communications to Dr. Cotton Mather, a clergyman of Bofton; being very credulous, that is, of great faith, when the fmall-pox appeared in Bofton, that he might have the imaginary honour of a new fangled notion, he furreptitioufly without my know- ledge fet a rafh undaunted operator [*p*] to work, and by three practitioners in town and country, about 286 were inoculated, whereof about one in forty-eight died in Bofton.

Thefe communications were regarded in England, only as virtuofo amufements, until 1721, M. Maitland, a furgeon in the retinue of Sir Robert Sutton, the Britifh ambaffador at Conftantinople, upon his arrival in Lon- don, from fome fcanty obfervations, but moftly from

---

[*p*] This undaunted operator imagined, that by going to London with a quack-bill of his inoculation performances in New-England, he might acquire a fortune in London: but fo it happened, that void of common difcretion to couch his ignorance and filly mean affurance, he returned to Bofton without being called upon to perform any ino- culation.

hear-fay,

hear-fay, with the merveilleux of a traveller, broached this novel practice, and a few were inoculated with fuccefs; which induced the royal family to think well of it, and by way of experiment fome condemned criminals were inoculated in Newgate with their own confent. In the fpring following by direction of the princefs of Wales, fix hofpital children, and foon after five more hofpital children from æt. fourteen weeks to twenty years of age were inoculated; fome did not receive the infection, as having had it formerly, or from fome other impediment, but none died or fuffered much: upon this encouragement, Mr. Amyand, ferjeant furgeon, was ordered to ingraft the fmall-pox on princefs Amelia, æt. 11, and princefs Carolina, æt. 9, they had them favourably; this encouraged the practice; and from the accounts of Dr. Jurin, fecretary to the royal fociety (a great promoter of inoculation) in the firft three years, 1721, 1722, and 1723, of the practice, in all Great-Britain were inoculated 477 perfons, whereof nine are fufpected to have died; and as of thefe twenty-nine did not receive the infection (this is one in fixteen) the deaths were nine in 448, or two per cent. in this period of three years: the principal inoculators in England, were Dr. Nettleton in Yorkfhire eighty patients; Mr. Amyand, ferjeant furgeon, fixty-two; Mr. Maitland eighty-five, &c.

The firft promoters were fo incredibly marvellous in their accounts, as would have difcouraged any fober man to have attempted it, if the fubfequent more moderate accounts of its fuccefs had not given a reafonable encouragement. Timonius wrote, that of many thoufands inoculated in the fpace of eight years none died. Le Duc writes, that in the fpace of about forty years, out of many thoufands inoculated by one Greek woman in and about Conftantinople, not fo much as one perfon had mifcarried, as is before hinted. Mr. Maitland in his printed account fays, " Dying is a cafe " which never happened in ingrafting; that the giving " of the fmall-pox by inoculation never yet failed, nor
ever

" ever can ; no head-akes, thirft, inquietudes, and other
" fever fymptoms ; not one in a thoufand, the puftules
" never leave any pitts behind them." Dr. Brady of
Portfmouth writes, " not one ever died of inoculation
" rightly performed ; it always is favourable." Dr.
Harris fays, that " inoculating is a certain remedy
" againft the confluent kind." Mr. Colman, a clergyman, and principal promoter of the practice in Bofton
of New-England, publifhed, that " none die, no blains
" or boils follow the practice." Mr. B——ton the
firft operator, publifhed, " there is no truth in the re-
" ports of people dying under inoculation ;" his accounts are fo abfurd they invalidate themfelves, and require no other animadverfion.— Other inoculators have
publifhed, the inoculated fmall-pox is always favourable,—never infecting ;—fo fafe as to require no phyfician ;—the puftules never exceed ten to a hundred, and
do not pit [*q*].

Dr. C. Mather, who firft fet up inoculation in Bofton,
in his publifhed accounts of it, fhews what fmall dependence there is upon weak authorities, " fome cats 1721,
" in Bofton, had a regular fmall-pox, and died of it [*r*]."
—— During the fmall-pox, the pigeons and dunghill
fowls did not lay nor hatch.—He never knew bliftering
mifs of faving life in the fmall-pox.—The patient is more
healthy after inoculation, it is ufeful to women in child-
bed,—it dries up tedious running ulcers,—makes the
crazy confumptive people hearty,—and rids people of
their former maladies [*s*].

[*q*] It would be idle in me, formally to confute thefe unguarded
affertions, daily experience evinces the contrary.

[*r*] He had not difcretion fufficient to obferve, that the fmall-pox
is a contagious diftemper, peculiar to mankind, as is alfo the meafles,
and plague ; that other animals have their peculiar epidemical or malignant diftempers, murrain among neat cattle, rot among fheep, and
the like: we may alfo obferve, that fome fpecies of trees only are fufceptible of peculiar blafts ; that male animals only impregnate females
of their own fpecies.

[*s*] Dr. Berkley's tar-water is lately recommended in the fame man-

In making of medium eftimates, we ought to take large numbers in a long feries of time, but not the cafes of fingular families, where fome may fay that notorious circumftances were not avoided or attended to, fuch as pregnant women, child-bed women, old negroes, and the like; we had a remarkable inftance in the inoculations of Bofton, 1752; of five perfons in one family, Mr. Sherburn's, inoculated by Mr. G—r [*t*] three died; — of 72 or 73 perfons inoculated 1721 in Roxbury and the adjacent country towns by Mr. B——n, five died; which is about one in fourteen.

In fhort the rifk feems to be only two to three per ct. and by the purging method, and fome prudential cautions might be further reduced.

¹ I am at a lofs for the reafons, why inoculation hitherto is not much ufed in our mother country, Great-Britain; confidering that it has with good fuccefs been practifed in our colonies or plantations, particularly in Bofton, New-York, Philadelphia, and Charles-town of South-Carolina.

The advantages of inoculation are, 1. The choice of fuitable feafons. 2. A previous proper regimen. 3. A laudable (this is the moft eligible) variolous pus or leaven. 4. We have no inftance of any who received the fmall-pox by inoculation, receiving the fmall-pox again. 5. By many trials for upwards of thirty years in the dominions of Great-Britain, it muft be acknowledged a more favourable manner of receiving the fmall-pox. 6. In a place of trade, it gives the fmall-pox a quick courfe, and the interruption of commerce fhort; in the very general fmall-pox of Bofton 1752, the ti-

ner as a panacea: the principal advantage I found in it, is, when a phyfician is tired out with fome tedious chronical cafe to turn the patient over to the ufe of the bifhop's tar-water; valeat quantum valere poteft.

[*t*] This is not defigned as a perfonal reflection upon my friend Mr. G——r, but to illuftrate that inoculation is very far from being a prefervative againft death, as was alledged by fome of its promoters.

morous

morous fled from the fmall-pox beginning of April, and with the trade generally returned beginning of September.

The difadvantages of inoculation, whereof fome are obviated. 1. Inoculated deaths being criminal: the royal family by their example, have removed this fufpicion. 2. Procuring of abortion to women with child, is a fin in foro divino, though connived at by us. 3. A fordid mercenary manner of perfuading child-bed women to receive the fmall-pox by inoculation, upon pretext of cleanfing: whereas the puerpera fret in the circulating juices, is by this leaven increafed, colliquative purgings enfue, and finally death: I can adduce fome notorious inftances in Bofton. 4. The communicating [*u*] of perfonal or family chronical and conftitutional diftempers to the inoculated (a man has or ought to have a proper regard for his progeny and fucceeding generations) has been a confiderable ftumbling block with me:. on the other hand, from many trials in the fpace of upwards of thirty years practice of inoculating the fmall-pox in the Britifh dominions, no fuch communications have been obferved; the itch itfelf, a notorious cutaneous diftemper, is not faid to have been

[*u*] Chronical diftempers have been received by cutaneous or external applications: we have a notorious inftance of this, fome years fince in Cork of Ireland; a nurfe reputed for drawing of child-bed women's breafts, from a venereal ulcer under her tongue, infected the nipples of her women; thefe women in coition infected their hufbands, and the city became generally poxed. All conftitutional diftempers have fome idea or feminium in every drop of our juices; the acute diftemper according to its nature foon fhews itfelf, the chronical ails act imperceptibly and flowly in the body; the diftempers ex traduce, fometimes intermit a generation or two, and again appear in fucceeding generations, fuch as the pfora of North-America, called a falt rheum, that is, a fcurvy, negro yaws, fcrophulous diforders or king's-evil, venereal difeafes, manias and other hereditary nervous diforders, arthritick or gouty ails, nephritick cafes, and the like, which may occafion inquietudes in the minds of the inoculated, and render them incapable of the greateft happinefs in life, mens fana in corpore fano. . . . .

thus

thus communicated: and if after a feries of years or generations any fuch fears fhould become real, fuch diftant
views cannot affect much where the prefent relief or
better chance are in the cafe. 5. It fpreads infection
very quick, and endangers the neighbourhood not prepared to receive it: this is one of the reafons that it
is felony or criminal for a man to fet his own houfe on
fire, becaufe it endangers the vicinity: it is a hardfhip
upon the publick, to oblige people abruptly to leave
their habitations and bufinefs; fome civil regulations
feem requifite to obviate fome difficulties which occur
in this practice. 6. It promotes the practice of P——
fraudes, as bifhop Tillotfon in another cafe writes, that
fome men had got the fcurvy trick of lying, in favour
of what they impofed upon people as truth, as lately
happened in the Bofton inoculations; upon an actual
furvey it was found that in about 2000 inoculations,
thirty-one had died (others including fome difputed cafes,
fay thirty-four) the promoters gave out 3500 inoculated,
but gradually reduced the number to 3000, and afterwards to 2500, (fee the Bofton gazettes publifhed in June
1752) and at laft acquiefced in the actual fcrutiny of about
2109 : in policy of infurance offices, this falfe reprefentation would be reckoned an impofition, becaufe people who would run a rifk at one per ct. may not run the
fame rifk at two or three per ct.

Virginia *fettlements.*

At firft there were only a few general patentees, but at
prefent every freeholder may be reckoned a patentee.

The government of Virginia pretend to extend their
fettlements fo far back weftward as the great lake Erie,
and fome branches of the Miffiffippi river, comprehending an immenfe quantity of land unfettled; and as their
fettlements extend gradually towards the mountains, they
create new counties from time to time, for the conveniency of attending inferior courts of judicature.

The

The frontier or fartheſt back counties being of great extent, no navigation, and not much foreign trade, hold quarterly county courts only ; all the others have monthly courts ; there are variations from time to time; at this time anno 1752, they are as follow.

Quarterly county courts.

Brunſwick,	⎱ Laſt Tueſdays in March, June,
Fairfax,	⎰ September, December.
Lunenburgh,	Firſt Tueſ. in Jan. April, July, Oct.
Frederick,	⎱ Second Tueſdays in February, May,
Albemarle,	⎰ Auguſt, November.
Auguſta.	Fourth Tueſdays in ſaid months.

Monthly county courts.

Henrico,	
Richmond,	Firſt Mondays in every month.
Williamſburg.	
James city,	
Northumberland,	Second Mondays.
Nanſemond,	
York,	Third Mondays.
Prince William,	Fourth Mondays.
Cumberland,	
Middleſex,	
Elizabeth city,	Firſt Tueſdays.
Spotſylvania,	
Prince George,	
King and Queen,	Second Tueſdays.
Northampton,	
Stafford,	
Eſſex,	
Gooch land,	Third Tueſdays.
Princeſs Anne,	
Surrey,	
Louiſa,	Fourth Tueſdays.

Weſt-

Weftmoreland, Accomack,	Laft Tuefdays.
Charles city,	Firft Wednefdays.
Warwick, Ifle of Wight, Hanover,	Firft Thurfdays.
New-Kent, Southampton,	Second Thurfdays.
Norfolk, Culpepper,	Third Thurfdays.
Gloucefter, Orange,	Fourth Thurfdays.
Chefterfield, King George,	Firft Fridays.
Lancafter, Carolina,	Second Fridays.
King William, Amelia.	Third Fridays each month.

Thus the government is divided into forty-five counties, whereof fix hold quarterly courts, and thirty-nine hold monthly courts; fee the proper article of legiflative and executive courts.

The country between James river and York river is the beft inhabited, cultivated, and produces the beft tobacco.

Lunenburgh, their remoteft fettlement, is about 100 miles S. W. from Hanover; Hanover is fixty miles from Williamfburg, the metropolis,

The lands weft of the Virginia fettlements are claimed by the Six nations, called by the French Iroquois, and by the Britifh, Mohawks; they are alfo claimed by the fouthern Indians; fee vol. I. p. 187; and by the French of Canada. The beft lands are above the falls of the rivers; the firft falls of each river muft be the barcadiers for the back or inland countries, and in time become great towns or corporations.

The E N D.